K. R. CONWAY

UNDERTOW

WICKED WHALE PUBLISHING

K.R. CONWAY

First Edition: August 2013
Second Edition: August 2014
Third Edition: December 2015

Conway, Kathleen R.
   Undertow / by Kathleen R. Conway

   Summary: Seventeen-year-old Eila Walker learns that she is the last descendant in a rare line of dangerous humans while being protected by four unlikely friends, including a young man who is her genetic enemy, as she hunts for answers to her own family's dark past and a destiny that wants her dead.

ISBN: 0-9897763-5-2 / 978-0-9897763-5-6

Wicked Whale Publishing
P.O. Box 264
Sagamore Beach, MA 02562-9998

www.WickedWhalePublishing.com

Published in the United States of America

DEDICATION

For Mom.

The most hyperactive, devoted cheerleader I have ever known in sky-high zebra pumps. I adore you.

K.R. CONWAY

UNDERTOW

BOOK 1

PROLOGUE

BARNSTABLE HARBOR, MASSACHUSETTS
OCTOBER 14, 1851

Killing Jacob Rysse would not be an issue.

Dying in the process, however, was more difficult for Elizabeth to stomach.

She didn't fear death, for sacrifice was both expected and inevitable in her race. She was a fighter after all and the carnage left behind by Rysse and her own family was nothing new.

But leaving behind those she loved was more painful than any form of torture she had known. Her infant son would never remember her, the Captain would mourn her, but Christian? Christian may very well never forgive her.

He would quickly figure out that she was not at the blacksmith's as they had agreed to meet. She had left him, instead, a letter and her necklace among the sawdust tables of the shop. In it she had written out her instructions in the same sweeping lines that had conveyed so much between them during the rebellion. What she asked of him was simple: protect the house, protect the necklace, and protect their secret. He would do it for her, just as she now was about to do for him and for the child.

Rysse was hunting her family and had succeeded at killing most of her kind. By taking him out, she was protecting them all. Christian would understand that hopefully. Eventually.

Her well-laid plan would draw Rysse in, and his perfection as a murderer should ensure her success.

He wanted her power.

He believed she would trade it for revenge.

He was about to die for his ignorance.

She hurried towards the harbor docks and though it was well past midnight, the moon opened the world before her. The harbor was glassy and black, strewn with fishing vessels and whaling ships whose masts seem to scrape along the stars. Soft wooden moans escaped the ships as they rolled lightly in the water and Elizabeth shifted her heavy skirt that scuffed the cobblestone street.

As she reached the fountain at the center square, Rysse stepped out of the shadows. He was as she remembered him: tall, stunning, and dangerously seductive. His dark eyes and ebony hair were useful to lure his victims, making him irresistible when it came to women. Unfortunately, few women ever lived long enough to realize their terrible error. On the rare occasion he left one alive, she would inevitably take her own life within a matter of hours.

He needed to die. Elizabeth would make sure he did.

"Mrs. Walker. I must say I was most pleased to receive your message, though meeting me alone . . ." Rysse shook his head in mock disapproval, "Overconfidence seems to run through your family's bloodlines. I was sure you understood that such a trait is a distinct disability in my presence."

Elizabeth watched as Rysse strolled towards her, his eyes skimming over her form-fitting corset and raven hair. His roving gaze disgusted her, but she didn't flinch. Rysse closed his eyes and breathed in her essence like the most exquisite bouquet. His close proximity lit Elizabeth's nerves on fire, but she forced herself forward as Rysse became instantly alert, tracking her movements cautiously.

His lips curved into a flawless grin. "It is truly a shame at your family's fixed desire to be eliminated. But you, I'm sure, may harbor your own delight in their demise," he purred while watching her carefully, as any enemy would. Elizabeth forced a neutral expression as she buried her rage and Rysse took it as confirmation that she was, indeed, like him.

Elizabeth drew herself up straighter. "I do not recognize such a thing as family anymore. Surely you know this. Tonight is solely about you and me," she lied, a hateful edge to her voice.

"They did not deserve to survive. How did it feel to be so treated by them?" he asked, attempting to ignite her fury. Elizabeth's mind flashed to her childhood and of Christian in the woods so long ago. His face filled her thoughts and cut through her heart, but she pushed his protective eyes from her memory.

She took a slow, deep breath and looked fiercely at the soulless man. "Retribution will be mine," she replied, quietly spooling her dangerous power. "Do we have an accord?"

"Oh yes," he laughed, looking lustfully over the gentle, perfect curves of her body. "You are a most unique creature, Elizabeth. A beautiful, fatal flower, aren't you?"

The question was pointless, as both her kind and his knew she was different. She was a flaw of evolution – a dark mark among a perfect race ~ and her kind saw her as a dangerous liability. Elizabeth knew, however, that Rysse and his clan saw her as the perfect weapon if she could be changed; if she could become like him. That was what he wanted – a soul-thief like himself with limitless power. He wanted a Lunaterra like her, which he could corrupt and then command.

She had told him she would do it.

He was about to learn that she lied.

Suddenly Elizabeth caught sight of two more like Rysse, standing in the shadows near the building behind them. She recognized their young faces and was pained to see what they had become. No doubt they now worked for Rysse – as killers, enslaved to his every whim. They were good men when they were human, but she held little hope they would survive what she was about to do.

"I do believe you are afraid of me, Jacob," taunted Elizabeth, breaking the silence and attempting to bait his inner demon.

Rysse, indignant at her apparent confidence, grabbed her roughly by the neck, causing her hair to cascade down his arm. She was face to face with him, separated by a thin veil of moonlight.

Behind them, the two witnesses straightened. No doubt intrigued by the exchange. No doubt completely unaware of what was about to unfold.

Elizabeth refocused and looked confidently back at Rysse as the marks began to surface on his face. The intricate black designs swirled over his cheekbones and brow, forming the ancient symbols of the one who had created his kind. His eyes bled to black as he began his attempt to turn Elizabeth. She didn't fight, didn't resist, and Rysse took it as an honest desire to become immortal.

Elizabeth's chest constricted as she felt Rysse begin to weave a stolen life-force into her potent soul, the marks extending onto her own skin as well. Rysse believed the exchange – the forced infection – should change her, just as it would for a human.

The moonlight filled Elizabeth's face as the telltale golden rings wrapped around the green of her eyes. It flared and pulsed like liquid stardust - a distinctive, genetic reaction to Rysse's markings.

But as their lives mixed, Rysse realized that this woman was entirely different from the others. Somehow Elizabeth forced her essence to reverse and pour into Rysse as if a dam had broken.

His face contorted as a burning sensation began coursing through his body, evolving into an excruciating pain. It was a fire inside him that slowly spread and raged hotter and more relentless by the second.

He closed his eyes, pummeled by the pain, knowing that what was happening should be impossible. No Lunaterra could reverse the flow, and yet Elizabeth was running him through with her essence like a hot sword. He tried to pull away, but he was locked to her by an invisible force as his muscles seized in pain.

Furious and confused, he roared through his clenched jaw at the injustice of his prey becoming predator. He began squeezing her throat, all previous plans to recruit her abandoned.

His only goal now was to kill her. Quickly.

Elizabeth, her eyes now radiant like the sun, began to falter as her body called one last time to the power she commanded. White light began to glow from her skin and wound around her and Rysse like a serpent, engulfing them both. He began screaming, but it was too late.

The town square shook with thunder as the ivory snake quickly evolved into a column of fire and vaulted skyward. With one last ricocheting crack, the tower of light collapsed and a massive wave of energy churned away from them. The boats in the harbor rocked violently, nearly capsizing in the shockwave that raced across the water. The energy rushed through the two onlookers and they fell to the ground, their bodies arching in agony, as their genetic code was forcefully re-written.

A dusting of ash at the foot of the fountain marked where Rysse had been incinerated. Beside it lay Elizabeth, her dark hair fanned on the cobblestone street. Not a single scorch-mark flawed her lifeless body.

The sudden stillness of the night was soon broken by a man's voice in the distance, calling desperately for her, pleading for a response. He called to her, over and over, from the direction of the blacksmith's, but his own painful echo was all that responded.

As his voice rang out in the night, the two from the shadows staggered to their feet, forever changed, and disappeared into the darkness of the surrounding town.

CENTERVILLE, MASSACHUSETTS
PRESENT DAY

When Mae and I first found out about the house a month ago it screamed fraud - especially since our luck was always worth dirt.

But according to Mr. Talbot, the auction house owner, the transaction was legit, though highly unusual. I never even knew about the house until my phone rang at the beginning of August and he was on the other end, deed in hand. Apparently, when the estate went up for auction, an anonymous buyer purchased it . . . and put my name as owner and rightful heir.

Yeah, talk about Twilight Zone.

I will admit that even Mr. Talbot was a bit stunned to learn I was still in high school, and I was sure he had the wrong person. I mean, seriously, what seventeen-year-old is given a million-dollar estate?

But he had my address in Kansas correct, scumball apartment

that it was, and the names of my parents, though he was unaware they had been dead for the past fifteen years. Mae, my mom's BFF and my legal guardian, had been my only family since I was two and she was working herself into the ground to keep that rotted roof over out heads. But with one call from Cape Cod, we were given the chance of a lifetime.

We couldn't say no. We didn't say no.

Thankfully the home, number 408 on Main Street, was in good shape and downright massive in size. It had been updated regularly, due to a trust fund that had cared for it until the money ran out. And yeah, the house still needed a bit of work and a nuclear-fueled weed whacker. As for the barn and carriage house, however- only a bulldozer could help. Or a time machine.

Mae and I had driven out to see the home two weeks after Mr. Talbot had called. During that three-day trip, I didn't really get a chance to feel out the Cape, though stunning definitely applied. It was a seaside paradise speckled with quaint little towns and outgoing locals. A few bumper stickers even claimed that the area was basically a "friendly drinking village with a fishing problem."

It turned out my 4th great grandparents, Elizabeth and Josiah, had built the place, an elegant, three-story black and white home, in 1850. It was graced with huge windows and a wrap around porch large enough to host my old high school's junior prom . . . not that I went. Not that I wanted to either.

The roof was topped with monstrous chimneystacks and a Widow's Walk that could see the glittering bay. And even though it was more than 160 years old, it was simply the most beautiful house I had ever seen. Surrounded by other antique homes, it was, without question, the best of the best.

I will admit that I had some serious reservations about the move from Kansas. I was torn between the tantalizing idea of living in such a spectacular home by the beach, and my reservations about a small town mentality.

And school . . . which would start in two days.

It was like a countdown to inevitable torture.

The mere mention of Barnstable High sent my stomach twisting into a sailor's knot. I had no desire to meet my classmates until I was forced to, especially given the fact that I was such an easy target in elementary school.

Back then I had even more freckles, was a tad chub, and had a funky scar on my lower back from a damn radiator incident when I was a baby. Top that off with being raised by Mae, who was barely an adult herself, and I became quite the bulls-eye.

Granted, I still had the freckles, the scar, and Mae, but the roundness sort of stretched-out, as I grew taller to five and a half feet. I was in no way a string bean, but I wasn't a sumo wrestler either. I also had become accustomed to living life as a reject and, quite frankly, enjoyed the nosebleed section. I had no desire to be dragged into the ridiculous, self-serving dramas that so often plagued the cliques of my old high school.

Yup – there was a plus side to being ignored.

The grand view from my four-poster bed however, suggested that anonymity might no longer be mine. One did not dodge the radar when they walked home to this house.

I lay in bed, staring at the ceiling of my new bedroom, noting that gravity had managed to chip away the antique plaster's stubborn resolve. Snuggling down further into my lush blankets, I was grateful that I located the moving boxes for my room when we arrived last night.

3

My personal stone fireplace was buried somewhere behind those boxes and my very own bathroom looked like a hair-tie tornado had struck. But I had a fireplace! And a bathroom! And who cared if they looked less than pristine at the moment?

Out of the eight - yes, EIGHT bedrooms we now had, I claimed the room above the front porch. Scoping it out last night, it appeared that I should be able to crawl through my window and hang out on top of the flat roof. Well, minus Mae obviously. Yes, I had to admit, Cape Cod, or at least the Walker homestead, might be a true piece of heaven after all.

The slant of the Saturday sunlight painting my floor tipped me off to how early it must be. Seven, maybe? Seven-thirty? No way I was getting out of bed yet. It was the weekend after all, and I should head to the beach after breakfast and get some sun. Enjoy these last, few days of freedom.

I lolled in bed running through my plan for the day. My wish list was waylaid, however, by the sound of footsteps coming up the main, mahogany staircase.

"Eila?" called Mae from somewhere in the outer hall.

How on earth did she know I was awake? I stayed silent, wishing that I had pushed the moving boxes against the entrance. Sure enough, there was a knock at the door and a slow squeak of the knob as it turned.

"Eila?"

Dang. I swear the woman had radar. "Hmmm - yeah?"

She peeked her head around the door, eyeing my pile of boxes and me, tucked happily into bed. "You need to get up. I have a lot to do today."

"Uh, I was hoping to head down to the beach today," I pleaded.

Okay, maybe whined.

"I need you to . . . geez, you have a lot of stuff," she declared, trying to pick her way through my minefield of boxes and bags. "Look. I need to do a ton of errands today and there are workers coming to do some things on the house. I need you to hold down the fort while I'm gone and show these guys what needs to be done."

She looked at me for a moment, assessing whether a battle of wills was to ensue. She decided to seal the deal, "We work as a team remember? I moved my life across the country for you, don't forget."

Ugh, I could see *that* pity card being played till it was flimsy and dog-eared. The fact that we moved from a run-down building with an ex-con neighbor seemed to have escaped her memory. I sighed, "Sure. Give me a few and I'll be down."

"Meet me in the kitchen." She started heading out of the room and closing the door behind her, but at the last second, the door opened slightly again, "And Eila?"

I semi-sulked, knowing my beach plans were just washed away.

She looked around the door to make sure I heard her. Her eyes connected with mine, "Hurry up," she said and the door closed.

I lay in bed a moment more. What was it I said before, about enjoying the beauty of an antique home? Yeah, let's scratch that off the list. Turns out you have to babysit homes like this. Turns out they need a ton of work and, as such, any plans for a relaxing day of sun and sand disappears. "You and me house – we need to have a chat," I muttered, stretching out of bed and onto the oak flooring.

I walked to one of the massive side windows that faced another antique home beside ours. Slipping my fingers into the lower sash handles, I gave a firm, upright pull. The pane rattled up about two inches and stuck. *Perfect.*

Through the 2-inch gap, the light smell of freshly cut grass and pine trickled in on a feathery breeze. I leaned down and breathed in deeply. It was cool and elegant and absolutely intoxicating.

I looked out at the home next door. Similar to ours, white with black trim, but its porch was enclosed with glass and the overall feel of the house was more feminine – tea and fancy little cakes came to mind.

It looked like no one was home.

Either that or they were still SLEEPING.

Lucky suckers.

Resigned to a beachless day, I ditched the idea of a shower until the evening. I rummaged through my junk, locating a navy tank top, sports bra and some very old cut-off jeans.

Stripping off the oversized Black Keys shirt I had worn to bed, I pulled on the bra and top and wiggled my way into the jeans. Thankfully they zipped, but my beloved cut-offs now looked more like Daisy Dukes. I hadn't worn them since last summer and this past year I really grew. Not just in height, but in curves as well. Shopping for end-of-summer clothes was now a priority, otherwise I wouldn't be able to leave the house. I quickly brushed my long, wild hair and twisted it into a coffee-black rope, managing to then jam it all up under my black pageboy cap.

I headed out my door into the large, curved second-floor landing. The air inside 408 was crisp and I rubbed my arms furiously as I headed down the grand staircase to the first floor, jumping the last three stairs with an echoing thud.

The ceilings on the first floor were easily 14 feet high and I noticed the windows on this level were opened to a full 12 inches. Either Mae was hiding some real biceps under those long-sleeve shirts or I was an absolute weakling. The latter seemed more probable.

As I came into the kitchen, the smell of coffee and sugary carbs filled the air. Mae stood washing a coffee mug at the sink and my eyes drifted to the stained glass window above her, which threw red and purple blobs of color on the tiled floor.

"The lady from down the street brought by muffins and the Cape Cod Times," said Mae, gesturing toward the table. Sure enough, a basket of the biggest blueberry creations ever was in the center of the pale pine table. I selected one as I sat and Mae opened the fridge. "You want milk?"

"Milk sounds good to me," I replied distractedly, my attention caught by the headline on the front page about a drowning. I quickly scanned the article, learning that a middle age tourist was assumed dead after going swimming and not returning.

Something about a current dragging him beneath the waves.

When I finally looked up Mae was across from me, her coffee in her hand. "I know. I read it too. And here I was thinking it was those sharks that will get ya."

"I read that Cape Cod doesn't usually have shark problems. That's a myth," I reminded her.

"Didn't you see JAWS?" asked Mae with a quirked smile. I just rolled my eyes as she slid a note pad to me. It was covered in her chicken-scratch handwriting that matched her crazy red hair and glasses.

"I'm heading out, but I thought you could tell the guys what we need done on this list. And while you're here, you might as well start looking for a vehicle. I pulled some money from the savings your parents had left so you could finally have your own car. You are going to need one soon, especially since my trip is coming up next month."

She drew a deep breath and sighed, "You know, I'm not so sure traveling overseas is a good idea anymore. I mean, when I booked the trip a year ago we had no clue we'd be moving. I could just cancel." She pulled her purse from the back of the counter and fished out her car keys. Her face was conflicted.

Mae had saved for years to finally be able to tour the castles and cities of Europe. She had an inner fairy-tale dreamer lurking beneath her bookworm looks and quiet nature. I knew that leaving me for two weeks in Kansas, where we did in fact know a few people, was okay with her. Leaving me in a new town with a giant, antique home however, was a different story – from her perspective at least. Not to me though.

"Don't worry about me," I said. "The Cape is so safe it's insane. I mean, what is their biggest crime? Stealing lobsters out of someone else's trap? I will be fine. You can trust me."

"I know I can, but I still get to worry," she said, kissing me on the top of the head as she strolled for the door. "Read the list so you know what needs to get done. The gardener is already out back working. Call me if you need anything. I love you."

"Love you too," I said, waving over my head, my mind now consumed with thoughts of my very own chariot. I flipped to the back of the paper and found the classified section and started scanning the ads. Unfortunately, everything seemed either on its last leg or way too much cash for the financially stunted such as myself.

As my finger slid down the third column, it slowed on an older, "Black and Chrome Jeep Wrangler." I hadn't really entertained the idea of a Jeep, but the tantalizing thought of climbing over the dunes in some convertible 4x4 was suddenly all I could think about.

My mind spun away from me, visions of the off-road creation being my ticket to absolute freedom. I got up and reached for the house phone hanging next to the kitchen's screen door. Excited, I punched the phone number in the ad. *Don't be sold. Don't be sold.*

"Hello?" a boy answered.

"Uh, Hi. I'm calling about the Jeep in the paper. Is it still for sale?"

"Sure is. I just listed it."

"Excellent! Where are you located?"

"I'm working at The Milk Way and it's here. With me."

He said it like I should know it: Milk Way? What in the heck is The Milk Way? Some hardcore dairy farm? "Um, I'm new to the Cape. What and where is The Milk Way?" I asked, feeling out of the loop.

"Ah. Washashore, eh? Well, welcome to the Cape. I'm MJ and The Milk Way is just the best ice cream parlor on the planet. It's in Centerville, near Craigville Beach. Do you know where Craigville is?"

Awareness in my head slowly brightened and I leaned back slightly, looking out the kitchen side door toward the street. Just barely visible through the trees and wedged behind the library I could see the four corner lights. Sitting at the lights was a gray, tilted building which I suddenly suspected was, in fact, The Milk Way. We had driven by it last night on our way to the house. I started chuckling.

"Something funny?" asked MJ.

"Yeah. I think I can see the place from my new home. I'm Eila by the way."

The line suddenly went quiet. I thought the call had been disconnected. "Um, Hello?"

"Sorry, yeah. I'm here," he replied, but his voice sounded tight. He paused briefly again, but then finally snapped back to the jovial boy who had originally answered the phone. "So, you live on Main? Lucky you," said MJ, slightly impressed. "Well, if you want to see the Jeep, it's here. Wander over from your home and it's on the side. Dirt lot. Check it out and then come check ME out. Look for the devastatingly handsome dude in an apron."

I snorted.

"Hey! Ye who is disrespectful to the ice cream gods will get none," said MJ feigning insult.

"See you in thirty, Apron Boy." I smiled into the phone.

"See ya."

I downed the rest of my milk and quickly glanced over the to do list from Mae. No one was supposed to be here till 11:30. I had time to see the Jeep. I jotted a quick addendum about my stubborn window then headed out the side door to check on the gardener, my mind still bouncing over the sand.

One long, LONG rambling history of the area later, I managed to excuse myself from our white-haired botanist. He was a very polite, slightly elderly man who loved to talk, possibly more than work, given the size of his waist. I made a mental note to avoid him, simply because I was not the most chatty of individuals.

That, and my brain had melted after the first ten minutes of his non-stop chatter.

I walked hurriedly past my new digs, glancing up at its glorious and imposing side. Believing that this mini mansion was mine was still unfathomable. Mae and I had great hopes for this place as a Bed and Breakfast sometime soon if the business loan came through. It better come through, because I sure didn't want to go back to Kansas and our crappy apartment.

I took a sharp right at the white washed fence that designated our property, and trotted past the creamy Victorian next door. Still no signs of anyone inside - I began to think it might be a summer place. I glanced around at the other stately homes. Some were Inns, some were shops, and some were private homes like mine.

I quickly crossed the road and soon approached The Milk Way, which was definitely a relic of the 1950s. With its sagging roof and chipped paint, I was surprised it had yet to make the town's list of unstable buildings. As I walked up to the screen door the smell of vanilla and raspberries hit me in a wave and I dragged in a deep breath of deliciousness. Perhaps MJ wasn't lying about being an ice cream deity.

I pulled on the white washed screen door, but it didn't budge. I stepped back slightly and glanced around the large front window for a sign.

The Milk Way

Open 7 days

11am to 9pm

I looked right and, sure enough, a beautiful black Jeep was sitting in the far lot. It looked perfect and I abandoned the storefront, heading to the parking lot.

As I passed the side of the building, I got another blast of sugar-laced air and looked over my shoulder. Standing in the side doorway with a towel in his hands and a stained apron hanging from his neck, was an athletic boy about my age and a half-foot taller than me. He was tan with a wild mop of sun-streaked brown hair that peeked out the sides of a ratty baseball cap and tumbled into his beautiful, gray eyes.

He looked insanely familiar as he smiled and stepped through the door, "You must be Eila."

I smiled and nodded. "MJ right? Aren't you here kinda early? I mean, who eats ice cream at 9am?"

"Oh. Well, my family owns this place and we make ice cream every morning. Remember: Ice Cream God," he proclaimed as he shut the door and locked it. He slipped out of his apron and hung it on the doorknob. "So, my Jeep, eh? Come on, I'll show you."

As I watched him walk across the lot, I couldn't shake the familiarity of his face. It was driving me crazy and I finally caved to my compulsive need to know where I had seen him before. "I give up," I said, drawing a deep breath, "How do I know you?"

He stopped and looked at me, "You don't. I'm damn sure I'd remember your freckled face."

I blushed, but persisted, "No seriously, you look so familiar."

A smile curved upward on his face, "Oh yeah . . . I do look like someone. Someone famous. Everyone tells me all the time," he said, reaching up to pull off his cap. He shook his hair and it fell haphazardly, framing his face. The transformation was instant and I was shocked.

"WOW! You look exactly like what's-his-name. From that movie, you know? A KNIGHTS TALE!" I said, triumphant.

"Yeah, I know. I could've been a body-double for Ledger. Don't you think?" he asked, striking a hero's pose. I wrinkled my nose slightly, not quite agreeing.

"What? I thought you said I looked just like him?" MJ protested, jamming his hat back on.

"I think he was a little more muscled."

"WHAT? Oh, you are *so* not my friend," he said, acting hurt. The smile pulled back to his face though.

"You can be a parts-double," I said, trying to make up for the muscularly-challenged comment, "You know, face, hair . . ."

"Butt?" he asked, "Cause I do have very nice parts, including my rear. At least, I think so." I just laughed as we walked towards the Jeep. He stopped at the driver's side, turning the key in the lock and swinging the door open, gesturing for me to hop in. "So, you just moved here, huh? Where ya from?"

"Kansas," I said, sliding into the saddle brown seat. "But I guess you could say I'm from here. Historically, that is, though I have never visited myself. Turns out I had a grandfather who was a sea captain." I put my hands on the wheel and glanced around at the décor.

"So you moved here without ever having been here before? Your folks must have been here though, right? I mean, who moves from land-locked Kansas to seaside Cape Cod without knowing what they are getting into? Unless you're nuts."

"I ask myself all the time if I have lost my marbles, so 'nuts' is entirely possible – especially because I'm fairly sure my parents had no idea about the house. I moved here with my guardian. She was my mom's best friend. She raised me since I was two, when my folks died. Car accident."

MJ was quiet for a moment, watching me flip open lock boxes and check out the back seat. I climbed out of the driver's side and started walking around the Jeep, looking for any signs of damage.

"I'm . . . sorry about your folks," he said, his silly demeanor slipping briefly. I just nodded. Everyone was always sorry about my parents, but no amount of apologies would ever bring them back.

He went to the hood and unlatched the rubber locks, freeing the engine to the sunlight. "So, this is my Jeep which has been maintained religiously by my friend who works at RC garage. It runs great and is loads of fun," he proudly announced. I raised my eyebrows in mock suspicion. The truth was, I fell in love with the 4x4 the moment I saw it.

"Why are you selling it, if it's the pinnacle of perfection?" I asked sarcastically.

"Need the cash for college," he said with a shrug. I continued to inspect the vehicle, not that I knew what the heck I was doing. I came over to the engine and he stepped next to me.

"So, you said you could see the shop from your house. Which place is yours?"

"The big white and black one sort of opposite the library."

"You mean 408? Captain Walker was your grandfather?" He sounded impressed - or shocked. He looked at me, almost as if he was seeing me for the first time. Sizing me up. It was . . . odd.

"Are you alright?" I asked, somewhat uneasy.

He seemed to snap out of his strange appraisal. "What? Oh yeah, I just thought that place was abandoned or the Historical Society, or rather hysterical society, owned it. Maybe even haunted. I just never imagined I'd meet someone who was actually related to the Captain and his wife," he said. "Cool history though."

"Really? Because I never knew about them and I'd love to hear what you know." I was damn curious now.

MJ shifted on his feet, almost . . . unsure. "Well, I don't know tons. Just rumors. I guess Elizabeth Walker, the Captain's wife, disappeared when she was young. Early twenties. Most people think she drowned but there was one urban legend-type thing that said she was struck by lightning."

"STRUCK BY LIGHTNING? Are you serious?" I looked at him like he was now the one with a screw loose.

He waved the idea off, "It's just a legend. Though I still wouldn't run around with a golf club during a storm." I just shook my head.

"Are you going to Barnstable?" A trickle of hope sparked in MJ's voice.

"Don't remind me," I muttered, "Yeah, I'm going to be a senior. What college did you say you go to?"

He was delighted by my assumption, "Ha, no, not there yet! I'm a senior at BHS as well. Kids are pretty friendly too. Maybe not the cheerleaders though, at least where you are concerned," he grinned as his hands slipped into his pockets.

"What? Are they some psycho clique that detests newcomers?"

"Only when the newcomers don't seem to be the type to blindly follow orders and therefore pose a threat to their godliness," he replied, suddenly closing the hood and putting space between us. "I get the sense that you're more the rebel-type, especially if you are bold enough to move cross-country to a place you've never been to."

I gave a knowing smile. No way I was some lemming that was going to follow a dictator who can do a cartwheel. I knew MJ wasn't either, since he obviously wasn't a fan of the Cheer Squad. Yup - I was definitely going to be pals with this kid.

He dangled a set of silver keys in front of my face. "So, test drive anyone?" he asked, a crooked smile on his face.

"Uh yeah, but you can drive. All I need is to wreck the car of the first classmate I've met. That would be awful." I climbed into the passenger seat.

"I know," he replied sarcastically, "Because that would really suck for you to not be pals with someone as cool as me. It would absolutely take you down a few pegs." I rolled my eyes and he turned the key, causing the engine to roar to life. I tugged on my seat belt to make sure I had a chance of walking away if his driving reflected his personality.

"Hang on," he winked, and the Jeep vaulted forward.

* * * *

Over the next hour or so, MJ was my tour guide, showing me the town I now called home. He drove me down to several beaches, some on the map and some only accessible by 4-wheeling fans. We eventually ventured down to the waterfront and the busy harbor.

Lining the endless rows of docks were all manner of sea-going vessels. There were bulky fishing boats, tiny sailboats and a wide array of aggressive-looking speedboats. There was also a sizable assortment of yachts, complete with bathing suit-clad ladies sunning themselves on the million dollar decks. MJ pulled up next to the front dock where the massive Island Ferry was offloading passengers and cars.

I watched the parade of people exiting the boat as one child dropped a small toy through the slats of the gangplank. It fell nearly fifteen feet to the water below, at which point the child turned into a screaming blob of jelly. The mother picked up the boneless kid and continued down toward the dock. Both she and her husband looked like they were just about 'vacationed' out.

"So," said MJ turning to me, "what's the 411?"

"The 411?" I asked, still watching the parents struggle with the child.

"Yeah. Like, how did you come to move into 408 if no one from your family knew it existed?"

I laughed and shook my head. It was still a crazy story. "An auction guy called me when I was in Kansas. He told me that an anonymous buyer signed the house over to me," I said, twirling a hair elastic around my wrist. "It was a complete shock, but I guess instinct, told me I should move here. I know – it's absurd."

"It's not absurd. It's just like some crazy, fairy tale come true."

"Hmm," I mused, dubious. "The verdict is still out on the fairy tale part. It could turn out to be a nightmare."

"A nightmare?" asked MJ, surprised. "Have you looked around you? Have you seen YOUR HOUSE?"

"Yes, but I recall a mention of aggressive cheerleaders, right?"

"Oh that . . . you're right. Jury is still out," he replied with the same, awesome grin.

We sat for a few minutes longer, watching the boats and the people. The harried parents were finally hailing a cab. As I looked across the harbor, I noticed a spectacular home situated on what appeared to be a long peninsula jutting out into the horizon.

"Who owns that house?" I asked, pointing to what looked like a mansion, possibly plucked from F. Scott Fitzgerald's vivid mind.

"Ah yes, the house at the end of Torrent Road. Also known as the *Island House*," said MJ, nodding knowingly, "Spectacular home and, like yours, rarely lived in. Not sure of the owners though."

"Island House? Why is it called the Island House?" I asked, stumped.

MJ looked at me as if I were joking, "Uh, because it is on it's own island. Sort of, anyway."

He leaned closer to me and pointed out toward the home, trying to show my eyes the way. "From here it looks like it's on its own island, but it's attached to Torrent Road by a narrow strip of sand. It's basically an island, hence *Island House*."

I let out a long, low whistle. "There is no shortage of spectacular homes here, is there?"

"Nope. Zillion dollar homes are plentiful here, all of which my family cannot afford," said MJ as he started the engine. We chatted about the finer points of ice cream making and Alternative Rock as we drove back to The Milk Way.

"So, what's the verdict? Is this going to be your Jeep, or stay in my garage until someone else comes along?" MJ parked the Wrangler back in its spot at the shop and cut the engine.

"Mine," I said firmly and we got down to the business of car ownership. We haggled on the price, when to finalize the money and papers, and when he could bring it by my house. I was thrilled with my purchase, but was frustrated it would take a week to get the Jeep as he said he needed to tweak a few things.

"So, does this purchase come with limo service to school for the next week?" I asked, suddenly bold. "After all, it won't be mine until Friday, so technically I'm still Jeepless."

"Are you asking me for a ride to school?"

My boldness wilted slightly, "Yeah, I guess I am."

"Well then, yeah, I can do that! Pick you up at 7:05. I can give you the lay of the land."

"And where the minefields are, right?"

"It won't be that bad," MJ said, a broad smile spreading across his face, "Of course, I did grow up here, so I may be biased."

I half groaned and then remembered I needed to get back for the workers. I told him I'd see him soon and kicked it into a run for home.

As I glanced back one more time I saw MJ talking on his cell phone. I found it odd that his face could change so quickly, for his happy, free spirited smile had been replaced with the squared jaw of someone who was very serious.

I could only wonder who was on the phone and why they stole his sunshine.

I spent the better half of Sunday organizing the endless sea of boxes that found their irksome way into my walking path wherever possible. By nightfall, I felt like I had eaten a jar of ants and they were line dancing in my stomach.

My nerves about the following morning at Barnstable clouded my mind. I had visions of spiteful cheerleaders and baffling miles of hallway. I was grateful that MJ was going to give me a ride, but asking him to be my personal anti-anxiety pill all day long was a remote option.

I barely touched dinner with Mae, who examined me carefully, but said few words. She was less than pleased with my vehicle choice, no doubt having hoped for something with ten airbags and a solid roof. She must have had a touch of sympathy about the new school however, as she kept her pointed opinions about my black beast to herself.

When I climbed into bed that night, I had trouble unwinding my racing imagination long enough to doze off. Finally, in the wee hours of what was technically Monday, I fell into a deep sleep, but my restless subconscious rose to the surface in the form of an uneasy dream.

I stood in the darkness, slowly making out landmarks. Timeless, tall-masted ships graced the harbor and the black water rolled under the white light of a full moon. I took everything in ~ the gas lamps, the cobblestone street and smell of the sea. My clothes were too heavy and the skirt I wore weighed me down, nearly rooting me in place. I heard the faint thrum of running water and turned to see a fountain, tall and pillar-like, next to me. I seemed to be in the center of a small square near the harbor.

A dark haired man, probably in his 40s, stood casually next to the fountain. As soon as my eyes met his however, I was seized with a crushing fear. It was as if I was alone in the sea and knew a hungry shark was circling beneath my flailing feet, waiting to pull me into the abyss.

The dark man started calmly walking toward me.

"Elizabeth," he purred.

As I drew a sharp breath, the view suddenly swiveled and I became the spectator watching the man and a young woman. She was dressed similarly to me and she had taken my place near the fountain. In one fluid movement, the man lunged at her and grabbed her by the throat.

My heart nearly leapt from my chest, my terror fueling it on, as I knew she was about to die. I screamed to her, willing her to live, but I was thrown to the ground by some potent, invisible force.

Suddenly I was awake and on my bedroom floor, wedged against the frame of my bed with my legs still hiked upright by the tangle of sheets. I lay there, eyes wide, taking in the cracked ceiling and allowing my heart to slow.

My hands tingled from the adrenaline still loose in my veins and

I quickly pulled myself up on my elbows and scanned the room looking for the man, but finding only the quiet of my bedroom surrounding me. It was a nightmare, but it felt far too real.

I stayed there on the cool floor as time slipped by, trying to cautiously remember the dream that had shook me, but was fading fast from memory. As I finally extracted myself from the sheets and reset myself into my bed, all I could remember of the dark night was a fountain, softly lit under the light of a full moon.

The nagging call of my alarm clock woke me at 6am and the vague recollection of sleeping like crap crept back into my mind. Of course, what really ruined the morning was the knowledge that BHS was looming in the very near future.

Dragging myself out of bed, I got ready for school and pulled my hair into a loose ponytail. I looked at my reflection in the bathroom mirror and realized I could hide better behind my mane, so I pulled the elastic free, releasing a mass of darkness around my face.

Forty minutes later I was waiting in the kitchen, looking over what little our chatty gardener had accomplished over the weekend. The protesting crunch of seashells heralded the arrival of MJ and his ancient SUV. Determined to face my classmates with a scrap of dignity, I sucked up my courage and grabbed my backpack, pushing through the screen door.

Approaching the old brown and black Bronco, I saw MJ through the passenger window reaching with all his might across the ripped vinyl seat. His long arm grabbed the old, silver door lock and he yanked it up with a snap and then pulled the handle, opening my door. I stood in the open passenger doorframe, looking at my classmate nearly flat on the bench seat, his arm still outstretched.

"No automatic door locks, eh?" I smiled.

"Hey Chicky, don't laugh!" he protested as he sat back up and I climbed in, "You did notice that the Jeep lacks power locks too, didn't ya?"

No, I didn't. "Of course I knew that, but at least the span isn't ten feet," I smiled.

"Ha ha," he said dryly. "Listen, don't knock the limo service, or you can take the mommy-mobile. This mechanical marvel was my Dad's," he declared, stroking the faded dash. "It has great sentimental value."

I raised an eyebrow suspiciously as I slammed the 4-ton door shut. He tried to stare me down, but I was a pro.

"Okay, FINE. It is a pile of scrap metal, *but* it was F-R-E-E!" He knocked the gearshift into reverse and backed the Bronco down the drive, hooking a left on to Main.

BHS was only a few miles from my place, but the neighborhood was centuries apart. Whereas Main Street was lined with declarations of wealth from yesteryear, the street that led to the high school was a reminder of the 1960s race to build small, cramped cottages by the sea. I watched out the window at the passage of time as defined by the homes that slipped by.

"So, how do you like the Cape so far?" MJ asked, one hand fiddling with the chipped radio dial, searching for a station.

"Well, I haven't actually had much time to see anything except the inside of my house and this weird ice cream shop called The Milk Way. Okay, and maybe the grocery store and the beach. But what little I have seen so far is welcoming. I hope I'll like it here."

"I think you will," said MJ, slowing the Bronco to a crawl behind the line of cars snaking their way into the BHS parking lot. "I mean, it's real quiet here in the winter, but everyone knows one another and I, at least, like that small, tight community. On the other hand, there are no secrets here, so don't badmouth too many people," he said with a wink. He pulled the rumbling chariot into a parking spot next to another large, fast-looking older car, though this one appeared to be a true classic by anyone's account.

As he cut the engine, the door to the black two-door opened and out stepped a lithe girl with short, spiked blonde hair. Her delicate features and huge blue eyes made her look like a pixie on the lam from the Lost Boys, though I was quite sure she could bench-press the Bronco on attitude alone.

She came over to MJ's side and he excitedly wound down the window. "Hey Ana! How the heck are ya? I haven't seen you for weeks!" proclaimed MJ, a happy smile beaming at the petite athlete.

"Dude, I was working on my baby at the shop most of this month," she replied, nodding towards her ride with the massive gold falcon on the hood. "Come to think of it, I was also working on YOUR tricked out Wrangler this summer, which begs the question: where is the source of so many slave hours? If you wrecked it, I may have to kill you!"

"Calm down, calm down. I had to sell it. Needed the cash and you knew my Dad had this fine automobile sitting out behind the shed." As if on cue, the Bronco's engine snapped with heat as it cooled. I cleared my throat.

"Oh yeah," added MJ, turning slightly in his seat, "This is Eila. She bought the Jeep over the weekend. And, get this . . . , " he added in a conspiratorial whisper, "She lives in the Walker place."

Ana raised a suspicious, dirt blonde eyebrow and looked at me with a slight grin, "Hey Eila. I'm Ana Lane." She hooked her arms over the driver's door. "I hope you plan on taking outstanding care of your new ride. Many hours went into that Wrangler, most of which could've happily been spent surfing Nauset if it weren't for old friends." She reached in and wildly rubbed MJ's head as he sat there like a contented dog.

I crisscrossed my finger over my heart, "Promise. I'll take great care of it."

I opened my door and hopped down, crossing in front of the Bronco as MJ stepped out his side. The sound of hip-hop music and someone wolf whistling caught my attention and I turned to see a white convertible slowly heading up the school's main driveway. Behind the wheel was a life-size Barbie doll, tossing her dark hair to the side as she chatted with another girl in the passenger seat. A third girl sat in the center back seat, her arms outstretched on the caramel leather.

Inadvertently, I caught the driver's eye and she stared me down, a superior smile to her candy-apple lips. I felt my cheeks burn as her roasting gaze dragged from my face down to my sneakers and up again. She inclined her head toward her co-pilot and said something brief, her eyes never leaving me. Her stick-thin passenger looked at me appraisingly and snickered. Before I knew it, they had passed by our parking spot and disappeared around the building to the other lot.

Ana had not missed our silent exchange and stepped next to me. She nodded to where the white car had disappeared, "Those, my friend, are to be avoided at all costs. They are part of the cheerleading squad and can make your life a living hell if you piss them off. But don't worry. You'll be fine." She slapped my back for encouragement, but it felt like she realigned my spine.

MJ slid up next to me and put his arm around my shoulder, giving me a quick, friendly squeeze. "Welcome to BHS!" he announced enthusiastically.

I had not even entered the building and already I wanted to toss my cookies. Resigned, I followed Ana and MJ into my new high school as they explained the finer points of avoiding sadistic cheerleader, Nikki Shae, and her PomPom Mustang Gang we had seen drive by.

After figuring out the maze of hallways thanks to my personal escort service in the form of MJ and Ana, I found myself at first period Literature class. I managed to claim a chair with a right-handed desk attached to it in the second row and dropped my backpack by my feet. I leaned over and fished out a pen and pad of paper as more students filtered in through the door, chattering to one another as they took seats.

A boy with dark velvet skin and a red and white letterman jacket sat down next to me and nodded. I gave a quick smile back. To my great relief, none of my English Lit classmates resembled the clique from the convertible.

Varsity Boy cleared his throat and I turned to him. "Hi. I'm Jesse," he said, extending his palm. I reached out and shook his wide hand.

"I'm Eila."

"I know who you are," said Jesse, smiling.

"Seriously? How?" I asked as a stray curl tickled my cheek and I absently brushed it away.

"It's a small town. That, and I have Nikki Shae in my homeroom and she was talking about a new girl who was hanging out with MJ and, well, I saw you get out of his retro Bronco in the front parking lot."

"Man! Word travels fast here."

"Better than fast - I'd say light speed," he said, leaning back slightly and crossing his arms, proud of his knowledge. "For instance, I also know that the Walker place has new residents. I know this because my family's slow-as-dirt landscaper, babbled on about the mother-and-daughter pair that now lives there," said Jesse, leaning in toward me and dropping his voice to a lower, conspiratorial tone.

"And he said the daughter was very sweet and had beautiful, long dark hair similar to the original Elizabeth Walker, whose photo is at the hysterical society's museum." He leaned back again in his chair, "So, using my brilliant deducing skills, I figured *you* must be none-other than Eila Walker."

I looked at him for a moment more, my eyes dropping to slits.

"Okay, okay, someone pointed you out in the hall and filled me in."

I laughed, "I see. Well, it's mostly true although I will say word gets around."

"Yeah, it's like six-degrees of separation the way people know each other here. And all their business!" said Jesse.

"More like two-degrees if you ask me."

"Damn straight! Welcome to the Cape, Eila!" he said, smiling.

"Thanks," I replied.

As the last few seats started to fill, a gray-haired, rounded man shuffled into the class, coffee mug in one hand and several folders tucked under the other arm. He placed both mug and paperwork on his desk at the front of the classroom and turned to write his name on the blackboard. As he wrote, the class quieted down with a few whispered conversations continuing.

The door opened again and another boy stepped into the classroom. He wore a gray hooded sweatshirt, which was pulled up over his short, dark blonde hair. Through his sweatshirt I could tell that he was well built, with broad shoulders and defined arms. Whereas MJ was athletically lean, like a swimmer, this boy was solid, like a member of the lacrosse team. His face was hard to make out under the hood, but I felt compelled to look at him.

Out of the corner of my eye, I saw that Jesse glanced at him as well, then surreptitiously at me. Sweatshirt Boy dropped a yellow slip of paper on the teacher's desk and continued to the back corner of the room and the last remaining seat.

I tried to look studious and scribbled on my notebook while attempting to glance sneakily over my arm towards Sweatshirt Boy. Instead I caught Jesse's eye. He gave me a knowing smile, clearly aware that I was checking out the boy that had just entered.

He leaned forward, speaking quietly, "He's new too, although. . ." he glanced back, his body language changing and his voice slowed, "I have no clue who he is, which is surprising."

"So much for you being the real Gossip Girl, eh?" I whispered, smiling broadly.

Jesse made a sad face, then smiled, "Seriously, I have no clue who that dude is, although by the look of him, he might be a candidate for the football team. I guess I'll have to check him out too, though the 'longing-for-a-liplock' interest can be yours alone," he said, laughing quietly.

"I am NOT!" I was grinning like a fool as my face blushed hot red.

We both turned back to the front of the room. Our teacher, a "Mr. Autler" as it now read on the blackboard just above **English Literature 322**, turned around, picking up his coffee mug and taking a sip. He took up the yellow paper and read the written name aloud. "Raef O'Reilly?" he asked looking around.

Sweatshirt Boy raised his hand, barely clearing the top of his head.

"It says you are a new student here at Barnstable and have added my class to your schedule," said Mr. Autler flatly. "I'm flattered you have decided to join us, but try to be earlier in the future. And no hats, Mr. O'Reilly, and that includes hoods."

The majority of the room had now turned to see Sweatshirt Boy, aka Raef. Well, the girls did at least. He pulled his hood back off his head, keeping his eyes on the notebook in front of him.

O . . . M . . .G

I bit my lip so I wouldn't sigh loudly at his classic, Abercrombie-esque face. He reminded me of a young cowboy via Hollywood: tossed and wavy dirty blonde hair, strong chin and flawless, golden skin.

With him in the room, I'm sure most of the boys in the class wanted to get on with the literary classics, using Clif Notes if needed to speed the process along. The females, on the other hand, could stay in English all day long, perhaps reading *War and Peace* cover-to-cover.

I was just about to pry my attention away from Raef, when he cautiously glanced up from his black and white notebook and connected with my gaze.

I was instantly seized with horrific and illogical fear.

It wasn't the quick, superficial burst of scariness that accompanies a spider on the wall, but the absolute certainty of imminent death that unleashed a torrent of adrenaline through my body. Raef must have sensed my startling change of mood because he quickly glanced back to his notebook.

My nerves on fire and my heart ricocheting in my throat, I barely heard Mr. Autler doing roll call. I stared at my desk, my eyes unseeing as I tried to calm myself, dearly hoping that whatever had just occurred was not love at first sight. My stomach flip-flopped neurotically.

"Eila!" I heard Jesse whispering urgently. I slowly became aware that someone was butchering my name.

"Ee-Ly-A Walker?" questioned Mr. Autler again, looking out over the class. As my heart slowed, I managed to bring my brain back to the present.

"Uh, here," I replied, meekly raising my hand. "But it's EYE-LA," I continued, trying to calmly correct him. My voice sounded squeaky in my ears.

"No chance you are related to Captain Walker?"

Oh please. Not now. "Uh, yeah. He was my Grandfather way back when." I was suddenly the new focus of attention and wanted to melt through the chipped linoleum floor.

"Very impressive," he mused taking another sip of his drink before turning his attention to our reading list for the year.

I glanced over at Jesse, who was watching me, his expression one of concern. He mouthed the words, "You alright?" I nodded rapidly, almost like a bobble head doll on a caffeine high, though my sanity was far from certain.

Through the rest of the class I fought a restless urge to look back at the boy in the corner. The two contrary emotions of an almost magnetic draw to him and primal fear of him tormented me through Mr. Autler's monologue. Self-preservation, however, won out and I was able to keep my eyes away from the back corner, instead attempting to focus on the class syllabus that was being discussed for the semester.

My body still tingled, as if wary and on edge. I tried to simply dismiss the whole thing as first day jitters and the fact that an outstandingly beautiful boy looked at me. By the time Mr. Autler was assigning us the first two chapters of *The Scarlet Letter*, I had convinced myself that Raef was a Greek god, fallen down from Olympus to make all the girls at Barnstable High mindless blobs of goo.

When the bell rang, Mount Olympus disappeared and I, heartbeat in check, gathered up my folders and notebook and made sure I was out the door before any immortal heroes.

The mob of students flowing through the corridor was surreal. I felt like a wayward tourist during rush hour in New York City. Not quite knowing which way to go, I got caught up in the stream of students while trying to look at the school map in my hands. Suddenly, my elbow was knocked hard and all the papers and folders I had hiked under my arm scattered like roadkill in the crammed hallway.

For a second I stood and stared at the carnage strewn on the floor, quickly calculating the probability of being trampled by my peers if I knelt down to recover my schoolwork. I hoped the school nurse was well trained in combat triage as I crouched down to retrieve my belongings.

As I did so, I heard a light laugh and looked up to see Nikki Shae and two cheerleaders walking away from me in the crowd, one glancing back and giving a petulant wave. The throngs of students didn't seem to impede their stride as the crowd parted for them, as if they were celebrities who could not be touched.

Farther ahead of them I saw Ana looking down the corridor at me, her sympathies projecting past the lockers. She had seen the whole incident and I realized that one of the girls had deliberately knocked into me.

I watched as Ana turned her attention from me to a frazzled freshman across the hall from her. She locked eyes with the skinny kid, who was fumbling with his books. The boy suddenly seemed lost in thought as he stared at Ana. He abruptly straightened and smiled, quickly shifting his books under one arm. He then turned his attention to Nikki, who was rapidly approaching the area where Ana and he stood.

As the cheerleaders strode along chattering, the now squared-shouldered boy burst forward, stepping out in front of the three girls.

The sudden obstacle in the parted sea of students broke their stride and caused Pompom #1 to careen off into a locker. Nikki and PomPom #2 came to an abrupt halt, with Nikki landing nose to nose with the boy who had a toothy, confident smile across his face. He seemed to be talking animatedly at her. Suddenly he held out his hand as if to shake hers.

Nikki looked stunned, then disgusted, and pushed past him. The PomPoms quickly filed in on either side of her. I glanced back to where Ana had been, a smile on my face, but she was nowhere in sight.

As I turned my attention back to where my papers were being crushed, a bolt of panic sent me tipping off my heels. Crouching in front of me, with all my belongings in his hands, was Raef. As I lost the precarious balance I had attained on the balls of my feet, he quickly reached out and grasped my elbow to steady me.

"I think we better get up, unless your plan was to be trampled. Though, being crushed on your first day may save you from being used as target practice," said Raef, nodding after Nikki. Stunned at suddenly being face to face with him and dazed by his oddly soothing voice, I was unable to move.

"I think we better get *up*," he said more urgently as backpacks and students whizzed by our heads.

Realizing I was currently without any survival instincts, he started to guide me to a standing position from my crouch, his hand firm but gentle on my elbow. I quickly judged my heartbeat and level of panic, but was surprised to find not fear, but excitement, as if I was about to bungee jump off the Sagamore Bridge.

Maybe I had misjudged our first eyeball encounter in the class? Maybe I misread my own flaming self-consciousness, in the face of this stunning boy, as fear? That had to be it, for as we stood among the passing river of kids, I felt nothing but a thrilling, magnetic pull towards Raef.

I realized I was staring at him like a fool, so I managed to form a few semi-coherent words, "Uh, thanks," I mumbled as he slowly released my arm, no doubt worried I'd slouch to the floor again. "It is Raef, right?" I asked, slightly straightening my back and trying to act remotely casual.

"Yes. Raef O'Reilly. And you're Eila Walker, correct?" he asked. That smooth, husky voice felt strangely familiar. It was an odd sensation, like when a smell triggers a potent memory that eludes identification. I held his voice in my mind, replaying it over and over.

"Uh, yeah, " I mumbled again, showing my scholarly command of the English language. He shuffled my papers into a neater stack and handed them to me. "Oh, thank you so much," I said. "I'd have been lost, literally, without this map."

I snapped out of my daze and looked over the campus map, frantically searching for my next classroom number as I realized there were very few students left in the halls. As if on cue, the bell rang, signaling next period. "Darn it," I gritted my teeth. "I have no idea where I'm going and now I'm late. Way to go, Eila," I hissed to myself.

Raef offered up a ray of hope as he glanced at my class schedule, "Chemistry. Fun. I passed it on the way in this morning. Come on, it's this way," he nodded down the hall.

As he looked at me, that same, original panic I had when I first saw him flashed through my veins. I quickly shooed it away as pure hormone-issued stupidity or a severe case of butterflies.

A hot guy that had saved me from being roadkill, rescued my academic scribblings, and now was acting as guide? Raging butterflies for sure. I glanced at his face and my stomach did calisthenics, "Uh, lead the way then."

We swung down the hallway, me trotting to keep up with Raef's long, fast strides. As we rounded a corner, a student hall monitor sitting at a rickety desk saw us coming. "Do you have a pass?" he called out.

Without breaking stride, I called back, "I'm new, slightly lost and now late. Give me a break!"

We continued down the hall for what I swear was a mile of dust bowl brown, finally slowing as we entered the science wing.

"What is the room number?" asked Raef, glancing at me.

I slowed, scanning my class schedule until I found my Chemistry class. "It says 115," I said, looking up at him and then quickly at the number on door closest to me. "It must be a few doors down. I'll find it. Thanks so much!"

I smiled and started past him down the hall. As I crossed near him, I could feel the air seem to thicken and the back of my neck chilled. If this is indeed what they call love at first sight, then the description is woefully lacking.

As I reached my class door, I looked back and he was still standing there, his backpack hitched over his shoulders and his hands in his jean pockets. I gave a quick wave and he nodded in return and turned, heading in the opposite direction.

The chemistry teacher understood about my being "new and lost," but quite frankly, she could've put me in detention for a month. I wouldn't have cared as long as I kept the face of Raef O'Reilly in my mind, with his warm voice making all my senses tingle.

Butterflies? Nah. This was more like the ravens from *The Birds*, when all the feathered friends attacked the people in a rage.

Chemistry slipped by in a blur of equations and periodic charts. It wasn't until homework was being distributed that I turned in my chair to fetch a folder from my backpack and saw her.

Seated one row over and three seats back was none other than Nikki. She seemed to be inspecting her manicure and my sudden lack of movement caught her attention. She raised her coal black eyelashes from her nails just long enough to convey a forceful, unspoken loathing.

My wide-eyed surprise slipped into a hardened glare, and Nikki seemed to prime herself for a drawn out battle. The ringing of the 3rd period bell broke off our stare-down. We both stood and she crossed the aisle to stand in front of me.

"Just because you live on Main and the hot, new guy showed you some mercy, does not mean you fit in with the elite crowd," she whispered, a sharp razor edge to her words belying her beautiful, crimson smile.

My brain jettisoned any sense of sanity and my words just tumbled out, "Ah, I see. So you haven't been able to climb the social stratosphere either, huh? Could it be that your fat head makes the climb too difficult?"

A vein nearly popped from the side of her head as I continued, "Oh and, uh, FYI, Raef's 'mercy' extended to walking me to class as well. He is very sweet." Without doubt, my mutinous mouth was looking to get slapped.

As I watched Nikki, I was sure her head was about to explode all over the taupe desks. She drew a deep, hateful breath, then turned quickly and strode out the door, her lithe cheerleader figure sashaying ever so slightly.

I kept up my grating smile until she disappeared out of the classroom and then allowed the rage to seep back into my bones. I finished packing up my things, now ramming the innocent chemistry book harshly into the leather pack. I fumed and had visions of this cheerleading twit getting mowed down by one of the buses.

After another two classes, the lunch bell finally rang and I wove my way through the chaotic hall, aiming towards what I hoped was the cafeteria. Like the jammed roads of Cape Cod, I quickly learned to not cross traffic unless I wanted to be in a head-on collision.

It took me almost five minutes to make it to the cafeteria entrance, though I may have only moved a few yards.

As I rounded the corner to head down the ramp towards the acres of tables, I saw MJ and Ana. MJ waved enthusiastically at me. I was so relieved to see friendly faces.

"So . . . is BHS all you ever dreamed of?" asked MJ sarcastically. "Come sit with us."

I followed the two of them to a table at the far corner near the back windows. I flopped into a garish orange chair, and MJ and Ana sat across from me.

"So, you look burnt. Long morning?" asked Ana, pulling her lunch from her messenger bag.

"That might be an understatement," I sighed, biting into my flattened ham sandwich. I probably should've taken my lunch out of my backpack *before* I hurled in the textbook.

"You awl wight?" asked MJ through a full mouth of cheese puffs.

"Yeah, yeah. I'm fine. Last period wasn't fabulous though. Turns out Nikki isn't a complete nitwit since she has AP Chemistry with me, and I have a feeling she'd like to use the Bunsen burner on me. Soon." I swallowed down my squishwich, but the tension made it go down my throat in lumps. "What's her issue anyway? I mean, I don't get it, she doesn't even know me."

"What? You want to be pals?" asked MJ with a snort of disgust. "Listen, here is the deal - Nikki surrounds herself with high-end mannequins who will bend to her every command. But you, well, I guess you come with a bit of mystique," said MJ, still happily chowing.

"I have a mystique? What are you talking about?" I gave up on the ham and cheese and moved on to the bottle of water.

Ana could see MJ was going to continue the conversation with a disgusting mouthful and mercifully took over, "He means that you are a Walker. Your family is old money and *you* own a spectacular and well-known home in one of the most beautiful areas on Cape Cod. No amount of new money that Nikki has can trump such old family history and wealth."

My face flushed, embarrassed. MJ mumbled something unintelligible to my ears, but Ana caught it, "Oh yeah, and you were talking to that new guy who she supposedly made a move on a few days ago at the beach. I heard he rebuffed her advances and she was pissed! It must have been epic." A reminiscent smile lit Ana's face. "Of course, I'm sure that she didn't miss his chivalry, and nothing irks her more than thinking she has to compete for the biggest boytoy in school. Nikki doesn't compete. She seeks and conquers. By my count that is two, huge strikes against you," said Ana, slugging her Powerade.

MJ nodded and muttered something again, his mouth still full. Ana nodded as well, "I agree with MJ. You were just an irritating fly on Nik's radar until that guy helped you out. Now, you are her bright red bullseye until she lands that poor sucker."

I put my hand to my face, trying to stave off a migraine, and rested my forehead on the cool, laminate table. I didn't know which was worse, being Nikki's target or worrying she might win over a certain, handsome boy. Suddenly I heard MJ humming something that sounded vaguely like a funeral march.

"Uh, Eila. I think someone wants you," said Ana poking my fingertip. Without picking up my head I swiped away her hand. That is when I heard the velvet voice again.

"Eila. Are you all right? Did you get trampled in another hall? I can't leave you for an instant."

My skin tingled and I swear I could feel the heat radiate off of Raef's body. I stayed frozen, my face to the table for a moment. I was excited he was here but wondering why on earth this boy was following me. Finally I picked my head up and brushed back my hair away from my face. Ana looked like she had swallowed a bug and MJ looked amused.

I glanced to the table where Nikki sat with her minions. She was watching Raef and me with rapt attention as she bit ruthlessly into a shiny, red apple. I hoped madly that it was poisoned.

I stretched my neck one way, then the other. "Yeah, yeah. I'm fine," I said, hoping to sound casual as I looked up at Raef. "Just a little headache. Long day, you know?"

"Yeah, I do know. Being the new target isn't so fun, I will agree," he said nodding toward a table draped in cheerleaders and jocks. I was a bit stunned. He knew Nikki was after him, but seemed uninterested. Was he immune to her curvy waist and ample chest? Good grief, was he *blind?*

He looked at me and smiled slightly, "Well, I hope you get rid of your headache soon, but, seeing as I am sort of new as well, can I join you?" he asked, still standing slightly behind me.

"Uh, yeah. Sure." I pulled my lunch out of his way while

mentally checking to see if my mouth was hanging open. As he sat down next to me, I began to introduce my two pals, "Raef, this is MJ and . . ."

"Ana Lane. I know," said Raef calmly.

Ana narrowed her eyes as she studied Raef's handsome face. "I'm sorry but . . . do I *know* you?" she asked, suspicious.

"Technically you know my brother. Kian," said Raef, extending his hand to hers. "It is a pleasure to finally meet you."

Ana's demeanor instantly changed. Her body grew stiff and the surrounding oxygen felt as though it fell a few degrees. Raef seemed to sense her unease, "I'm sorry, you *do* know my brother, correct? He spoke well of you. He said you are a very talented mechanic."

Raef left his hand outstretched, waiting for her to shake it. MJ had stopped chewing as well, flicking his eyes back and forth between the two of them, his chronic smile long gone.

She finally reached out and shook his hand briefly, but she never took her eyes off his face. "I didn't know he had a brother. Is Kian here?" asked Ana, still rigid, her hand quickly back in her lap.

"He is and he'd like for you to do some work for him. He has a new Corvette."

Ana snorted. "Ha, sounds like him," she said, almost distastefully. "I'm busy at the shop, so tell him he can take it somewhere else. I'm not the only gear-head in town."

"My brother only trusts you," replied Raef, looking at Ana.

"She said she is busy," clipped MJ, a hard, almost defensive edge to his voice. Perhaps he did know this Kian character.

MJ and Raef watched each other carefully. The stare down was broken by MJ's cell phone chirping. He glanced quickly at Ana, who was looking off into the distance, then dug his phone from his pocket to read the text.

I glanced at Raef and realized he had been looking at me. "What?" I asked, sounding a tad demanding, the tension between my classmates apparently contagious.

"Nothing, you just remind me of someone," he said, his face oddly serious.

"Who?"

Raef shook his head, "You wouldn't know her, just someone I knew in passing."

I wanted to ask him more. Was it a girlfriend? A relative? His seriousness seemed to speak volumes. I got the distinct impression that whomever I reminded him of, she had demanded a heavy emotional toll. I could tell his deep blue eyes were no longer in the present.

He was rerunning my twin in his mind, and I was dying to know who she was. Was this phantom girl from his past the reason he was sitting with me at lunch? And what the heck went on between Kian and Ana and possibly even MJ? I had so many questions and had a feeling no one wanted to cough up the answers.

MJ snapped his phone shut and I jumped, yanked out of my mental monologue.

"Well, seems that I have to go to CatBird Farm for fresh raspberries for the shop, and my dad wants me to head out after 6th period, since 7th I have free. I'm sorry Eila, I know I was supposed to give you a ride. Can you call Mae?" questioned MJ genuinely sorry. He looked at Ana, hopeful.

Ana glanced from MJ to me and sighed, "Oh fine. I can take you home. I just have to stop off somewhere. It isn't far from your house."

"That would be great. I would've walked rather than have Mae come get me," I said, trying to bring a smile to her hardened face.

"I'll see you at my car right after last bell," replied Ana, no nonsense. "Don't dawdle, this place gets backed up quickly between the buses and cars."

Just then the bell rang and lunch was over. I turned to say bye to Raef, but he had already left. I didn't even hear him get up.

I scanned the sea of students making their way out of the cavernous cafeteria, but the mysterious boy in the gray hoodie was nowhere to be seen.

Ana's car seemed to lack shocks as every dip in the road rebounded through my spine. I tried to creep my butt over to a more cushioned part of the Trans Am's seat.

"So, where are we going again?" I asked, another bump rattling my teeth.

"We're stopping by Dalca Anescu's place," replied Ana. "She knew my Dad and has an old house like yours, but made the first floor into an herb and essence store called The Crimson Moon. Pretty cool stuff, though some people think she has a screw loose. I think she's harmless though. Just earthy."

"*Knew* your Dad?" I asked, not missing the past tense in her vernacular.

"Yeah. My Dad was a scallop fisherman. Last year he had a heart attack while out at sea and ended up in a coma. He died a few days later.

The doctors said he didn't have a chance, even if he had been on land and closer to the hospital, but I'm still not sure about that," she said, her eyes not leaving the road.

Whereas I had come to accept the loss of my parents, the buffer of many years helping greatly, Ana's pain was still raw. I felt for her and understood her anger.

"After his death, I proved to the courts that I could act as an adult and was allowed to move into the apartment above RC Garage. The owner lets me work off some of the rent. I really like my freedom," said Ana.

"What about your mom?" I asked, unable to stop myself from prying.

Ana shrugged, "She left when I was just a baby. Drug problems I'm told. I have no idea where she is."

"I'm really sorry Ana," I said, looking at her profile as she drove.

She was silent for a few moments then finally turned to me, "You too. MJ filled me in at school." Ana and I were more alike than I could've imagined. Damaged, but defiant.

She swung the wheel to the right, turning her boat of a vehicle down my street.

"She lives on Main?" I asked, surprised.

"Yeah, told you she was close to your place." Ana turned left into the driveway of a home similar to mine, but the angles of the roof were different. It was also missing the porch that I had come to love on 408. She parked near the side door and cut the engine. The sign hanging from a weathered shingle read, "The Crimson Moon - Herbs and Essence."

"Come on, I will introduce you to the only Gypsy around," she said, hopping out of the car.

I quickly followed. "Gypsy?" I asked. Ana nodded as she opened the back door to the home for me and I stepped through, but stopped cold when I saw the massive black dog lying in the middle of the floor. "Uh, there seems to be a bear on the floor," I said, my voice staccato.

Ana pushed past me. "Huh. I'm surprised he's here," she said, looking at the enormous canine with an eyebrow raised. "Anyway, this is just Marsh. He looks intimidating, but he's harmless." She leaned down and patted the massive dog on the head. "Looking a little chub there, eh Marsh?"

I could've sworn I heard the dog breathe out a low growl, but reminded myself that a dog can't understand a putdown when he hears one.

"He is huge. What is he?" I asked, amazed at the animal's mammoth size. Without a doubt, he would tower over my head if he reared up.

"Dalca says he's a cross between ancient Romanian breeds. I think he's just a cross between mutts."

"I think he's a cross between a horse and lion," I muttered, but Ana was already wandering through to the next room. I stepped gingerly around Marsh and followed Ana into the front where the store was located.

The area took my breath away.

It was as if I had stepped into an enchanted forest. The high ceilings were painted dark purple and strewn with little white twinkle lights. Suspended from the ceiling were long, knotty branches draped in dried flowers, crystals, woven dream catchers and delicate paper butterflies. Heavy drapes hung low on the windows, enabling the room to stay dark even at midday.

As I took in the fairy-tale lair, I heard the shuffling of something heavy. From around the corner came a dark-haired woman, pushing a large cardboard box.

"Oh hey, let me help ya," said Ana, hurrying over to help the woman lift the box onto the desk.

"It is so good to see you Ana!" the woman declared as they hugged, her ebony hair gathered in a long braid down her back. She was in her 60s from what I guessed, but fit. She wore a brightly colored blouse and soft, pleated skirt that dusted the floor. Her long, elegant neck was hung with at least 20 necklaces, the longest of which dangled past her breasts with a small vial of something gray.

"So, I wanted you to meet Eila Walker. She just moved here and is living in her family's place on Main. Eila, this is Dalca Anescu," said Ana gesturing to me.

"Pleasure to meet you, Eila," said Dalca, extending a hand adorned with a wild assortment of rings.

"Nice to meet you," I said, shaking her hand as I glanced around the room "This place is awesome. It smells fabulous too!"

Dalca laughed, "Why thanks. You girls hungry? I just made scones and ground some coffee."

Ana looked at me, "Can we? Or do you need to get back?"

"No, we can stay. I'd love whatever you are making," I said to Dalca. I was starving after passing on my squishwich.

"Excellent. Give me a few minutes to get things together. Feel free to look around." Dalca swooped into the next room with Marsh following her.

I walked along the shelves admiring an endless row of beautiful bottles, all in different, radiant colors. I glanced over my shoulder at Ana on the other side of the room. She was next to a wall of literature. *The Hound of the Baskervilles* stood out in a red binding and Ana pulled it from the shelf, flipping through the well-worn pages.

I turned back to the bottles and selected a lavender one, popping the glass stopper off the top. I gingerly took a whiff and the smell reminded me of the bushes near my house.

"These are essential oils," said Ana coming up behind me. "They are thought to have healing powers. What you have there is lilac. I like . . ." Ana scanned the wall, looking for something, "Ah ha! I like this one." She selected a deep green bottle and unscrewed the top. She handed it to me and I smelled. The aroma was exquisite.

"What is this?" I asked, highly impressed.

"Night Queen – a southwestern desert flower that blooms only one night. I love that it smells like Lilac and Lily of the Valley and Rose. I think it's like a combination of all the best flowers."

"It is fabulous! I may have to get some," I replied, looking around the room.

"Dalca has shown me how to combine some of the oils with herbs to make healing salves. I actually used one concoction on myself when I burned my hand working on an engine. It took away the pain and healed really fast. Pretty cool. People like Dalca have some amazing knowledge."

"You mean Gypsies?" I said, jokingly.

"Gypsies and witches and some more earthy individuals," replied Ana matter-of-factly.

"Wait a second. You're serious, aren't you?" I asked, stunned. "You're telling me that she really is a Gypsy? And that, what? Witches exist?"

"Just because you read all sorts of crazy stories, doesn't mean there aren't people out there who have special abilities and insights into the natural world," said Ana, picking up a sea green bottle with swirls of silver lacing through it.

I thought back to that morning, in the hall, and the freshman with the glasses. "What do you mean, 'abilities'," I asked, unable to shake the vision of the shy boy who had looked at Ana and then was suddenly confident.

Ana seemed to chose her words carefully, "I just mean there are all different kinds of people out there, that's all."

I could tell that a conversation about whatever I saw in the hall was not going to happen. I'd pry it out of her eventually though.

She changed the subject abruptly, dodging any further questions, "Come on, let's go eat."

I followed her into the kitchen, which was laden with so many objects it was a visual overload. More books and countless baskets with herbs and root veggies hung from overhead beams.

Dalca had laid out quite a snack spread on the dark oval table, and I pulled out a chair and sat down, starving, "Oh, thanks, I'm famished!"

"More than happy to feed you, my dear," said Dalca with a warm smile. She sat down opposite Ana and me. "So, how do you like the Cape so far?" asked Dalca, pouring me a cup of dark coffee.

"It is a lot different from where I lived in Kansas, but the people are really nice for the most part," I said smiling and glancing at Ana. "And I love your shop. Such great stuff. How did you get into all of that?" I asked, taking a bite of steaming scone.

"I am sure Ana told you that I'm from Gypsy blood. Our family has handed down our traditions through centuries. We are more or less born with the instinctive knowledge and taught the finer points by elders as we grow up."

I turned and looked at Ana, who seemed to be studying the book she had brought with her from the shop. It was an obvious attempt to avoid any questions I may have aimed at her. Ana had a talent, I was sure. Earthy my ass.

I sipped the hot coffee. It was strong enough to make hair grow in unwanted places.

"Understanding elements and nature can be truly helpful," said Dalca, warming her long hands on her mug of coffee. "Essential oils, for instance, can be very powerful at healing and reducing pain. Some herbs are more potent than any modern medicine when in the hands of the right person."

I nodded, as if I understood a darn thing she was saying. "The room is magical. I love all the crystals and bottles. And your necklaces are just fabulous." I looked at her array of jewelry.

"Gypsies wear a variety of accessories to ward off evil intent or carry protective powers," said Dalca, absently touching the collection at her neck.

I glanced at the gray vial that hung from her collarbone, nestled among the other stones. For some reason, I couldn't stop thinking about it. "What is the gray stuff?" I nodded toward the longest necklace.

For a brief moment Dalca seemed to debate something in her head. I glanced at Ana, whose eyes were looking at her carefully. I completely felt like I was missing the elephant in the room that seemed so obvious to them.

"What? What is it?" I asked, unnerved.

Dalca unwrapped the long, braided leather necklace from around her neck and placed it with the vial attached on the table between us. Ana was no longer interested in her book and closed it, sliding it to one side.

"Why don't you take a guess?" asked Dalca.

"It isn't a dead relative or something is it? Because that would really gross me out," I said, very worried it was Dear Uncle So-and-So's ashes.

"No, no," said Dalca with a dismissive wave, "Not a relative. We Gypsies believe that the soul can reveal itself through how one perceives certain elements. This ash contains many elements and people all smell something different, but what they smell reveals part of who they are."

I looked at Ana and she shrugged.

I was suspicious, but went with bold. I reached for the vial and looked through the smooth glass sides at the sand-like contents. I was taking my time and Ana started to drum her fingers impatiently.

"Oh, for crying out loud. Look, I'll smell it first," she huffed, taking the vial from my hand and unscrewed the metal top. She held it to her nose and sniffed. I watched carefully to make sure she didn't turn green.

"See? Nothing. No one ever smells anything. Dalca wants you to sniff to see if you have a hidden talent or creepy spirit. It is an old Gypsy belief."

I looked at Dalca and she gave a quick nod. I warily glanced at the re-capped vial being offered to me in Ana's hand.

"Okay fine," I said, quickly grabbing the vial and unscrewing the top before I lost my nerve. Some strange instinct told me not to draw breath over the glass container, but I didn't want to look like a complete wimp. I brought the vial to my nose and took a little sniff.

The smell was unimaginable.

I dropped the vial and nearly fell to the floor, gasping though my mouth to rid myself of the burn that had assaulted me.

Dalca and Ana vaulted to their feet and ushered me quickly out the back door of the house into the fresh air. I could hear them arguing under their breath, but I felt too ill to care. My head was spinning and I closed my eyes to keep from throwing up.

My entire body felt weak.

"Here, sit her down," I heard Dalca command, and Ana sat me on the cold, granite step.

Soon I smelled something altogether different and opened my eyes. Dalca had a bunch of leafy greens with white tips under my nose. I started to feel better, almost normal. Another minute passed and I felt fine.

Ana and Dalca watched me for a few more minutes before either one of them spoke.

"What did you smell?" asked Ana, almost in a whisper as all signs of sarcasm had vaporized.

I looked at her for a long time, debating screaming at her for such an awful trick, but decided I might be wrong. Maybe it wasn't a trick, because Ana seemed fine, as if she really didn't smell anything.

She leaned toward me, her eyes full of concern. "Eila, what did it smell like?" she asked again, slowly.

I could only think of one thing that came remotely close. That distinctive, telltale sent of an animal that didn't make it across the road. I looked at her and Dalca, trying to forget that horrific odor.

"It smelled like death," I said, swallowing back the urge to puke.

After the fiasco at Dalca's, I was hurried out of her place under the notion that she needed to do some research about why I smelled, well . . . what I smelled. I, however, wasn't buying it. Ana drove me home and when we reached 408, she cut the engine as we sat for a moment in the driveway.

"I think she knows something. I think she already knew before I opened the vial," I said staring out the windshield.

"Knew what?" asked Ana.

"Whatever it is about me that she can tell from that stupid vial," I replied hotly, the memory making my stomach turn.

"Oh please. It is just Gypsy weirdness. It probably means you have a freakish sense of smell. Don't go all Super Girl on me just because you almost tossed your cookies after smelling the salt flat's sand," said Ana with a snort.

"Salt flats?"

"Yeah. Look Miss Landlocked, here in the world of tides and oceans, the bay can stink to high heaven during low tides. It can smell like dead animals or a backed-up sewer. I wouldn't read into it if I were you. You just have a great sense of smell."

I looked at Ana, seeking a chink in the armor of her story. I didn't see the slightest bit of tall tale.

"Really?" I asked. Though she seemed to be telling the truth, I didn't ever recall low tide smelling so horrific. And 408 was definitely close enough to the water to smell something THAT bad. I wanted to believe her, but something was wrong with the contents of that vial. I felt as though I knew what it was, but the information was hiding from my comprehension.

"Yes, really. Look, just take a breath and relax. I'll see you at school tomorrow, okay?"

"All right. I'll see you tomorrow. And Ana?"

"Yeah?"

"Sorry I freaked on you just then. Moving here has been a big change for me," I said, eating some humility. She may really believe that there was just sand in the vial.

"Hey, no worries" she replied.

I stepped out of her Trans Am and she started the engine, backing down the driveway. As she drove away, I saw her talking into her cell phone and she glanced back at me.

She wasn't smiling and her look was a familiar one. It was the same expression I had seen on MJs face when I left The Milk Way. Something was up.

My new town, though small by many standards, has a frustratingly enormous high school. You could hide a small army inside and never know it. So I was very proud that I had finally learned the labyrinth of halls by the end of my first week (well, almost) and how to avoid collisions, planned and accidental. Occasionally, Nikki would see me in the hall, but I'd manage to tuck in next to someone else and avoid further confrontation.

I also avoided The Crimson Moon like the plague.

Dalca was nice and all, but the vial on her neck kept me far away, like a talisman conspiring against me. I knew I was just being paranoid . . . I hoped.

Crap, what if she HAD murdered somebody? What if the gray stuff really WAS a dead person's ashes? Did cremated people even stink? Good grief, I sounded like a crazy person. This is Cape Cod for crying out loud; no one is murdering ANYBODY.

Well, except maybe Nikki, who wants to kill me.

On the plus side, I had found my little niche in school in which I felt comfortable. And the students, for the most part, were very welcoming. Jesse talked with me everyday in English, and I had met a nice girl in gym class - a redhead named Cara. She talked a mile a minute to the point that I was unsure how she didn't pass out from lack of oxygen.

I even managed to swap out Chemistry for Ecology, accomplished with no small amount of begging in the guidance office. Kids had begun to say "hi" to me in the halls and though I was terrible at remembering names, I was good with faces and always returned the greeting. Nikki and her cronies, however, never smiled at anyone who was not on her 'A' list. Or anyone who remotely said "hello" to me for that matter.

She made no attempt to hide her distaste for me, a fact that was undoubtedly accentuated by Raef. That girl loathed me and I knew it. Most of the school knew it too. On the plus side, most of the school didn't like her either, but they sucked up to her in order to avoid her wrath.

It wasn't that she scared me - I simply didn't want the drama that followed Nikki everywhere. And drama was Nikki's middle name. She lived it, breathed it, damn near held court with it.

I did have one thing going for me when it came to Nikki . . . I wasn't her only target. Everyone was on Nikki's radar and if you were anything less than a perfect, adoring fan, life could be plagued with high school misery. For the large majority of Barnstable High, it seemed that students fell into one of four categories in regards to Nikki:

1. You actually worshiped her, in which case you were part of her "in crowd."
2. You feared her like an ancient deity and therefore sacrificed your dignity to appease her.
3. You were enough of a geek that your existence was of insignificance.

And lastly . . .

4. You were a most-loathed heathen and would be crushed like a bug.

I fell into fun category 4. Raef, I suspected, was on his way there as well, given his strange desire to be my friend. Why the most handsome boy in school seemed to enjoy my company was a fabulous surprise, but completely stumped my average self.

We would talk briefly after English and he'd often wave to me in the hall. He had even started to "eat" lunch regularly with MJ, Ana, and me, though technically he only drank protein shakes (no doubt a huge asset to his stunning physique).

I did feel bad for Ana and MJ, whom I suspected had enjoyed the anonymity of category 3 until I descended on the school. Being my friend meant you were fair game in Nikki's eyes. It was a fact that I apologized for profusely many times, though they all said that pissing her off was completely worth every moment of pain.

Pain included writing not-so-nice observations on MJ and Ana's lockers in ruby-red lipstick, stealing MJ's backpack and papering the restroom with his academic accomplishments, and other such irksome issues.

I could feel my irritation evolving into rage, but I managed to keep myself distracted, especially since I was due to take possession of a certain Jeep within hours.

Thank the stars it was Friday.

Ana gave me a ride home from school in the afternoon. When we pulled up to my house, I saw it, my Wrangler, gleaming in the falling sunlight. I thanked her for the ride and hopped out, waving to her as she backed out of the driveway.

After watching her car disappear in the distance, I walked . . . okay SKIPPED, over to my beautiful black and chrome vehicle. Any and all memories of the week and near trampling in the BHS hall were a distant past as I basked in the thrill of such a fabulous ride. I went to open the door, but it was locked. *What the . . .?*

I put my hand to the glass to shade the sun from my eyes and looked inside. On the seat was a note with a dweebish smiley face:

Come find me at THE MILK WAY and I will give ya the keys! Sniff . . . I MISS IT ALREADY!!! -MJ

I smiled broadly and trotted down the seashell driveway and across the road.

Sixty seconds later I was pulling open the door to the fragrant shop as the rusted cowbell heralded my arrival. The place was mobbed with classmates and the long chrome and green counter was jammed to capacity. Even the smaller, side area of the shop where there were little booths and tables was standing room only.

MJ and another girl sporting a mocha-streaked ponytail were zipping around the back of the counter, occasionally stopping to laugh with a friend while rapidly multitasking. I decided to wait until MJ had a moment to breathe and stood against the wall near the entrance.

I was reading down the chalkboard menu when I heard someone call my name from the table area. I looked over and saw Cara and Jesse waving wildly. "Eila! Hey Eila! Get your butt over here!" yelled Cara in her high voice. I wandered over to where she and Jesse were sitting.

"Come for a root beer float?" asked Jesse, smiling warmly.

"The food is awesome and the ice cream is killer," said Cara, her bubbly personality shining, near blindingly so. "Move over a bit, Jes! We can squeeze her butt in with us!"

"Absolutely!" said Jesse, obediently starting to slide farther to the right.

"Oh thanks, but that's okay." I said, waving off the warm invite. "I'm just grabbing something from MJ. I'm waiting for him to have a second."

"Honey – look around," said Cara. "This place will be crazy for at least another half hour. So please, SIT!"

I looked around. MJ and the girl seemed to be on rollerblades as they flew around the shop. Cara was right. There was no way I was getting those keys for a while.

The wafting, warm scent of fresh cream and fried food made my stomach growl. I was fairly certain that if I licked the air, I could taste a mint chocolate chip French fry. I nodded, "You know what? You're right! Live a little, eh?" I squeezed in next to Jesse who pulled a red basket of mini, circle shaped fries toward me.

"Help yourself, best around," he announced cheerfully.

"They do smell awesome. I did hear the fries were great," I said, tossing one into my mouth.

Jesse looked at me, an eyebrow raised. "Uh, that's not a . . ."

As soon as I chomped down on the "fry" I knew it wasn't a spud. I shifted the crispy, but chewy lump to one side in my mouth so I could speak. "Is this fish?" I nearly whispered, my stomach starting to twist. Even the thought of eating something with gills made me ill.

"No, no," he said, waving off my panic. "Nope, not fish."

I eyed him carefully and took a tentative chew. It still didn't taste like a fry.

"Seriously - it isn't a fish," protested Jesse at my obvious disbelief. I finished chewing and swallowed, trying to convince myself it was some sort of veggie, but was having a hard time buying it.

I wiped my mouth with a napkin and narrowed my eyes at him and the basket of suspicious, fried rings. "Not fish? Really?"

"Nope," said Jesse, taking a swig of his root beer float. "It was a CLAM BELLY!"

"ACK! CLAM? Oh gross!" I wanted to puke, preferably all over Jesse.

Cara was chuckling. "Here - have some," she said, sliding her milkshake toward me, a huge smile on her face.

"Oh thank god!" I said and greedily took a cool, creamy gulp to eliminate all remnants of my briny snack. The ice cream was truly a gift from the gods. "Wow. Now *that* is ice cream," I gushed.

Jesse's cell phone rang and he snapped it open, greeting the caller loudly in some male-jock lingo that was tough to get a grasp on. I tuned him out.

"So, you're buying MJ's Wrangler, huh? Nice ride! I'm envious," said Cara.

I looked at her, surprised that she knew I bought it and more floored that she actually knew what the 4x4 was called. "Uh, yeah. Came here to get the keys. How did you know?"

"Hun - this is the Cape. Small town. That and, well, have you seen the hunk of junk he is driving now? No way he'd willingly park the

Wrangler and drive that old thing," laughed Cara. She began chatting a mile-a-minute about who's dating who and the local gossip, barely pausing to take a breath. She was nice, but standing by the screen door seemed like a much better option in retrospect.

The weathered bell heralded the arrival of another patron and I glanced over. Coming through the door was none other than Nikki and one of the Pompoms.

She didn't see me seated in the far corner with Cara and Jesse. She strode in, her superior mentality obvious in her every move. Two younger girls, probably freshmen, were seated at the counter, chatting happily. She laid her hand on the shorter one's shoulder and squeezed. The girl looked up and quickly vacated her seat with her friend, making room for the Queen and her Lady-in-Waiting.

Just the sight of her – the way she treated everyone around her – was infuriating.

My two tablemates didn't seem to notice her. Cara's phone had chirped, breaking her monologue, and she was now texting someone, while Jesse was still on his cell. I sat there, watching Nikki, the ambient noise in the room fading fast. It was as if I could see only her, my peripheral awareness Gonesville.

MJ hadn't noticed the two, irritating new patrons at the counter. He was madly scooping ice cream when Nikki reached past the counter and grabbed onto his sleeve. MJ, jerked short by her grasp, dropped the large sundae he had slaved over, and the tin bowl created a resounding clang on the tile floor.

He turned, stunned, and saw Nikki. From her gestures, I could tell that she wanted to be served, quickly, and ahead of the already waiting customers. MJ, no doubt using all his willpower to not strangle her with his apron, nodded dutifully as he started cleaning the mess.

Nikki tossed her flawless locks and turned to talk with her subservient sidekick.

I felt the darkness of rage, laced with a need for vengeance, overtake the saner part of my brain. The Queen had already shown her absolute distaste for me. I might as well kick the hornet's nest and bring the rain.

All sense of sanity gone, I turned to Cara, whose thumbs were flying over the microscopic keyboard of her phone. "How much is a milkshake?" I asked calmly, stroking the sweating, icy glass, which was nearly full.

"Hmmm?" asked Cara absently, her eyes never leaving the phone, "Uh, three-fifty."

"Then I owe you three-fifty," I said calmly, my plan solidified in my head. I stood up from the bench seat, the milkshake firmly in my hand.

"Wait. What?" said Cara, finally looking up from her phone, but I was already making my way through the packed room.

Stealthily.

Deliberately.

I could feel my body tingle with excitement and an absolutely fabulous feeling of imminent justice.

As I approached the far end of the counter, luck was for once on my side. Nikki had her back to me and was still deep in self-absorbed conversation with the Pompom, who was nodding obediently at everything she said.

I caught MJ's eye and he, understanding my devious intent, started to frantically shake his head 'no.' I simply smiled back to him. If this girl was going to make our lives a nightmare, then it was my duty to repay the courtesy.

I saw MJ, still behind the counter, also start towards Nikki's seat. I was almost to her, when she saw MJ out of the corner of her eye.

She turned slightly and yelled to him, "You know, if you were any slower, it would be prom season before I got what I wanted!"

The twit sealed her fate.

I pretended to trip, letting out a yelp. Nikki turned toward the sound of my voice just as a double thick chocolate shake splashed all over her face and perfect hair, soaking her True Religion jeans and top.

She launched to her feet, howling in rage and disbelief. Her mascara began a southern trek down her face, adding to her ridiculous appearance as she frantically wiped the ice cream from her eyes. The entire shop went completely silent.

Pompom was stunned.

It was as if I was David and got Goliath square between the eyes. No one could believe that I had just taken on the wrath of the beast. I heard someone at the end of the bar swear and looked over to MJ whose eyes were huge, but his mouth barely contained a grin.

When she was finally able to open her eyes, Nikki was beyond livid. She was shaking with fury and when she saw me with the glass, I actually thought she would combust.

"I . . . am . . . going to KILL you!" she roared and launched herself at me.

I threw my hands up, ready to defend myself, but there was suddenly a wall of black between us.

"Ladies," said a rich voice emanating from the wall. I looked up and all I saw was broad shoulders cloaked in a black t-shirt, topped with a head of straight, shoulder-length ash blonde hair.

Whoever he was, he had a solid build, but I couldn't see his face since his attention was turned to Nikki. He was bracing the roaring cheerleader so her arms couldn't reach around him and tear my limbs off. He seemed to contain her easily, even though she was channeling the aggression of a rabid hyena.

"Calm down. Calm Down! It was an accident," said the wall.

"Like Hell it was!" screamed Nikki. She let loose with a tirade of what she was going to do to my life, accentuated with more foul language than most sailors could muster.

Over her ranting, MJ called out to my defender. "Get her out of here, Kian!" he said, pointing to the door.

Kian? This wall of black is Raef's brother?

As if on cue, Kian glanced over one shoulder and down at me. He must have been at least a foot or more taller than me. Like his brother Raef, Kian was handsome on a whole different level. He looked like he had been picked out of a broody, high-end clothing ad.

"You okay?" he asked me, his voice cool and deep.

"Uh, yeah. I'm fine," I said, though the hairs on my neck stood on end. Adrenaline is a funky chemical.

Nikki managed to twist herself around Kian to look me in the eye. A tsunami didn't throw as much fury. "You just made the biggest mistake of your life," she growled.

"You're right. Wasting a milkshake from this place is a true crime. We will all mourn the loss."

I had a death wish, without doubt.

Someone snickered and Nikki made one last attempt to launch herself at my throat, but Kian was unyielding. MJ pointed firmly to the door again and Kian nodded, hauling the chocolate covered teen from the shop. Her minion, finally regaining her senses, hurried out to her owner. Chairs scraped along the tile floor as everyone stood in near unison and watched her through the windows.

Kian dragged her to her convertible and she screamed at him. He stood there, arms crossed, not reacting to her tirade. Eventually, she got into her car with PomPom and tore out of the parking lot onto Main Street. She must have been doing 60 by the time she was roaring past my home. We all watched out the windows as her engine's sound faded.

Jesse and Cara were standing at their booth, staring at me in amazement. A sophomore sitting at the counter finally looked over to me and broke the strange silence in the shop, "You are some type of brave, but completely suicidal."

I turned to her, my legs getting wobbly with the fast-fading adrenaline vacating my system. "Some things are just worth the pain," I said, smiling. "Besides, who wants to live forever?"

Apparently not me, the way I was going.

"Jeez woman! You are crazy," said MJ with a bold smile. "Here, have a seat before you keel over!" MJ turned to the crowded shop, which was slowly starting to regain its normalcy, "Sorry folks! All over now! Please enjoy yourselves!" He reached up to a high shelf and turned the station up a little louder to coax the casual back into the stunned patrons.

The cowbell rang as Kian returned. "Well, she was delightful," he said, his voice rich and smooth.

"Thanks Kian," responded MJ, somewhat stiffly. He came around the counter to clean up the milkshake that had cascaded all over Nikki and the floor. I felt bad that I made a mess.

"Oh here, let me clean it up," I said to MJ, reaching for the rag.

He quickly put up a hand to stop me, "You, my friend, earned all the brownie points tonight. It is my pleasure to tidy such a historic moment."

I sat back down on my stool. Kian took a seat next to me and MJ glanced at him briefly, almost coldly. Kian may have been a big help, but MJ didn't seem thrilled he was here.

Kian's presence made me nervous. It was a sensation not unlike when I first saw Raef, though not nearly as strong. I made a mental note that I needed some more practice being calm around gorgeous guys.

"So, you must be Eila Walker. I'm Kian O'Reilly."

Seated next to me, I was able to more closely size him up. I guessed him to be 20 or 21. His hair framed his angular face in such a way that he looked exactly like one of those obscenely hot, surfer guys from California.

"I guess I must," I said, shaking his hand. My whole arm tingled and I quickly released his hand. "You're . . . uh, Raef's brother," I said, the electricity fading. The O'Reilly boys had some serious talent at making females weak. "Thanks for the quick save."

"Not a problem, I was passing by and saw what you did through the window."

"Accident," I corrected.

"Uh huh, yeah. Sure it was. Anyway, she was going to blow a screw and I decided to step in."

"So glad you did," I replied, truly grateful.

"So, how is my little brother adjusting to Barnstable?"

"Good. He speaks highly of you," I fibbed. Technically Raef acted about as close to an only-child as I had ever been.

Kian raised one suspicious eyebrow and leaned back slightly to where MJ was wiping up the floor, "Dude. This chick is a rotten liar." MJ didn't react.

"Hey now!" I protested.

"Eila, my brother would never sing my praises. Ever. But thanks for trying." He got up from his stool and started heading for the door. "I need to go grab dinner, but I'm sure I will see you around again Eila."

"Wait! Why don't you eat here? Food is great," I said, hoping to get some details about the O'Reilly brothers and possibly Ana. MJ glanced up at Kian, but kept cleaning.

"Not today. I already have plans." He looked thoughtful for a moment. "Take-out."

I was disappointed, but nodded. "Nice to meet you."

"You too," he said, "And MJ - tell Ana I'm looking for her. We need to talk." MJ made a somewhat disgusted snort and shook his head, never looking up.

Kian headed to the door, but looked back at me. "Try not to piss off the rest of the squad, will ya?" he said, smiling as he let the screen door slap the frame behind him. I shook my head, still trying to grasp all that I had just done.

I heard jingling and looked down to see that MJ was fishing something from his pocket. He held up a pair of silvery car keys and dropped them in my hand. "Next time I will just leave the keys with Mae," he said with a wink.

* * * *

The woman's body lay crumpled on the ground and the man, gone. Next to it, the fountain poured peacefully, but was now dusted in ash. The same gray material that I recognized covered the road, the edge of the woman's skirt, and the ornate pillar at the fountain's center.

I turned as I heard someone calling through the darkness and caught sight of two figures staggering to their feet near a building. I called out to one of them, pleading for help, but he stood like stone, unflinching, uncaring . . . and 100% recognizable. I screamed his name over and over, and he turned to look at *me. His doll-black eyes reflected no emotion and his gaze sent an electric shock of panic through my chest.*

My heart was pounding madly, sweat soaking my tank top. I sat up too fast in my tangle of sheets and the sudden motion made my head spin. Disoriented in the darkness, I was quickly losing the memory of the nightmare once again. I tried to replay it in my mind – tried to remember something about the repetitive scene that was plaguing my dreams.

I scrambled out of bed and hurried over to my desk, fumbling in the darkness for paper and pencil. I scrawled the words *fountain* and *ash* on the pale sheet. I knew a woman died near a fountain, but the details of how her life ended were gone once again. I tapped the pencil against the paper, as if it would start writing on its own.

The yellow light drifting up from the street lamp across the road cast the slightest, golden glow to my paper. I took a deep, cleansing breath, and dropped the pencil down on the worn, wooden desk. Someday I'd be fast enough to recall the dream that was haunting me.

I glanced out toward the street and was shocked to see a man standing under the lamp, directly across from my house. He was just standing there, in the dead of the night, partially in the shadows.

His face was hidden from the light thanks to his dark hooded sweatshirt and he dodged out of the light, disappearing into the darkness. I stepped quickly away from the direct view of my window and looked toward the street from behind the curtain. What the frick? Was some degenerate casing my house for a robbery?

The street was quiet and the man nowhere to be seen. I rubbed my eyes, questioning my mind, uncertain he had been there in the first place. Maybe the house had lead paint and it was messing with my brain. Of course, if the walls were harboring a toxin, it wouldn't explain Dalca's vial. Nothing made sense anymore. At least my friends were normal.

I slowly drew the curtains closed across the window and climbed back into bed, pulling the covers up tightly around my neck trying to shake off my goose bumps. I closed my eyes and pictured myself holding Raef's hand and I instantly felt safe. Calm. Protected.

The next morning revealed itself as a spectacular day to be a Cape Codder. It was sunny and unusually warm, all in all the perfect beach day. I was determined to put the vial, the dreams, and the man that I may have hallucinated to the back of my frayed brain.

I was also thrilled with my awesome new ride, so I called Ana and MJ at the irrationally early hour of 8 a.m. to make plans to head to the off-road portion of Sandy Neck.

MJ was groggy but thrilled at the idea when he answered the phone, mumbling something about a new skim board. Ana however, wasn't such a ray of sunshine in the wee morning hours. After explaining the finer points of never calling her so early and the repercussions of doing so in the future, she agreed to come along. I even debated calling Raef, but lost my nerve when I went to dial his number.

An hour later, both Ana and MJ arrived at my home. While Ana and I packed up beach necessities, MJ proceeded to remove the doors from the Wrangler - a task I had attempted and failed miserably at earlier.

With top down and the doors off, we all jumped in and headed down King's Highway towards the off-road section of Sandy Neck. The north-facing beach stretches miles from one end of the Cape to the other and is a spectacular site to behold.

I paid the gatekeeper at the entrance and MJ signaled me to pull over. I assumed he wanted to drive. Typical male.

"I think I can drive this section. I'm not a complete female fruit," I protested.

"Well, you can drive . . . and be dug in within a half mile if I don't let some air out of the tires," said MJ with a wry grin as he climbed out.

"Ahh . . . gotcha," I replied, feeling off-road ignorant. I glanced back at Ana in the backseat. She was absorbed in some book she was reading, though her barely disguised smile told me she thought my poor sense of 4-wheeling was amusing.

It took us about 15 minutes to get out to a more remote area of the beach. The scenery was gorgeous, with softly rolling mounds of powdery sand and tall dune grass. Here and there a weather beaten fence would show up. Ana explained that the fences helped stave off destruction during storms.

"Someday that home of yours will be waterfront property due to the erosion."

"Be serious," I laughed, "I'm like a quarter mile from Craigville. There is no way I will be sitting on my own private beach anytime soon."

"Note I didn't say you would still be *alive* when it happens," she said with a smile.

I gave her a knowing wink, but the reality was, I rarely knew exactly what Ana was thinking. In fact, I wasn't sure she actually liked me much. She seemed often distant, as if she wore armor all the time.

I watched as she leaned forward from her seat behind MJ and said something in his ear as she pointed towards the ocean. He nodded, and she sat back to watch the view.

I found it interesting that Ana and MJ seemed so well connected yet were not boyfriend and girlfriend. Every moment they spent together, the subtle ways they knew each other, spoke to the way they adored one another. I was fairly certain, however, that neither was bold enough to pursue anything other than the friendship they had known for so long. But no one could ignore the fact that these two people, so different, were ideal for each other.

"Ana said that there is a nice sandbar down and off to the left." MJ pointed to where Ana had also directed. "Drive a bit more toward the water and we'll park and set up our stuff."

Fifteen minutes later, we had set up a great sunbathing area, complete with picnic lunch, cooler of drinks, fluffy towels, and my ratty old blanket.

I couldn't get past how odd it felt to be on the beach with my car. I could lean back against the hubcap to read or lay down by the bumper for shade. It was just so weird . . . but so much fun.

Before I knew it, MJ had stripped himself of his t-shirt and taken off with his super-thin, mini-surfboard. He'd run along the edge of the water and, at just the right moment, drop the boogie board down to the water and hop on. He'd ride the thin piece of wood along the waves in about five inches of water. It was amazing to watch. I also knew that I'd break my neck trying to do it.

Ana and I sat for a while in silence, taking in the view and the salt breeze. I finally broke the silence. "Do you mind if I ask you something personal?" I questioned, always slightly nervous around Ana.

"You can certainly try. It's a free country," she replied, turning her attention to me, her dark sunglasses obscuring her eyes.

"Well . . . do you like me?" I asked, morbidly curious.

"Oh man. Are you one of those insecure chicks? I was really hoping you weren't a Cling-On," she said flatly.

"No, no. Not asking as a needy twit! It's just that you are hard to read," I replied, fiddling with a shell.

"Oh." Ana picked up a pebble and tossed it toward the water. "Yeah. I like you Eila . . . I just, keep my emotions and thoughts to myself," she said. "Better to be a locked vault than an open book I guess."

I nodded. "I think that's probably smart . . . And just for the record, I think you are a great friend to have." I smiled but Ana, the locked vault, simply nodded.

We hung at the beach till almost dinnertime. I wished I had packed more than just lunch as I watched the sun start to set. Some people around us were gathering wood for bonfires and I wanted to stay.

"No worries," said MJ, offering to drive us out in the falling light. "We will be back! There are lots of parties out here during the fall!"

I was looking forward to returning but then noted that the tide had receded into the bay and there was no smell.

Salt flats? I think not. Something else was in that vial for sure.

* * * *

That evening, I had made a small dent in my volume of Kansas junk that was still piled around my room. It was a vain attempt on my part to not think about the Crimson Moon sniffing incident, now fresh in my mind thanks to the smell-free low tide. I ended up sniffing every old, beloved t-shirt I owned, testing my nose. They all smelled like a boxed-up version of me, which actually didn't smell half bad. Raef, I already knew, smelled downright divine.

Mae was busy in the kitchen making dinner and once I caught the scent of something tomato-laden and zesty wafting up the back staircase, I ditched my pitiful attempt at organizing.

I entered the kitchen just as Mae was pulling a pan of bubbling Italian goodness from the oven. "Your room spotless yet?" she asked, shaking Parmesan on top of her oozy creation.

"Ummm. Sort of," I replied with a shrug. She looked at me and rolled her eyes.

"Did you know we have a visitor?" she asked, smiling at me. "He's been hanging out on the front porch for at least a half hour. He's quite hard to miss."

I raised my eyebrows at Mae, questioning. Raef? She left Raef on the front porch for THIRTY MINUTES? What the heck!

Suddenly I was completely self-conscious of how I smelled from the hours of digging through dust bunnies and musty clothes. "Uh, I'll be right back," I said, hurrying out of the kitchen through the parlor and to the front door.

I glanced quickly at the hall mirror and attempted to fix my hair and sniffed at my shirt. I opened the front door and stepped out onto the porch to greet . . . "Marsh?"

Dalca's massive black dog was lying on the front porch and looked up at me expectantly, his huge tail thumping the wooden decking rhythmically.

"Marsh, what the heck are you doing here? Where's Dalca?" I

asked the dog, absurdly. As if he was Lassie and knew where Timmy fell in the darn well.

His tail thumped faster as he slowly got to his feet and wandered over to me, rolling his head under my hand. I stroked his thick fur as one of his huge, brown eyes looked at me. I had the strangest sense that he could understand me, and I fluffed his thick ears, a bit unnerved.

"I should've had you out here last night. No way that guy would have been hanging around if you were here . . . although, I'm not sure there was actually anyone out here."

Marsh pulled his head away from me and looked at my face, his eyes studying my own.

"What?" I asked, only half aware I was talking to a dog. I was losing my mind, I was sure. Two words: lead paint.

"I thought I saw a guy outside last night. No biggie – I'm sure it was just my imagination," I said, defending my story to a canine. To my amazement, he actually let out a low growl.

"Alright. You know what? I have had enough of a ride on the Crazy Train for the weekend. You need to go home." I crossed my arms defiantly in front of me.

Was I actually arguing with a dog? Good grief I was!

He looked at me and snorted.

"I'm fine! And I'm hungry, and Mae is going to be pissed if her homemade lasagna gets cold." He licked his lips, pushing the ridiculous into down right creepy.

"Ana said you were getting chunky, so no lasagna for you. Now go home!" I demanded, pointing sternly in the direction of The Crimson Moon.

He let out a low grunt and turned, heading down the front porch steps. I watched him go and as he reached the sidewalk, he turned and

73

looked at me. "Bye Marsh," I said, as he trotted for home. I watched him leave and made a mental note to Google intelligence in dogs.

Back inside the table was set for dinner. Mae was pouring ice tea as I sat down. "So, has the dog gone home?" She seemed remarkably nonplussed about the giant that had taken up a quarter of the porch.

"Yeah. I sent him home. He's huge but harmless. He belongs to this lady named Dalca. She owns that herb shop down the street," I said, pulling a piece of garlic bread from the basket in the middle of the table.

"Oh, I know where he's from. Dalca is the one who gave us the muffins our first morning here." replied Mae. "I met Marsh the other day when I popped into her store. Such a great little place!" Mae sat down across from me. "I picked up a witch ball."

I stared at her, as if she spoke in a foreign tongue, "A what-what?"

"A witch ball. Dalca was insistent that old homes like this traditionally had one. I hung it over the sink," she said, nodding to the counter behind me.

I swiveled around in my chair, still chewing on the bread. Hanging delicately above the kitchen sink was a stunning glass orb, the size of a man's fist. It was translucent, swirling with purples, blues and touches of gold.

"It's beautiful. Not sure what it does with witches, but it sure is stunning," I said turning back to Mae.

"Supposedly it will attract malicious spirits and they will become trapped inside," replied Mae, proud of her knowledge.

"Casper will not be pleased," I muttered.

"You know, Eila, I actually like that big beast hanging out on the porch. Especially since I'm going to be leaving in a month." I could tell the wheels of Mae's mind were furiously spinning. Truth be told however, I also felt safer with Marsh at the house, especially given the possible stalker I had seen.

"I know a friend of Dalca pretty well," I said. "That girl, Ana, from school - she's pals with her. I'm pretty sure she would let Marsh come live with me while you were away. He seems to like it here anyway."

Mae nodded, thoughtful. "Please be careful while I'm away. I'm still not sure this is a great idea."

"I'll be fine," I said, my mind jumping to one particular boy. "You deserve this, and it took you forever to save for it." I got up from the table and walked around to her, bending down to hug her, "I love you and I will be fine. I'm boring, remember?"

Monday morning dawned with a dusting of crystal dew on the ground. I cranked the heat in the Jeep as I drove to school, my teeth chattering since my jean jacket did not suffice in the Cape's suddenly cooler temps. I made a mental note to try and locate the box of winter clothes that were stashed somewhere in the house. How Cape Cod could be sunny and warm one day, and frosty cool the next was maddening.

Walking past some of the still unlit rooms, I couldn't help but think of the dude that hid so well in the shadows across from my house. By the time I reached my locker, I was consumed with thoughts of creepy stalkers.

As I shuffled books and folders into the steel box well past its prime, I reflected on how fast that blissful life I was daydreaming about only hours earlier at the beach, had taken such a wrong turn.

I jammed one last book in the locker and slammed the door shut and let out a howling scream. Raef had been standing behind the locker door and the sudden sight of him scared the life out of me.

"Eila! I'm so sorry," he said, amused but a bit alarmed. "I didn't mean to scare you like that."

I leaned back against my locker and took a deep breath. I felt exhausted, and the stress swirled through my body like a wayward river. "It's not your fault," I said, looking first at the ceiling, then to his beautiful, worried face. "I'm just . . . tired."

"Just tired, huh? Usually 'just tired' people yawn, they don't scream to shatter glass," said Raef, questioning my lame excuse. "You look drained. Is everything alright?"

I debated telling him about the man I thought I saw, but worried that he'd take it upon himself to go looking for the dark stalker and end up in a dangerous situation. I decided to keep the incident to myself.

"I just didn't sleep well due to nightmares," I lied. Sort of.

"Nightmares? What about?"

"You don't want to know. You'll think I have a seriously twisted psyche."

"Try me," he said, leaning a broad shoulder against the adjoining locker.

I looked at him for a moment, debating whether to skirt the issue, but went with it instead. "I keep dreaming about a woman who seems to get . . . murdered. I only get quick snapshots though, once I'm awake, so it's kind of jumbled and hazy."

Raef seemed to stiffen, "Seriously? You think it's some sort of future premonition?"

"No. I think I just read about it somewhere, because the scene looks like it is from the past. Like, WAY past." I glanced up at Raef and sighed. "You know what? Do me a favor and don't tell anyone. They think I'm weird anyway."

He laughed a bit. "That's probably wise. Especially after what Kian told me about you and a certain aggressive toothpick with pompoms. You sure do steer yourself into the lion's den. Tripped huh?"

I moaned. "Please just tell me to duck when she hurls something at my skull, will ya?"

"Will do. I've always got your back," he said, lifting my backpack from the floor and pitching it over his shoulder. We headed out to first period English together, my improbable companion and I.

By the time lunch rolled around I was amazed at my luck, as I had not seen Nikki at all. I mentioned her absence to Raef as we walked to the cafeteria. He was as pleased as I was, especially since he had to leave school early to meet his brother. I missed him, almost painfully, the moment he was gone.

I sat down across from Ana and MJ. Our seating arrangement never changed, as if the chairs only fit each of us and couldn't be traded. MJ, as always, was chowing the instant he sat down. How he remained so slim and toned while consuming so many calories was beyond me. Hello envy.

I decided to feel out the dog-borrowing idea with Ana before asking Dalca. "So, guess who visited me last night?" I asked, though the stalker from the road immediately burst into my mind.

"Do tell," replied Ana, but my brain had fallen back into the night. "Hello?" she said, louder, "Earth-to-Eila. Who visited?"

I yanked myself back to the present. "Uh, Dalca's dog, hung out on my porch," I said, twisting the cap off my water.

Ana's silence made me look up. She was staring at me. "Really?" She seemed almost annoyed. "That dog really gets around."

"I'm sorry. Is he not supposed to be out?"

MJ snorted. "He's not Dalca's dog," he replied, managing to actually speak without food in his mouth. "He's a . . ."

"Mangy stray," finished Ana.

"I was going to say 'adventurous rogue'." MJ shot Ana a pointed look. He turned his attention back to me. "No one owns Marsh. He goes where he wants."

I was surprised. "The town doesn't mind some massive, black dog wandering around?"

"Nah. Everyone loves him," said MJ, cheerfully. Ana just shook her head, clearly not a platinum member of the Marsh Fan Club.

"So I don't have to ask Dalca if he could come and stay with me while Mae is gone?" Both MJ and Ana were silent, looking at me like I sprouted another head.

Finally MJ spoke up, "Uh, no. You don't have to ask her permission. Just open the door to the house and call him when you see him. I'm sure he'll come in."

"I'm sure," said Ana dryly. "And don't forget to feed him. That dog loves to eat."

I looked at both of them as Ana flipped open a notebook and MJ waved to someone across the room. Sometimes you just know you are in the dark about something, and I knew I just missed a lot of info on Marsh.

With my luck, he'd end up being Cujo.

Fantastic.

* * * *

My last class of the day, New England History, was slowly

becoming 90 minutes of my academic schedule that I actually debated skipping. Daily.

For the first few days, I really found the information about the area fascinating. New England, especially Cape Cod, was so old and rich in history. The volumes of information and the fortitude of the settlers in the darkest winters amazed me. The class kept my attention and I thoroughly enjoyed it. That was until Mr. Grant, our somewhat creepy teacher, started asking me to wait at the end of class.

Frequently.

It wasn't that he screamed "pedophile," but he seemed somewhat obsessed with the history of my family and especially, my house. Even more disgusting was the fact that the girls in class regularly drooled over him like he was some hot, older rock star. And yeah, he was real good-looking – almost like Tony Stark from the Iron Man movies. Heck, he even had the goatee and everything. But still . . . it was just plain gross.

Many times our after-class chats were just a quick, semi-interrogation. He'd ask if I had found anything interesting in the home, learned anything else about my family. He often mentioned that he'd like to stop by sometime to see the house from the inside, which was SO not happening.

The dude just plain made me nervous, especially the way he moved when we were alone. He kept an appropriate distance, but I felt like he almost prowled around my perimeter.

Freakin' weirdo.

Today, thankfully, Mr. Grant was absent, replaced by a female teacher sitting at his desk. Though I knew the smart money was that she was a substitute for the day, I hoped like mad that she'd find her position permanent.

As I sat and listened to her talk about the whaling industry, I reminded myself that I needed to swing into the Guidance Office before heading home. I wanted to pick up some information on colleges and, more importantly, scholarship opportunities. Though 408 was worth nearly two million, I was far, FAR from a millionaire.

By the time I had gotten out of the guidance office, a good portion of the students and teachers had left for the day. I headed out to the parking lot and my beloved vehicle. As I unlocked the door I heard the low rumble of a motorcycle approaching me. I turned and saw Raef pull up on an alien looking, coal-black bike. He turned the key off on the top of the beast he was riding, and swung his leg off.

"I drove by your house just a few minutes ago and your car wasn't there," he said, walking over to me. A flash of adrenaline cut through my body as he approached. Would I ever get used to his presence?

"I was getting some college stuff, so I was running late." I raised an eyebrow, curious, "Are you spying on me?" *Not that I mind.*

Raef shook his head. "Of course not. I was just on my way home and noticed your Jeep was missing. I swung back here to make sure you weren't having problems with it," said Raef taking a black helmet off the bike's seat. He held it out to me, "But since you're here, come take a ride with me."

My heart leapt into my throat. "You've got to be kidding." This would, without doubt, end up as a lesson in what not to do.

"I've been riding for years. You'll be safe with me," he said, still holding the helmet out to me.

"I'm more worried about the old lady with the two-ton Caddy that doesn't see us," I mumbled. I took the helmet and shoved it on my head. Raef adjusted the strap for me and as his hand brushed against my chin, my heart nearly skidded to a halt.

"Uh, you know these things are called Donor Cycles for a reason, right?" I said, nervous. "What is this thing anyway?"

Raef stepped back from me. "It is called a MO-TOR-CYCLE," he said slowly, smiling ever so slightly.

"Ha ha, no kidding? I meant what *kind* is it, because it looks like a NASA reject." The bike's body had twisted pipes and a sweeping look unlike anything I had ever seen before.

"It's a Night-Rod, but Ana added a few things for me," said Raef, getting on the bike and standing it upright so I could join him. He nodded his head toward the seat behind him.

"What did she add?" I asked, trying to calm my nerves with senseless questions as I carefully climbed aboard and lightly placed my hands on his waist.

"I asked her to give it a bigger seat in case I had a passenger," he said plainly.

"Oh . . . have you had a lot of, uh, passengers?" I reminded myself a boy this handsome must have had girlfriends in his past. I prayed I didn't sound jealous. I wasn't . . . was I?

"You're the first," he replied, starting the bike. It rumbled to life and made my spine vibrate. "I had her put it on the day I met you," he continued, over the engine's growl.

I sat there, stunned.

He reached down to my hands and pushed them into his sides. "Hang on, alright?" he said, putting on his own black helmet. I nodded, the butterflies going psycho in my gut for multiple reasons.

He pulled out of the parking lot and onto the main road, his bike fast and agile. The first corner he took, I instinctively feared crashing down to the ground as the bike leaned heavily into the curve. I tried to counter it, leaning away from the road that seemed dangerously close and conspiring with gravity to flatten me.

When we stopped at the next street light, Raef set his feet down to balance the heavy machine. He turned slightly and I could see his chiseled profile as he glanced back towards me. "Lean with me, okay?" he asked loudly over the rumble of the bike. "Don't worry. I won't let you fall."

I nodded. "Sorry," I yelled, a bit embarrassed at my terribly poor biker skills. The light turned green and we were off again. I could feel the subtle change of the bike's forward motion every time Raef shifted gears and it made me clutch onto his jacket even tighter.

I found that every time he slowed, I would slip down the angled, leather seat and become wedged against his back. I'd wiggle myself back, but within minutes be pressed against him again. Eventually I gave up, allowing myself to relax and enjoy the tight closeness of his strong back. He changed gears so smoothly that the motion of the bike became a steady heartbeat. It was soothing, as I sat tucked into the double seat he had installed . . . for me.

I couldn't get past that amazing revelation; that Raef O'Reilly, the *day* he met me, modified his bike in the hopes of someday fitting me into his life. I smiled so wide that I nearly started to laugh. I took a deep breath in an attempt to act more composed as I watched now familiar roads zip by. I soon realized we were headed toward the harbor.

I tipped my chin forward to Raef's helmet, "Where are we going?" I yelled over the wind, confused.

"My place," said Raef, his voice muffled by the engine.

Suddenly I was wishing beyond words that I had dressed better for the occasion. "So, um, will your parents be home or do they work?" I hoped they were type-A workaholics.

"It's just me and Kian," said Raef, as he leaned the bike into a right turn heading toward the harbor. I gripped him tightly, still not 100% sure that gravity would play fair.

As we approached the water, I noticed the ferry dock was lacking the Nantucket Steamship. The workers, however, were busy organizing ropes and talking to one another. No doubt the ferry was in transit from the island.

I was surprised when Raef hooked a left into one of the parking areas for boat owners. He drove slowly through the parking lot, parallel to the docks, the boats growing in size and price tag. We approached the end of the lot, where the largest boats - well, YACHTS - were tied, each one taking up its own expanse of dock.

Raef pulled into a spot next to a sleek, gunmetal gray sports car with a small, raised "ZR1" on the side. He planted his feet to steady the bike and cut the engine, the void of noise making my ears ring.

"We're here. You can take your helmet off now," he said, removing his. I pulled mine off and tossed my hair slightly with my hand, hoping my locks didn't look too ridiculous.

"I thought we were going to your house," I said, looking at the amazing, sea-faring vessels.

"I never said 'house'," replied Raef casually, dismounting the bike and helping me do the same.

We started walking toward the long line of bank-busting boats. He jumped down off the seawall and onto the pier, then turned to help me down, but I hesitated as that strange flash of caution passed through my body.

"You coming?" he asked, looking up to me.

It was only then that I realized that the place Raef called home was one of these multi-million dollar yachts. "You live on a boat?" I nearly whispered, finally taking his hand and jumping down next to him. Though the caution was gone, my hand tingled at his touch.

"Well, yeah," he said, looking almost ashamed. "I know it isn't like your house, but it's all we have."

I couldn't believe that he thought these yachts were anything less than jaw dropping. *All we have* I mouthed to myself, amazed at the marvels of engineering, barely rocking in the sea. "Trust me when I say that I'm seriously impressed by your home."

He turned to me and smiled, "Well, that pleases me then."

We walked along the dock and each yacht we passed seemed larger than the last. Most had broad arched sterns with stairs built into their polished skins. Each had been named and included such stellar choices as *Making Waves*, *Sea Urging*, and *Beauty N Boat*.

Raef suddenly stepped away from me and onto the dive deck of an enormous yacht named *Cerberus*. It was a magnificent boat, beautifully crafted with a mirror-like ruby hull and a streak of black windows. I looked at Raef, who was still standing on the platform waiting for me.

"Oh, right! Permission to come aboard?" I asked.

"Permission granted, Miss Walker," he replied, helping me step aboard. He pulled me so close on the narrow dive deck that our bodies touched and my face flushed pink as my heart hammered away. He looked down at me and I tried to distract us from the moment, "So, uh, someone a Greek mythology fan?" I asked.

"What?"

"The name? *Cerberus*? Isn't that the three-headed dog that guards the Underworld?"

"Oh that. Yeah, though technically Cerberus sort of works for the living, keeping them out of Hell. Well, at least he tries."

"I stand corrected," I said, as he moved slightly so I could walk up the bow stairs onto the yacht deck. The inside of the top deck was all polished dark woods accented with modern tones of burgundy. There was a curved, white lounging bed built into the back of the yacht and a gleaming wood table centered the outside aft area.

An upper section of the boat, what Raef called the flybridge, overhung the table and an expanse of tinted glass centered with an ornate, stained-glass door. Raef opened the door and stood aside so I could enter what I could only describe as the parlor, complete with furniture and a bar. I instantly felt as though I had trespassed onto some Hollywood hotshot's private oasis.

Raef smiled as he took my hand, "Come on and I'll show you around." I was so dumbfounded by the yacht's glory, that I could only manage a lame nod.

He led me through the parlor and to a chrome staircase that wound lower beneath our feet. I followed him down into a spectacular modern kitchen and I let out a long whistle, impressed. Raef just smiled and nodded toward the hallway connecting to the kitchen. The hallway itself had a white, polished floor with little blue lights lining the wall. Raef opened a variety of doors along the hall, which revealed a beautiful bathroom with glass shower, and two bedrooms, one of which was Kian's.

"This is my room," he said opening the last door. The same color tones and fabrics continued into his room and splashed over a beautiful, round bed.

"Wow. What an awesome bed," I said, impressed at the unusual design, but quickly realizing I complimented his bed . . . in his bedroom. I started to feel flustered. Raef tried to control his smile and cleared his throat.

"It was part of the design of the boat. I actually prefer old architecture like your home," he said, moving around the opposite side of the room. "I mean, workmanship like that requires a passion for the trade. Your four-poster is just beautiful. It's a piece of art." He stopped short and seemed suddenly at a loss for words.

We stood there for a moment, just looking around the room, my feet glued in place. I couldn't believe I was in his bedroom. Finally Raef cleared his throat, "So, uh, want to see the flybridge?" He acted restless, as if he'd never had a girl in his bedroom before. His nervousness I found cute.

Nevertheless, I was ready to spontaneously combust and rapidly agreed. We both moved quickly out of his room, which I swear got hotter by ten degrees while we were in it.

As we walked back up the staircase I realized I needed to call Mae and let her know I was running late, though my whereabouts might require some creative editing. "I should call Mae. She is going to start to worry and she can stress on a whole different level, if you know what I mean."

"Of course. If you go outside there's a set of stairs going up to the flybridge. Reception on a cell is best up there." He smiled at me. "Want something to drink?"

"Sure. Thanks," I replied, fishing my cell from my hip pocket and heading up the stairs.

The view from the top of the yacht was spectacular. The harbor water reflected the setting sun and the light wind ruffled the wrapped masts of the sailboats. The homes along the shoreline were slowly winking on their lights.

I took a deep breath, drawing in the crispy, salt-air oxygen and smiled at the peace I felt. I dialed my cell and left a message for Mae about studying with some friends. Deleting the bit about a certain boy I was falling for was a necessity if she was going to keep her trip plans and, therefore, the freedom of having the house to myself.

I closed my eyes and let the cold air run across my face and twist my hair. So relaxing, so peaceful . . .

"Stalking is against the law," said a deep voice, so close to me that the hairs stood on the nape of my neck. My eyes flew open and standing right in front of me was Kian.

"I mean, I know I have that effect on women, but really? Next time you want to snuggle, just ask," he said with a wiry smile.

"Jeez, Kian, you almost gave me a coronary! Are you trying to kill me?" I demanded, only half furious. It was hard to be livid with the devastating O'Reilly brothers. One could only wonder what the rest of the family looked like.

"Definitely not trying to kill you," said Kian, still intimately close. Too close.

My personal space feeling squeezed and my skin prickling, I casually stepped back but my leg caught on the low table and I lost my balance.

I didn't even see him move, but my swan dive was halted by Kian, who now had his arm hooked around my back. He held me for an extra second, his brilliant blue eyes studying me with an unnerving intensity. When he released me, my brain was on fire and every nerve in my body was raw. I swallowed hard and glanced over my shoulder to see where the heck Raef was, but Surfer Boy cleared his throat.

He stepped over to a white lounge chair, flopping into it. "So how do you enjoy your new home?" he asked.

"It's, uh, really nice. I still can't believe I was so lucky." I swallowed, an odd chill flowing up my spine.

"Somehow I doubt luck was involved," said Kian, glancing behind me. I heard footsteps on the stairs and turned to see Raef appear with a glass of soda. He walked over to me and placed it in my hand. Thank goodness.

"Kian. Didn't know you would be here," said Raef, standing next to me, his arm brushing against mine. He almost seemed . . . possessive. "You remember Eila, I'm sure."

"She is quite unforgettable." Kian's voice was rich and smooth like Raef's. My brain was filled with cross-wired neurons thanks to being stuck between the two local gods.

"Uh . . . are you in school, Kian?" I asked, trying desperately to pull my thoughts together.

Kian just gave a stunning smile, "You could say I'm studying risk management. Assets and what not." He pushed off the couch and headed for the stairs, but paused in front of me, as if he was searching for a perfume. "I'm headed out for the evening. Take care Miss Walker," he said quietly, then left Raef and me standing alone.

I'm not sure whether it was the coolness of the coming night, or the fact that Kian made me ill at ease, but suddenly I felt cold. Raef saw me shiver, "Let's get inside and warmed up."

I nodded, but in the distance I could see Kian open the door to the fancy sports car. He paused as he was about to get in, and looked back at me. Even at the distance he was, my body felt panicky. Raef must have picked up on my stiffness. "Are you alright?" he asked as I watched Kian drive out of the parking lot.

"Yeah. Just cold," I said, smiling weakly at him.

His brow furrowed, "You sure?"

I glanced back to the lot and seeing the empty parking spot made me feel better. I smiled, a more calm and happy state settling in,

"Absolutely. I'm fine."

He looked at me like he was debating whether or not to believe me, but then smiled, "How about something hot to eat? It's nearly dinner."

"That sounds fabulous!" I declared and we went down the stairs, back into the yacht.

In the kitchen of the *Cerberus*, Raef and I gathered vegetables and cooked chicken to make soup. It was the perfect night for warm comfort food.

We stood next to each other at the counter working on our mutually assigned tasks. Raef pulled the meat from a cooked hen while I chopped a variety of vegetables. I pulled a second celery stalk from the bunch beside me and started cutting it. "So, where exactly are your folks?" I asked, trying to be nonchalant, though truly curious.

"Well it's, uh, just Kian and me," said Raef, glancing in my direction. "Our folks were older when they had us. My dad died when we were younger and my mom died a while ago too. Our parents left us well off, financially. We've done well on our own." He reached over to my celery that I had finished chopping. "Here, let me put this in the pot."

"I'm sorry about your family," I said as he gathered the little green pieces.

He looked at me and gave a small smile. "Thanks," he said as he took my assignment over to the pot.

I grabbed a skinned potato and sliced it through. "You know, my folks are gone too," I said, slowly cutting. The knife looked razor sharp and brand new. Out of the corner of my eye, I saw Raef's hands pause briefly over the chicken.

"I had heard that at school," he said quietly, "I'm very sorry."

"It's okay," I said, flipping the spud sideways to make another cut. "I never really knew them. A friend of my mom's raised me. I love her like a sister. To me, she *is* my real sister," I said, confident in the truth I just spoke.

Raef added the chicken to our soup, then walked around the counter and sat down on a stool opposite me, watching me slice. "I also heard that you inherited the house."

"Well, not really inherited, more like, *won*," I said, remembering back to that day the auction house called. "I still don't know why, but some random person bid on the house when it was up for auction. I guess a trust fund for it had run out, so it was put up for sale. This buyer, whoever the heck he is, then said the house was to go back to its rightful owner and gave MY name."

"So you're related then? To the original owners?" asked Raef.

"Well, yeah, but I mean I never knew about them, or the house. It was built by my great great great great grandfather, or something like that," I said, losing track of the "greats."

"Well, it had to be a family member that bought the house. Eccentric Uncle or something?"

"That's the thing," I said, knotting my forehead. "I don't have any living relatives that I know of. Nobody. So how this person found me, I just have no idea." I shook my head. "Oh, and here is the real kicker! He paid cash and never used his name on *anything*, so I can't even thank him."

"No offense, but that didn't strike you as strange?" asked Raef, watching me.

"Well yeah, but . . ." I sighed, "We had nothing to lose. Mae and I were barely making ends meet. She was working these awful jobs and I knew my fate was going to be the same. We saw this crazy gift as a chance to start again. Leave behind all the crap and just reinvent ourselves, you know? And so far, the Cape is such a perfect place for us." Well, except for the weirdo outside my window the other night. Okay, maybe *perfect* is a tad too strong of a word.

I quickly changed the subject. "Can I ask why you live on a yacht?"

"Kian and I like to travel a lot," said Raef. "And we don't want to be locked into any one place. If we bought a house, we would have to deal with what to do with it if we wanted to leave. This house goes wherever we want as long as there is water."

He went quiet for a moment and then looked at me, "And we have never had a reason to stay in any one place . . . in the past."

Was he telling me that he had a reason to finally settle into one place? Could that reason be *me*? Or was he saying he wasn't planning on staying? UGH! He was maddening to decipher.

My phone began vibrating in my pocket. I fumbled for it and snapped it open. "Yeah, I'm just studying with a friend," I said to Mae, who wanted details. I sort of skirted some of the finer points as I watched Raef head over to the pot on the stove and pulled down a bowl as I talked. I told Mae I'd be home within an hour and she seemed fine with that answer.

I tucked the phone back in my pocket as Raef slid a bowl of soup across the counter to me along with a glass of ice water.

"Studying with a friend, huh?"

"Yeah, uh, she'd probably flip if she knew about the motorcycle." *And you,* I thought to myself. "She's leaving on this two week trip to Europe in a few weeks and she has saved for it forever. I just don't want her to think she can't trust me enough not to go. It's her dream to travel overseas. We had discussed it all before moving here."

I looked to Raef who was leaning against the sink. "Aren't you going to have some?" I asked, feeling like a glutton.

"No. I'm fine."

"You sure? It's really good."

"Nah. Soup is not really my thing," he said with a smile.

Weirdest. Boy. Ever.

A half hour later, Raef had brought me back to the high school parking lot. As I drove home in my Jeep, I replayed the moment Raef and I shared in his bedroom, adding a few fictional rewrites as I daydreamed.

Soon, however, something began nagging me.

By the time I pulled into the driveway of my magnificent home, I knew what it was.

Raef had complimented my bed, which would have been fine except for the fact that he had never been in my bedroom. Ever.

I looked up at my room's window and suddenly felt uneasy.

Tuesday was destined to suck, mainly because Nikki had yet to retaliate. Surprisingly, however, I hadn't seen the bitter bombshell anywhere. When gym rolled around just before lunch, I was downright giddy.

Walking out to the soccer field, I actually started to believe another day would squeak by without retribution. But once I got onto the field, my scrap of hope was shredded. Nikki, curvy co-captain of the BHS WAVES field hockey squad, was standing mid-field, waiting with her team to play *our* class.

I always did loathe Tuesdays.

Forty minutes later, my hatred for field hockey was in full bloom, courtesy of Nikki. Whoever thought it was a good idea to combine Tag with wooden golf clubs and a rodent-size ball should be beaten senseless.

Attempting to do all three was a bad combination for me, and I ended up tripping one of Nikki's teammates, who took a digger in the dirt. Nikki retuned the favor a few minutes later by "accidentally" knocking me hard into the goal post, face first.

It was like kissing concrete at a high rate of speed.

The impact nearly knocked me out, and I was sure that I was going to have a permanent indent on the side of my face.

As we walked back to the locker room, I could hear Nikki laughing with her teammates, no doubt at me. All I wanted was a hot shower and to get through the last two hours of the day without committing a homicide.

In the locker room, my face continued to pound under the shower's warm spray, but I took my time, not wanting to face any of the other girls. I listened carefully and the voices dwindled until only the sound of the shower echoed in the musty room.

I knew I was going to be late for lunch, but I no longer cared. I simply wanted the water to wash away the day. I started visualizing smacking Nikki repeatedly with the wooden stick, but exhaustion from her constant harassment was starting to take its toll.

My throat started to tighten, but I fought back the tears, taking slow breaths to quell my mutinous emotions. I turned my face up into the shower stream one last time and reluctantly turned the flow off.

Squeezing out my rope of hair, I pulled the towel off its hook and wrapped it around me. But as I pulled the curtain back, I knew with absolute certainty that Nikki was the Devil. The clothes that I had left so neatly folded on the bench outside the shower, were GONE. I frantically scanned the room, but saw no clothes. Anywhere.

"No! Oh no no no!" I stepped out of the shower and onto the cold concrete floor. I rushed around the room, searching for my missing jeans and top. My steps were leaving a detailed map of wet footprints chronicling my frantic search.

Finally I found them, crumpled and soaked, in the furthest sink. I started ringing them out, my towel providing scant warmth against the chilly locker room. *"See Eila,"* I thought, chastising myself, *"This, THIS is why we should never leave our clothes unattended with serial nut jobs lurking!"*

As I finished squeezing the last of the water from my jeans, I realized that my gym clothes AND UNDERWEAR were not among the dripping pile. Where I was simply irritated before at being stuck in dirty gym clothes for the remainder of the school day, now I was horrified. I had nothing to wear. AT ALL! I stood there, staring down at my pile of clothes in the creamy sink, debating what to do next.

Did I dare walk out of the room, wrapped in a towel, and try to make it to my locker to get my keys? Then what? Drive home half naked?

I could see myself walking through the sea of students, enduring stares and laughs. I had a nightmarish vision of accidentally dropping my towel as I passed the guidance office.

Dashing to my locker was clearly not an option.

As the realization of my predicament set in, I could feel my face getting hot - a combination of rage and humiliation that made the sudden tears running down my cheeks feel like fire.

I slumped down against the center row of gray lockers, feeling defeated as I rested my forehead on my knees. I tried to figure out what would happen if I were stuck in the locker room for hours on end when I heard a quiet knock on the locker room door.

The heavy steel door cracked open and Raef's voice rolled through from the outside. "Eila? Are you in here?" he said in a near whisper.

I hurriedly wiped my tears and nose and staggered to my feet. I cleared my throat so he wouldn't know I had been crying. "Uh, yeah. I'm here," I responded, padding in my bare feet over to the door. The large mirror on the wall displayed my half-naked form, complete with a growing bruise on my face. I was going to look like a Jack-O-Lantern two weeks after Halloween once it formed.

I spoke to the door, but kept myself tucked behind it and out of sight. "I seem to be having a, uh, wardrobe issue."

"I suspected as much," he said reaching through the door without showing his face, his hand mercifully holding my ratty gym clothes. "I think you are missing these."

"My clothes! How did you find them?" I asked, highly relieved and yet mortified that he was holding muddy sweats *and* undies.

"I was worried when you weren't at lunch. When MJ got to the cafeteria, he said the school was buzzing about you and Nikki having quite the fisticuffs on the soccer field. I came here figuring you were getting cleaned up, but found your clothes scattered in the hallway."

I stood there in my towel for a moment, replaying the incident. My face throbbed and I knew it would look quite horrific in a few more hours. I quickly made up my mind to tell Mae I was just a fumble-footed teen who damaged herself during gym. She need not know about the hellish prom queen or my knight.

I stepped forward and took the clothes from his hand. My fingers brushed his and as he released my clothes, he grasped my hand firmly. His voice was right on the opposite side of the door.

"Let me see," he said, his words quiet, but laced with anger. He wanted to know what Nikki had done on the field.

He squeezed my hand, encouragingly. "Eila, let me see," he said again, softly this time. Embarrassed though I was, I forced myself forward, peeking my face through the crack in the door. His deep blue eyes came into view and nearly took my breath away.

I could see his face reflect a torrent of emotions, from pain and frustration to rage. He reached up slowly, and gingerly touched the edge of the welting bruise. His hand continued tracing my face and he gently felt my brow bone and under my eye. I winced and he carefully softened his touch.

"Sorry," he said quickly. "I didn't mean to hurt you. I was worried she might have broken something." His hand slowly slid down my jaw line and came to rest at the side of my neck. My body was electrified by his touch and I was certain he could feel my now racing pulse.

Watching him, I started to notice that his irises seem to darken, the ocean blue becoming a shade of midnight. The slow evolution of color was mesmerizing . . . until it suddenly shifted to jet-black.

I gasped and stiffened.

Raef quickly dropped his hand, alarmed. "Are you alright?" he asked shaken, his own breath quick. His eyes were back to their normal yet spectacular deep blue.

My heart had been jolted into a sprint. "I, uh should probably get, um, dressed," I said uneasily. I gathered my clothes close to my chest and looked one more time at his eyes.

"Are you sure you are alright? You could have a concussion," said Raef, controlled, but his face now worried.

I was slowly recovering my mental state. "Yeah, uh, I'm okay, though my face is humming," I said, still watching him carefully. What in the hell was that? Good grief maybe I do have a concussion. I managed to pull my scrambled brain together. "I'm going to look hideous though in a few hours," I said, a half-hearted smile crossing my face.

"Nah," he said, raising my face with his hand under my chin so he could see me. "You could never be hideous."

My eye was starting to water from the sting of the bruise, forcing a tear down the battered curve of my face and into his palm. His smile fell as he wiped away the path of my tear with his thumb.

I wanted to be strong. I wanted to be unbreakable, but with him it was difficult to continue to fuel the charade. My throat was once again tightening, and I took a deep breath, trying to squelch my mental and physical scars. He saw my struggle – my attempt to be brave, but my stoicism was wilting away.

Watching me, his usually reserved demeanor disappeared. He pushed the door open and pulled me into his strong arms. I rubbed my face on his warm sweatshirt and he held me tighter in a safe embrace.

The magnetic draw he had on me was a near-audible hum in my head. While I could've remained ensconced in his arms for hours, he seemed to recover his "friendship-only" badge after a minute and released me, but held my shoulders. I wobbled slightly, woozy and high from our close encounter.

"You'll be okay, Eila. You are stronger than you think," he said, a tad too serious. I nodded drunkenly. "I'm still worried though, about a concussion. You look a bit unstable." I bet I did.

I managed to solidify my legs and focus on the task of getting dressed. "I'm fine," I said, rubbing my forehead and debating the veracity of that statement. "I just have a pounding headache."

"Well, I'm still going to stand outside the door, but if I hear the thud of your unconscious self hitting the floor, I'm coming in," he said, releasing me. "I'll be right here," and he pulled the door shut.

I stood there for a moment more, staring at the door and absorbing our brief, but intimate, moment. It was something I had desired from him for so long, yet something just felt off. Of course, my face meeting the goal post may have something to do with my stomach doing flip-flops.

I couldn't get past the fact, however, that the butterflies I developed around Raef always behaved like a panicked mob. And what on earth did I see in his eyes?

That wasn't even possible, was it?

I let out a long, slow breath and turned toward the counter, the mirror watching me approach. I dropped my towel and got dressed, thanking every star in heaven that Raef had decided to come looking for me.

When I finally emerged, my humiliation had been replaced by a strong desire to choke Nikki. Raef was waiting for me as promised, leaning against the wall.

"I'm so done with this place for today, maybe even for the week!" I said, infuriated. "My head is pounding, I have on smelly gym clothes and there are grass burns in places I can't mention." I tied my sneakers in a brutish fashion, nearly snapping off a shoelace.

"I agree. Done for the day sounds good. I'll drive you home," said Raef, watching me.

"You don't have to do that," I replied, though not protesting his chivalry nearly enough.

"You can't drive after a blow to the head like that. I would feel better taking you myself." He opened the exit door, which let out a chirp. "Don't worry. I already had the nurse clear you to leave."

"Thanks Raef," I said.

"Anytime," he replied.

Later that night over dinner, Mae wanted every detail of why I looked like Two-Face from the Batman Comics. I went through the whole field hockey game, but changed the ending. I told her I had stumbled and fallen into the goal post. Adding the deranged cheerleader would have been counter-productive if I wanted her to still go on her trip. I also left out my handsome hero.

That night I lay in bed with a cold cloth on my throbbing face. I replayed the day, skipping the more unappealing instances and dwelling more on the fantasy portion involving Raef.

The way he touched me, and how I felt when he did, was near intoxicating. I toyed with the moment repeatedly while staring at my ceiling. As I started to sway towards sleep, the memory of the day started to take on a life of its own and, unbidden, I saw Raef's eyes turn black.

Every time I tried to ignore the moment and throw it to the back of my mind, it would slowly rise to the surface. *Not possible,* I kept telling myself over and over, and eventually my memory began to bend in the direction I wanted it to.

Finally content with my dreaming, I drifted off to sleep, but my mind stopped replaying my edited version of Raef and proceeded back to the man who had watched me from the shadows. I pulled my blankets tighter around me and not even my memory of Raef could comfort me.

I had gotten settled into school and Cape life, and before I knew it, mid-October had arrived. The shadow stalker never reappeared, Raef's eyes stayed blue, and the vial? I gave up on the vial. It had to contain just some nasty-smelling herb and I was just being a freak. Not to mention, life had been perfectly normal and I was with friends who I really enjoyed.

It was a good thing too – the normal part – since Mae had left on her trip a few hours earlier at the crack of dawn, heading to London and beyond. While I'd miss her, I was thrilled for the freedom. I fully intended to keep an eye out for Marsh and invite him for a sleepover when I saw his furry frame.

Mae had been flip-flopping on whether or not to go for weeks. Getting her to not cancel took some fast-talking and perhaps ten promises founded on certain house arrest if they were broken. In the end, however, my non-existent social life and perpetual lack of boyfriend seemed to assure her that I'd be having an outstandingly dull and chaste fortnight.

Mae, for the most part, was right. With the exception of MJ, Ana and, to my delight, Raef, I really had no set social network here. But it didn't matter to me - I had made three good friends and they made all the difference. And, bless the Fates, Nikki and I had not had any further confrontations.

I had come to actually look forward to BHS. I started every morning by parking my very cool Wrangler next to MJ's equally uncool hunk of sputtering junk. Ana would park somewhere near us, and we would all walk into school together. We had plans to hang out at my home that night, maybe get pizza and watch a movie. It was the first time that they would actually be in my home and I was excited to have visitors to entertain, including Raef.

As I walked through the parking lot alongside Ana and MJ, arguing once again about musical preferences, I couldn't help but be lost in my own thoughts. In a few hours I'd be enjoying a movie night with my friends and the one boy who set my soul ablaze. The thought of him sent an odd flurry of emotions rippling through my skin.

One part of me knew he was a strong, faithful friend to have - the boy you wanted in the foxhole when all hell broke loose. Yet there were still fleeting moments when I would look at him and could not be sure whether I was in the right foxhole to begin with. My inner voice would question the sanity of being near him, but it was a voice that shrank day by day and now was barely a whisper.

It was easy to imagine kissing him, but thus far he only seemed to be in a "friendship" mode. I reminded myself that I was lucky to have him as a friend and tried to push aside any further desire. The problem was, it wasn't just a desire. It was a magnetic pull cranked to a thousand and impossible to turn off.

Since my brain seemed to continuously dwell on Raef, I utilized my occupied mind to devise three possible explanations for his behavior towards me: a) he was interested in me, but shy, b) he was not interested romantically, but a good friend or c) he saw himself as a big brother. Gag.

Option "c" I buried in the back of my mind because it would eliminate all hope of him becoming more than a friend. Of course, there could be an option "d" that I had not thought of yet, but option "a" kept me preoccupied with hope for the future.

When the last bell finally rang for the day, my head was already calculating what I needed to buy at the grocery store for the four of us. I was making a mental list as I navigated my way to my locker when Jesse caught up to me, calling my name and waving a bright yellow paper in his hand. I stopped in the hall, trying to dodge the masses fleeing academia.

"Eila! Wait up!" he yelled, finally reaching me. He handed me the flier for a beach bonfire scheduled for the evening. "This is the first party of the fall and it's always a blast. You, as a washashore, must come! We have music and bonfires. Perhaps a few brewskies," he said with a knowing smile.

"Thanks for thinking of me, Jess, but I have plans." I started to hand the paper back to him, but he refused it.

"You mean you *had* plans! Trust me, this is too damn fun to miss."

I stood there, debating what to do. The flier said that the event was the seniors' yearly party on the beach near Town Neck. I thought about the sand, the surf and the stars.

I thought about enjoying all three with Raef.

Suddenly pizza and a movie seemed to pale by comparison.

"I *did* have plans, but I may be able to change them," I said, a completely new, snuggly, beach-at-night to-do list forming in my head.

"Excellent! I'll see you there," said Jesse and bounded off as a few other random males yelled to him as he passed. Being the captain of the football team meant that a virtual spotlight followed him wherever he went. He seemed to enjoy the fame. I would've hated it.

Thank goodness I was an extra in life and not the star.

I headed to my locker and found Raef and Ana waiting for me. I was a little surprised to see Ana still at school. She usually bolted in her Trans Am to get out in front of the belching, diesel buses.

"Hey. What's up?" I asked, twirling the combination lock on my locker.

"MJ said someone called in sick and now he has to work tonight," said Ana, hiking her backpack higher on her shoulder. "He's pissed he's missing the pizza and grand tour of *su casa*."

"I was actually thinking maybe we should postpone the pizza and movie and do this instead." I handed her the paper. She didn't even look at it, but passed it to Raef, who read it carefully.

"I already know what that is. It's the beach bonfire. One of many different parties all year long, each used as an excuse to either get laid, get drunk or both," she replied. I flushed a little at her brutal honesty.

"Well, who says we can't go and enjoy ourselves without such intoxicated debauchery? I've yet to go to the beach at night or bonfire by the ocean." I glanced at Raef, who was now folding the paper, hoping for agreement.

"It's fine with me," he said, knowing I wanted to go.

Ana sighed. "Okay fine. Sheesh. Flipping beach-bonfire virgins. So demanding," she said with a grin. "Dang washashores are ruining the Cape."

I laughed and Raef smiled. "That is what Jesse called me too when he gave me the flier."

"A bonfire virgin?" asked Raef, an eyebrow raised.

I nearly choked. "No, no! A washashore! He called me a 'washashore,'" I babbled, an even darker pink dusting my cheeks. Kill me now.

Ana put her arm around my shoulder and leaned in to my ear, pretending to whisper but to be sure Raef also heard. "I think Jesse wouldn't mind deflowering more than your bonfire innocence," she said, a devious curve to her mouth.

I shrugged her arm off of me with a jerk, "You have a dirty mind, Ana Lane." I was now absolutely red-faced.

Raef picked up my backpack off the floor and slung it over his shoulder, clearing his throat. "I can't think of anyone who would want to be plucked by that player, though I bet he has plucked plenty."

"Oh, ouch. So much for a brotherhood among boys!" I declared, but I suspected Raef was testing my state of mind regarding Jesse. "Shall I warn the other chaste girls in school?"

"I wouldn't bother. I think you are the only one left," he said as he started to walk towards the door. Ana punched him hard in the arm and he feigned pain, "OW! Okay, you AND Ana."

I laughed, but I wasn't sure whether to take what he said as a compliment or not. Did he applaud our honor or think us shrews? I decided not to ask for clarification and let the subject drop as we walked out to the parking lot.

Students were heading out in their vehicles, the seniors no doubt excited about tonight. Ana turned to me, "I'll meet you at the boardwalk around 9:30," she said, climbing into her Trans Am.

"Doesn't it start at nine?" I asked, walking up to my Wrangler that was parked next to her.

"Fashionably late," she replied and backed out of her spot.

Raef was standing next to me, still holding my backpack. I unlocked my door and climbed in. He tossed the backpack on the passenger seat then closed my driver's door and leaned on the open window. If I didn't know him better, I would've thought he was about to kiss me. His closeness made my heart hiccup. "I'm shocked this is held on a school night," I said, trying to calm myself.

"The flier says that seniors are exempt from school tomorrow. Not sure how they pulled that off, but I guess tonight is technically Friday as far as school is concerned. For us anyway."

I nodded and glanced at Raef's black beast of a motorcycle parked next to me. "Want me to pick you up at the boat so you can leave the bike behind?"

"No – it's fine. I'll just meet you and Ana at the parking lot by the boardwalk. Nine-thirty, right?"

I nodded.

"I'll see you then. Drive safe," he said and walked over to his motorcycle. I started up my Jeep and pulled out of the lot as Raef climbed onto his bike. I headed back to my house debating what to wear as I drove.

Tonight was going to be awesome and couldn't come fast enough.

* * * *

By the time nine o'clock rolled around, I could barely manage my excitement. It had taken me forever to pick what to wear, not that my wardrobe was very broad in selection.

In the end I went for cozy-casual, with a blue flannel button-down shirt, a gray tank top with a few little sparkles at the front, and dark blue jeans. I pulled on a pair of leather boots, and tucked my mass of unruly locks into a large clip with just a few, petulant strands falling loose.

I grabbed my leather jacket and an extra sweatshirt as I headed out to my Jeep, flinging the spare clothing in the back. It landed on top of the two red blankets, shovel and small wooden board that I had learned were necessities in a Cape Cod four-wheeler.

It took me about fifteen minutes to reach the curving stretch of northern beach known as Town Neck. A long, twisting boardwalk reached out over the dark salt marsh to the dunes where the ocean rolled. I had heard that you could see to the outer curve of Provincetown, miles and miles away from the beach. I couldn't wait to see what it looked like with a bonfire.

I drove into the packed parking lot and immediately saw Raef leaning against his motorcycle, which was parked next to Ana's Trans Am. The golden bird on the hood seemed to glow under the cosmic light.

I pulled into the spot next to Raef and cut the engine as he walked around and opened the driver's door for me. The air by the water was raw and cold and caused my breath to trail off into the night air. "Wow. I didn't think it would be this chilly down here," I said, leaning into the back seat to grab one of the two blankets. I looked briefly at the sweatshirt, but decided I'd be warm enough in the jacket.

Plus, if I shivered, Raef might decide to keep me warm.

A smile sprang to my face, but I quickly contorted my lips until I wasn't such a grinning fool. Blanket in hand, I climbed out of the Jeep. Raef shut the door behind me and I locked it, stuffing the key in my pocket.

"Shall we?" he asked.

"We shall!" I glanced to the Trans Am, "Where's Ana?"

"She's already on the beach. Someone's truck broke down on its way out there and she had to help get it going again. It was carrying all the amplifiers for the music."

"Handy, isn't she?" I asked, laughing.

"That she is." He took the blanket from me and we walked side by side onto the beginning of the boardwalk, the wood decking giving off a low luster. When we passed other students, we were forced to form a single line, as the narrow boardwalk could not contain more than two people side-by-side.

A few times, I wobbled dangerously close to the edge, but felt Raef reach out from behind me and place his hand on my waist to keep me from toppling over and falling fifteen feet into the black marsh. The boardwalk was busy, especially since it seemed a large portion of the 300 seniors actually came out for the event.

Toward the middle of the boardwalk was an incline and the highest point, a bridge, almost 25 feet above the snaking, black river that raced through the marsh on its way out to the ocean. People had said that only the highly brave (or terminally stupid) attempted jumping from the bridge, since the water was like a melted glacier and the current could drag you out to sea in seconds.

Even in the night, the moonlight revealed the speed at which the current plowed through the land. It was beauty, power, and hostility all rolled into one elegant statement of nature. Unforgiving and untamable, it was why people lived here, by the ocean, and were careful to respect it. I glanced back at Raef, "Wanna jump?"

"I think I'll pass, but thanks."

A couple classmates raced past us and over the bridge, laughing and screaming something. We could soon hear the low boom of a deep beat as we neared the dunes. We hopped down at the end of the boardwalk onto the soft, fine sand and followed the flow of students coming in and out of a break in the dunes that lead to the beach.

When we reached the water, I simply gasped.

Bonfires dotted the beach and a green pick-up truck was parked near the center of activity, two monster size speakers poised at the edge of the open tailgate. It pumped out some thunderous pop song, while a cluster of about fifty kids were dancing near it. Their shadows, thrown by the fire, traveled in a circle around them, like spirits from the dark side. Little bits of flaming confetti from the fire traveled gently upward into the night air as the wood popped and crackled.

The beach was strewn with students, laughing, playing volleyball, and drinking under the intense, blue light of the largest moon I had ever seen. It seemed to rise above the tip of the Cape and nearly swallow half the sky as it climbed. Stars filled the sky as if some celestial payload was lost on its way to heaven, spilling millions of diamonds all over the night's canvas.

"I'm so glad we opted out of the pizza thing," I nearly whispered. Raef, however, looked at all the students partying and didn't seem so sure we chose correctly.

"The night is spectacular, but it's hard to enjoy in such insanity," he said, gesturing to the hundreds of classmates around us. "Let's go stake out our own area. We can see the sky better away from the fires."

I nodded and looked back to the blasting truck. It was then that I noticed a very familiar, petite friend climb over the cab and jump into the bed.

Ana, dressed in someone's varsity jacket, was fiddling with something in the back of the truck. She stood up and banged on the cab hood with her fist. In response, the music suddenly jumped exponentially in volume. You could physically feel the music pound mercilessly through your chest. The entire crowd roared in approval and she raised her hands, victorious.

"It's Ana!" I yelled at Raef above the musical onslaught. He nodded. "I'm going to go talk to her!" I yelled again.

I must have looked ridiculous, screaming above the pounding beat, because he gave a broad smile and then yelled back, "I'll stay here and wait for you!" I nodded and trotted off into the pulsating crowd.

When I finally reached the edge of the truck, I was sure I was deaf. Ana, still in the back coiling up cables, was oblivious to my appearance. I banged on the truck's side to get her attention. She looked up and waved and I gestured for her to come lean down to me so I could talk to her.

"Raef and I are going to find a spot away from the crowd," I yelled, "Wanna come?" The blasting music seemed to cancel out my voice.

She gave me a knowing look and shook her head, "no," and then made kissing motion with her mouth. I narrowed my eyes at her and shook my head, but my face was smiling.

I motioned to the varsity jacket she was wearing and gave a questioning look. She stood back up and pounded on the cab roof again. This time the door opened and one of the football players poked his head out. I recognized his face, but could not recall his name. I looked at her and grinned, mimicking her kissing motion. She just shook her head and waved me off.

I trotted back out of the crowd and found Raef waiting for me, "Okay. Let's go!" I yelled.

We walked for a couple of minutes, and the pounding music faded to mere background tunes, gently complementing the fires that glowed softer with distance. We found a spot by the dunes near a large home that faced the water. The stretch of beach was probably private, considering the row of huge houses that sat among the tall grass, but I figured the owners would not care as long as we left *Fergie* and her musical crew farther down the beach.

Raef shook out the blanket and I helped smooth it wide, then sat down and slowly zipped off my boots so I could stick my toes in the cold sand. Raef sat down next to me and looked up at the stars.

He was right.

Away from the blaze of the fires, the stars were all the more brilliant. The massive moon continued to climb higher, causing the luminous pathway on the water to slowly stretch toward the horizon. I just smiled at the good fortune that granted me a chance to live here.

I glanced over at Raef and caught him looking at me. "Yes?" I asked, an odd combination of unease and desire flashing through my veins.

"I was just wondering what you were thinking about."

"I was thinking how amazing this view is, and how unbelievable it is that I get to enjoy it because I live here," I said, my nerves slowly calming. "It's just incredible. I'm waiting to wake from this dream."

I looked back at the stars and then leaned back onto the blanket so I could enjoy the broad view of space, "Perhaps I'm not really here. Maybe I'm in a coma somewhere and this is just my brain misfiring. I think that is more plausible, especially the way my luck normally runs."

He leaned down next to me, propping himself on one elbow as he looked at me. "You are not in a coma."

"Oh yeah? How do you know? Maybe you're in a coma too. Maybe we had some tragic accident and now we're both carrots in a hospital bed somewhere."

He reached over to my arm and pinched me. I let out a yelp. "What the heck?"

"See? Not vegetables," he said with a smile, then looked a bit more serious. "This is real. This is your life now."

I looked at him, debating how to phrase what I was about to say, fearing his answer as well. "And your life? Is this your life as well, or is this temporary?"

He rolled over on his back to study the sky with me, "I think this is my life now as well. Kian and I are not planning on leaving anytime soon."

I nearly sighed audibly in relief, but managed to control myself. We lay there, staring at the stars and watching the moonrise. Finally he spoke up, "You know, as a true native, you should know your constellations."

I didn't follow. "Why is that?"

"Well, Cape Cod is an ocean-going community. Your own grandparents were a big part of that as well. And, as such, knowing how to navigate by the heavens is part of being a native."

"And I take it, as a brilliant boat-dweller, you know such things?"

"Heck yeah. Care to learn?"

"Go for it, but be forewarned – I'm a slow study."

"Then I guess it is a good thing we don't have school tomorrow," he laughed.

For the next hour, Raef explained the stars and the pictures they made in the sky. He told me about the stories of the gods they represented, and how to find your way based on the characters that rose in the universe nightly. I was pleased when I was able to find Sirius with his help.

"I'm a true Cape Codder," I said proudly, thanks to my limited, but accurate constellation identification. He was silent for a moment as he lay next to me and I turned to him.

He looked at me, eye to eye for a moment, then slowly sat up. "A true Cape Codder needs a badge of belonging," he said as he looked back at me lying on the faded blanket. He reached into his jacket pocket and pulled out a little velvet bag.

Intrigued, I sat up next to him and pulled my chilled feet under me. He reached out and took my hand, unfurling my fingers as he placed the soft bag in my palm.

"What's this?" I asked, my heart pounding.

"A gift that says you belong to this area," said Raef, watching me.

I swallowed and slowly untied the black string, tipping the bag upside down into my other hand. A beautiful silver bangle bracelet with a glistening ball in the center slid out into my hand. The ball had a thousand little facets cut into it, making it pulse with moonlight.

"It's . . . beautiful," I said, breathless and stunned.

He picked it up and untwisted the ball, causing the bracelet to spring open slightly. He took my other arm and slid the bracelet onto my wrist, then tightened the ball down again to link the hoop together. He turned it slightly so the ball faced the moon, twinkling.

"This is made here. Most locals have one and it's distinctive to Cape Cod. I wanted you to have one, so that whenever you felt like you didn't belong, you could look at it and remember that someone says differently."

I sat there, turning my wrist slightly, watching it shine like the moonlit path on the water. I looked up at Raef, who was watching me with a serious look on his face that I found unsettling and impossible to read.

"Thank you," I said, trying to understand what this gift from him meant. Was it just a gift of friendship, or something more?

I was about to ask where I stood with him, when the jovial voice of Jesse broke our silence.

"Well HELLO. What are you two doing way out here. In the dark. ALL ALONE," asked Jesse, a huge smile on his face, directed at me. I may just murder him if he embarrassed me. All I could think of was the way he had watched me check out Raef our first day of school.

Raef got to his feet. He reached down and took my hand, pulling me to mine. "Ana has the music a bit too deafening for my taste," said Raef with a brief smile.

"Plus we wanted to see the stars better," I blurted out. Jesse gave me a look that screamed he didn't believe I had been stargazing. As if to prove I wasn't lying, I pointed skyward without looking up. "Cepheus. Right above us."

"Sure," said Jesse, the smile still on his face. He turned to Raef, "Since you're out here, can you help me grab a few cases of beer from my house?"

Raef looked at me, as if seeking permission, and Jesse's smile got even more irritatingly huge. "Go ahead. I'll just hang out here and wait for you," I said, sliding Jesse a look of death.

"You sure?" asked Raef.

"Yeah," I said, nodding toward the house. Raef's fingertips gently touched mine, but so surreptitiously that Jesse didn't see. The sensation, so simple, gave me a rush of heat.

He turned away from me and followed Jesse toward the large house nestled among the dunes. I could hear Jesse talking to Raef, his voice fading as they walked down the beach toward the staircase that led to his property. I sat back down on the blanket and looked out over the water, feeling my bracelet cool against my skin.

Here, on the bayside of the Cape, the waves slowly lapped at the shoreline, leaving a delicate line of perfectly polished stones along the water's edge. I made a mental note to come back over the weekend and gather a few to line part of the side garden near the kitchen door. Mae would like it when she got back from her trip, calling it "seaside chic" or something like that.

I smiled, dreaming of her exploring the castles of some foreign land. Mae would be in her glory. She loved all that stuff. As I thought about her wandering some limestone hall, a figure caught my attention out of the corner of my eye.

I turned and could see someone, broad in shape, walking . . . no, *stumbling*, toward me. In the darkness, he was hard to make out, but seemed decidedly drunk. "Hello?" I called.

"Hey! Who's dat?" called a deep, slobbery voice.

"It's Eila. Eila Walker," I called back, finally seeing his face. It was the footballer from the truck! I noted that he had his varsity jacket back on and I wondered where Ana had gone. What the heck was his name? Tom? Ted?

"Eila!" he said in a booming, friendly voice, as if he was my best buddy since forever. "How the heck are ya?"

He kept stumbling towards me and I suddenly realized he was going to trip on me. I tried to scramble to my feet, but I was too late. His foot got caught up in the end of the blanket and he fell on top of me, pinning me underneath his massive frame and spilling his beer all over my shirt and jacket. I struggled under his weight, trying to shift him.

"Dude! Get off me! You weigh a ton," I gasped, trying to push his shoulders upwards so I could breathe. He shifted his weight so he was nose to nose with me. He smelled like a day-old keg that had been left in the sun.

"Hey girl, you're kinda cute," he slurred, smiling wide.

"Oh, hell no," I said, realizing where this was going. "Ted? Fred? Whoever the heck you are, you need to get off me. Like NOW!" I said, louder and more irritated.

He laughed, "You are so hot when you're feisty!" He grabbed my face and kissed me forcefully. I was horrified, and pushed and shoved until he finally broke the lip lock.

But then his massive hands started to travel south and my irritation transformed into panic. I knew he was drunk and hopefully wouldn't act like such a moron when he was sober, but the alcohol was clouding any decent judgment he had. I needed to get him off me. Fast.

"Get up!" I yelled into his face, hoping to break through his beer haze, "Get off me you idiot!" I reached for his hands to keep them from wandering further, but in doing so, his weight became even heavier on me. It was hard to draw a full breath to yell. I was starting to really freak out and I drew what air I could. "GET OFF ME!" I screamed.

Suddenly I could hear Raef and Jesse's voices yelling. Within seconds, Raef was above me, his voice commanding and hard, "Get off her! NOW!" He grabbed the back of What's-His-Face's shirt and hauled him off me. He landed on the sand about five feet away.

I drew a long deep breath and just laid there for a moment, grateful for the oxygen. I turned my head and saw Jesse bending down to the footballer to roll him over onto his back.

"Teddy, you moron," he said, shaking his head. He turned to me,

"Sorry, Eila. He has a low tolerance for beer even though he's a big guy."

"Well, maybe you shouldn't provide him with so much alcohol!" snapped Raef, angry. He dropped to his knees beside me. "Please tell me you're okay," he asked, putting his arm around my back and slowly helping me to sit up.

I drew another deep, grateful breath, "Yeah, I'm fine, but I think I left a permanent indent of my butt in the sand. He weighs a ton!" I nodded to the unmoving mountain in the sand. "Is he okay?"

"Eila, who cares?" asked Raef, a raw rage barely contained in his voice. "He almost . . ." He drew a deep breath and his body seemed to actually vibrate with anger.

"Actually, he tripped and fell on me, and then got other ideas," I said, trying to calm Raef. His dark intensity unnerved me and I placed my hand on his forearm, trying to soothe him.

"Well, he's passed out now," said Jesse, oblivious to Raef's iron glare. "And he's not *that* type of guy. He's going to feel like an ass in the morning. Well, if he remembers." He looked over to Raef, "I know you would rather leave him here for the sand fleas, but the tide is going to eventually come in and he may not wake up before then. Can you please help me get him to his house? It's the third one down, past mine."

Raef looked down the beach, his body so tense I could probably bounce a nickel off his arm and have it ricochet a mile. "Why don't we just drop his molesting ass in *your* house, since you provided the booze?"

"And have him puke all over my mom's furniture? No way!"

Raef leaned next to my face and spoke quietly, the anger darkening his eyes, "Are you *sure* you're okay?"

I nodded.

He sat back and wrinkled his nose, "Is it him that smells like a brewery . . . or you?"

"I've been drenched in his Bud, unfortunately," I replied.

A muscle in Raef's jaw twitched. For a moment I actually thought he wouldn't mind killing Ted, and worse, capable of doing so.

He seemed to reign in his rage as he got to his feet and walked over to the linebacker, who was snoring. "Let's do this," he said tightly. Together they managed to stir Teddy enough to get him to his feet and dragged him towards his house.

I watched them disappear into the darkness. This evening had not gone quite according to my hoped-for plan. I sniffed my shirt and the powerful smell of beer emanated from it.

Yup, I was definitely Eila, because this was my type of luck.

I decided to run back to my Jeep and grab the smell-free sweatshirt that was on the backseat. I got up, barefoot, and jogged back along the beach and past the throngs of classmates, cutting through the dunes once again. I hopped up onto the boardwalk and started to walk back to the parking lot.

Unlike the beach that was in full party mode, the boardwalk was now deserted. The wind blew in gusts that were cold and raw across the salt marsh, and I was looking forward to getting into a dry top.

As I approached the bridge, I saw that there was another partygoer headed my way. I dutifully started to walk farther to the outer edge of the bridge and its low railing. As the figure approached, however, my instincts started to stir and the hairs on my neck rose. I slowed, but the figure kept coming.

He was tall and slim, with a baseball hat and a young man's stride. I didn't think I knew him, but it was hard to see anything in the colorless moonlight.

I told my gut that I was just freaking myself out, since I couldn't recognize him and we were all alone. I told myself that the incident with

Teddy had made me more edgy of figures heading my way in the dark, and this kid, most likely, was harmless.

Most likely.

And then a frightening thought came into my mind: that the beach and the crowd were too far away to help me if this guy was not so friendly. I started to speed up, thinking that if I could just get to my Jeep, I'd be fine.

Soon we were both nearing the top of the bridge and my instincts were screaming, but it was too late. Just as I was about to pass him, he reached out and in one powerful move, knocked me over the railing.

I tumbled from the bridge, striking my ankle against a piling as I fell and hit the black water, back first, before I could even scream.

The impact with the river knocked the wind out of me and the brutal cold felt like a thousand shards of glass. I plunged deeply into the water, swimming recklessly in the thick blackness, disoriented as to which way was salvation.

I pulled with all my might toward what I hoped was air and reached the racing surface, gasping for breath. My muscles were seizing from the frigid ocean temperature and the current was mercilessly dragging me away from the bridge.

I was coughing and retching from the water I had inhaled, but I still managed to yell for help. I was fighting the powerful current, trying to keep my head above the icy depths. I yelled again glancing toward the bridge and caught sight of someone racing along the boardwalk.

I watched, stunned, as he climbed the railing and jumped.

I heard him hit the water and then there was silence for a moment. My body was starting to weaken in the biting cold, but I continued to fight, my desperate pleas becoming softer. Then I heard him in the night, calling my name. Raef.

"Eila!" he yelled from somewhere in the river.

I opened my mouth to call back to him, but just as I did, something grasped hold of my leg and hauled me down into the blackness.

It dragged me under, toward the river bottom, and I willed myself not to bend to my screaming lungs and pure fear. I kicked with my free leg furiously, but did not seem to connect with anything. My chest started to burn, the instinct to breathe soon to overthrow my will. I was going to drown, and my desire to live made me flail at the creature that was dragging me.

But then suddenly whatever had me started to jerk, back and forth, swirling the water around me. As if it was having some sort of spasm.

It released me, but the rip current was now dragging me far from hope. My lungs had hit their limit when something clutched desperately at my arm and hauled me to the surface. As my face broke through the water, I gasped for air.

Raef pulled me to him and held me fast, grasping me tightly to his chest. "Eila! Breathe! Do you hear me? Breathe!" he commanded, a reckless, wild fear ringing clearly in his voice.

I drew a deep, sputtering lungful of the night air as relief ran through me. His powerful arms wrapped defensively around my frozen body, one strong hand wedged between my shoulder blades, holding me upright.

As he heard me draw another, life-giving breath, he pressed his icy cheek against mine. He whispered, quietly in my ear, a word of thanks to a greater power, as his voice cracked slightly.

I forced myself to control my chattering mouth, well aware that something may be in the water with us. I managed to breathe the warning into his soaked hair, my body vibrating from the violent shivering. "Sssomething's in the waterrr."

"Not anymore," he replied darkly, but my frozen mind couldn't process his words. He swam quickly through the current to the edge of the river, towing me effortlessly in his arms. He tried to get me to my feet on the riverbank, but I crumbled under the throb of my ankle.

"Can you stand?" he asked, latching onto my waist to support my weight.

I shook my head. "Hit my ankle," I gasped.

He instantly gathered me into his arms and I clutched him tightly, as he ran along the river's edge back to the parking lot and my Jeep.

It was as if I weighed nothing. I never knew he was so strong.

I felt exhausted, succumbing to a fatigue that I never knew existed and my chest seemed tight. I was shaking so badly that I thought my teeth would break.

Raef ripped off one of the soft-sided windows from my 4x4 and reached through to unlock the door. He set me down on the passenger seat and I wrapped my arms around me, trying to contain the little heat my body was vainly attempting to produce.

Raef climbed in the other side and looked at me shivering uncontrollably. "Strip down to your underwear. Your clothes are going to speed up hypothermia," he instructed, handing me the blanket from the backseat. I started to strip, too freakin' cold to be self-conscious.

"Where are your keys?" Raef demanded urgently, as he searched my soaked jacket. I pointed toward the river, my shaking preventing me from speaking clearly. Without hesitating, he grabbed the drive column just below the steering wheel and ripped the cover off, hot-wiring the

Jeep to life in mere seconds.

He looked at me and reached over, stroking the back of my neck, as if to let me know he was going to make it all right. He then grabbed my cell phone from the glove box and called Ana, letting her know what happened. She told him to meet her at Dalca's house, as she was there catching up on some reading.

Slowly, my body started to warm, just trembling in spurts. Within a few minutes, Raef had turned onto Main Street and pulled into Dalca's house.

It was only then that I started to feel it - a burn that was starting to claw at my leg.

A pain unlike anything I had ever felt before.

Raef carried me quickly through Dalca's backdoor and into the kitchen, stopping at the table to hook one foot under the chair nearest us and pulling it out away from the table. Gingerly, he sat me down in the chair, keeping my left leg in his arm.

He reached for the empty seat to his side and looked up to Ana, who had rounded the kitchen entrance, a pillow in her hand. Raef took it and in one smooth movement, tucked the pillow under my leg and rested both on the chair.

As gentle as he was, my face betrayed my outward stoicism and I winced at the burn, still twisting itself around the wounded ankle. It was as if someone had branded my leg, then continued to drag a burlap rope around it.

The sensation was brutal.

Raef, kneeling next to me, didn't miss the flash of pain cross my face. "I should never have left you alone," he said, furious at himself.

"It's not your fault. I decided to go back to the car. How would either of us have known that some lowlife was going to be such a jerk and send me for a swim," I said, wrapping the old blanket tighter around me. He was right about getting out of my wet clothes as fast as possible. I had warmed up fairly quickly now that I was down to just my skivvies and a fleece blanket. Raef, however, was still in ice-cold apparel.

"You really should get changed," I said, amazed he wasn't shivering like I had been. "You're going to catch pneumonia. Maybe Dalca has something here." I looked to Ana, hopeful as my leg started to throb harder.

Ana rolled her eyes, "Oh fine. I think Dalca left some stuff here for me to bring to Goodwill. Let me go look."

She disappeared around the kitchen doorway, and I could hear her footsteps heading up the staircase to the second floor. I looked back down at Raef, who was still kneeling next to me. "Thanks, by the way, for jumping in after me."

Raef reached out and caressed my cheek with his wide hand, "Always, Eila. Always."

Just then Ana came in with a t-shirt and jeans. "Alright, Michael Phelps, here are some clothes. Now strip." Raef turned to Ana who was holding out the clothes.

"We need to take a look at Eila's ankle. She said she hit it falling into the water. And . . . there was also *something* in the water with her," he said, looking almost . . . dangerous.

Ana's normally flippant demeanor was crossed with a fleeting shadow of fear. "Good thing you were there," she replied slowly.

It was strange, but I had a sneaky suspicion that they had a shared idea of what hauled me down into the frigid channel.

Raef pulled the soaking t-shirt over his head and I gasped. He spun around, "What? Are you alright?" he asked, worried.

"Uh, yeah. But YOU aren't!" I reached out to touch his flawless physique that was now marred by a deep gash on his back, but he turned deftly out of my reach. His move to avoid my touch surprised me a little.

Ana leaned over and inspected Raef's back and then glanced at him, her jaw tight. "What? I didn't feel it!" Raef said defensively.

She looked over to where I sat. "If you don't mind I need to take your personal lifeguard upstairs where I have a first aid kit. Can I borrow him?" There was a sparkle in her knowing eye and I returned her gaze with a half-hearted look of death. She knew I liked him, but it was mortifying to have her flaunt it in front of him. Of course, I thought he liked me too, since he did jump into 55-degree water to save me, sea creature and all.

"We need to call her," said Raef, apparently not listening to Ana about the Band-Aids.

"I will, but you need to be fixed first," said Ana, her eyes darting to me for a moment.

Finally Raef followed Ana out of the kitchen, "I'll be fine Eila." Oddly enough, I heard Ana mumble something under her breath. It made no sense, but I could've sworn she said, "*Speak for yourself.*"

In the silence of the kitchen I suddenly felt very alone. My ankle was starting to really burn, and I knew I must have seriously raked it on the side of the boardwalk. I had no desire to look at the damage yet however, as I tended towards squeamish when it came to my own blood. I took a deep breath, attempting to shake off the pain.

What I could not shake off, however, was the feeling that something far more dangerous than a seal or squid was in the water with me tonight.

I started to replay the events of the evening in my head. Of walking back to my car via the narrow, elevated boardwalk. Of approaching the bridge that spanned the channel and realizing I had to pass that kid. I remembered my danger instinct switched to red alert, but I thought I was just insane. I should've listened to my screaming, internal alarm.

I remembered the water was like breaking through ice, the cold physically burning and sucking the air from my lungs. I remembered looking up to the bridge to see Raef running to the highest point to jump to me.

And then something bit me.

No, that's not right.

I searched for a reference point to the sensation. It wasn't a bite. *A bite would involve sharpness, right? Teeth?* It was something else. Something completely different. My leg started to flare even hotter. The pain was starting to become unbearable.

Just then, Ana appeared followed by a dry-clothed Raef. Ana had a few Band-Aids on her lower arm. "What happened to you?" I asked her.

"I slipped while cutting the gauze for Raef. It's nothing," said Ana. "You, however, don't look so grand. I'm calling Dalca." Ana moved a tad quicker than I would've liked. Her urgency made me nervous. She hurried out of the kitchen and I heard her cell phone dialing.

Raef pulled a chair over to me and sat down. He looked very concerned. Too concerned. I was certain they knew something that they weren't sharing.

I was about to pry the information I sought from them, but was waylaid by a razor-like shot of pain. Instinctively I drew a sharp breath through my clenched teeth. "Jeez, my ankle is just about on fire," I said with a shiver that was more from the memory of being dragged under the water than my body temperature.

"It burns?" asked Raef, now alarmed. "I thought you said you hit the wooden boardwalk when you fell." He leaned forward to start quickly unwrapping my leg from the red, tattered blanket.

He looked toward my face for a moment as he worked, his expression a mix of concern and . . . pain? No, not pain. Self-torture. His eyes, such an incredible shade of cobalt, seemed to try and free me from the pain. Even in my agony, my heart tripped over itself at the sight of him and his gentle touch on my cold skin. I tried to control my face, but the burn was simply too much, and my eyes started to pool with tears.

As his fingers brushed near the top of my thigh his voice became fast and serious. "Ana! She has been exposed. She's been . . . poisoned," said Raef, his eyes on my leg.

Poisoned? I looked down and was horrified to see red cracks slowly extending up from the wound. They were actually lengthening *while* I looked on.

I'm not sure if it was pure panic or the sea creature's intense venom, but my heart started to race and the room began to spin. I closed my eyes to try to offset the dizziness, but with each passing second it became more difficult to breathe. Some invisible force was crushing my chest.

"Eila?" I heard Raef ask, then swear sharply. "Eila! Can you hear me?"

I felt his hands on my face and I finally forced my eyes to open, but I gasped, terrified at what I saw.

The blue of Raef's eyes had turned to a merciless black once again.

Adrenaline flooded my body and I tried to push away from him and his otherworldly glare but I was so damn weak. He looked away from me for a moment, and when he turned back, his eyes were blue.

Holy crap, I was really losing it.

My head was spinning and now apparently hallucinating once again. I couldn't breathe and the room was fading away from me. I could hear Raef pleading with me to respond, but I couldn't.

"Ana, hurry! It's spreading into her blood stream!" I could hear the alarm in Raef's voice, followed by Ana demanding how it was possible that I wasn't already dead.

WASN'T ALREADY DEAD? What the heck!

I was hearing things. Seeing things. My mind was a lying fog of confusion.

I was exhausted from the cold water, from the burning pain, and from my body battling back some strange poison. I fought against unconsciousness, but I could feel my body start to slide sideways from the chair. Raef called my name again as his powerful arms snatched me into a tight embrace, holding me desperately against his warm chest as the darkness overtook me.

* * * *

Someone was speaking in whispered tones. At least, I think that's what I was hearing. It was hard to concentrate through my slamming headache and as I slowly woke, I realized I was tucked into a bed.

Cautiously I opened my eyes to a ceiling that was strewn with branches and crystals. The sun brought a soft light into the bedroom, which was decidedly not mine. How long had I been asleep? Where was I?

As I searched my memory for the pieces of what had happened

to land me in a strange bed, the horror of the night before came racing back. I heard the voices again and slowly turned toward the sound, my eyes slits against the sun, which seemed to scream through my head. I could feel something moist wrapped around my leg and as I moved something cool slumped forward over my eyes. I grabbed at the damp cloth that had slipped off my forehead and the voices came to an abrupt halt.

Blinking once again, I saw Raef and Kian by the door. They had been talking to one another, but now they were both looking at me. Realizing I was awake, Raef's expression radiated sheer relief.

He turned back to Kian briefly. "I'll be down in a bit," he said and Kian left, shutting the door behind him.

Crossing the room, Raef reached out and touched my cheek and forehead, as if checking my temperature. He sat slowly on the edge of the bed and softly took my hand, turning it over to feel my pulse. I watched him carefully. Cautiously.

He glanced to my face then back to my fingers, "Your fever finally broke. How do you feel?"

I didn't answer and pulled my tingling hand gently from his warm palm. Something dangerous happened to me last night and I had strong concerns that Raef was involved, and not just in a lifeguard capacity. Suddenly I wasn't so sure I knew Raef O'Reilly at all. In fact, I wasn't so sure I knew anything anymore.

Raef watched me as I moved away from him slightly, but I was quickly reminded of the damage I sustained in the dark water under the boardwalk. My entire leg felt like it had endured a supernova sunburn, but compared to last night, it was a vast improvement.

As I edged away from Raef, he shook his head, as if ashamed. "Eila . . . I'm sorry. I should've been with you. I forgot for a moment.

Who I am – who we are – and I was careless. It won't happen again, I swear to you. I just . . ."

I interrupted his plea for forgiveness, "Something was in the water last night. You know what it was . . . don't you?" Time seemed to freeze and Raef nodded. "What was it?" I never asked such a loaded question in all my life.

Raef cleared his throat, "What do you remember of last night?"

I watched him carefully as I answered. "Most of it." Unfortunately. "I remember being pushed. Being dragged under the water by something damn stronger than a jellyfish. You . . . saving me."

I shifted slightly, my mind playing vivid flashes of the night. "Was I hallucinating or did I see what I think I saw? In the kitchen and the locker room?" I needed answers but was uneasy with the truth that may be lurking.

Raef answered quietly, "You weren't hallucinating."

"Your eyes changed color," I whispered, the memory of his dark pupils expanding outward and swallowing the blue replaying in my mind.

"As did yours," he replied calmly.

WHAT? No way. Not possible.

I was definitely stuck in some way-too-realistic nightmare. I rubbed my face furiously, as if I could dig my way out of the obvious insanity.

Raef gently pulled my hands from my face and leaned in slightly, "Would you like to see what *you* can do?"

I froze. Panic, fear, and excitement were twisting through my chest. I wasn't so sure I wanted to know.

Raef got up, retrieving a hand-held mirror from the nearby bureau. Thanks to the interesting décor, this had to be the living quarters of the Crimson Moon.

He sat down next to me and flicked his head signaling me to come closer and I slid carefully next to him. While his eyes may have changed, I believed his heart to be true. I trusted him. It was that simple.

Our faces, close together, looked back at us in the glass. "Don't be afraid," breathed Raef, the words caressing the side of my cheek with prickling electricity.

I turned to reply, but the words halted in my mouth. The blue of Raef's eyes were slipping away into the black centers, like quicksand into the abyss. It was absolutely mesmerizing and darkly elegant.

He gently touched my chin and I turned toward the mirror. My own reflection, so familiar, had altered. The chocolate of my own eyes was now rimmed in a shimmering, liquid copper.

My heart rate took off like a rocket, startled by my own face now so foreign.

I felt Raef's hand touch softly between my shoulders, attempting to calm my heart. In the mirror, the blue of his eyes gracefully returned and my golden ring faded out like a dying flame.

I stared at our reflection, trying to process what I had just witnessed. Finally I turned to Raef, who sat with an eerie stillness, no doubt wondering if I was going to freak out on a nuclear level.

"What . . . was that?" I asked, the fear giving way to awe.

Raef lowered the mirror, content that I apparently wasn't going to flip out. "The truth of what we are," he replied.

"Which is?" I whispered, leaning closer as if the walls would spill our secrets.

"Dangerous," he replied.

It wasn't exactly the explanation I was looking for, that's for damn sure. But my need-to-know-what-sort-of-weirdo-mutants-we-were instantly fell to a distant second.

Dangerous? Me? That was just laughable. I must have been holding my breath, because Raef slowly reached up toward my face and tucked one stray curl behind my ear. "Are you okay?"

"I uh . . . have a lot of . . ." I shook my head. "Dangerous? Are you sure? There is just no way."

I was arguing, but my train of thought skittered off the tracks as he took my hand in his. He slowly traced the lines that crisscrossed my palm, his pensive silence worrying me. His touch was electric; the voltage a lot higher than it had been previously.

"See this," he asked me, his finger following a deep line that crossed my palm.

"Yes," I croaked, as my skin seemed to spark under his touch.

"This is supposed to represent your life line. Yours is very deep," he continued, but he seemed to be speaking more to himself than to me.

He traced it softly again, and the sensation sent my nerves ablaze. He reached out with his other hand and sandwiched my lifeline between his own, holding it there for several seconds. "Eila. I *am* trying desperately to protect this lifeline. Never doubt that, alright?"

I nodded as the gravity of his words hit me. From the look on his face, I began to believe that I might actually need to have a shield in the form of this handsome boy. A shield against what, however, I wasn't quite so sure.

He took a deep breath, as if to clear his thoughts, and then smiled at me softly. "You have to be hungry. Let's go have some breakfast."

"What about the thing in the water? You never answered me."

"I will answer all your questions, but you really could use some food first. Brain processing power, you know?"

I sighed. "Fine."

Raef gently pulled me to my feet, but my leg throbbed and I winced, sucking in a quick breath. "Allow me," he said and in one gentle motion, he picked me up and carried me out the bedroom door. I could feel the warmth of his strong arm around my back, cradling me softly to his heart.

Once again, he carried me effortlessly. Apparently exceptional strength went along with black eyeballs. I noted that he had never sparkled nor fried in the sun, so I scratched "vampire" off the insane list of possibilities for Raef . . . and me.

"Do the others know? About you?" I asked.

Raef nodded, "They know about both of us."

I was a bit ticked off, "Seriously? And no one wanted to clue me in? Well, thanks for nada."

"We weren't sure about you, at first. Last night confirmed some . . . stuff," said Raef, finally reaching the first floor. I opened my mouth to demand further clarification, but Raef cut me off, "Food first. And we need to check your leg. That was the deal."

I gave a small growl and Raef smiled. As we approached the kitchen, I could hear a whispered, but heated, debate raging between Ana and what sounded like Kian. Raef had slowed his walking, as if he too was eavesdropping. I could hear Dalca's voice, followed by Kian's, which was seriously short-fused.

"Like hell! You had no right to push her into this! Ana, you can't be here! It's obviously not safe." Kian was really pissed.

Ana's angry voice rolled over Dalca's attempted reply, "Don't you dare think, for one second, you get to tell me what to do. I told you to stay the hell away from me, and yet . . ." Ana's voice dropped so low I could no longer hear what she was saying.

When Kian replied, his voice had lost its biting edge, "I just wanted to make sure you were alright. I never intended all of this . . . of us, being . . . Look, I'm sorry, but I'm not leaving now."

Raef shifted his weight and stepped forward. His movement caused a pine board under his foot to protest and the kitchen became silent. I looked at Raef, who was watching the kitchen entrance as we heard a chair slide along the floor and footsteps coming toward us.

Dalca appeared in the doorway. She looked at my escort coolly. "Raef," she nodded to him stiffly.

"M'am," he replied, equally formal. Okay. Obviously not super chummy.

Dalca turned her attention to me. "Hi Eila," she said, her voice now comforting and kind. "How are you feeling? How's the leg?"

"Loads better. I mean, it's still sore, but nothing like last night." I could feel Raef hold me tighter.

"You gave us quite a scare. Try not to do that too often, alright?" she said with a smile. "You need to eat and I need to redress your wound. Breakfast is already out. I will be there in a minute." She headed past us into the front room and Raef looked down at me, still snug in his strong arms.

"So you guys are real pals, huh?" I asked, a twist of a smile on my face.

Raef rolled his eyes, "Oh yeah. Two peas in a pod."

I snickered as he carried me through the kitchen door and sat me on a familiar chair. He once again lifted my leg up onto another chair, stuffing the same pillow from last night underneath my foot, then pulled a glass of orange juice and a selection of pastries towards me.

Across from us, Ana was still simmering. Kian, however, stood casually near the side door. I selected a cinnamon concoction and took a bite.

"Eila, you know my brother," said Raef, nodding toward the tall blonde. I wondered if Kian and Raef shared . . . talents.

I swallowed, my stomach clenching. "Uh, yeah. It's good to see you again Kian."

"You too. Word is you flirted with the darkside last night . . . and I don't mean Raef. Though . . . ," Kian, pulled out a chair to sit down, " . . . perhaps the next time he talks about you - and he does so a lot, to the point of irritation - he will tell me what you two were really doing so far from the crowd." He gave me a bold wink.

My cheeks flushed hot and breakfast flipped in my tummy. I glanced at Raef who was staring at his brother, his jaw set. Kian flashed him a triumphant smile.

Dalca returned carrying a bowl of suspicious green stuff. I took a sip of O.J., eyeing her concoction warily. She looked at Raef and flicked her head to the side, signaling him to get out of the way. He looked at me, as if to get my approval, and then walked over to the counter to wait.

"Alright missy. Let's put some more of this on you," said Dalca, starting to unwrap my leg.

I realized then that I was wearing an over-sized t-shirt and an old pair of sweat pants, with one leg cut off. I pulled the t-shirt away from me in an attempt to read what was on it. I was mortified.

"Vanilla Ice? Seriously?" I asked, my eyebrows raised, "Ana? Is this *yours*? And why am I wearing it?"

"Okay. First of all, have a bit more respect for my taste in music," said Ana, crossing her arms. "That thing I found in with the Goodwill bag, though I will admit that I did like a couple of his songs when I was *five*. And second of all, I needed to get you into some dry clothes. Your skivvies were soaked. I washed your stuff. It's in the dryer now."

I mouthed the words *"You stripped me?"* to her without Raef seeing my face. She nodded and I sighed, relieved that a certain, heroic boy didn't help in THAT department. Thankfully he was too focused on what Dalca was doing to notice Ana and I.

A sudden shot of pain radiated from my ankle and I jumped. Raef immediately stood up straight, no longer leaning against the counter. My fingers dug into the seat as I looked over to Raef. He looked concerned and I gave a weak smile.

"Sorry Eila. I'll try to be more careful," Dalca apologized. I nodded, nervous that her version of careful may not be up to my pain-free standards.

"Okay then, so this right here is where your ankle struck the decking of the bridge," she pointed to a dark gash in the center of an odd-shaped burn. "It must have sliced open your skin, causing it to bleed. It is also exactly where you were grabbed, resulting in this burn."

She traced above a four-pronged wound that seemed to wrap around the front of my upper ankle. Another line extended around the back of my ankle. All five, thick lines were connected by a solid, circular burn on the outside of my leg.

"When I looked at it last night, it was hard to discern the outline, because the poison had spread so aggressively," said Dalca, shaking her head.

I looked at the Gypsy, confused. "I don't remember you looking at it last night at all."

"You don't remember Ana dressing you up like a dime-store mannequin either, dear. You were unconscious."

Yeah. Thanks for that reminder. I blushed at the thought of myself, floppy and unaware, being examined by this elderly lady. Maybe I even drooled in my unconscious state. My stomach twitched at my fertile imagination.

Raef walked over to look at my wound. Kian and Ana came around the table as well to inspect the damage. They were all quiet for a few minutes as they looked at the burn.

"I was under the impression that touch can't cause such a severe reaction," said Raef finally, glancing to Dalca.

"It can't," said Dalca. "And I don't think it did. I believe her attacker came in contact with her blood due to the cut on her ankle. Once that happened, his skin began to decay and bleed as well. She reacted when his blood made contact with her own. It's a miracle she wasn't dead inside of a minute. She must have some sort of blood tolerance that bought her some time."

I have a blood tolerance? To what? And it sounded like they were referring to a person, not a thing. Any inclination I had toward my breakfast was long gone.

Raef looked almost ill at the mention of my near demise. He turned to his brother, "Did you find a body?"

A . . . BODY? WHAT THE . . . ?

Kian nodded, "It got dragged out toward the west beach. MJ and I took care of it. Good work by the way."

"Did you say MJ?" I asked, floored. Did my ice cream hurling pal help move a . . . BODY? I swallowed, a sickening feeling sliding through me.

Raef didn't seem to hear me. He looked tense, "It wasn't me. By the time I got to Eila, I could see he was already dead. His body was being dragged away by the current. It was stupid of me to have left her on the beach alone. He could've killed her."

"Stop for a minute," I interrupted. Food be damned, I wanted answers. "Who's dead? Are you talking about the guy from the bridge?"

Kian looked at Raef, eyes narrowed, "I thought you brought her up to speed."

"And what? Give her the low-down on centuries of history the instant she finally woke up? Of course not. I didn't want to drop all this on her when she was . . ." he glanced to me, " . . . in pain."

"Well give her the abridged version now, damn it!" demanded Ana. "There is obviously more than one, since SOMEBODY shoved her. I warned you both! But does anyone listen to me? Of course not!"

She grabbed the newspaper off the table and pointed to one of the stories on the front page, nearly jamming her finger clean through the headline. "Look! I knew this was way too many. What does that make? Eight? Yeah. I think it's eight now. And no way there's just one, picking off this many. There have to be at *least* two, if not more. We're screwed," she moaned.

Raef motioned for the paper and Ana shoved it into his hand. The headline read, **Beach-Goers urged to use caution: Two more swimmers assumed dead.**

"Oh, come on now, think positive," said Kian.

Ana glared at him, then burst into a huge, excessive smile. "We're screwed!" she declared in an upbeat tone, completely the opposite of her current state of stress.

"Ah, see? Much better!" encouraged Kian.

I was sure Ana was going to flip out and slap him.

Dalca shook her head. "They may not have known. It could've been just horrible luck. There were a lot of beach-goers out there last night and it could've attracted them. And it had to be a young one who didn't understand the rules and grabbed her over her open wound. There's one less in the area now though," said Dalca, still looking at the oddly shaped burn.

She turned my ankle slightly and I gripped the seat harder. I couldn't figure out what in the world they were talking about. What rules? Who's young?

Dalca sighed and shook her head, "I will tell you one thing though. If they were in the dark before, they definitely know now."

My patience was gone. "What are you all talking about? Who is 'they?' What do they know? What the hell is going on and, for crying out loud, WHO IS DEAD?" I demanded, angry I was left out and because my ankle was being fooled with.

They all looked at one another. I searched their faces, but they seemed torn. I finally looked at Raef. He was holding the paper with one hand.

"Raef, what is going on?" I pleaded.

He came over slowly and knelt beside me, looking up to Ana and Kian. His brother nodded, but Ana didn't move, her face hard.

He took his right hand and held it just millimeters from the angry burn on my ankle, spreading his fingers to line up with the marks. To my absolute horror, his hand was a near perfect match to the burn.

It wasn't some*thing* that had tried to drag me to a watery grave.

It was some*one*.

"GOOD GRIEF! What is going on?" I yelled. My heart was racing as Raef withdrew his hand and backed up to the counter. I was looking at all of them, rapidly searching their faces. "Oh my God! Why is there a handprint - a BURNED handprint - on my leg?" I was breathing rapidly and the room was tilting slightly.

Dalca sighed, "Eila. Listen to me. Calm down or you are going to hyperventilate."

"Calm down? Are you insane? Someone tried to kill me!

140

HELLO? KILL ME!" The room was definitely starting to spin.

"Ana, grab me a brown bag from the cabinet. And some lavender," instructed Dalca calmly. "Eila, listen to me. We will explain everything, but you need to calm down. You are safe now."

I heard Kian snort, apparently not of the same mind as Dalca. Raef shot him a lethal look.

Ana came back with the brown bag and handed it to me. "Here Eila, breathe into this," she instructed, handing me the bag. "Slow breaths Eila, slow breaths."

As I breathed into the bag, I could feel my body calm. My heartbeat slowed and the room stopped spinning. I started to study the faces of those I had come to know and one I had come to love. They held knowledge of something terrifying and I seemed to be part of it, dragged into their dark secrets.

I looked at Raef who was standing by the counter, in some ways, defeated. He studied me sadly, as if I was already lost. As if he had not saved me from the water and whoever had dragged me down.

I found his despondency the most frightening of all

I have learned many things since coming to Cape Cod.

The cheerleaders are pukes, the ice cream is to die for, and that owning a Wrangler makes you part of some strange secret society where the other drivers wave to you whenever you pass.

There is also the fact that, nagging or otherwise, hurrying a Gypsy will get you nowhere fast. I wanted answers instantly. Come to think of it, answers would've been helpful *before* I moved to this cursed strip of sand.

Why couldn't Mr. Talbot have said, "Oh yes, the home is lovely. There are some sea monsters with hands like Schwarzenegger and your eyeballs may start to glow in the dark, but other than that, the place is great."

Information like *that* I would've considered critical in deciding whether to leave peaceful Kansas and, I don't know, maybe SOLD a multimillion-dollar piece of property and avoided being a target.

Yes, answers. Right now!

But Dalca insisted on rewrapping my wound and making me finish breakfast. She also made sure no one answered my repetitive questions until she had time to gather a few "things." It felt like hours, but when I glanced at the clock, she was ready to talk 20 minutes later.

She set a heavy, leather-bound book on the kitchen table and turned to me. "Eila, what do you know of Elizabeth Walker?"

She wanted to talk family? I was surprised at the question. I wanted to demand what my grandmother had to do with my throbbing leg, but instead decided to answer the stubborn Gypsy.

"Um, I know that she and my Grandfather Josiah built my house. MJ also told me about her disappearance, but no one knows what happened to her. He said there was an urban legend she was hit by lightning," I looked around the room at my audience. "That's about all I know."

Dalca cleared her throat and opened the book. It seemed to be a journal, but she was flipping past the handwritten pages too fast for me to read anything.

She stopped at a page with a yellowed photograph of a woman. Her corset top and heavy skirt told me it was taken a long time ago. She was beautiful, her tangled black hair not unlike my own curling down towards her chest. A round necklace, containing an oval stone, lay just above her breasts. She looked . . . like the woman from my nightmares.

Dalca touched her hand to the photo on the page, "This is Elizabeth, your 4th Great Grandmother. This photo was taken a few months before she disappeared. Before she was murdered."

"Murdered?" I asked slowly, as bits and pieces of the woman by the fountain flicked across my memory. I had a sinking feeling that my dreams were rooted in historical fact, but that wasn't even possible . . .

was it?

I glanced at Raef and he didn't seem shocked. "You knew this?" I asked him. He nodded and shifted his weight to lean back against the counter.

"History says that Elizabeth Walker vanished on December 14, 1851," started Dalca. "History also says her disappearance was never solved. We, however, believe that she was killed in the harbor square, not far from here, by a man named Jacob Rysse."

Crap. It was my dream. Even though it never remained clear and I only had pieces of it, I knew Elizabeth was the woman by the fountain. I also had an instinctive feeling that the man didn't just disappear.

"What happened to the man?" I nearly whispered.

Dalca looked at me and some strange emotion flickered across her face. "We are not sure. We think he died that night as well. Neither body was ever found. The surprising part of the equation is you," she said, watching my expression.

"Me?"

"Elizabeth Walker never had any children that we know of, and yet you are obviously a blood relative. That part is without dispute."

The room was quiet and Dalca sat back in her chair, lost in thought. I wondered how they knew for certain I was actually related to Elizabeth. It wasn't like I took a blood test to confirm our mutual history.

I was about to ask when the screen door creaked open. MJ's voice broke the silence and my train of thought. "Eila is up. Alright!" he declared as he entered, quickly appraising the room.

I snapped my attention to him, and all other thoughts in my head vanished but one. "Did you move some person's body? That's completely illegal!" I accused, jamming my paintless fingernail in his direction.

"Well, yeah, but I wouldn't call him a person. Soul-sucking demons deserve to be off-ed anyway. And if you don't want me shuttling bodies around with Kian, don't swan dive off the boardwalk at night anymore. For crying out loud, the water isn't always safe, ya know? Forget the sharks. It's the half-human undertow that will get ya."

I looked at him, irritated, "Please, MJ. I'm not in the mood for poor jokes."

MJ looked around the room. He seemed confused as all eyes were glaring at him.

"Oh, uh . . ." he laughed uneasily, "I, um, guess we didn't get to that part, huh?"

Ana whacked him in the back of his head with her hand. "Ow!" protested MJ, "What the heck? How was I supposed to know?"

I leaned slowly back in my chair. The issue of what had hauled me under the water had not been settled, my attention diverted by a dead grandmother's murder and the thought of MJ dragging a body around.

And while MJ was prone to a few poorly delivered jokes now and again, no one was laughing. Their faces showed no emotion. They were, however, all looking at me. I felt like they were waiting for me to do something. Or react. Maybe waiting for my head to pop off.

My eyes grew wide, "Are you kidding me? Is that what grabbed me? Some sort of, what? Zombie?" I sat there, unable to move, cemented by a newfound fear of the world around me.

"Thanks a lot MJ," hissed Ana coldly. "Way to give the girl a heart attack."

"I'm sorry alright, but I mean, what did she think grabbed her?" pleaded MJ, desperate for a bit of forgiveness. "The Little Mermaid?"

"Well in my world Ariel is just as likely as a person who has risen from the grave!" I yelled at him. As much as I wanted to deny what I had just learned, I couldn't. The throbbing evidence was a bright red mark on my leg. I remembered the excruciating pain of the night before and the near certainty of drowning.

Dalca put her hand on mine gently, "First of all, they are not zombies."

THEY are not Zombies? Terrific. That leaves what exactly? Aliens? Vampires? Swamp monsters from the deep?

"They are known as *Mortis* and they are an extremely dangerous, extremely old race of immortal humans," said Dalca. "Occasionally they hunt swimmers, since their death is easily covered up as a drowning."

My internal voice snapped shut. She had my undivided attention now. I silently pledged my undying love of the land, never to set foot in the ocean again.

"Raef. Why don't you try and fill Eila in on some history. I'm going to make a phone call and see if I can find us some further information on . . . a few things."

As Dalca left, I looked back at Raef. "Okay, now spill," I said. Oddly the fear had melted away. I was, however, pissed at my ignorance.

"I'm just going to say, for the record, that I'm not convinced she's gifted," said Ana, always the optimist.

"Please," snorted Kian, "I'd say the fact that her kick-ass grandmother was most likely killed by a soul-thief and now Eila almost bought the farm as well, ensures she has some glow-stick properties."

My mind was spinning.

My grandmother was murdered by the same super-human race that made an attempt on my life last night? And . . . glow-stick? What the hell does that mean?

Kian and Ana were starting to argue some more when Raef interrupted them. "First of all, she carries the mark. I saw it when she stripped in the Jeep."

"Mark? What mark?" I asked, trying to picture myself naked in a mirror, scanning my body. "You mean my stupid radiator-burn?" I demanded.

"*You stripped in the Jeep?*" whispered MJ to me, shocked. Or impressed.

Raef didn't seem to hear my question and he just continued on, "Second, her skin burned once in contact with her attacker's blood. The average human doesn't have that reaction to Mortis blood, but she would." He pushed off the counter and walked over to the table.

All eyes, including mine, were on him. He continued, confident in his train of thought, wherever it was headed. "Eila killed her attacker simply with her blood. Not even knowing about it. Not even trying. So do I think she is gifted? Absolutely." He sighed, sitting down next to me, "Which also makes you, Eila . . ."

"Their number one target," finished Kian, looking at his brother. He then furrowed his brow, "She really has the mark? It isn't some old wives' tale?"

Raef nodded.

I was irritated now, "It's a FRIGGIN' BURN from babyhood! And there is no way I killed anyone!" I felt nausea climbing in my throat. I didn't want to be a murderous, Halloween light-up accessory. My head was pounding.

"Do you remember getting burned as a baby?" asked Raef.

Well . . . no. Mae just said that was the doctor's explanation for the mark when she took custody of me. My silence seemed to boost his confidence.

"Trust me, it's not a radiator burn and you did kill him," said Raef. "But if it makes you feel any better, you executed him by accident. Plus, if you didn't kill him, I would have."

"ALRIGHT THAT'S IT!" I yelled. "I want answers. Right now. Got it? Right now!"

Kian leaned back in his seat, a smile twisting on his lips. "Have fun man."

Raef glared at his brother, "Thanks a lot. How am I going to explain this?"

"Oh, I know!" said MJ, enthusiastic as always. "Show her the chart thing. Like you did for me."

"Oh my god," said Ana, exasperated and rubbing her face. "If this takes as long as it did to explain to you, MJ, then we will all start to age."

"Actually, that's not a bad way to start," said Raef, searching the counter for something. He found a piece of paper and a pen and sat down next to me. He drew a triangle, with horizontal lines going through it. He then turned to me and started to explain.

"Okay, so this," he pointed to the drawing, "is kind of like a food chain."

"Food Chain? What happened to the marky thing?" I said, rubbing my back, as if I could feel it.

"First things first. Trust me," he said, a slight smile to his face.

I huffed, "Fine. Radiator burn later. Keep going."

"It's not a . . . nevermind. So, anyway," continued Raef, "you know what a food chain is, right?"

I nodded, "Yeah, like, the stronger animals eat the weaker. Humans are at the top and then, like, sharks and lions and stuff."

MJ looked on expectantly, listening to Raef.

"That's right, except what you just told me is the humans' version and it isn't a very accurate depiction of the truth. Dalca's family and, well, Kian and I, know a different pyramid. Your Grandmother did as well."

Ana smiled, "Yeah, I know a different one too. If we are going for accuracy, the new food pyramid has vertical lines."

"Oh yeah. You're right," agreed MJ, leaning across the table to point at Raef's drawing. "Yeah, see, like from the peak down. You just take a line and . . ."

Raef glared at him and MJ sat back in his chair. "Right. Pointless information. Got it." He gestured for Raef to continue.

"Anyway, as I was saying with my POORLY DEPICTED hierarchy, which is a *food chain*, you moron, not a USDA food pyramid," snapped Raef, his patience fading. "In the human version of the food chain, they are on top. In our version, the real version, soul-thieves are on top." He scribbled a word at the top of the pyramid.

I looked down to see *Mortis* scrawled on the paper.

"Humans are under them, food for them, of sorts. The Mortis survive off the life-force of others, having no souls themselves. Many of their victims simply appear to have died from natural causes or, in seaside communities like the Cape, apparently drowned."

I shivered as Raef wrote *humans* under the word *Mortis*.

He turned and looked at me, his face stunning. "But Eila, this picture is missing something. It is missing an ancient family of humans called the Lunaterra." He wrote *Lunaterra* in larger letters alongside *Mortis*.

"The Lunaterra are the only people, only thing, a Mortis fears. The Lunattera do have weaknesses, as their body is as fragile as any human, but they command an intense power, which is absolutely lethal

149

to those who are soulless."

"Such as a soul-thief," I mumbled, not thrilled with the new food chain.

"Yes, exactly," said Raef. "A human's soul, or conscience as some people think of it, is destroyed when they evolve, or turn, into one of the Mortis."

"Evolve? From what?"

"Humans. Everyday, normal, mortal humans," said Raef. "Humans that become Mortis do so when they are infected with the disease that destroys the soul. The disease was the result of a fallen angel who tried to 'recruit,' shall we say, a human army. The resulting genetic reaction caused the disease."

"So they are . . . fallen angels?"

"No. They are the genetic remnants of one fallen angel," said Raef. "And the Lunaterra are descended from the Archangel who attempted to stop the Fallen one. The two races are perfectly matched, genetic enemies. They are humans with unique DNA."

My mouth had nearly hit the floor. Two races, descended from warring angels, locked in a genetic loathing for centuries. I had a hard time wrapping my head around it. I was so floored I couldn't even respond.

Raef touched my hand to get my attention. "Eila. Listen to me. You need to understand what we are up against. The Mortis are fast and strong. They are also immortal, living forever off the life-force, the essence, of others unless they are *killed*. And they can only be killed by a broken neck, fire, or at the hands of a Lunaterra," said Raef.

"That's it?" I asked, alarmed. "No sunshine? No garlic? No crosses? Three things and that's it?"

MJ laughed, "Girl, they are not vampires. Sheesh."

Raef let me sit, looking around the room, my thoughts racing. He let me mull this information over for a minute. I looked back down at the paper and tapped my finger above the pyramid, "Okay, so who are these people? These Lunaterra?"

"Like the Mortis, their line also goes back thousands of years. We also know that their ability to channel power can be handed down through generations. Unlike the Mortis, the Lunaterra are born, not infected. Their ability is a birthright," said Raef, watching my face.

"Why do these Mortis fear them?" I asked, absorbed with the story.

"A Lunaterra can channel the Web of Souls. It is the energy that humans give off to one another and links each human soul together. A highly skilled Lunaterra can invoke their will on the Web, wherever they are, and use its force to incinerate any soulless creature. Like Kian said: glow-stick, but on steroids."

I sat there, absorbing all this information. The death of my grandmother, the burn on my leg, the vague dreams, the mark on my back. Connections were starting to form in my mind. All eyes were on me, especially Raef's.

I turned to him. "You said 'gifted.' That you thought I was gifted," I said to him slowly. He nodded.

I added the idea that I had some sort of ability into what I had learned that morning. Then I thought about being knocked down in the hall and shoved off a bridge. I thought about the fact that I didn't have the strength to carry some of the moving boxes up the stairs before school started, or lift the door off my Jeep.

I realized what they were thinking and I was sure they were wrong.

Very, very wrong.

"Wait just one minute," I said, my face incredulous. "You believe I'm one of these Lunaterra people, don't you? You think my radiator burn is some sort of sign?"

"It's a mark of your kind. A rare mark, even within your race, but it only belongs to the Lunaterra," said Raef.

"Oh yeah? Well, tell that to the Birmingham company that built the darn radiator. It's their emblem."

Raef still shook his head, "No it's not. It's the mark of talent."

"Talent within an already powerful race? Go ahead then, Mr. Know-it-all. What's it mean?"

Raef didn't speak for a moment, then seemed to actually stiffen. "It is a lethality mark. A sign of the most deadly. A gifted killer's badge."

The room looked serious, no one cracked a smile. They obviously didn't see the ridiculousness of their logic.

"Oh please," I laughed. "That is absurd. I have the worst luck and no talent whatsoever." I was trying to educate them on their faulty ideas, but the burn on my leg and fiery edge hidden within my eyes was nagging me. Still I refused to believe it.

"Seriously, there is no way. I mean, come on, if I'm one of the Lunaterra, what does that make you? Some sort of superhero?" I asked, smiling at Raef.

He looked at me, but he wasn't smiling. His face was like stone.

"Mortis," was all he replied.

Oh, hell.

I looked at Raef, his beautiful face lined with trepidation. His was supposedly the face of a true demon. A hunter of humankind who had irrationally decided to protect me, his brilliant enemy, or so it seemed.

Like any sane human, I would've predicted that I'd run screaming from the room. But then again, we humans are full of surprises, even to ourselves. And I, for one, have always questioned my sanity.

I looked at him, a fury of emotions bouncing off one another inside me. Betrayal, Passion, Hate, Love, Trust. A million emotions, yet fear was not one of them.

I looked forcefully into his eyes. "Prove it. Prove you are what you say you are," I said in a solid but determined voice, the image of his black eyes returning to my mind.

Confusion and surprise briefly raced across Raef's face. He

could've easily hurt me. Snapped my neck in one sickening yank and ended my existence.

My world was so fantastically twisted that, at this point, I could've readily believed any horror story. Most likely it was true. Perhaps I was . . . what? Fearless? Suicidal? Generally nuts?

Or maybe I already knew in my heart that he was different. Maybe my confidence was because they *were* right. Maybe it wasn't that I should fear him, but that *he* should fear me.

Maybe I was the true killer in the room.

He got to his feet and looked down at me, rumpled in a poor-taste top and sweats. He took a deep breath and pulled his shirt over his head, revealing a chiseled, smooth chest and well-toned arms. He looked like any other human. Well, an exceedingly handsome, athletic one, but nothing that denoted soulless immortal.

I raised my eyebrows, impatient. My heart was racing, no doubt due to the view and to what I knew to be true.

He turned his back to me. Running along his rib was a barely noticeable light pink line. Last night it had been a deep, weeping slash mark. This morning, he was nearly healed.

"How?" I asked him plainly, as he looked over his shoulder at me.

He nodded toward Ana. "Show her," he said in the same, smooth voice I had come to wrap myself in. She sighed, and reluctantly held out her left arm, displaying the bandage on her forearm.

As sore as I was, I launched to my feet remarkably fast. Raef spun around, alarmed that I was going to keel over.

"What the? Did you . . . cut her? Bite her?" I yelled at him. Somewhere in the more sane and repressed part of my mind, I was being reminded that I was yelling at a member of a murderous race. I stomped on the voice and shoved Raef in the chest, furious.

"How could you?" I yelled, incensed that he had done something terrible to my friend. That he had lied to me. That he had made me love him and in doing so, had betrayed me.

I kept hitting him and he let me. I was so angry, for so many reasons, none of which, however, was fear.

I must have struck him 20 times before he reached up and softly held my wrists, preventing me from hitting him anymore. I struggled in his iron grasp, but I was becoming exhausted, both mentally and physically.

"Eila! Stop!" demanded Ana. "It isn't his fault. I offered, and for crying out loud, he didn't bite me. I cut myself so he could drink my blood."

She got up and came around the table to face me. "It was the only way to heal the wound quickly and I wasn't about to let him tap my life-force. Blood carries a similar essence of the soul. It was a quick fix and you need his protection!"

"Oh please," I spat back, still angry and unbelieving.

"No, it's true!" said Ana, looking from me to Raef. He was still holding onto my arms and looked heartbroken and guilt-ridden. "His blood, no matter how small the amount, is lethal to a Lunaterra. You found that out last night! He couldn't be bleeding around you. He could've killed you by accident."

The new world I was now part of had simply become too much to understand. I dropped my head, my heart in pieces. Tears soaked my face as Raef released my wrists and cautiously wrapped his strong arms around me. He held me to his smooth, warm chest as my adrenaline high faded and the burden of last night's near death experience made me heavy with exhaustion.

I could feel the room fade to darkness as I slipped into unconsciousness, Raef's arms still holding me securely.

* * * *

An hour later, I woke to find myself on Dalca's bed. This time, however, I had a clear head and a new reality. As I stared at the ceiling, I heard the chair in the corner creak and looked over to it.

Raef was sitting there, the heavy leather book from earlier open in his lap. He looked absorbed in what he was reading. The window next to him was open and his dirty blonde hair was moving slightly in the sun-sparkled breeze.

I studied him, trying to see the darkness of his kind, but he looked human. If anything, he really did look like an angel's descendant.

As he sat there reading, I made the greatest leap of faith I had ever made in my life – to trust my most deadly enemy. To trust that he would not deceive me, and that his intentions were in my best interest.

Some strange instinct told me I was supposed to trust him. It felt like the same instinct that brought me here in the first place.

He had told me he'd be my sentinel and that he would not fail me. I believed him with all my soul. But, I needed to know why an enemy so ingrained in history, even in our bloodlines, would choose to protect me. I was sure there were volumes more I needed to understand.

I slowly sat up in bed and my movement caught Raef's attention. He looked up from his book, his sapphire eyes calm but focused.

I smoothed back my tangled bed head of hair the best I could, and gave him a weak smile, but he didn't mirror my face. Instead he closed the book, laying it on the windowsill, and walked over to the bed. He reached out his hand to mine, gesturing for me to take it.

"I think you could use some fresh air," he offered.

I looked at his hand for a few seconds and I knew I was about to officially cross a line that could never be redrawn. What would my ancestors think? Would they be turning in their graves to know I was falling hard for the deadliest of soul assassins?

But then again, Raef was also betraying his own. Protecting me meant potentially killing his kind. And though I had no understanding or command of my supposed "abilities," guarding me was to defend a potential mass-murderer. I tensed at the thought that I could be such a violent person deep down.

I flexed my ankle and found it completely, miraculously pain free. Deciding that I could stand on my own two feet, I finally reached out for his hand and he pulled me up, steadying me with his strong hands.

I looked at his beautiful face. "Yeah, I think some fresh air is a great idea," I said, and this time he gave me a slight smile.

On our way out of the house, I noticed that everyone had disappeared. Raef led me out to the back stoop, the same granite step that saw me almost throw up after sniffing Dalca's vial.

The vial. Dalca must have used it to see if I was one of Elizabeth's kind, though what exactly it was still remained a mystery. A stomach-churning mystery.

Thankfully, the need to vomit was nowhere near and the fragrant vine climbing the back of the house was intense. The warmth of the day was retreating, shooed away by a cool, late afternoon breeze riding in from the ocean.

Dalca owned several acres of land at the back of her home, most of which was a large field of late season wildflowers, with the grandest weeping beech tree standing alone in the center of the field. It was a magnificent tree laden with abundant, oval leaves. Its lower branches curved toward the ground, creating its own crisp and cool secret garden.

The field drifted down a sloping hill towards a thicket of pines and beyond where the waters of the Atlantic glistened. The fairy-tale tree swayed lazily in unison with the flowers, tickled by the salty air.

It would've been a destination postcard, except for the two of us, who substantially decreased the allure of the area.

I walked out through the meadow, Raef following a few steps behind. He was always there, whether in my head or by my side, he designated himself my keeper.

I, however, saw him as far more than a simple protection detail. He was more to me than a way to survive. Every last molecule of my design pulled me toward him, illogically, like an undertow, towards salvation . . . or potential death.

As my hand grazed lazily over the tops of the flowers, I let my mind wander and, for one moment, I was not on Cape Cod. Not caught up in the frenzy of desperation that had begun to define and consume my life here. For just one moment I was your average teen in love with the boy who was following me.

In love. It was true.

I was IN LOVE with Raef, as absurd as it seemed. I dreamed that he wanted me as much as I desired him, and that this field was where he would kiss me, declare his love for me and pull me down gently into the tall grass . . .

"It's nice to escape, isn't it?" asked Raef, breaking me from my illusion. I turned and realized he had been watching me play with the tops of the flowers. My face blushed hot at being caught in my fantasy, now terrified he had another ability known as mind reading. I laughed, a little too nervously.

"Uh, yeah," I confessed. "Though I'm not sure I'm okay with you reading my thoughts."

"I can't read your mind," said Raef, sincerely. "But I can read your face. You were far from here for a moment. Peaceful."

I targeted a daisy and plucked the blossom from the stem. I neurotically started to remove each petal from the yellow center, still wary he knew my thoughts. Whatever momentary lapse from reality I had, it was long gone now.

"I am so very sorry for bringing all of this on you so suddenly. It must be quite a shock," said Raef, truly apologetic, though his gaze was off toward the distance. He seemed unable to look at me, ashamed of the nuclear stress he had thrown like a bomb into my life.

A shock? A shock to find out that we are descendants of an angelic war? That my grandmother had been murdered and that I command her same devastating talent? Yeah, "shock" didn't quite cover my state of mind. But as I ran this news once again through my head, I couldn't escape one fact: that subconsciously I may have known all along.

I stopped walking, and my lack of movement made Raef stop short too. He looked at me, that all too common protective worry creeping over his face.

"It wasn't a shock," I managed to whisper, staring at my mangled flower. I heard Raef move closer to me and looked up to his face. The falling sun reflected off the corners of his eyes and revealed chips of bronze in the sea of blue. I took a deep breath and solidified my knowledge. "It wasn't a shock," I said again, steadily this time.

Raef was surprised, "I guess that would explain why you didn't bolt from the house when I told you what I was. How did you. . . ?" His voice trailed off, as if something was occurring to him. "You mean Elizabeth. Your dreams," he said, awed. He shook his head and smiled, "Your kind truly is on a different, supernatural plane."

"Baby steps please," I moaned. "I'm still adjusting to the human sparkler aspect of my nature."

I continued on, walking slowly through the fields and attempting to replay a few of my nightmares. "I should tell Dalca I've been having the dreams."

Raef grimaced, "I'd rather you not. Not yet anyway. I do not trust people easily and Dalca is someone I have known for a very short period of time. She also dabbles in a weird sort of earth magic and I'm worried she will fry your brain trying to get you to remember your dreams."

I recalled the vial and me wanting to puke. Yeah – Dalca, though nice, was a bit too experimental for me. I nodded. "You know, I've got to tell you. I think I may be defective as a Lunatorra."

"LunaTERRA," Raef corrected, one dark eyebrow raised in a curious curve. "Defective? Somehow I doubt you are the least bit defective, Eila."

"Seriously!" I demanded. "I mean, as one of these LunaTERRA people, don't you think I should have the scruples to be able to recall a dream clearly? I mean, I barely remember them at all. And they weren't even the sweet, fuzzy type of dreams that make you all happy inside when you wake up. They were nightmares! I'd wake up tangled in the sheets on the floor with the dust bunnies, and all I can remember are the emotions. I get snippets. I'm like a stupid radio with poor reception!" I moaned, frustrated. I ended the daisy's misery and popped the blossom off. I looked at him, aggravated. "I feel like she's trying to tell me something and I sense it's so damn important!"

Raef looked at me, sympathetic to my thick head, "When we

know, we know. Don't beat yourself up about it. Maybe she was just trying to tell you about who you are. Well, who *we* are, I guess. Maybe the house triggered the dreams."

I looked at him as I started walking toward the tree again. As always, Raef fell into step with me like a chaperone shadow. I wrenched another innocent flower from the ground, venting my frustration over my lousy dream recall. "I have so many questions," I muttered, almost to myself.

"I know you do," replied Raef, looking at me. "I'll tell you what I know if you'll meet me under the tree."

"Meet you under the tree?" I asked, but as soon as I said it, he had disappeared before my eyes. I may have seen it in a sci-fi flick ten times, but seeing a person vanish in front of you is quite creepy. Hollywood doesn't do it justice.

"Raef?" I whispered to the space in front of me. I reached out at the nothingness and swished my hand around to see if he was somehow there, but invisible. There was only the briny, sea air.

I glanced over to the tree and then back at the empty field. I started thinking about soul-stealing stalkers and started jogging toward the mammoth hardwood. I seemed to speed up the closer I got to my destination. As I breached the edge of the tree's branches I nearly plowed into Raef.

I was breathing fast from my sprint and brief panic. "Don't do that!" I said, poking him in the chest. "Showing off in disturbing ways is unacceptable. You freaked me out!"

"Sorry," he said with a little smirk.

I was trying to slow my heart. "Did you disappear or are you supersonic?" I asked, breathing fast. I was face to face with him in the cool darkness of the tree.

"We can't disappear. The speed is, well, a perk of my kind, I guess." I slowed my breathing and gazed at the elegance of the massive tree that surrounded us. Looking up into its upper branches was a dizzying experience.

"It's beautiful," I said to him quietly, and he stepped aside, gesturing for me to look around. My breathing was finally calming.

"I remember this tree as a boy," he said as I walked slowly around the inner perimeter of the beech. I reached out as I walked and let the soft, rounded leaves roll through my fingertips.

"It was just a sapling back then. If it had been this massive, I would've loved hiding in here," said Raef, who had slowly begun to also walk around the outer circle of the tree, his direction opposite from mine.

"I'm sorry for what happened to you. Becoming a Mortis," I said quietly, wondering how old he was exactly. He could be any age, but his strong body and silky skin revealed no age past 18 years. It also didn't reveal his true, violent nature.

I realized I had failed to ask a critical question.

I stopped walking and playing with the swaying boughs. I looked at him for a few seconds before I spoke, observing how he moved, so fluidly, gracefully, and no doubt, lethally. I was looking at the true Raef for the very first time, yet my feelings toward him didn't waver.

"Why are you protecting me?" I asked, a slight bit of suspicion crossing my face. He stopped and looked at me, his own face looking uneasy.

"Eila, you do know that I will never hurt you?"

The briefest second of caution crossed my mind, but my instinct that I was safe with him was potent and solid, "I trust you."

He walked slowly over to me. "This is a bit of a long explanation.

We should sit. You still need to take it easy."

He held out his hand and helped me to the ground, then sat down next to me, crossing his arms over his knees. I could tell he was debating how to begin and I gave him time to get his thoughts together. His solid arm brushed ever so slightly against mine and sent my nerves into a chain reaction.

"I knew Elizabeth for a few months before she was killed. I knew her before I became what I am now. I helped finish building your home. I was good with my hands and my father was a brilliant woodworker, so I learned a lot from him," he said glancing at me. I was floored – he knew Elizabeth *and* built my home?

"I had a little sister as well, and my mother, Beth. We lived on the outskirts of Barnstable as we could never afford a home in this area. But we got along fine and I enjoyed working with my father," said Raef, reaching out to pick up a small stick. He started rolling it in his hand.

"And Kian. He lived with you too, right?" I asked.

Raef shook his head. "No. Kian isn't my real brother. I didn't really know Kian before I was infected. I actually really didn't know him well until this summer. I think Ana was pretty shocked when she met me at school that first day – and especially when I mentioned Kian. After that day at lunch, Kian and I knew we had to talk to Ana and MJ. They had been told about you and your family thanks to Dalca, but Dalca had no idea about Kian and I. We were a big surprise to her. We started working together. Well – coordinating at least. Dalca doesn't like Kian and me. Can't say I blame her. As a Gypsy, our histories entwine and not often in a good way. When she found out about you inheriting the house in the summer, she let Ana and MJ in on your real history. She wanted them to keep an eye on you, but you bumped into MJ by sheer luck when you called about his Wrangler."

163

He looked at me for a moment, to see how I was appraising the story. I remembered MJ calling someone after I had left the ice cream shop the first day he met me. He was probably calling Ana or Dalca to tell them I had arrived.

I also vividly remembered the first day of school, especially since Raef rescued me in the hall. "So, if Kian isn't your brother, who the heck is he?" I said, in a near conspiratorial whisper.

"Another Mortis who was in the right place at the right time a very long time ago. My last name is actually Paris."

"Raef Paris," I said, trying out the name. It sounded like someone famous.

"The summer that I turned 18, my family decided to move south. They heard that the winters were easier in Virginia and that the south was excellent to live in. I, however, preferred to stay here, on Cape Cod. My father, seeing that I was a man and could care for myself as a carpenter, let me stay," said Raef. I was listening intently.

"Elizabeth knew I had no family here and offered me steady work. She hosted some very fancy parties, as she was a sea captain's wife. She once told me that such pursuits bored her nearly to death and that she preferred the quiet of her books and the beach," said Raef looking out toward Dalca's house.

"She was beautiful, but more than that, she commanded a room. In an age where women were expected to be an accessory in life, she broke all the rules. When she spoke people, even men, really listened. She was a warrior hiding in plain sight – a powerful Lunaterra - but I didn't know it back then. I never knew she was hiding a pregnancy either." I could see Raef's mind trailing back to a time when his life was still human.

"You seem to have been a fan of hers," I said, trying to figure out if it was okay for the boy I was falling for to have a crush on my ancestral grandmother.

"She was well respected and could read a person like a book. The fact that she never treated me like a hired hand, but like a craftsman with great skill, endeared her to me," Raef looked at me, his face quiet. "I considered her my friend."

I couldn't help but swallow, "I wish I could've known her."

He laughed slightly and shook his head, "You are more like her than you know." Raef's eyes lingered on me for a few extra seconds, as if lost in thought. He continued to fiddle with the stick, which was getting shorter by the minute.

"It was the day of one of those parties that I met Kian when he was still human." Raef broke another piece off the twig and flicked it aside. "Kian's family had a lot of wealth - old money and grand homes on the Cape, Nantucket and Boston. So Kian, though young at almost 20, was well respected. Word was that he could also be an arrogant ass and a complete playboy, but he was unbelievably smart."

"I can see that," I mumbled and Raef smiled.

"I met him when I was finishing work on one of the bedrooms just before a party. He was an invitee, but Elizabeth still introduced me as her 'gifted woodsmith.' He barely blinked. My station in life, even in her favor, did not register me on Kian's radar. I excused myself and left. That's the last time I ever saw Elizabeth in my human form. I'll never forget the date. It was December 29th, 1850. Almost a year later, your grandmother would die."

I swallowed hard. Raef was over 162 years old. My mind refused to grasp any reality that demanded he be more than a high school Senior.

Raef sat there quietly for a while, remembering back to that day.

No doubt wondering what he could've done differently, as if fate allows us a do-over. He tossed aside the small remainder of the stick, which now looked more like a toothpick.

"I don't remember much about the night of the party. I had driven my horse and carriage back home. I remember untacking her from the hitch and locking her in her stall. I shut the barn doors behind me and then . . . nothing," said Raef, looking frustrated.

"I woke up two days later in the forest surrounding what is now Sandy Neck. My mind was on fire and all I cared about was this burning need to get my hands, viciously, on someone. Anyone. Nothing registered but the lust to steal someone's essence. I couldn't remember who I was, nor did I care to try and find out," said Raef, his voice haunted.

"I was a killer, a Mortis, and no one could stop me from my desires. Sometimes I ended their existence quickly and other times I would slowly, torturously pull their life-force from their body," he shook his head, disgusted at himself. "I was good at it and soon was recruited for my flair as a killer."

"Did you kill . . . many?" I asked my voice small.

Raef nodded, "But Kian and I mainly hunt animals now. When we have no other option, human blood will do - usually blood bank stuff, which we vastly prefer to inject. That's how Ana helped me. She healed me by allowing me to drink her blood. I must say, it tastes terrible though."

"Do you still hunt people?" A clawing unease wound through me at the idea that the boy I adored could kill.

He paused, watching me, "Yes. But trust me when I say they deserve it."

I swallowed hard. I reached out to that instinct that told me he was my salvation, despite the terrifying truth of what he was. I could feel that powerful bond linking me to him hold steady.

Raef seemed surprised I was still sitting calmly next to him. "I don't frighten you?" he asked, his eyes searching mine.

"I will admit that the first time I saw you, in English class, I had this horrific sense of danger," I said, my gaze not leaving his face.

He nodded, "I remember. I could hear your heart rate change so fast I was sure you were going into cardiac arrest."

The fact that he could hear my heart beat worried me. Did he know how it raced when he was near? He must. I tried to push that mortifying notion aside. "I no longer have that fear and haven't had it for quite a while."

He looked like he was mulling over this information, his eyes searching my face. I could tell he was debating something in his head. I decided to break the silence. "So you have no idea who infected you?" I trailed off, not sure I had the term right.

"You mean 'turned' me? No. But I will tell you this: if I ever find the one responsible for stealing my soul from me, I will kill them. They took my life away and I will return the favor in kind," he said darkly. His vengeance surprised me.

"Is that normal? To not know who did this?" I asked.

"Of all the Mortis I have ever met, and I have known my fair share over the past century and a half, I have only known one other who also has no memory of their turning." Raef looked at me, waiting for me to catch on.

"Kian?" I asked, stunned.

He nodded. "And on the same night I was turned. Of course, I didn't know that detail about him until he was recruited as well. We weren't exactly confidantes even though we were technically comrades," said Raef, angling toward me slightly.

"Comrades? What do you mean?"

"We were recruited for our abilities by the Rysse Clan – by Jacob Rysse."

I stiffened. Kian and Raef had worked for the man that killed Elizabeth. I slowly rose to my feet and Raef followed, but gave me space. "You worked . . . for Rysse?" I asked, tension coiling in my belly.

Raef nodded slowly. "We both were there, in the harbor square, the night Elizabeth and Rysse died," said Raef, watching me cautiously.

"You saw her *die?*" I asked, my voice like a wisp of dry air, taking an instinctive step back. Raef looked pained. He started to reach for me, but I widened the gap between us and he drew his hand back.

"Eila, please understand that for all that I am now, at one time I was the polar opposite. I did not recognize her as Elizabeth, my friend." His voice sounded desperate, "It was not within me to save her back then. We were there because we had heard that a Lunaterra would be there, that night, and neither of us had ever seen one. Neither of us had ever fought in the wars with your kind. I mean, to us, your kind was just a myth. It was a distant war in a distant land with a foreign enemy we had never seen."

I looked over at his face, seeing his concern. The boy in front of me now was somehow different than the one who watched my grandmother die. He had protected me. He was defending me.

He looked down to the ground. "I have no idea what happened that night, between Elizabeth and Rysse. The memory isn't clear for me, so I'm not much help on precise details. But in her death, she released a burst of energy so massive that when it reached Kian and me, it was as though I had been struck by a freight train. That energy should have killed us, like it did Rysse," said Raef, finally looking back to me.

"Whatever was part of that energy, it changed us. Our ability to control our rage, our memories, and the immunity, all came from Elizabeth, I am certain."

"The immunity?" I asked, confused.

He reached out cautiously and touched my face. "Immunity," he said, "To you."

I was stunned. Raef was immune? To ME? His hand dropped away from my face as I stepped towards him. "Elizabeth did something to you both," I breathed, amazed. "She made you... human?"

"No, not human, but a chance to be close. There is no cure for what we are. And understand that we still, on a very basic level, retain all the violence and cruelty that is the hallmark of our kind. We chose to fight that portion of who we are and it is a daily battle." Raef's face looked frightened, not for himself, but for me. He stepped back toward the edge of the tree.

As much as he had explained, there was still one major question that remained unanswered. "If you are Mortis and I'm Lunaterra . . . Answer me, Raef. Why are you and Kian protecting me?"

"At the beginning of the summer Kian bumped into me again in Miami. We got talking and he mentioned he was bringing his yacht up to the Cape to possibly sell it. He asked if I wanted to help him crew the boat. I agreed as I hadn't been back to the Cape in decades."

"Once here, I found out that 408 was once again owned by a Walker. I convinced Kian that we should check out who owned the house. But you hadn't arrived permanently yet and the locals started giving us the fish-eye, so we built the whole wealthy-brothers-dead-parents thing. When you finally returned, I saw you, up in your bedroom one night. I realized you were in high school and I figured I needed to find out more about you and, well, keep an eye on you. If necessary."

"It was you, wasn't it?" I asked, realizing that Raef was the one outside my window. I didn't have some creepy stalker. I had Raef.

"I've been watching the house most nights. If I'm not there, Kian sits guard. I was worried you may have recognized me that night. I was surprised you were awake so late. Did you have a nightmare?" he asked.

I nodded as Raef stepped towards me. "Eila - I did not help Elizabeth the night she died and I owe it to her to protect you now. I will not fail her again."

It hit me then, like a bullet to the chest.

I was not loved by this beautiful, imperfect boy. To him, I was nothing more than a chance at redemption. Nothing more than a way to ease the guilt.

My chest tightened and I was waging a desperate battle with my face, trying to control the pain that ran me through like a hot sword. I could feel the burn of my throat constricting and I knew I was losing the battle.

I slipped around the backside of the gnarled trunk where he couldn't see my face and I wanted to gasp for air. I had been such a silly fool. To believe a boy like Raef could ever fall for a girl like me. I shook my head, mentally chastising myself.

All the time together, his concern for my safety, it was all just part of his self-assigned guard duty. I shut my eyes to block the tears from escaping, and dragged in a slow, hot breath. I pulled with all my might to halt the pain in my heart, but even with my eyes closed, I could sense that he was now standing in front of me.

"Eila?" he asked quietly.

I thought about all the time we had together and how gentle and caring he always was. I erroneously believed I had understood his behavior and had picked the right option from choices I understood. I never dreamed his actions were derived from a fourth option.

I managed to clear my throat and speak without hitching my voice. "It is just . . . a lot to take in. You are my bodyguard then?"

The silence was torture. My skin tingled and I knew he was very close to me now, probably inches.

"Yes. I'm trying to be," he said quietly. I felt his warm hand carefully cradle my chin, and he lifted my face. His touch sent heat over my neck, spreading out from his fingers. I could hear him sigh and I finally opened my eyes, a tear fleeing down the curve of my cheek.

"I'm so sorry this all has happened to you. You can't know how horrible I feel about last night. Eila, please forgive me for not being there." His face was a combination of sadness and frustration, his touch making my pulse pound. His hand released my chin and slipped down to my chest, right above my heart.

I thought I might burst into flames.

"When I first saw you," he said quietly, "I heard your heart race and your face was that of barely controlled panic. From then on, I continued to hear this whenever I came too close." He spread his fingers slightly over my speeding heart. "I could feel it roll off you and vibrate through me. It was your instinct, built into your genetic code – a fight or flight response to my presence. You react to me – your eyes, your pulse, your instinct. I've noticed it still happens, but the fear does not seem to accompany it."

No kidding. My heart had rocketed away due to an entirely different reason, now destroyed.

"I . . . I trust you. You still cause my system to short circuit, but I trust you," I said, my stomach twisting into a painful knot. He was only my bodyguard. How stupid I was all this time. Anger laced the pain, but not at Raef. I was furious at myself to let my heart fall for this boy.

Raef's brow fell as he watched me, "Are you feeling alright?"

"Yeah Raef. I'm just . . . fine," I replied as Ana's voice called out to us to come in for pizza.

Raef, oblivious to my shattered heart, smiled at me and nodded toward the house, "Come on, let's get you fed." We started walking toward the house, Raef's hands tucked lazily in his pockets.

I could do this. Be normal with him, like nothing changed. He obviously cared about my safety. He was a good friend who I could not blame for my blindness.

I glanced over to him as we walked, his eyes scanning the woodline. "I just realized I have never seen you really eat anything," I said, watching him.

"And with any luck, you never will," he replied.

"What does that mean?"

"Eila, come on. What do you think Kian and I eat?"

"I'm guessing not pizza," I said, having worrisome visions about Kian and him *eating.*

"We mainly survive off the life-forces we take. It is all we need, nourishment-wise. But our prey here is mostly the flippered variety."

I stepped through the door and stopped in front of him,

"Seriously?"

Raef just gave a devious smile. I enjoyed seeing it, despite our circumstance. Yes, he was a good friend.

I stuck out my tongue, acting grossed out. "I think you're right. I don't want to see you eat, especially if it's seafood. I hate seafood." I had a flashback to the un-french fry incident. Yuck.

"What delinquent hates seafood?" asked MJ as he squeezed past me through the back door. "Nobody hates seafood. You can't live here and hate seafood," he said smiling broadly at me. "I mean, heck. I can't be friends with someone who is anti-fishy." He gave me a bear hug. "So glad you are on your feet once again! Come on and eat. Ana and I hit up DJs for some pies."

MJ flung an arm around my shoulders and ushered me into the dining room. "Oh, and Ana said no worries about the damage to the Jeep. She already fixed it." He looked back at Raef, "Keys, man. Shiny, silver things with little teeth marks - much more effective than ripping the steering column apart, you know, for future FYI."

Raef just gave him an incredulous look, "Uh huh. I'll try to remember that in the future."

I entered the dining room as Ana was opening a pizza box. The fabulous cheesy aroma hit me and I was suddenly famished. "Oh man. I'm starved," I said as Raef pulled out a chair for me to sit.

"Ditto!" said MJ.

"You think you're hungry! Try being a meal and then see how hungry you are afterward," said Ana, looking at Raef.

"Ana. I'm really sorry. We'll be better prepared in the future. I'm truly grateful for your help," replied Raef.

"You mean my blood. We might as well get the lingo straight," said Ana, dryly. I got the distinct impression that she wasn't Raef's biggest fan, probably because he was "brothers" with Kian. Basically blacklisted by association.

I wondered where Raef's other least-favorite fan had gone. "Where's Dalca?" I asked, selecting a slice of plain cheese.

MJ took a gulp of soda. "She headed for Salem about two hours ago. She said something about finding help. Ana's got her cell number," he said, taking another bite.

I was a little surprised she left, but comprehending her weird ways was like unraveling a mind-teaser game.

Kian waltzed into the kitchen from the front room. "Oh yum. Pizza," he said sarcastically. He looked over to his brother, "Are you ready?"

"I'm not leaving them alone. You go. I'll stay here," replied Raef.

"You need to hunt and I can't go alone. Someone needs to watch my back. Dalca's house is safe. They will be fine," argued Kian.

"I don't care. I'm not risking leaving them here. You go first and then when you're back, we'll switch."

I looked up at him. "You're hunting? Now?"

"We need to be in top form to protect you and Ana," Raef replied. "Kian and I need to go hunt. But Kian's right. We shouldn't go alone and risk attack."

"Attack from what?" I was trying to imagine them tackling a great white shark. The visual was right out of Jaws.

"Other Mortis," said Raef, plainly. I was shocked.

Kian stifled a laugh, "You don't really think that our kind would welcome us with open arms when we are protecting a Lunaterra, do you?"

I looked around the room. Ana and MJ seemed unaffected by this revelation. Raef knelt down beside me. "Eila. Don't worry about it.

It's not like our kind is one, big happy family. No honor among thieves, you know? We've been sort of outcasts since Elizabeth died and we disappeared from the Clan."

"Oh yeah. And it's been a blast ever since," said Kian, flatly. "Can we go now? I'm running on empty and Ana still smells tasty."

Ana shot Kian a brain-melting look, then grabbed a slice and headed into the living room.

"Eila - you'll be fine in here," said Kian. "Dalca's house is cast against other Mortis. It's very powerful magic. Just stay inside."

I looked at Raef. He reached out and squeezed my hand, but the darkness outside suddenly seemed all the more menacing. *Stay inside.* As if the night would consume me the moment I stepped past the screen door.

Raef didn't budge. "I'm not leaving you alone."

Kian sighed and looked at MJ who was gobbling down another slice. "Fine. We switch off. MJ - you're with me."

"Oh come on. I'm stawved," replied MJ through a mouthful of bread and sauce.

"You can grab something on the go," said Kian smiling. I was completely lost as to why MJ would be headed into the night with him. And I was worried.

"Wait! Why are *you* going?" I demanded, pointing to MJ.

MJ wiped his mouth. "Cause I got skills, baby," he said, grinning his silly, idiotic smile. He was so going to get killed.

"What skills?" I demanded, fearful for my friend's safety.

"Let's just say that I'm the motion detector. I can see the Mortis coming and smell them. Oh! And I know some KA-RA-TE!" he yelled, jumping to his feet.

Obviously my dear pal was taking his Heroic Heath delusion to a whole new level and Kian and Raef were unaware of his mental impairment. "He can't go!" I shouted, pointing in the direction of MJ. "Are you insane? He'll be snapped like a pretzel!"

"Actually," said Raef, calmly, "MJ has been of great value to us on our hunts and he did kill a vacationing Mortis who had picked off a tourist."

"This is not the time to joke!" I was irritated.

MJ, nonplussed by my protests, walked past me into the living room. "I'll meet you in the truck!" he called back to Kian.

Raef looked at me, "Trust me. He'll be fine."

"He better come back in one solid piece," I warned.

"Oh, he always does and then some," said Kian, heading out the side door. A few seconds later I heard the front door slam as well.

"I'm going to go check the house's perimeter. You going to hang with Ana for a while?" asked Raef.

"Yeah. You go do what you need to."

Raef nodded and headed out of the kitchen, commencing his official guard duty. I headed into the living room with a slice of pizza to join Ana, who had relocated herself to the floral couch.

The rumble of MJ's Bronco signaled their departure and I glanced out the side window that faced the driveway. I saw Kian in the front seat with Marsh riding shotgun. MJ must have been in there as well, but the dark tint to the windows made it difficult to visualize the Bronco's interior, though I had no idea Kian was so fond of the dog. I didn't even realize the massive animal was here.

I watched them back down the driveway and then hook a left onto Main Street, driving away. My heart was in my throat as I prayed that MJ would be safe. Kian and Marsh too.

Thinking about them, I lost my appetite and flopped down on an old, blue armchair. I watched Ana, who was now pulling a book from the shelf near the fireplace. She glanced at me and then sat back down on the couch, drawing her legs up under her Indian style. Placing the book open in her lap, she started eating her pizza.

She glanced at me again, clearly unsure what to do with me now that we were alone and the "alarming information about my life" class had been dismissed. She was probably waiting for my brain to finish processing all the info I had received, which would then lead to a total nervous breakdown.

I was actually doing okay with my new information, blistered heart aside. But I realized I wasn't sure exactly what Ana and MJ brought to our theater of war in the first place. Ana could obviously do something. At school, I saw her make a self-conscious geek into a self-assured god in seconds. I studied her profile as she slowly turned a page in the ratty book and cleared my throat.

Her eyes glanced up, "Yes?"

"I was just wondering how you did it. At school, I mean. You know, made that boy walk up to Nikki."

She continued to look at me, finally shutting her book and placing it aside. "You want to know what I am? Is that what you're asking?"

"Yeah. I guess so."

"The answer is I don't know," said Ana, picking up her bottle of water and taking a swig. "For as long as I can remember, I could read most people. Basically understand their true desires in emotional form. I could sense that kid at school liked Nikki, but his shyness would forever keep him from approaching her. And yeah, he was obviously a bad judge of human character, but hey, he wanted her. So I just gave him a push."

"A push?"

"Yeah, like, mentally enhanced the desire that was already there and boosted the scrap of confidence he had. A push."

"That is . . . somewhat creepy. What if someone was angry? Are you saying you can push them over the edge?"

Ana nodded.

"Damn. That is one heck of a talent," I said, very impressed and a bit concerned.

"I have my limits though. I once tried to get it to work on Kian, but it didn't seem to have an impact, so I assume that Mortis may be immune. I've been practicing though, you know, trying to get faster and more forceful. I can get a strong read off of Kian and Raef about what they really want, I just can't enhance it," said Ana, a knowing twinkle in her eye.

I swallowed back my nerves, realizing she most likely sensed my infatuation with Raef. She continued, probably reading my sensitivity on the subject, "I hope that I can get a fast read off of anyone we may run into and be able to list them as friend or foe before we find out the hard way."

"If you can get a read off of someone's emotions, can you also read their minds?"

"No, but I'm hoping that someday I might." She held up the book slightly, "This is a book on telepathy and ESP. I've been studying how scientists think it may work and I hope to be able to read someone's memories soon."

A crazy idea hit me. "You can try it on me! I've been trying to recall a dream for a while now . . . regarding Elizabeth. I get snippets, but nothing solid. Think it would work on me?" I asked, my heart rate creeping up faster.

Ana looked surprised. "Wait - you knew about your

grandmother and didn't tell Dalca?"

"Raef thought it would be best if some things, for now, were just kept amongst us. I hope that is okay with you." She seemed to debate whether to agree or not, but finally did. Trolling through my mind, however, was a different story.

"I don't know, Eila. It might not be safe for me to read you. Uncontrolled, I may melt your brain cells, or worse, mine."

"Melt my brain cells? Really? Come on, I think that is a bit extreme." I said, a tad shocked I was encouraging her. I was starting to wonder if my new attitude had to do with my DNA.

I was never this bold in Kansas.

Ana looked at me for a while then finally tossed the book down next to her. "Oh, what the heck. Let's try it," she said.

She pulled a chair next to me and sat down. I turned to her, waiting expectantly.

"Okay, so, according to the book, touching the one you're reading can help establish a connection. So I'm going to . . ." she reached up with both hands and carefully touched her cool fingers to my temples and forehead. "Okay, so now focus on what little of the dream you remember."

"I remember the fountain and some of Elizabeth's dress."

"Go with that then," said Ana, slowly dropping her head and closing her eyes. "Just don't move or talk. Close your eyes and focus on the images."

I did as Ana requested and for a while I just sat there, feeling her cool touch and the ticking of the grandfather clock in the corner. I tried to keep my mind on the fountain and the dress, but my mind started to wander, unbidden, to my bedroom at night.

I was suddenly hit with a vivid, almost blinding flash of Raef watching me from the darkened street. I could feel my panic and the chill of the wood floor against my feet. I was there, in my bedroom, and I gasped at the vividness.

Ana quickly took her hands away, her eyes wide and breath coming fast. The scene vanished the instant she let her hands drop from my face.

She looked at me with fear and confusion on her face, "What the hell was that?" she whispered.

"You saw that? That's amazing! But, uh, my mind kinda wandered. Sorry."

"No kidding!" said Ana, sitting straighter, "But what was *that?*"

"That was Raef, watching my house a while ago. Back then I didn't realize it was him and I thought some weirdo was going to rob me." I gave an involuntary shiver. "Damn - your ability brought with it the emotions from that night. Man, Ana! You have talent," I breathed, impressed.

"So, wait a minute. Back then you thought someone was going to rob you and you never told Raef or Kian?"

I shook my head, "Well, no. I thought it was just some crazy hallucination, though now I know it was real and just Raef guarding me. I did mention it to Marsh though, the night after it happened. God only knows why."

"You mean MJ?" asked Ana, as she leaned back, looking over the room, amazed no doubt that she was able to link with me.

"No, I didn't tell MJ. Just the dog . . . not that the dog would actually know what the heck I was saying. You know what is weird though? I could've sworn he was listening to me that night on the porch."

I sounded like a raving Looney.

Eventually they were all going to realize this, and save themselves the effort of rescuing my butt by simply tossing me back into the river. "Well, I sure sound like a nut."

I noticed that Ana was looking at me with a questioning eye and then a smile crept over her lips like a Cheshire cat. Her eyes twinkled and the grin grew.

"What?" I asked.

"You don't know, do you?" she laughed. "I thought Raef would've told you!"

"What? What don't I know?" I was lost. Dang it, why was she laughing?

"The dog, Marsh, IS MJ. He's a shape-shifter. You really think for a second that that boy, in his lanky form, had a chance against a Mortis? Jeez girl!" she laughed.

"He's a . . . DOG? No he's not! Are you SERIOUS?" I said, trying to figure out if she was telling the truth. *No way. A shape-shifter? No way.*

She nodded enthusiastically, still laughing, "Seriously! He's a Therian. And you almost had him sleep over when Mae left!" Ana was in tears, laughing so hard.

"I would've fed him dog food, poor guy," I muttered, looking at Ana, who was now absolutely roaring, nearly choking on her tears. I couldn't help it. My life was so absurd that I started laughing too.

"Here MJ, I got some Alpo!" cried Ana, another laughing fit striking.

I was laughing so hard, my eyes were pooling, "Milk-Bone anyone?" I gasped.

I was wiping the tears from my eyes, trying to calm down. So that's why I didn't see MJ in the truck. He was in dog-form. Good grief, my life was one traveling freak show.

A few minutes later I was finally able to speak, "On the plus side, you can read minds."

Ana shook her head. "No, I'm learning to read memories," she said, a huge smile on her face, "And that means that I can see the past."

I looked at her and narrowed my eyes. "School's in session, girl. Show me my dream. Show me my grandmother's death," I said, leaning in close to her.

She nodded, concentration and determination crossing her face as she placed her hands back to my temples to try once again.

This time, she succeeded.

A few hours later, each of our two immortal guards had gotten a chance to . . . feed. Ick.

I told them about what Ana and I had accomplished and a clearer version of Elizabeth's death. They were confused when they learned that Elizabeth allowed Rysse to touch her, and that her own power appeared to have killed both of them, though whether by accident or not we didn't know.

According to Raef, Elizabeth would've never allowed someone like Rysse near her, nor would Rysse be dumb enough to approach. We could come to only one conclusion: Rysse, and possibly Elizabeth, didn't plan to die that night. It seemed that my dream lead only to more questions and no answers.

Unfortunately for Ana, reading my mind caused her to acquire a slamming migraine and she had crawled into the recliner, spent. Kian took up residence near her, watching her sleep. I eventually crashed on the couch, torn between wanting to scream in frustration or kiss Raef until my lips fell off.

When I woke the next morning, Dalca was still gone, though she did call leaving instructions for the five of us to get back to my house and locate Elizabeth's diary. She said that she was positive Elizabeth kept one and it should give us much better insight into what I needed to do to protect myself. With her reassurance that she'd be back that evening, we all headed out to my house.

Once at 408, I led my friends up the front porch and unlocked the door, walking in. Ana followed me with MJ, in his furry form, trotting past us into the living room. I realized that I'd most likely be seeing him as a dog a lot more, now that we knew there were Mortis in the area. I turned to talk to Raef, but both he and Kian were still standing just outside the threshold of the front door. They were both looking at the mahogany frame.

"What? What is it?" I asked, alarmed.

Raef cleared his throat, "It's uh, just that we are playing a whole new ballgame now and neither of us ever thought we would be entering your house. We didn't plan for it or for much of what is happening." He continued to look warily at the rectangular opening.

"What Raef is trying to say is that you need to invite us in. We, being what we are, can't enter your house without being invited," said Kian flatly. "It's a life-thief thing."

"Oh," I said, a bit surprised. "Well, then, come on in." I gestured dramatically to the long hallway behind me. Both Kian and Raef looked at each other, but didn't move.

"Well, here's the thing," said Raef, clearing his throat. "If Elizabeth was a fraction of the goddess she was supposed to be, then this house is . . ."

"Booby-trapped," finished Kian, darkly.

"What do you mean, 'booby-trapped'?" I asked, instantly thinking of strings attached to bowling balls and poisoned arrows.

Ana stepped next to me and looked more closely at the door. "He means that they might be crispy critters the second they step inside, whether they were invited or not." She ran her hand down the woodwork lining the door. The two boys watched her carefully.

"What are you looking for?" I whispered, as if the door could hear me. I bent down next to her, as she was now running her hand along the bottom threshold.

"A way to cast the door against a formidable foe. A back-up security system, in case you let the wrong sort of soulless person inside," replied Ana, the tips of her fingers following a groove near the corner bottom of the door. "Bingo!" she said, satisfied. "I need something to pry up the wood on the threshold. I think there may be something underneath."

I jumped to my feet, "I have tools in the laundry room. Hang on!" I ran towards the back of the house and the laundry area off the kitchen. Digging through a box of carpentry stuff, I managed to find a screwdriver with a long shaft. I ran back to Ana with my makeshift pry bar.

"Here you go," I said, handing her the screwdriver. Ana bent down to jam the tool under the wooden slab, but MJ's large black head appeared and blocked her view, his brown eyes looking straight at Ana.

"Dude. You are in my way - MOVE!" scolded Ana, trying to push his head away. He whined and grabbed hold of the screwdriver with his mouth and wouldn't let go. "MJ! What the heck is wrong with you?"

Finally, I realized what he was trying to say, "Wait! Ana, wait. He's right. Let me do it. If it does contain a trap, I would think it could only be removed by another . . . Lunaterra." I couldn't believe I said the word in reference to myself. I stood there, dazed.

"Eila? You okay?" asked Ana, still holding the tool in her hand. I looked over to Raef who was smiling slightly.

"Uh, yeah. I think so," I replied, trying to understand the magnitude of what I had just admitted out loud.

Ana got to her feet and held out the screwdriver for me to take, "Well, have at it then." She turned to MJ, "And YOU do not need to be a dog right now. I hate charades, so go change into a homo sapien. And you SMELL!" said Ana.

Marsh, or rather MJ, cocked his head and turned to me. He let out a *woof!*

"Sorry pal, but you do stink a little bit," I said, shrugging and patting his head. He moaned and trotted off, no doubt to do as he was told.

"Um, ladies," said Kian, pointing to the screwdriver, "the door? Any day now would be great."

I wedged the screwdriver in the wood threshold of the door jam and started to pry ever so slightly, inching the screwdriver along. I was certain that if I broke the doorframe, Mae would have questions, all of which I wouldn't want to answer.

"This is just ironic," I said shaking my head as I thought back to my all-too-friendly history teacher.

"What is?" asked Kian, leaning lazily against the outside of the house. Raef, always the guardian, scanned the street in both directions.

"Just this. Something hidden under the door jam for luck. I thought Mr. Grant was just kidding about these old homes," I said,

187

working the slat of wood methodically away from the nails that held it fast.

I noticed Raef and Kian's black boots suddenly just across the threshold from where I worked. I heard Raef's voice, dark and serious, "What, *exactly*, did Mr. Grant say?"

I sat back and took a deep breath and flexed my hands. I swept a stray hair from my face as I looked up at Raef and Kian. "He just said that many of these old homes had pennies or letters under the threshold of the door. It was some sort of good luck. He said I should look to see if such things existed in my own home. That it would be an *interesting find.*"

My last words slowly rolled out of my mouth as an unnerving idea was starting to form in my head. "In fact, he seems fairly obsessed with this place in general."

My two bodyguards seemed a lot more tense. I knew exactly what they were thinking, "Wait a minute! No way. I mean, I've been alone with him at least five times and I'm still kicking!"

"I'm thinking that Mr. Grant's resume is probably missing a few critical facts," said Kian. He looked over at Ana, who seemed shocked, no doubt from the realization that she had come so close to one of the *real* bad guys. "Go grab a flashlight, Ana," instructed Kian as MJ walked back into the room on two human feet. He must have overheard the conversation.

"No way! I'd have known he was immortal," said MJ, helping Ana to her feet. Ana still looked amazed. Or horrified. Some emotions just blend together after you have seen them too many times.

"Actually, you would've only known if you were in your more handsome form and doggies are not allowed in the school. Turn your brain on please," said Kian. MJ glared at Kian as he led a stunned Ana into the kitchen to fetch a flashlight.

I stood up and faced Raef. "Do you think he's a Rysse clansman? Isn't it possible he's just, I don't know, an average, uh, Mortis?" I asked, hopeful but in that naïve way that never ends well.

Raef raised an eyebrow, "Really? You really think that just on some fluke, a fellow Mortis decided he would like to become a substitute history teacher, right here? Right now? When you just happen to move here?"

"And when Maureen Cooper happened to suddenly leave town?" added Ana, now composed and back with the requested item and MJ. "What, exactly, are we doing with this?" she asked Kian, holding up the flashlight.

"Trying to see under the threshold without disturbing any good luck charms," said Kian.

"Who the heck is Maureen Cooper?" I asked, confused.

MJ answered, while Ana sank to her knees on the floor beside me, "Ms. Cooper was the American History teacher for the past 20 years at BHS. She was due to retire next year, but it seems she made an abrupt departure without notifying anyone. Mr. Grant was new to town and had the required background to take her place."

"How serendipitous," I muttered.

"Most likely Mr. Grant dined with, or rather on, Maureen, making her exit a permanent one," said Kian.

Raef shook his head and looked at Kian, "We should've been suspicious of a new teacher from the start. Anybody new, for that matter."

"We're doing our best," said Kian, slightly heated.

"Our best nearly got her killed!" snapped Raef, now angry. He leaned in closer to Kian and hissed through his teeth. "Our best better be a hell of a lot better in the future or we're all dead."

"Well, I hate to burst your bubble, *brother*, but so far the clan is undefeated in their quest to eliminate her line. Hell – she is probably the last one! If I was a betting man, I'd bet against us!"

I was the last one? The last . . . Lunaterra?

"I'm all that's left?" I asked, my voice so small that I wasn't sure anyone heard me. Had every one of my kind been killed? If true fighters didn't make it, how on earth were we ever going to come out alive?

Raef had heard me.

He stopped arguing and looked down to where I knelt by the door. Sadness and anger brushed across his face. "Possibly. Probably," he replied, dropping down to find my eyes. "You are not going to die. We are going to keep you safe, do you understand?" His voice curled with a dark, knightly devotion that almost made me believe him.

I glanced at Ana and MJ, who were watching Raef and I. They could easily have taken their talents and chosen not to stand and protect me. They could've hidden from Dalca's screwed up assignment and declined what was beginning to sound like a suicide mission.

I needed to find my ability. I needed to perfect my lethal talent if I was to protect my two friends and two boys who no doubt had a bounty on their immortal heads. I needed to shift the balance of power in our favor and I needed to evolve on a seriously accelerated timeframe.

I pulled at the confidence that swam beneath my fear, dragging it to the surface. "I'm going to get you all inside and then we're going to find her journal," I said to my friends. Raef allowed a second more to pass between us and then rose to his feet.

I took the flashlight from Ana's hand and dropped to my former spot on the floor. I jammed the screwdriver under the oak threshold and pried it slightly, aiming the light into the shadow. Pressing my face to the floor I carefully looked underneath. No one made a sound as I scanned the floor.

"Hmmm," I muttered, "Well, I may be blind, but I sure as heck don't see anything. No, wait! There's a hollowed out area in the floor, but there isn't anything in it." I sat up and flicked off the flashlight. "What's the chance that Mr. Grant was able to remove something from the door?"

"And still be alive?" asked Kian, "Zero. He would've been long past dead."

Ana looked at Raef and Kian, "Is it possible that one of Eila's kind removed it? Or maybe it was never there to begin with?"

"It's possible, but either way, we need to know why there is an empty space in the threshold," said Raef.

MJ, impatient, huffed. "Well, on the plus side, it appears to be an average door! Let's get on with the treasure hunt. Come on, you *soul suckers*," he said, still sore from his olfactory shortcomings.

"Listen, Fido," said Kian a grin spreading on his face, "I may prefer the essence of humans, but you'll do in a pinch."

"HA! I'd like to see you try," snapped MJ.

Ana rolled her eyes. "Men," she moaned and got to her feet. "MJ is right. You guys should be able to come through. Come on in."

Raef and Kian started toward the door, but I panicked, visions of the boy I adored being incinerated flashing through my head. "WAIT! What if we're wrong?" I protested.

Kian and Raef stopped short.

"You invited them in," said Ana. "Technically that should afford them the ability to enter safely, since you own the house."

I got to my feet and looked at my two keepers.

"Your call," said Raef, putting his existence potentially in my hands.

I tried to sort the odds of them turning into a pile of dust. They should be okay. The house was MINE. I invited them in and the door was clear. "Okay. Fine," I finally replied.

They stepped forward but I second-guessed myself again, "No, wait!"

"Oh, come on," said Ana, dramatically. "This is like Red Light Green Light during 2nd grade recess."

"No, wait. I have an idea. Give me your hand Raef," I said, reaching through the doorway, my hand extended to him. He looked at me and I gestured with my hand for him to take it. I spoke loudly, with a clear, probably ridiculous, voice, "Raef O'Reilly – crap, I mean *Paris* - I invite you into my home."

Raef took my hand, instantly causing a riot of sensation to engulf my arm, and I pulled him quickly through the door to me. I looked up to his flawless face smiling down at me, free of burning embers, and relief washed over me. I remained clutched to him for another moment, lost in his closeness until Kian loudly cleared his throat. I released Raef, who gave my arm one last squeeze.

I reached once again through the doorway and Kian took my hand. His index finger gently stroked the underside of my wrist and I gave him a squinty-eyed look. He simply grinned.

I took a deep, slightly disgusted breath, "Kian O'Reilly. I invite you into this home." Unlike Raef however, Kian did not need to be pulled through the door. Instead he strode through the threshold in one giant step and squashed himself firmly against me, my hand still in his. Taller than Raef, I had to crane my neck upwards to look at Kian's wide smile.

"Thanks Eila," he purred sarcastically. I shoved him back.

"I figured after 160 years your hormones would've dulled," I whispered to Kian.

"Thankfully, no," he said with a wink.

I gave him an irritated look and he backed away.

I composed my thoughts and looked over my four unlikely allies. "So, um, welcome to the Walker house," I said, trying to act like a hostess who was not running from a death squad.

The four slowly looked around the great foyer with its grand, central staircase. Kian walked forward toward the curve of the staircase and reached out, caressing the ornate handrail. He looked back toward Raef, who seemed lost in thought.

"Looks the same doesn't it?" asked Kian.

"Very. I can't believe it's so well preserved," replied Raef, slowly walking into the right parlor. I was thoroughly confused, but then remembered what Raef had said under the tree.

"Wait a minute. You two *have* been in here before. So, what the heck was the dog and pony show over at the door?" I asked, baffled.

Kian looked over at Raef, who had wandered further into the parlor. "We entered as humans, never as Mortis," said Kian, still looking around. "There was a time when I was part of the mortal, but privileged, society. Elizabeth held grand parties here," said Kian, still looking about the foyer. "This home holds detailed memories for me."

"Me too," said Raef, reappearing. He took in the expanse of the staircase. "I wasn't part of Kian's upper echelon, though."

"That's for damn sure," replied Kian with a snort.

Raef just shook his head. "I remember crafting so much of this house and the furniture, including this staircase and your bed," said Raef, stroking the lush, smooth curve of the arm rail as if it were velvet. Now I understood why he knew I had a four-post bed. He made it.

His index finger traced the swirl at the top of the finial. "Of course back then I had no clue what she was or anything about whom she fought," he said dropping his hand from the woodwork.

I watched both him and Kian, and realized that these two boys had basically been a part of my life, my history, for a century and a half. They had walked with, talked with, Elizabeth. And now, more than a century later, they were with me, her descendant, in an attempt to save my life. The knowledge was humbling.

MJ, for once, looked more serious than usual, "You know, call me crazy, but I think it would be wise to find out who bought this home and signed it over to Eila."

I felt suddenly uneasy in my own home, having now let two legendary enemies of my previously unknown family tree inside. And while my heart said they were here to protect me, my head was having conflicting thoughts once again. Thanks to MJ, I now worried that my house wasn't really a gift after all.

"MJ's right," said Raef. "We need to find out how this person knew about Eila in the first place. And why they would be so generous as to give the house back."

"I agree," said Kian. "What made you come and take the house anyway? I mean, some random stranger buys a home and signs it back to you and you just take it on faith?"

"Kian. Don't . . ." said Raef, but Kian continued on, "Because I mean, really Eila, had you *not* come back we . . . ," he whipped his finger around the room to the others, " . . .would not be here, sticking our necks out. Had you not come back, our lives would've stayed sane."

The brimming anger and frustration in Kian's voice made my throat tighten. I felt responsible, but resentful as well. It wasn't just their lives. I was the center of the vortex.

The one marked to die.

"Look," I said, my voice sharper than I intended, "I took the deal because it seemed legit, and it is. I took the deal because I had nothing. NOTHING in Kansas and Mae was working herself into the ground to keep a roof over our heads and food on the table. And most of all, I took the deal because I had no clue that craziness like this," I mimicked his finger twirling about the room, though slightly more manic, "was waiting here! Do you really think, for one ludicrous moment, that I'd ever, ever come back to this home if I knew what I know now? Do you? I WANT MY LIFE BACK!"

I was livid, and now only mere inches from Kian's face. The rest of the audience remained frozen for a few seconds, no doubt floored at my outburst.

"Oooo kaaay," said MJ, stepping up to our face-off. "Let's just take a breather and not point fingers, shall we? However we got here, whatever our past, doesn't matter. What matters is what we do with our situation now. Together, we will hopefully remain in one piece, but fractured, we're probably dead. Personally, I always liked the Three Musketeers. 'All for one and one for . . .',"

I put my hand quickly over his mouth to halt his monologue, while looking at Kian. I was still angry that I was being blamed. I knew MJ was right, no matter how much Kian and I would clash. I drew a long, cleansing breath. "Let's just get this over with," I muttered, trying to release the rage.

Raef nodded. "I agree that we need to learn who bought back the home for Eila," he glanced between Kian and me.

I could feel MJ's warm breath on my hand and I dropped it from his mouth. He let out a quiet 'all' to finish his enthusiastic chant.

"But right now, daylight's on our side and the clan will not risk coming out when they can be easily seen. Our kind hunts best in the darkness. I say we find the diary and anything else we can from Elizabeth," he looked directly at Kian. "Preferably before someone decides to make another try for Eila."

The gravity of our situation created a void of sound within our company.

"Right," said MJ, breaking that silence. "And since this place is, like, twelve million square feet, we should be done when we are in our 90's. I hear retirement is highly overrated anyway."

Raef looked at MJ. "We need to condense your timeline."

Kian walked over to Raef. "One of us should head to the Registry of Deeds. See what paperwork we can find on the house," he glanced at me, then Raef. "I can go."

Raef shook his head, "You aren't exactly the studious kind, nor the most polite of men when you are frustrated. Digging through mountains of legal papers at the dusty Registry is not going to bring out your best side." Raef looked to me, "I'll go, if it's okay with you. I'll make sure to be back well before dark. Kian and MJ will keep you and Ana safe."

"I can take care of myself!" yelled Ana snappily from the other room.

Kian lowered his voice, "I'll keep them safe."

"WE'LL keep them safe," correct MJ.

"Whatever, Fido," replied Kian.

Just then, something occurred to me. "I thought that this home is safe from the Mortis, ergo, safe from the clan. What is the daytime rush?" I asked, uneasy.

"Mortis who regularly steal from humans are able to blend into the darkness. They pull the shadows over their skin, like a cloak," said

Kian "It makes them near impossible to see after sunset, though MJ can usually sense them in his other form. Nighttime becomes their best shot at succeeding."

What a sucktastic development. It was entirely possible that I'd never sleep again. Flashlights. I needed lots and lots of flashlights.

Raef reached out and touched my hand, "With the clan, we assume nothing. The sun is just a way to, 'strengthen the safety net,' shall we say?"

"This is my house, though. I live here," I argued, confused. "Are you telling me that I can no longer stay here? I thought this house, of all houses, is supposed to be Fort Knox."

Raef gave my hand a squeeze, "It probably *is* Fort Knox, but until we know for sure, you only can be here in the daytime. For your safety, you cannot be alone in the night."

I couldn't help but tense at the idea that a killer could hide in any shadow, possibly in my house. Maybe in my closet or under the bed. I needed to turn my imagination off before I flipped out. "When will we know for sure the house is safe?" My voice seemed to drown in the space around the hallway.

"When one tries to get in," said Raef.

Kian gave a clipped laugh. "Yeah, and then we quickly rip their head off," he said with his megawatt smile.

"If they are bold enough to walk through that door," said Raef stepping closer to me as he pointed to the entrance that he just came through, "they should be ready for a speedy demise."

MJ came over to me. "Eila, they won't get in without you inviting them in. That's an unbreakable supernatural law, right?" he asked looking over at Kian and Raef.

Raef nodded. Kian just stood there.

"I said, *RIGHT?*"

"Most likely," said Kian, finally answering MJ.

"MJ's right. They need to be invited in. You'll be okay here," said Raef. I was having trouble reading whether or not he was concerned about leaving me at the present time, but he seemed okay. It gave me more confidence to be without him.

"I have got to go so I can get back by sundown," said Raef. "You'll be safe here until then, and when I get back, we can decide what to do about sleeping arrangements. I promise."

"Sleeping. Right. Like that will happen for me." What an absurd idea.

"You'll be alright," said Raef, placing his hand on my shoulder and looking into my eyes. "We'll find the diary and learn how to activate your power, and then no soul-thief will be crazy enough to make an attempt on your life."

"Except for the clan," added Kian. Raef shot him a dark look.

I wanted him to stay, to be my protective shadow all day long, every day, for the rest of my life, but I knew he only trusted himself with the task of finding the buyer. I told myself I was safe in my home, among my talented friends. I nodded and he rubbed my shoulders one last time.

He leaned in towards me slightly and spoke softer, "I will be back before the sun sets. I promise."

"Yeah, yeah, yeah. We get it. Time's ticking," said Kian, tossing his head toward the door, "We'll see you soon."

Raef released me and headed out, looking back to me as he closed the door behind him.

"Finally. Now we can get this party started!" said Kian, rubbing his hands. I gave him my best *"give me a break"* look.

"Such party-killers," sighed Kian. "I'm heading upstairs to start looking." In a burst of speed, he disappeared up the main staircase and out of sight. His sudden shot of speed made me nearly jump out of my skin.

I looked at Ana, my hand on my now racing heart, "Damn, he's fast!"

"All of them are. He's nothing special," said Ana, shortly. She was completely unshaken by Kian's sonic-like speed.

"I heard that," shouted Kian from the 3rd floor. My mouth dropped open slightly. I mouthed the words, "*He can HEAR me?!*"

She picked at a peeling piece of plaster on the wall, looking a bit annoyed. "You know, if you are going to be this jumpy about everyday stuff, you will never be able to handle this lifestyle."

"Be nice, Ana," reprimanded MJ. "This is all new to her. Some of it is new to me too, Eila. You'll get used to it."

"Thanks MJ." I smiled at him. He was trying to be kind but Ana seemed on edge. I couldn't really blame her though. I turned and headed into the library as MJ followed me. Ana, on the other hand, walked down the hall to the back parlor and out of sight.

She was mumbling something about a needle in a haystack.

"She can be so . . . prickly, at times," I said, now standing in front of the monstrous floor-to-ceiling bookcases stuffed with leather-bound books.

"I know, but it's not really her," replied MJ, trying to defend Ana. "Last year she even looked different – long hair, a touch of lip-gloss. She is very different now."

In some ways I knew this was the truth. That somewhere under all the anger, and probably pain, was a different, though no less bold, Ana.

While I was certain that the loss of her father was a tremendous blow to her, I didn't think it was the trigger for her current personality disorder. Her dysphoria, I was fairly certain, had something to do with Kian. I was dying to find out what went on between them because Ana KNEW him, but I managed to control my urge to blurt out a million demanding questions.

I looked over at MJ who was systematically pulling out books and flipping through them, looking for the diary. He glanced at me, as he placed yet another book in the reject pile. "How many books do you think are in here?" he asked.

"Honestly, I don't want to know," I laughed. I started pulling books from the other end of the wall, sitting cross-legged on the floor in front of the lowest shelf. Book after book was typewritten and nothing like a diary.

Novels, battles, history books, geography. A few were even art books. It took us nearly an hour to get through just the first shelf during which I got a most fascinating, though abridged, history of MJ's Chinese ancestors. I still was having a hard time even believing he could change.

"Thus far, I have only learned how to shift into the Black Shuck that you've come to know," said MJ. "I chose that because I was a big fan of Sherlock Holmes novels and the Hound of the Baskervilles. I guess I thought it was appropriate for taking on the Mortis, as a shuck is supposed to be a supernatural creature. Plus, people wouldn't be shocked to see a dog named 'Marsh' walking around town. It's short for my full name, Marshall James. If I chose something with more, uh, *flair* I guess, I would've stood out like a whale on the beach."

"So you're saying you could turn into other animals? Potentially?" I asked, my attention rapt. MJ's ability was too damn cool.

"Potentially is a loaded word there. Turning into a variety of animals, rather than just maintaining one, takes an enormous amount of focus and training. I just don't have what it takes," replied MJ, humbly.

"My Chinese ancestors on my mom's side were known for being able to shift seamlessly between multiple creatures at once. Almost like a domino effect of changes, one right on top of another. To be able to do that, without pausing to come back to your baseline human form, just blows my mind. I have a tough enough time trying to stay focused long enough to pull off one change into just a dog. Those Therians were legends. They were freakin' gods," he said, awed. "But me? I'm just an oversized dog with a fast reaction time when it comes to the soulless."

He grabbed yet another book from the shelf, flipped through it quickly and tossed it aside. The pile behind us was growing exponentially and yet, no diary. Thank you Elizabeth for making this so darn easy.

I set another book aside and looked at MJ. "Okay, first of all, YOU have an incredible, mind-twisting skill. And I fully believe there is a shape-shifting god in you somewhere," I said, confident in my assessment.

I tossed aside another book on some small, stick-legged bird called a Piping Plover. I could've sworn I saw a bumper sticker about those birds tasting like chicken. Cape people are so strange.

"I really appreciate your confidence in me, but it's unwarranted. I'm not a superhero."

"Well, last time I checked, I was the figurehead of this train wreck and if I say you are a superhero, you are. Heck you're, um. . ." I stopped to think of an appropriate comparison. "You're Underdog!"

"Underdog?" said MJ, mock horror on his face. "That stupid, poorly animated beagle from TV? Are you kidding me? I mean, at least make me cool, like uh, Rin Tin Tin."

"How about Wolverine? The X-Men dude with the claw things?" I asked, smiling.

He snapped his fingers, enthused, "Yes! Yes, much better! I'm Wolverine, just, you know, without the claw-things and, well, bad hair cut. I wasn't a big fan of those yellow and blue suits either. They looked pretty dorky."

I stared at him, a smile crossing my face. MJ was trying to control his face, but a smile was climbing up the corners of his mouth. "Underdog then?"

"Yup" said MJ, sighing dramatically.

"Look. I'll make a deal with you," I said, but MJ moaned. "You work on turning into another creature, something fancier than a naked mole rat, and I'll work on figuring out how to become a human glow stick. Deal?"

MJ started to laugh. "Well, when you pitch it that way, how can anyone refuse?" he asked, still laughing.

I started laughing as well. The complete absurdity of our situation combined with the stress level at code red combined to short circuit our brains. We laughed and laughed till tears filled our eyes. It felt good, a release of tension and an ability to just forget the situation we were in, if only briefly. When I asked him to show me how he changes, he flatly refused, explaining that he had to be stark naked to transform. I burst out laughing again and he gave me a good-natured shove.

When we finally regained our senses and I had wiped the tears from my face, I felt renewed, and I think MJ did too. We continued our mission with the books and worked once again in silence, an occasional chuckle escaping us.

Another half hour had passed without any luck and the sun had yet to stop its march across the sky. I couldn't help glancing at the shadows as they slowly slipped up the walls in the library. I heard a creak of the wood floor behind us and turned around. Ana was standing in the doorway, hands in her pockets.

"Any luck?" she asked.

"No. Not yet," I replied. "You?"

"Nope. I'm going to go find Kian and see if that slacker has come across anything," she said, shifting her weight.

"K. Sounds good," I said, glancing at MJ who seemed to be pulling books a bit rougher. He didn't turn to look at Ana. I couldn't quite read his mood. I thought he might be getting overwhelmed at the monotony of our new sport known as book hurling. "Is that fine with you, MJ, or do we need extra help here?" I asked.

"Whatever," he replied, curtly.

Ana set her mouth in a tight line and disappeared out of the doorway. I could hear her footsteps taking the stairs two at a time up to the second floor.

For a while we worked in silence, until the nagging question I wanted to ask MJ from before could not be contained anymore. I cleared my throat. "Uh, any luck?" I asked, trying to warm up the conversation again after another near half-hour of silence.

"Nah, but this one . . ." MJ twisted to a pile behind him grabbing a faded black, leather book with deep etching carved into the cover, " . . . at least has some cool, old photos."

"Really? Can I see?"

"Here," he said, sliding the dense book towards me. I looked at the intricate pattern on the cover. The exact center had an oval indentation with more scrollwork around it. I suspected that some ornament had once fit there but had long since fallen out.

I gently opened the weathered binding and looked at the black and white photos on the first page, some of which looked older than the house. I flipped through the first few pages, then jumped ahead in the book, but it seemed that the album was unfinished.

I glanced over at MJ who was still pulling books from the bottom shelf, now seated like I was on the floor. "So, um, what is the deal between Kian and Ana?" I asked, amazed I had the nerve to bring it up.

MJ paused briefly. "That's not for me to share," he said, and continued pulling books.

"But she knew him, right? Before I arrived, she knew him?"

MJ put down a book and looked at me, "Yeah, she knew him before this whole thing."

"Were they in a relationship?" I asked, reflecting on the fact that her anger with Kian seemed more like bitterness. As if she was half of a couple whose relationship went south.

"I can't talk about this with you," said MJ, going back to his books.

I closed the photo album and put it aside, intending to take the time to truly enjoy it later. Perhaps when I wasn't being hunted. I reached for the next black, leather-bound book on the bottom shelf. The miles of books between MJ and I on the first shelf had condensed down to only a handful left, though hundreds remained on the rows above.

He slid sideways toward me to reach the next few books in line. We were almost close enough to reach out and touch. I heard him sigh and I looked over at him. Something was bugging him.

He finally spoke up, "Look, I can't talk about what did or did not happen between the two of them, but I know you like Raef. We all know." My faced started to flush and I looked away toward the books. "But, Eila, you should not - cannot - have a relationship with him. It's not safe."

"You don't know what you are talking about. He is just a friend," I said, not looking at MJ. I was always a lousy liar.

"Uh huh," he replied, not buying my tale for one second. "Look, he's not human. He's not one of us. He looks like one of us, but he isn't."

I was slightly taken aback and defensive of the boy I had fallen for, "That's the reason? Because Raef is not a human? Talk about not looking in the mirror! Last I checked, you turn into some mythical canine, I supposedly can light up like a nuclear warhead, and Ana has some weird ability to convince people to do things. Last time I checked, none of us were completely human."

"No, we are not, but he is truly *in*human. He and Kian are faster, stronger. I mean, they barely keep their moral centers functioning. Their true calling is to steal the life-force of people. Their normal state of existence is one of selfish, murderous desires. To start a relationship with one risks the possibility of their biological-selves returning. He could hurt you. He could kill you."

"I know all that," I said, angry. Possibly at myself for knowing everything he was saying was true, but unable to turn off my desire to be near Raef.

It was then that I realized what had occurred between Kian and Ana. "Kian hurt Ana. That's it isn't it? They were a couple and something happened and he hurt her, didn't he?"

MJ got to his feet and looked down at me, his jaw squared, "We're done talking about this. Ana will kick my ass if she knew I even mentioned her past with Kian." He started to walk out of the library.

"Wait! What about the diary? Look at all these books," I asked, nearly pleading, as I had no desire to go through them alone.

"It occurred to me that Elizabeth would not have been crazy enough to leave her diary in a reading library for everyone to peruse," he replied.

I felt mildly stupid. "Uh, good point."

I was about to leave the room, but remembered the photo book. I thought Mae would like to see it as well when she returned home, so I picked it up and took it into the kitchen with me, following MJ.

Mae. What on earth was I going to tell her? Or was I not going to say anything? And if I kept her in the dark, would it threaten her life? My chest started to tighten, panic rising. I placed the book on the table, staring at it, lost in thought.

MJ headed over to the fridge but saw my furrowed brow. "What?" he asked, looking at me.

"I'm just . . . I mean, what do I say to Mae? And for that matter, what will you tell your parents?"

MJ opened the refrigerator and pulled out a bottle of water. "Ah. Good question," he nodded. "You want one?" he asked, holding the water up slightly.

"No thanks. I'm going to get some tea going." I walked around the table and pulled the kettle from the back burner.

I took it to the sink and started filling it, glancing at the witch ball that Dalca had given Mae as a housewarming gift. It glowed softly as the sun filtered through it. I checked the clock on the microwave as I finished filling the kettle. It blinked "4:36" repeatedly. I was hoping Raef would be back very soon.

I turned off the tap and carried the full kettle to the stovetop and clicked on the gas flame. I looked over at MJ, who was now standing by the book on the table and running his finger along the leather cover.

"My parents know of our family history and tales of our ancestors who could change into other creatures. But for many decades my family has just chalked it up to myth and poor translation over the years of native stories," said MJ, still tracing the elaborate cover.

I looked at him, gesturing for an answer.

He shook his head, "Nope. Haven't told them. Hoping I won't have to and that we can curb this thing before we need to tell them, Mae included. I've been pitching them some BS about having a huge project that is part of a study group, so they have been letting me slide at the shop."

"What if we can't 'curb' this thing?"

"Then not telling them is to turn a blind eye to their safety. On the other hand we may never get a chance to tell them and, if this thing goes badly, the Clan may have no desire to pursue them. I mean technically, they are only gunning for you. Ana and I would just be, well, you know."

"You guys would be collateral damage. I get it," I said, strongly questioning the sanity of MJ and Ana joining the fight. "You guys shouldn't be part of this. I think you two should just bow out."

He held up a hand to stop me. "Shut up now. Please. You're our friend. You aren't going through this alone. Plus, I think Elizabeth wants something from you – maybe from all of us. Between your dreams and Raef and Kian being there when she died? Yeah – she wants something from us all, or at least Fate does."

"It would be nice to know what exactly that was, don't you think? Couldn't she, I don't know, ELABORATE?" I asked, frustrated.

"She probably did in the diary. When we find it, we'll know," said MJ, cracking the cap off the water bottle.

"What if she didn't have a diary? I don't keep a stupid diary. What makes everyone think she had a diary?"

"Dalca said she should've and Kian said he saw her writing in it," said MJ, taking another drink.

"Well, what if it was like, a flipping grocery list or something!"

"You know, you need to learn how to relax. You might need to look into yoga or something," said MJ, trying to look serious. "Negativity is bad for your health. Of course, so are soul-suckers." His face started to crack a smile.

"No kidding? Perhaps yoga could cure that problem as well?" I said, trying to be cross, but a determined smile crept onto my face.

MJ walked over to me and held my hand, giving it a squeeze as if it could fill me with his confidence, "We're going to win."

"How can you be so sure?" I asked, trying to draw from his strength.

"Because I believe nothing is just chance. I think we were all flung together for a reason. And I think that type of crazy destiny is bound to give us a hand."

He was right. My failing faith in our motley crew was not what Elizabeth would've wanted and was a liability to us. From what Raef said, she embodied confidence, bravery and authority. She'd expect a granddaughter to embody no less, even at 17. If I was to be of any help to my friends, I needed to act like Elizabeth.

"You're absolutely right. If we are going down, it will be in a blaze of glory," I said, doing my best to sound confident. It was a new state of being for me and would take getting used to. Like breaking in new jeans that cling too tight and leave rib lines on your body after you wear them for too long. Eventually they break in and become your favorite pair, but it takes a while.

"Damn straight! We are gonna ride this sucker 'til the wheels fall off!" said MJ, enthusiastically. I smiled broadly, feeling silly for my negativity in the face of brave, selfless friends.

"I'm sorry I pushed for information about Ana," I said, feeling a bit ashamed.

"No worries. If I had blabbed and she found out, I'd just have blamed you and she would've beaten the crap out of ya," said MJ, winking.

"So much for protecting me!" I protested.

"I protect you against the Mortis. Ana however is a whole different type of scary when she's pissed."

"Gee, thanks," I laughed.

Suddenly MJ started fishing for his cell phone in his pocket. He flipped it open and answered it. He seemed frustrated with the caller. "Now? Really? It's just that I'm. . . Yeah, but . . ." he sighed heavily. "Fine. I'll be there in five minutes. Yes, I know Dad . . .Yup, five minutes. OKAY . . . Bye."

He snapped the phone shut and swore, aggravated and turned to me.

"Eila. My dad is having a cow that I didn't do inventory this morning. I completely forgot, being here with you guys. I have to go, but I won't be long. And Kian's here," he added truly apologetic.

I nodded, slightly nervous that we were down yet another guard, but relieved MJ would be close.

He must have read my mind, "I'm just down the street. Call me if you need anything and I'll come right back, pissed parent or not. Okay?"

"Go ahead, MJ. We'll be alright."

He headed for the screen door and looked back one more time. "I'll be back soon. I promise," he said and headed out.

I watched the white, screen door lazily bounce in its frame and suddenly felt uneasy. I quickly latched the screen and shut the oak door as well, dead-bolting it.

"They can't get in without my say so," I said, trying to convince myself of the safety of the house, but just to be sure, I rechecked the dead-bolt.

I looked around the kitchen and suddenly the first floor seemed very lonely. I headed out of the kitchen and toward the stairs to find

Kian and Ana.

As I approached the landing I could hear the heated voices of the two of them upstairs. I couldn't quite make out the entirety of what they were saying. I stood there, at the bottom of the grand staircase, debating what to do.

Should I head up the stairs quietly and try to hear what they're saying? Should I run up and sound like an elephant so they know I'm here?

Finally I just decided that straight forward was the best approach, so I simply yelled up the stairs, "Hey guys? Anyone want some tea?"

The arguing from upstairs stopped. It was dead silent for a moment then I heard footsteps. Kian appeared at the top of the staircase and made his way quickly down to the landing.

"I'm going outside to check the barn and carriage shed. Maybe she hid the diary out there, where she figured no one would bother looking. Text me if you find something."

He pushed out the front door and stalked around the side of the house and down the hill to where the barn's roof was barely visible.

Man, he was pissed, but he was controlling it.

While the barn was on our property, it felt miles away since Ana and I were completely alone. I realized then that Kian had no clue MJ was gone as well.

"ANA!" I yelled.

Ana appeared at the top of the stairs. "Now what?" she asked, visibly raw from her argument with Kian.

"Kian just left to check out the barn," I said, thumbing towards the door.

"Thank goodness for small blessings," she replied, icily.

"You don't understand. MJ isn't here either. He's at work. His father called in full meltdown mode about inventory! Kian didn't realize he was gone."

For the first time since I met her, Ana's brave façade slipped slightly, "So, it's just us? In the house?"

I nodded, "Just us."

She shifted her weight and took a deep breath. "It's fine. It's daytime and neither of them are far away. We'll be fine. We're not going to freak out and start calling them back. We can handle this."

I tried to draw off her confidence. It seemed to work, on a near microscopic level at least. My house used to feel so safe to me. Well, until I found out about my real family tree.

"Right. We'll be fine. I'll just lock up and then we can keep looking," I said, dead-bolting the front door. I kept chanting, *"We'll be fine"* over and over in my head.

"Kian and I started looking in the back bedroom up here, but didn't find anything," said Ana.

"Well, we might as well check my room. There are some nooks and crannies in there too," I said, starting up the stairs but stopping when I heard the shrill whistle of the kettle.

"Oh. I forgot the tea. Be right back," I said to Ana, heading back into the kitchen. I gathered up a tray and a couple teacups, small kettle and some crackers. Ana saw me with the tray as I approached the stairs, trying to balance the heavy load. She looked at me and sighed, no doubt sure I was going to drop everything.

"Here, let me help you," she said, picking up the kettle from the tray. We started up the stairs in silence until she finally cleared her throat. "Did the house come with all this furniture? It looks old," she asked walking up the stairs beside me.

"Most of this stuff came with the house. Some of it is a bit too, elaborate, I guess, for me. My bed, though, is awesome," I said, truly pleased with the spectacular 4-poster bed.

"You mean the one Raef built? Can't wait to see it," said Ana. She looked at me out of the corner of her eye. "I bet Raef would like to see it again too."

"What?" I asked, embarrassed.

"Please. You know what I mean."

"Raef and I are just friends." Well, at least from his standpoint. I however wanted something more. A lot more. My cheeks were a bit too hot as we reached the landing.

"Yeah, right," said Ana, knowingly. I suspected she had more abilities than she let on. Maybe some sort of psychic dowsing.

"We're friends. Besides, the priority is to keep us all safe, and mixing business with pleasure might endanger you guys."

I led Ana down the hall and to my bedroom door, opening it for her. She stopped and looked at me, "Life's short, even when you are not being hunted. Know what I'm saying?"

I nodded, stunned. And confused. Ana had a bad experience with Kian and she was encouraging me to live a little with Raef? She walked into my room while I was left standing in the doorway, trying to make sense of her mind.

"Nice digs," she said, looking around the room. Her eyes fell on the ornate bed. "And really nice bed. Plenty of room to maneuver. Well done, Raef," she said, grinning.

I turned to her, making sure she was in fact Ana, the petulant pixie, and not some doppelganger. "Have you been smoking something?"

"No," said Ana with a laugh.

"Okay, don't get me wrong, but you ain't exactly all warm and fuzzy in regards to Kian and Raef. What's up?" I put the tray down on my desk and she placed the kettle next to it. She leaned back against the desk, her hands in her pockets.

"Truth?" she asked. I nodded. "I'm thinking that I better Carpe Diem while I can and you should do the same."

"While you can?" I asked, suspecting I already knew the answer.

"I just don't think we'll be the team to score the winning touchdown, and the game clock is running is all."

I had no response. I knew she was probably right and bold enough to say it. While MJ had a good point about Elizabeth and destiny, the fact was Elizabeth died at the hands of Jacob Rysse and she was only a few years older than me.

I also knew that if we were going to lose anyway, it was senseless for Ana to be part of the team. I wasn't even sure what she could bring to the fight besides trying to read my dream. Heck, I wasn't sure there was anything I'd bring to the fight either. I felt like a liability.

"Ana. I appreciate your help but you don't need to risk your life for me. Why don't you step out of this? It's okay," I said, truthfully. If we couldn't win then staying in the game was suicide for the players. And senseless to continue on with me, especially when they weren't the targets in the first place.

I felt old.

As if I just blew through my teenhood and had been slammed into adulthood. I wasn't ready for it. I didn't want it, but had no choice. My life felt surreal. How on earth did I go from being Eila Walker, invisible Kansas girl, to Eila Walker, natural born killer and public enemy number one of the Mortis?

I had lived my whole life believing in one type of world, where monsters stayed in fairytales and legends are only resurrected by Hollywood. Now I had been dropkicked into the real world, where nothing's impossible. I guessed ignorance could be bliss, because my reality really sucked.

"While it has crossed my mind to bolt, you grew on me. You're my friend and so is MJ. I'm not leaving either of you to fight without me," said Ana, walking along the length of my bureau to my stereo. "And arguing that you don't like Mr. Abercrombie is pointless, especially with me."

My face blossomed once again, but she ignored my embarrassment. "Got tunes?" she asked, looking at me.

I handed her my iPhone and she docked it between the speakers. She touched the screen to scan over to my music library and flipped through the songs with a toss of her finger. "Your music is, uh, interesting," she said, the compliment hiding a distaste for my acoustic preferences.

She flicked on some *Citizen Cope* and started nodding her head slightly to the beat. "Not half bad," she said, letting the thrumming guitar fill the room.

I watched her, as her hand trailed over my jewelry and haphazard knick-nacks on my bureau; an old photo of my parents, Mae and me laughing at dinner in a restaurant, a photo of me at the lake in my old bikini, my scar barely visible.

They were brief snapshots of my life as it used to be, so far from me now. My life, which was no longer my own, was now driven and ruled by a new understanding and permanent career assignment.

How could I live like this? I was drafted into a war I didn't understand and never knew existed. And my tour of duty would never end. My world was a new form of prison with only two options: fight or die.

On a very real level, the old Eila was already dead. The loss of her, of me, was difficult to accept and I could feel a tear trace my face. I quickly wiped it away, not wanting Ana to see. I took a deep breath and decided to shelve my former-self's wake for a later date.

It was too much to take on right now. One day at a time would keep me safe. One day at a time might just keep us all alive. I walked over to my closet and pulled open the heavy, protesting door. Ana watched me.

"Are we playing dress-up, because I'm not a good choice for that game," she asked dryly.

"Me neither," I said, my hanging clothes ranging from jeans and sweats to tees and tanks. Not a single dress or skirt to be found. "When I was putting stuff in here I noticed a trap door way up high in the corner, but I was too wigged out by the possibility of spiders to mess with it. I think I can climb up onto the shelf here and be able to reach it," I said, heading over to my desk and dragging back a chair for height.

"You're afraid of spiders, but not the two killers that hang with us?" asked Ana, her hands on her hips.

I stopped in front of her, the chair grasped firmly in my hand. "Dude. They're SPIDERS," I said, looking at her. She laughed as I continued on to the closet with my chair.

"I hope Mothra isn't up there as well," taunted Ana, snickering.

"Shut up," I said, acting pissed. I tried to fit the chair inside the closet, but my mountain of boxes was blocking any access. "Terrific," I said sarcastically. "Looks like we need to move a bunch of junk to get in here."

Together, Ana and I started hauling out boxes. The music continued to play through my giant catalog. I glanced at Ana, pushing a box across the room.

"So what's the deal with you and Kian?" I couldn't believe I asked. It was as if the edit button in my brain failed.

She stopped pushing and looked at me, surprised.

"Sorry," I said quickly. "Sooo not my business."

I set to pulling out another box, but the silence behind me was deafening. I was afraid to look at her. Any ground we just gained as friends was probably gone. When she spoke I nearly jumped out of my skin.

"We were an item last year," she said plainly.

I couldn't believe she told me. My stupid edit button failed again, "What happened?"

"I met him when school let out for summer break. He had come into town to buy this antique car and it broke down. The shop I worked at was the only one open and I happened to be there. That's how we met and from there we just slowly got to know each other," said Ana, sitting on the box she had moved. I felt frozen in place, afraid if I took a single step she'd realize she was opening up about Kian.

"Anyway, when he came by that night, the attraction to him was potent. I had never, in my life, felt that kind of electrical draw towards anyone. He felt it as well, though I only learned that later. It took me about a month before I found out he wasn't human, but by then I knew he wouldn't hurt me. After that, we became inseparable. He had bought the *Cerberus* and planned on staying. That yacht holds many memories."

I snapped my mouth shut, which had been hanging open in amazement. "Did you two . . .?" I asked, floored.

Ana looked offended, "Please! I'm not that wild. Not to mention, he wasn't keen on the idea since he was worried I might be hurt. I guess their kind of . . . well you know, can get pretty rough and that is all he had been exposed to for over a century. He was worried that old habits would die hard and so would I."

She just shook her head, "Sometimes it's hard for me to remember that he's not really twenty years old. I mean, physically he is, but mentally he has had more experiences that any other human man on the face of the planet. He has lived, like, FOUR lifetimes. The same goes for Raef. He looks like a teen, but his maturity is way beyond that. That kind of experience, especially intimate, makes me nervous, you know? What if I don't meet his expectations? But on the other hand, he never expected me to be experienced at all."

She shrugged her shoulders, "I guess, in the end, it's better to experience your first time with someone like him, than with one of the morons from high school who are solely hormone-driven."

My stomach tightened thinking of such "moments" with Raef, but she was so right. "So what happened? You two seem to not be very chummy now," I asked.

"My Dad. Kian was not a fan of my father. He was a good guy, but he had a tendency to drink a bit too much and he wasn't a friendly drunk, if you know what I mean. But he was my *Dad*. He was all I had. Kian begged me to move out and live with him on the yacht. He had almost convinced me when I got a call from my Dad's fishing boat in late summer that he had suffered a massive heart attack. They had airlifted him back to Boston and Kian drove me up to see him, but he was in a coma. I pleaded with Kian to save him, but he refused. He said that it wouldn't work because he was too weak. His heart had stopped repeatedly and he wouldn't be healed. That he may end up turning."

Ana was getting upset, "I know it was bullshit. He could've saved my Dad, but he didn't want to. He thought he wasn't worth saving because he had gotten physical when he was drunk, but he was still my FATHER. Kian should've tried. Instead, he let him die!" Ana clenched her hands. "I told him to leave and never come back. That he was a murderer. He was desperate for me to understand, but I couldn't forgive him."

My head was spinning and I sat down on a box next to her. "Oh Ana. I'm so sorry, I didn't know."

"It's okay," she replied, looking at her hands.

"What do you mean Kian could have 'saved' him?"

"Mortis can both take and give life-forces. Because they store life-forces inside themselves, they can also give some of what they have stolen. When they give, they heal. They can heal just about any injury on anyone, but *supposedly* they cannot fix someone whose heart has stopped, even if it has been restarted. That, and it cannot cure a genetic disease. Because my father's heart had stopped and then been restarted, Kian feared that if he shared a stolen life-force with my father, his weakened body may become infected and cause him to turn. To become a Mortis. Kian said that whoever you were as a human becomes amplified once you are turned and my Dad had a temper."

"So, he would've become a killer?" I asked, the hairs rising on my arms. Ana nodded. "And you didn't believe him?"

"No. I believed he could heal him and that, even if he did turn, he could be helped and shown how to live a life in peace with humans, like Kian. But Kian said it didn't work that way. But I knew he just wanted him dead. My father had hurt me in the past and Kian wanted vengeance."

I didn't know what to say. I felt for her. To love someone so completely then feel so terribly betrayed. And yet, I saw Kian's side. He loved Ana and didn't want to see her continue to be hurt by her father. Perhaps her father could've been saved or maybe the truth was he was destined to die anyway. How could one ever know? More importantly, did it matter?

"For what it's worth, if you had never met Kian, your Dad would never have lived anyway, right?" I asked, looking at Ana.

She turned to me as she played with her bracelet. It was nearly the same one that Raef had given me a few nights ago. I felt as though years had passed since the bonfire.

"At the time I wasn't thinking about that fact, but I know it now. When I learned that Kian had returned I was very angry. And seeing him all the time is like reliving the good and the bad. I'm just trying to come to terms with everything," said Ana, getting back to her feet.

"Will you ever forgive him?" I asked.

"I don't know," she said, "But he's hoping I will."

"Do you still have feelings for him?"

She paused, her look distant. Remembering. She nodded, "As strong as ever." She turned to me, "Eila. You should know that if you feel a connection with Raef, he undoubtedly feels it as well. It is one of the most potent links in their supernatural world. For either party to feel that electrical draw, the other must as well. Like magnets, you would not feel it unless he did equally."

Her voice became quiet, "You feel it, don't you? A need so

powerful it's like reaching for air when you're drowning. Finding water when you have been lost in the desert."

I swallowed and nodded.

"Make no mistake. Raef feels all that you do as well."

I sat there, frozen. In my mind's eye, I ran through all of the moments I had spent with Raef. When he pulled me from the hall at BHS. When he touched my face outside the locker room. When he slid the bracelet onto my wrist that night at the beach.

Those were not moments of a guard and his charge. Those were moments of affection. Of caring, for me, and not because I was Lunaterra. He felt for me as I did for him, but he refused to let it through. Absently I twisted the gift on my wrist.

I had not noticed Ana had begun moving boxes again until she dropped one loudly on the floor by the bed. "Let's get this done. There's a big, hairy arachnid waiting for you," she said with a smile.

"You know, you could let a girl's mind wander briefly once in a while," I replied in mock protest. The music switched again to a pop chart song. It was infectious. Perhaps it was the understanding that we loved two immortal boys, or the understanding that they loved us, but the need to break loose was uncontrollable.

Ana and I started to dance and lip sync. We acted like we were twelve with not a care in the world. We needed to be kids. We needed to be free.

Ana slid over to the radio and cranked up the music. I hopped onto a box and danced like my life depended on it. Ana started singing at the top of her lungs and I was laughing at her crazy rendition of the song.

When the song finally ended and switched to a slower tempo our faces were flushed, but our smiles were huge. Ana wiped her short hair back from her face, "Oh man. I need some ice water. You too?" she asked, still laughing.

I nodded, still trying to catch my breath.

"I'll be right back," she said leaving my room. I waved her on and hopped down off the box. As I was reaching for the radio to turn it down, I heard a horrific crash, then silence. I froze.

"Ana?" I yelled, but nothing was retuned but silence.

I knew with chilling certainty that she had fallen down the stairs.

"ANA!" I screamed and ripped the phone from my radio to call Kian. As I ran for the door, dialing, the phone slipped from my fingers.

I looked down to find where I dropped it and as I did something rock hard struck me in the chest. I was knocked backwards onto the floor, my lungs screaming for air.

It took a moment to focus on the figure in the door. I gasped as I made out the face of the young man from the bridge, with one distinct difference: his eyes were like asphalt.

I drew breath to scream, but he reached down and grabbed me by the throat. I hung onto his forearm as he pulled me from the floor and carried me by the neck with his one outstretched arm, slamming me against the far wall, causing a crack in the rock-hard horsehair plaster. My sight was swimming with little flashes of black stars and I blinked madly, trying to clear my vision.

He leaned close to my face, his hand on my throat as his lifeless eyes studied my own. "Where's the diary?" he growled. I was on my tiptoes as I tried to keep his grip on my neck from becoming a hangman's noose. He didn't look like he was more than seventeen himself.

"I don't know," I managed to say.

His face was mere inches from my own. "Do not lie," he hissed, his hand tightening around my neck causing my head to feel like it would burst.

"I'm not lying," I wheezed. "We've been searching for it."

The boy looked at me closely, his eyes the color of a raven's feather, obscuring any whiteness. They reminded me of a doll's soulless, glass eyes.

He raised his free arm and traced his finger down the curve of my face. My fear slowly gave way to a strange form of brutal confidence – a darkness within me that whispered murderous thoughts.

"I can feel your rage," he whispered, brushing his lips near my neck, tempting his senses as he felt my life-force pulse. His hand traced farther down my face, down my jaw, and along the artery in my neck.

The voice inside my head sung words I didn't understand, but I could feel the desire to kill build within me. My sight began to blur around the edges, tunneling my focus on my attacker.

"While I cannot draw from you, I could still snap your spine," he said forcing my head to slowly turn, exposing my neck to him fully. "What a thrill it would be to kill the last of your race. To hear your neck crack and watch the life flee your frail body."

My peripheral vision snapped to black and the voice became a physical hum, which burned in my chest and flowed down my arms. The heat pooled in my hands that were clutched tightly to his arms. His grip on my neck loosened and for a fleeting moment, his face looked strained . . . and surprised.

He glanced down at my hands and ground out several choice words as he leaned in close to my face, "Don't piss me off girl," he said, and slammed me back against the wall once more.

I instantly saw the disco ball stars again, and a searing headache replaced my burning hands.

"Try that again and I *will* kill you, orders or not. They want you and that damn diary, but that bitch Elizabeth has done something with her beloved book, therefore you will have to do for now."

He hauled me away from the wall and started to drag me toward the door, but I was knocked free of his grasp by what felt like a wall of iron. I crashed into the boxes and tumbled to the floor. From behind me, I could hear glass breaking and what sounded like furniture being smashed.

I managed to scramble to my feet and I saw Kian fighting with the boy. His face was paler than usual, his eyes entirely black and he growled like a beast from the underworld. Gone was the handsome, young man that I knew and Ana loved, replaced by an enraged, avenging angel trying to protect me.

They wrestled, smashing into furniture, pounding on one another. Their movements were lightning fast and hard to follow, while the carnage within my room grew. Suddenly they were still and Bridge Boy was standing over Kian, who had been stabbed through the side with the broken leg of one of the chairs.

I screamed for him, terrified he was going to die. Kian, clearly injured, slowly pulled the sharp wooden spear from his body as he tried to get to his feet.

My attacker strode toward me, but in a blur of snarling blackness, he was slammed up against the far wall that he had pinned me to moments before. The boy struggled against Marsh, who had suddenly launched into the room and now was attempting to rip out his throat. As he fought to keep the snapping jaws away from his face, Bridge Boy didn't see Kian coming.

In one coordinated movement, Marsh leapt away as Kian reached in to the boy and swiftly snapped his neck. The boy's instantly still body crumpled to the floor at my feet. His black eyes, fading to a normal green, stared at me, lifeless. I could barely catch my breath. I was unable to look away from the unmoving teenager at my feet.

"Eila? EILA!" said Kian, stooping down. "Are you hurt? Are you alright?"

I was so shocked at what had just occurred I couldn't find words to answer him. He finally managed to put himself in my line of sight and placed his strong hands on my shoulders. He looked directly at me and I saw that his eyes were back to that spectacular blue.

I swallowed and finally managed to speak, "I think I'm okay. Thank you." I said breathlessly. Blood was soaking through his white shirt. "No! You're hurt!"

I reached out to his side but he quickly grabbed my hand. "Don't touch it! You can't touch my blood Eila. Remember?" I nodded slowly, recalling the deadly nature of his blood for my kind.

"Don't worry, it heals fast. Eila, this is important: Did you invite him in?" asked Kian, nodding toward the boy's body.

"No," I replied, certain.

"Are you absolutely sure?" asked Kian.

"Absolutely. I did not invite him in," I said, solid in my recall. I glanced at the teen, crumpled near me. "Is he . . . dead?" I asked, feeling a bit sick.

"Very," said Kian, somewhat absently, his mind lost in thought. He sat back on his heels, thinking for a moment. "The house has been breached. We have to get out," he said, standing and pulling me to my feet. He looked at Marsh who seemed to know exactly what he meant. The massive black animal darted out of the room.

"What do you mean 'breached'?" I asked, worried by Kian's own stratospheric sense of guard.

"Something allowed him to enter. If he can enter, so can others. We need to get to the boat. We will be safe there."

From the floor below, Marsh started barking rapidly. "ANA!" I gasped, remembering the crash I heard before I saw Bridge Boy. Kian looked at me sharply.

"I heard her fall down the stairs. Before he attacked me. She must have been thrown. Or pushed!"

Kian and I ran out of my room, though I was having trouble with my balance. I braced myself against the hall, my head pounding from the impact with the wall.

We got to the top of the back staircase that led to the kitchen and, to my horror, Ana lay at the bottom of the stairs, motionless. Marsh was standing over her and barking up at us. Kian was down the stairs in the blink of an eye as I made my wobbly way down as best I could.

Kian looked to Marsh, "Go check the rest of the house and the grounds! NOW!" Marsh looked one more time at Ana and bolted out of the hallway and toward the parlor.

Kian leaned down next to Ana. He touched her face lightly. "Ana?" he asked. Her eyes fluttered opened and searched the room, finally settling her gaze on Kian. Her breathing was ragged.

"I'm going to help you," he said running his hands down the back of her neck and along her rib cage. Ana winced as he touched her side and rage flooded his face. "I'm sorry, baby. I'll make it better, I promise. You're going to be okay," said Kian, caressing her face with the same hands that just broke my attacker's neck.

He leaned across to me and spoke under his breath. "She has several broken ribs and one has punctured her lung. It's causing her to have trouble breathing and is filling with blood."

"WHAT? Oh my god, we need an ambulance!" My hands shook

as I tried to organize my thoughts. I needed my phone. Where the hell was it? SHIT - it's still in my room! I started for the stairs but stopped in my tracks when Ana spoke.

"Can't . . . breathe," she rasped. I knelt down next to my friend and clutched her hand.

Kian touched her face, "I know, but I can fix it." Ana looked panicked and shook her head *no*. Kian leaned down to her.

"Ana, listen to me. I can fix this, but I need to hurry. Your lungs are filling with blood. Please, let me help you," he pleaded.

"KIAN! We need to call 911! NOW!" I yelled, starting to fear for my friend.

"There is no time," he snapped, looking back to me. "She will not survive that long."

Fear gripped me like a vise as I realized my friend might only have minutes left. I was instantly on Kian's side and dropped to the floor beside her. "Ana. Let him help you. PLEASE," I pleaded, my voice cracking as I fought back tears.

"Dad," said Ana, her voice starting to gurgle as she slowly began to drown.

Kian was becoming more desperate, talking faster. "I couldn't save your father. I know you don't believe that but it's the truth. If I could have, I would've saved him. I will not turn you. Your heart has not stopped. Please let me help you," he begged. Leaning down, he placed his forehead to hers and whispered, "Do not leave me. Please."

She looked up into his eyes then to me. I was mouthing the word "please" over and over as a tear escaped the corner of my eye. She looked back to Kian whose own face pleaded the same and finally gave a small nod.

Relief flooded his body and he quickly brought his hands back to her face. His sea-blue eyes became swallowed by the blackness that poured from his pupils, sending a chill down my back. He leaned forward over Ana and his body tensed as beautiful, black lacey designs appeared on his face. They were the same marks that Rysse had when he killed Elizabeth and I was so shocked, that I fell backwards off my heels, landing on my rear with a thud. He didn't break his concentration however, and the markings lengthened, disappearing down his neck and under his shirt.

Reappearing on his arms and hands, the design flowed outward onto Ana and down her own chest. The markings pulsed softly, creating a warm glow that covered Ana's body. After a few moments, Kian released her and the markings on both of them vanished.

I couldn't move, amazed at what I just witnessed.

His eyes fading back to blue, Kian slumped slightly, as if all the strength was drained from him. I noticed that his shirt began to darken further, as if he began bleeding more, but he didn't take his eyes off Ana. He moved his hands to either of her arms as if he was pinning her to the floor.

"What are you doing?" I asked, alarm flashing through me as Ana started to moan and I pulled myself back to kneeling.

"Healing at an accelerated rate will save her life, but it can be. . . painful." He looked at my worried face then to Ana's, which was beginning to look strained. "Holding her keeps her from further injuring herself."

Ana began to moan louder. She began to make jerking motions with her pinned arms and her legs started to kick, as if trying to gain traction on the floor. She began to plead, crying out for Kian to make it stop, as if she was in a fog. It was torturous to watch as she writhed. Begging quickly turned to screaming as she arched her back against a hidden assault on her body.

Kian, still holding her to the floor had to look away at one point, the sight of her in such agony clearly too much, even for him. I held her hand, telling her it was going to be okay, but her screams drowned out my voice.

MJ raced in from the parlor, disheveled with just a pair of pants on. He saw Kian pinning her to the floor as she twisted and arched in pain.

"What the hell are you doing!" he yelled at Kian, collapsing to the floor next to him. "Stop it! You're killing her!" he said reaching for Kian who was focused only on Ana.

I reached quickly over Ana and grabbed MJ. "Don't! He's healing her!" I yelled over Ana's screams.

"Like hell he is!" barked MJ back at me.

"Trust me! It will work!" I yelled with a false confidence, but then the room suddenly went quiet and Ana's body fell stone still. "Ana?" I asked, panic flowing up my body.

Kian didn't move, but slowly released her arms. MJ was about to say something, but Kian snapped his head around towards him, glaring. He turned back to Ana and lowered his head close to her chest, then sat slowly back up, his body visually relaxing.

"She's okay. She just passed out from the pain, thankfully." He scooped Ana's rag doll form into his arms and shifted his shoulder so her head rested over his heart. Carrying her, his shirt stained red, he slowly got to his feet. MJ and I rose with him.

"Did it work?" I asked, finally releasing her motionless hand.

He nodded. "Her heart and lungs sound excellent. It worked, but we need to get out of here. Now."

"House and property are clear, but the sun is setting fast. We definitely need to split, preferably five minutes ago. I'm going to pull the Wrangler around," he said, dashing out the front door.

"What about the boy from the bridge?" I asked, always the practical one.

"Trust me, he's dead," replied Kian, adjusting his grip on Ana.

"Well there's a BODY in my room!" I demanded, foreseeing the police asking many questions.

"I'll take care of it later. If we stay here, the body count will definitely be higher," said Kian, walking out towards the backdoor in the kitchen with Ana. He turned to me, "Eila. It's time to go. NOW. I'll call Raef when we're in the car."

I glanced up the staircase to my room one last time and quickly followed Kian out through the kitchen, grabbing the book of my past family as I left. As we climbed into the Jeep, the sun continued its descent over the curve of Earth, pulling with it the blanket of night.

Kian carefully handed Ana off to MJ, who climbed in the back with her. Her body lay motionless on the leather seat, her head in MJ's lap. He stroked her blonde hair to let her know he was near, but whether she understood or not, was beyond our knowledge.

Driving along the roads to the dock, I watched the cheap cottages whiz past my window. It was the same landscape I had watched float past MJ's car when he drove me to school that first, fateful day. The day I met Raef, who had come to school posing as a student to find me. To protect me for the sake of a grandmother I had never known.

Why had Elizabeth met Rysse in the town square? Why did she even let him get close enough to grab her? Even worse, it appeared as though she didn't fight back in my dreams when he grabbed her, instead allowing a white fire to encompass them both, ending their lives. Was that planned? Did she intend to die or was it a horrible accident? The questions were maddening, as if we were navigating a burning house, blindfolded.

But something was wrong with the way she died. Something we were missing. We needed the diary desperately and I gripped the photo book in my lap tightly, watching Kian drive. The hard lines of his face unsettled me as did the memory of him killing the seventeen-year-old in my room.

Even worse, I had felt my own need to murder the boy flow inside my veins and, had I been more adept at my power, I would've killed him without remorse. I knew there was a violence that waited silently inside me, marked only by a brand on my back, and I was terrified. Was it possible I was worse than the Mortis?

I glanced at Kian who was on the phone with Raef and while I could only hear one side of the conversation, it was decidedly heated. From what I could gather, we were going to head to Boston and meet up with Raef. He had followed a lead to the city and may finally have located some useful information relating to the buyer.

Kian quickly dialed the dock, asking that the *Cerberus* be readied to leave ASAP. He ended the call and looked in the rear view mirror. "MJ? Does Ana have her phone on her?" asked Kian.

"Not sure. Hang on," said MJ and he reached in her pant pockets searching for her mobile phone. A few seconds passed, then he held up Ana's lime green phone. "Bingo!"

"Check for Dalca's cell number. We need to let her know what's going on. She could be in danger as well," said Kian, turning down North Street. We were only a couple miles from the docks now. The sun was hidden behind the trees, falling fast.

"Damn. The phone is cracked," said MJ. "I can't get it to turn on. It must have been crushed when she fell."

Kian looked at MJ in the rearview mirror, "Do you have her number?"

"No man. Only Ana did."

Kian glanced at her still profile and his jaw was set in a hard line. "It's alright. We'll deal with it later."

As we swung around the last brick building on North Street, the *Cerberus* came into view, lit up and elegant in its slip. I could see workers walking along the wooden dock beside her, untying thick white ropes and tossing them onboard. I looked back at Ana who was still unconscious. I realized we were going to have to carry her past the workers. "What are we going to say about her?" I asked, worried.

"We'll just say she drank too much and we're getting her back to her family," he said, pulling my Jeep into the parking spot next to the yacht. I was about to protest, but he was already out of the car and reaching carefully for the girl he loved last summer.

Kian carried her to the *Cerberus* and climbed quickly onboard. I followed, watching the quizzical looks of two dockworkers. I gestured to Ana and just said, "drunk," with a weak smile. I wasn't sure if they bought it, but they continued working.

MJ hurried around the main deck, making sure we were free from the dock. The last streak of sunlight was causing the water to glow like fading embers in a fire. Certain we were no longer tied, MJ headed up to the top-most fly deck where there was a full, second wheelhouse. I heard the engine roar to life.

I looked through the glass doors to the parlor and saw Kian gently laying Ana on one of the black couches. He pulled a luxurious red throw blanket off a nearby chair and draped it over her.

"Eila? Get in here!" demanded Kian as the yacht shifted slightly under my feet, pulling free of its slip. I wobbled for an instant, then pulled open the glass door and entered the parlor.

The view of boats slipping past us surrounded the room's view. I looked down at Ana. "How long will she be out?" I asked.

"Probably an hour or two," said Kian, laying her hands gently over the blanket. He walked to the mahogany bar and pulled open a mirror-smooth black fridge. Inside were stacks of blood in plastic bags. A stack of hypodermic needles was in a glass case beside the bags. *Red Bull*, I thought with a nauseating twist.

He grabbed one bag and ripped the little red tip off the top. He started drinking it, nearly chugging it down without pausing. My stomach turned as he finished the bag within seconds, tossing the empty bag in a nearby sink. He leaned on the counter and drew a long, deep breath then glanced out the window. He almost looked like he was going to be sick. Just thinking about what he had guzzled made my stomach sympathetic as well.

We started to exit the harbor, heading to open water. He leaned forward and reached out to the wall, pushing a button that was attached to a small, silver speaker. He seemed suddenly exhausted, as if all the power he had was finally gone from his body. He was already injured when he gave his strength to Ana and I had a strong suspicion he had pushed himself to a near lethal brink when he saved her.

"When we reach the last buoy, open her up. We need to get to Boston," said Kian into the speaker. He released the button and held his side as MJ's voice came back confirming the plan.

Slowly he began unbuttoning his shirt and sliding it off, but the deep gash in his side slowed him down. I walked over to him to help, but he held up his hand to signal me to stop.

"I know. Don't touch the blood. I got it. Let me help you," I said. Carefully I grabbed his shirt and pulled it down off of him. The gash where he had been stabbed was an angry, dark slice on a god-like physique. "I thought you said that will heal fast," I said, alarmed.

"Well, it ain't bleeding anymore, is it?" snapped Kian, a little short. I just looked at him. "Sorry," he said, "Normally it would, but I shared some of my ability with Ana. The blood we have here will reset my system and speed up the healing once again. Still hurts like hell, though. I'll be fine by the time we reach Boston."

"Thank you. You saved my life," I said, reaching out and taking his hand.

Kian looked uneasy with the praise and surprised at my touch. He cleared his throat. "You shouldn't be thanking me," he said, releasing my hand. "I should never have left. I was just frustrated with Ana. I don't want her to be part of this – it's too damn dangerous," he said, looking over to her on the couch. "Now look at her. Two or three minutes later and both of you would've been dead. And that *is* my fault." He shook his head.

"Look," I reasoned, trying to get in his line of sight. "That kid got in against all known rules, right? I mean, how would we have ever known the house was broken?"

"Breached," corrected Kian.

"Right. Breached. How were we supposed to know that? It's Elizabeth's house for crying out loud!"

"It's *your house* Eila. Don't forget that," said Kian. "You should expect more of me. Elizabeth would." I looked at him, as if I truly saw him for the first time. He was angry with himself, but he shouldn't take the full burden of responsibility. We had all been too foolish with our assumptions.

"You made sure Ana and I would live to see another day, and I get to thank you for that." I looked him in the eye, "We are alive because you risked your own life for us. Don't forget that, because I won't."

Kian looked at me, then Ana. "You know I can't help you like I did for Ana, right? It won't work for you. Linking life-forces like that would be fatal for you and probably for us. Raef and I may be immune to your power, but your life force would most likely kill us." In reality, it had not occurred to me that they couldn't heal me, only hurt me. I swallowed and nodded.

"Guarding you means not allowing these mistakes to occur. If you are gravely injured, only a hospital and real doctor can possibly help you. Understand?"

I looked out the window. I knew he was right.

From beneath our feet I could hear the engine growl deeper and the angle of the floor slanted up slightly as the bow of the boat rose from the water. I steadied myself slightly on the edge of the counter, listening to the engine. The tension needed release so I broke the silence. "Boston?" I asked.

Kian nodded, "It makes more sense to head to Boston and pick up Raef than hang around here, where we obviously have uninvited visitors. The boat is safe."

"I've heard that before," I muttered, unconvinced. "You said Raef had found something?"

"He said he had followed a lead to Boston. That he had a possible name," said Kian, reaching into the fridge for another, uh, drink. This time, however, he loaded several of the hypodermics with blood from a bag and systematically injected himself on the upper arm. I looked away so I wouldn't puke.

When he finished tossing the last syringe into the sink, he spoke again, "To be honest, most of the conversation with Raef was about me being a screw-up. He was livid that you had been in danger."

I didn't know how to respond to that, but secretly I was pleased that Raef was so upset. It was another sign that I was more than just someone to guard.

Kian reached into one of the cabinets and pulled out a small, black flashlight. He stepped close to me. "Look at me," he instructed, flicking on the flashlight. He tested the light strength by shining it in his palm.

"What are you doing?"

"Checking your eyes to make sure you don't have a concussion. You may be Lunaterra but you are still very breakable." He shone the light in and out of each of my eyes and had me follow his finger as he moved it in and out of my peripheral vision. He then placed the flashlight down on the counter and felt my head, his hands slowly traveling over my skull to the back of my neck. His touch caused every inch of my skin he grazed to tingle.

"You got a good bump on the back of your head, but no signs of a concussion. Your head must be like a rock," said Kian.

"Yeah, that's what Mae says." My heart clenched thinking of her.

"You were off-balance at the house. Are you still dizzy?"

"No. I'm good." For the most part anyway. Processing what went down was a whole other issue.

Kian stretched his neck and looked down at his side. Sure enough, the wound had grown smaller. "Impressive," I said, nodding to his rib, but he was already walking over to Ana.

He reached down and gently swept a blonde hair from her face. He sat down next to her on the couch and picked up her wrist, turning it over in his hand so he could feel her pulse. He sat there for a minute, watching her face and feeling the reassuring thrum of her heart through her veins. Finally he rested her hand back on her chest and pulled her blanket higher.

He looked over to me, "Can you watch her while I go grab some clean clothes?"

"Of course," I said walking over to the chair next to Ana and sitting down.

Kian looked at her one more time and then stood. Before he could walk away, I spoke up, "She is going to forgive you, you know."

He turned to me and just gave a weak, unconvinced smile. He then gathered up the contents of the sink and walked out of the parlor. I could hear him descend the stairs to the floor below.

The splash of the waves combined with the hum of the engine was like its own lullaby. The adrenaline that had flooded my body was now long gone, replaced with a body-soaking fatigue. I watched Ana, but as I did, my eyes got heavier and heavier. I closed my eyes, just to rest for a moment, but sleep came quickly and I nodded off.

I woke with a jolt almost an hour and a half later. My heart was racing as the nightmare of Bridge Boy attacking me all over again faded from my mind's eye. For a moment I forgot where I was.

I looked around the parlor, which was now only lit by a few table lamps. Outside the windows the softly lit decking could be seen, as the ocean beyond was now black. In the distance I could see the lights of Boston.

MJ walked by on the outside deck. He seemed to be organizing the ropes that had tied us to the docks in Barnstable Harbor. I looked over to where Ana was sleeping, but was surprised to see the couch empty. I stood up, looking around the room.

MJ must have seen me move and opened the back glass door. "You're awake," he said, smiling.

"Uh, yeah. But where's Ana?" I asked, concerned.

"She's in the galley, eating. I made some chicken parm for us. Go help yourself. You must be starving."

I was, in fact, famished. I glanced back out the window, "Where are we?"

"We just passed Hull and are coming into Quincy Bay. We're going to dock at the marina in about twenty minutes." I nodded and got to my feet. "How are you feeling?" he asked.

"Fine," I said plainly. It was the truth, to a point. I couldn't figure out whether I was fine or numb. I really didn't want to think about any of it. Reflecting on my current state of wellbeing meant reflecting on the past few hours. I had no desire to think about it. I thumbed toward the stairs behind me. "I'm going to go indulge in your culinary skills and check on Ana." MJ just nodded and went back to whatever sea-faring activity he had been engaged in.

I walked down the stairs to the galley, just as I had that evening after riding with Raef on the back of his bike. That evening seemed decades ago.

I took a deep breath, controlling the chaotic emotions that were trying to surface. Rage. Pain. Fear. Loss. I stopped at the bottom of the stairs, before I rounded the corner into the galley. I could smell the food and hear the clink of a fork against a plate. I tightened my grip on the railing until my palm burned. The distraction allowed me to gain control of myself. "*Confidence jeans,*" I whispered as I pushed myself around the corner.

Ana looked up from the table where she was sitting. She was still wrapped in the red blanket Kian had covered her in and she looked as though she had just recovered from the flu. A small plate of MJ's creation was in front of her. It actually did look excellent, but she was only taking tiny bites. She looked up at me.

"Hey. You're conscious," I said, walking over to her and sitting up on one of the stools near the counter. "How are you feeling?"

"Like I got run over by Kian's 'Vette. Twice." She tried a small smile. She did look like she went a few rounds with a hangover.

"MJ said we'll be docking soon. Maybe twenty minutes."

"Thank goodness. I'm all done with the rocking motion," said Ana, though the *Cerberus* seemed to barely feel the waves. She tapped her fork on her plate, "You should have some of this. It's pretty good."

I got up and made myself a plate of the chicken parm, then returned to my stool.

"Did you hear that Raef may have found the buyer?" I asked. She shook her head no. "I guess he followed a lead up to Boston. That is why we're headed up there. To pick him up," I said. The thought of Raef filled me with fuzzy warmth. "Kian didn't tell you when you woke up?"

"I haven't seen Kian. MJ brought me down here. He said Kian is piloting the boat due to a difficult navigation. I think it's BS. He's just avoiding me," said Ana.

"Are you . . . angry with him?" I asked, trying to figure out her state of mind.

"Honestly, I don't know what to think anymore. I'm grateful he helped me even though I don't remember it, but at the same time it makes me believe all the more he could've saved my Dad. I don't know. Is it even okay to forgive him?"

"I don't think it dishonors your father to forgive him. If Kian was just a man, you would never have blamed him, right?"

She looked at me and I knew she understood what I was saying. That it made sense to her, but was still hard to accept. "Would you forgive Raef if he let Mae die?" she asked.

I had no solid answer, "I'm not sure, but I would hope I could understand his decision and from there, either forgive him or not."

We sat in silence for a while, Ana lost in her own mind, simply playing with her food. I ate slowly as my stomach was still off, whether from stress or injury I wasn't sure. Soon I heard men's voices as the boat's engine slowed, then stopped. We must have docked.

Within minutes I heard the glass door to the parlor open and the sound of Kian and Raef arguing. Raef must have been waiting for the boat. Their argument was brief and I heard footsteps come down the stairs quickly. As Raef appeared around the corner, a wave of relief washed over me.

He stopped as soon as he entered the galley. "You two okay?" he asked, his eyes trailing over every inch of my body.

"We're okay," I said, "Ana took the worst of it." I nodded toward my friend.

"I'll be fine," said Ana and I realized that 'fine' could mean a variety of things. Between Ana and I, I could see it becoming our go-to word with about ten levels of "fine."

She slowly got up, still bruised and stiff. I got to my feet as well, thinking she needed help, but she put up her hand to stop me.

"I'm going to take a hot shower. Any chance you grabbed us clothes before you vacated the house?" she asked, looking at me while leaning on the table. She was still weak.

"I didn't. I'm sorry."

She waved it off, "Don't stress, I'll just steal a t-shirt from Kian."

Raef cleared his throat, glancing at her almost sideways, "Your clothes from last summer are still in Kian's room."

"He kept my stuff?" she asked, clearly floored. Raef nodded.

"Uh, well, that works," she said, still looking a bit shocked. "Eila,

I may have some brand new, um, intimates with tags still on them. And some clothes you can use, it seems."

"Sounds good to me," I said, slightly wigged out that we were discussing undies in front of Raef. Plus, Kian kept her clothes, which sort of screamed funky fetish.

Ana headed slowly down the hall toward the lure of a hot shower. As she disappeared into the bathroom Raef turned to me, concern and relief radiating from him.

"Raef. I'm okay," I said, trying to soothe his clearly stressed mental-state and hold myself together. "Kian said I don't have a concussion. Really, I'm okay."

I tried to sound strong but my courage was fraying. I nearly died. So did Ana. Reality tried to rush into me, like a bitter gust of wind. Raef saw it in my face and crossed the galley, pulling me into his arms in a powerful embrace. It was as if he was trying to absorb my body into his and I would've willingly climbed inside him to hide. Holding me as if he'd never let me go again, he rested his cheek on my head.

"Thank God you're safe," he breathed into my cheek. He brought his face in front of mine, sweeping my hair back with his strong hands. "I am so sorry you were in danger! Again!" he swore under his breath, clearly angry with himself. "Saints, Eila - I have made so many mistakes . . ."

"It's not your fault," I whispered as my arms reached around him, and I pulled his chest to my face. I rubbed my forehead against his soft shirt and his warmth radiated through the fabric, heating my entire body.

Guilt clawed inside me.

I should've never come to Cape Cod. The chaos we were in was my fault. "This is my doing. I should've never come here in the first place."

Raef stilled and his breath hitched as his arms tightened around me. "Don't you dare think that. Ever. I should be able to protect you better than I am. A Mortis nearly killed you! If he . . . I can't . . ," I could feel his body coiled tight with fury, no doubt trying to imagine what went down in my bedroom. "I should have been there. I should have killed him."

"You're here now," I said and his hand drew up my back to the nape of my neck, his face dipping to my collarbone as his breath teased my skin. The sensation lit a trail of fire that ran from my neck all the way down my back. I felt light headed as my body buzzed in response to his hands. Though my reaction could've been my own genetic warning system, I was fairly certain it had more to do with a magnetic need demanded by my body. I wanted him closer, tighter. I wanted the lines between us to blend into one.

I drew a deep breath to speak, but the sound of someone coming down the stairs made Raef ease his embrace slightly so we could see who was there. He didn't release me however, as MJ rounded the corner.

He stopped short when he saw us. "Oh! Sorry," he blurted, obviously feeling as though he tripped into an intimate moment. "I was just going to grab a bite, but I can come back."

Raef finally let go of me and I was instantly cold. I let my hand drift down his arm and remain in his fingers for a moment before letting go, "No, no. It's cool MJ. We were just talking."

"You, uh, sure?" he said, looking from me to Raef.

Raef nodded in agreement, "Absolutely."

I heard more footsteps on the stairs and Kian appeared. He looked toward me, "Feeling okay?" I nodded as he looked around the galley, "Where's Ana?"

"Taking a shower," said Raef.

"Good . . . I'm glad she is feeling up to it. When she gets out you can tell us what you learned. That way, we're all on the same page," said Kian, almost casually. If he was stressing from Ana cheating death, he was covering it well. Real well.

"I will," replied Raef. "And Kian, thank you. You too MJ," he said, looking to each of them. MJ was already making his plate of dinner. He just waved.

"That's the job, *brother*," said Kian as he walked down the hall to his bedroom. I just smiled because I knew his selfish persona was just a front. He cared, especially for Ana. I saw it when he saved her. In fact, I knew he loved her. Why else would anyone keep an ex's clothes, except to hope to someday have that person back. Perhaps her clothes were a reminder of what he used to have with her. Perhaps a way to keep her close. Well . . . unless he really did have some twisted obsession with underwear. Ew.

MJ was sitting at the corner table enjoying his meal. He looked up at Raef between bites, "Dying to hear what you found out."

"Don't get too excited. It isn't that much. Certainly not worth risking lives over," said Raef, looking at me.

I leaned back against the counter, taking a deep breath. "If it's any consolation, I don't think he was there to kill me," I said, trying to squelch the vision of my attacker in my room. MJ and Raef looked at me, suspicion on their faces.

"Why do you say that?" asked Raef.

"Because he said that his job was to collect me and the diary, though he did say he *wished* he could kill me. He said he fantasized about it." A little shiver crawled through me at the memory of his black eyes so close to mine. Raef and MJ looked confused.

MJ pushed his plate away, his appetite no longer so demanding and looked to Raef. "Why wouldn't he just kill her? And why the diary?" he asked, voicing the million-dollar questions. The idea that I wasn't just marked to die as quickly as possible seemed irrational.

Raef shook his head. "I have no idea. It makes no sense to leave Eila alive when they had a chance to . . . ," trailed Raef, unable to physically speak of my potential demise.

Something strange was going on – possibly more twisted than being hunted by immortal soul-thieves who were just out to murder me. Well, okay – maybe not more crazy than the Mortis, but definitely on the same level.

I looked at my two guards, "We need to find that diary. Especially since Bridge Boy wanted it. He was pissed that I didn't have it."

"The diary is critical. Dalca was right about that," said Raef, but then glancing to me with a curious look on his face, "Bridge Boy?"

The door to the bathroom opened and wisps of steam curled out the door. Ana stepped out with a towel wrapped around her lean frame. She didn't look at us, but instead crossed the hall to Kian's room, no doubt to unearth her last-year's clothing.

I was about to tell her Kian was in there, but she shut the door before I could speak. Raef and MJ were still lost in thought and seemed to miss the fact that Ana was in Kian's room with him. They began discussing where in the house the diary might be and if there was a way to get back in safely.

I, however, wasn't really listening. Instead, I was watching the door to Kian's room, expecting it to burst open any second and Kian being kicked out. Instead, all remained quiet from his room.

A few minutes passed and Ana finally emerged in a white robe with Kian behind her. The back of the robe had slipped off Ana's slim shoulder and Kian carefully lifted it back into place. It was such a natural moment between the two of them. Perhaps she had finally forgiven him. Perhaps they had come to peace.

Kian interrupted MJ and Raef as he and Ana reached the galley. "Alright. Let's hear it. What did you find out?" he said, looking to his un-brother.

"Come on up to the parlor. I'll show you what I brought," said Raef, looping a warm hand behind my back as if to guide me. The electricity we shared followed the path of his hand around my hip.

We all headed up the stairs and sat down in various chairs in the parlor. Raef picked up some papers that had been placed beside the photo book I had brought from the house. He gestured to the book, "What's that?"

"Just some old photos from the house. I grabbed it in case I never get to go home again." No one replied. The truth was, they didn't know whether 408 would ever be my haven again. What was I going to do if I couldn't go back? What would I tell Mae? A headache played behind my eyes, and I rubbed my temple.

Raef cleared his throat, "Okay, so I had gone to the registry but they said that all paperwork related to any auctions, including 408, were in Boston, so I headed up here. According to these papers, the house was originally cared for in several trusts since the 1800's, starting right after Elizabeth's death. Apparently the home was never lived in after Elizabeth."

"That's strange," MJ said, leaning back in his chair. "What's the point of not living in it or making a buck on it?"

"That's what I thought," said Raef. "The last trust was continuously funded until fifteen years ago. Right after Eila's parents died. After that, the money that was in the account never grew, it just whittled away on house expenses until this spring when the money finally ran out and the house went up for auction. There are no records of a buyer, which is really strange. Oh, and that auctioneer that called you? Ed Talbot? I can't find him anywhere."

I narrowed my eyes as I looked at Raef. "So the man who handled the transaction for my house is missing *and* someone stopped funding the care of the home when my parents died? Is that just a coincidence with the timing?" I asked, though I knew it was rhetorical.

Kian gave a half-laugh. "I'm going to go out on a limb and say that it probably wasn't," he said. "I also think Mr. Talbot probably met an untimely end thanks to someone who needed him gone."

This was a nightmare.

A true, living, hellish nightmare.

MJ and Kian had dumped the body of my first attacker heck-knows-where and there was currently a dead kid in my bedroom at home. Poor Mr. Talbot and Ms. Cooper must have also been caught in whatever plot was going down and probably both ended up dead. And last night we almost added Ana to the body count. With the eight swimmers either declared missing or drowned since I accepted the house, the mortality rate around me was sky high.

It had to stop. No one else was going to die for me.

"I agree completely," Raef was saying " . . . and I found the name of the company that last held the trust. It's called North Star Historic Estates and, when I called them, they said that the past manager of 408 is the president of North Star. His name is Christian Raines," said Raef, handing me the papers. I was still shaken by how many people had died because of me, but I managed to not drop the sheets all over the floor. "Mr. Raines will be in Newport tomorrow hosting the annual Fire and

Ice Ball at The Breakers."

"Fire and Ice Ball?" I asked, trying to drag myself back into our current situation, as much as it sucked.

"It's North Star's premier fundraiser for historic homes, and at five thousand a plate, it must rake in a fortune."

"I'm sorry - did you say FIVE THOUSAND DOLLARS? Per person?" MJ asked, stunned. "Seriously? That's crazy!"

Ana shifted forward in her seat suddenly, "Hold on a second. Did you say Christian Raines?"

"Yes. Why?" asked Raef, glancing to the tiny blonde wrapped in a thick robe.

Ana looked over at Kian who was sitting across from her, "You got your phone? I need to look something up."

Kian fished it out of his shirt pocket. "Ana, what's going on?" he asked, handing the phone to her. She touched the screen of the phone rapidly, typing something.

"HA! I knew it. Christian Raines was Newport's most eligible bachelor three years running. His Fire and Ice Ball is the hottest ticket on the east coast. Here - Look," she handed the phone to me.

The man looking back at me from the small screen was in his late 20's and defined the word handsome. He had a mop of wavy, somewhat wild mahogany hair with streaks of gold. Combined with his deep auburn eyes, angular nose and strong, dimpled chin, he was the physical embodiment of the athletic aristocrat.

He was a flipping Kennedy if they bred with Roman gladiators.

Something about his stunning face however, tickled my memory. "He looks familiar," I said slowly, not taking my eyes off the phone's screen.

"You probably saw him in People Magazine," offered Ana.

"No. That's not it," I said, finally handing the phone to Raef and picking the photo book off the table. I started flipping through the book.

Raef was studying the picture on the phone as well. "She's right. He does look familiar," he said, surprise in his own voice.

Intrigued, Kian got up and took the phone from Raef. MJ, now curious, walked over to look at the picture as well. "I think I know this guy as well," said Kian.

Flipping through my photo book I finally found the page I was searching for. I carried the book over to them. "Look!" I said, pointing to a picture from the mid 1800's of Elizabeth dressed in a formal gown, standing by the staircase in my home. Behind her, plain as day, was Christian Raines.

Ana's mouth dropped open slightly as she gasped, "No way! He's a Mortis?"

M.J. crossed his arms and shook his head in exaggerated disgust, "I think Christian may be cheating at the Most Eligible Bachelor competition. Mortis have an unfair advantage in the looks department."

He glanced at Kian, who was smiling proudly. MJ smiled even wider, "Thank goodness such an advantage doesn't nearly make up for their pea-sized brains, however."

Kian just shook his head and looked away at the ceiling, clearly biting his tongue at a snappy comeback.

I poked the book hard to get the two males back on target, "GUYS! Pay attention! This guy, Raines, is a Mortis who *knew* Elizabeth and *maintained* the house," I said. "We absolutely need to talk to him."

Kian suddenly snapped his fingers. "That's how I recognize him. From Elizabeth's parties," he exclaimed. "And you're absolutely right. We need to talk to him, but to be on the safe side, we're going to need to catch him when his guard is down. Let's not forewarn him of our coming just in case he's not the friendly sort."

Raef stepped closer to me, "I guess it's a good thing I bought these, though at the time I didn't think Mr. Raines would be immortal." He pulled five red and white velvet invitations out of an envelope on the table.

MJ picked one up. "These are tickets to the ball! We're going to crash this guy's own million-dollar fundraiser?"

Kian put his hands in his pockets. He looked at Raef and smiled, "This is perfect. Among the crowds and all the meet-and-greet, he won't be paying attention to all the invitees. We can slip in unnoticed."

Ana shook her head, unconvinced. "Won't he recognize you and Raef?"

"I haven't seen this guy in more than 160 years. Somehow I doubt he'll remember us. And as for you three, he has no idea who you are."

I looked at Ana. "Won't he sense Kian and Raef are Mortis?" I asked, unsure if this plan was the smartest route to take.

"No," said Ana, clearly confident. "Mortis can't sense one another, same as humans can't. I'm sure the boy from the bridge was fairly shocked to find Kian in your house." The room was quiet and seemed to be looking to me for direction.

"Well, I'm willing to give this a shot," I said, drawing a deep breath. "We need some tactical advantage, right? This Raines guy may be able to give us some. And if he is more foe than friend, I doubt he will make a scene in front of hundreds of deep-pocketed patrons."

Ana crossed her arms, "The ball is tomorrow night. Call me a pessimist, but *what* are we supposed to wear? I'm assuming sweats are not up to par at a black tie event at The Breakers."

"What's the Breakers?" I whispered to Raef.

"Big mansion in Newport. Owned by the Vanderbilts back in the day," he quietly responded.

"Um, HELLO? What are we going to do about apparel?" demanded Ana.

Raef looked at Kian, who seemed to know what he was thinking. "No way. I'm not calling her," said Kian firmly.

"She'd have some top notch stuff and she's right in Chinatown," encouraged Raef.

Kian's eyes grew wide, "She is a NUT job!"

"No she's not. You just don't want to be stuck in a room with her!" Raef had a devious smile across his face.

"Who are we talking about?" I asked.

"About a decade ago, Kian was seeing a couture clothing designer. Gorgeous stuff. She made him a couple of suits to rival Armani," said Raef, glancing at the tall, irritated soul thief who appeared ready to throttle him. "According to Kian, she got kind of possessive though, after a while."

"KIND OF?" demanded Kian. "I told you she was a lunatic!"

"Anyway, like I was saying, according to Kian, she got a bit too possessive and he broke it off. In return she nearly ripped his arms off. All's fair in love and war among our kind." Raef was thoroughly enjoying Kian's silent fuming.

"She's one of you?" I asked, now worried. "Isn't she going to want to "off me" since I'm Lunaterra and all?"

"Kian can go pick some things up from her. We won't be taking you anywhere near her,'" said Raef.

Kian glared at his un-brother.

"Oh, come on," prodded Raef. "You know that on short notice, she would be ideal. Tell her we'll bring her a case of her favorite vintage.

I have some in the cooler."

"She drinks wine?" Ana asked.

"O-negative," said Raef, referring to a rare human blood type. I stuck out my tongue, disgusted.

"She *is* a bit of a lush," replied Kian, thinking. Everyone was looking at him. "FINE. I'll call her," he muttered angrily as he left the parlor and walked outside onto the deck with his phone. He looked back in at the four of us and Raef gave him a thumbs-up. Kian returned the gesture with a different finger.

"Was she really a stalker?" asked MJ.

"Probably a complete sociopath," said Raef, laughing. Ana and I joined him.

MJ looked at the three of us laughing, "Hey, you know what is going to make my day?"

"What?" I asked, finally calming myself.

"The sight of you and Ana finally wearing something other than jeans and t-shirts."

Ana and I groaned.

It took Kian almost twenty minutes to convince his personal stalker, Collette, to dress us for the coming ball. Considering that the event was less than 24 hours away, I was surprised to learn she was placated with the owner's papers to Kian's Corvette and not one of his appendages. I'd have thought being allowed to keep one's arms would've been a plus, but Kian seemed highly displeased with the loss of his favorite automobile.

Collette, Kian explained, was almost 120 years old and originally from Paris. She studied under great designers like Paul Poiret, Coco Chanel and numerous others, but she currently favored Versace-esque designs. I was sure they had no clue she was an immortal when she was a student, although with THAT haute crowd, one never was sure they were all human to begin with.

"Is this really necessary?" asked Ana as she wrote our sizes on a piece of paper for Kian to take to Collette. Ana was obviously not thrilled with the idea of Kian having to face a former lover. "Can't we just grab something at a department store?"

Raef shook his head, "At five thousand dollars a ticket, no one there will wear anything less than runway designs. If we want to blend, we need to look like we belong."

"I'm going to look SICK in a custom tux!" said MJ, enthusiastically. He threw his arm around Ana and reached out with his other arm and pulled me over to him. "And you two are going to look devastating in these foreign things called 'dresses'!" He smiled widely.

"Ha ha," said Ana dryly as she handed the paper to Kian. "But seriously - does he really need to go and meet up with this chick? I'm not sure it's safe."

For a moment, Kian's face flickered with something tender, but he recovered, clearing his throat. "I, um - I'll be fine. I'm to meet her around 2 am at her loft."

"I'll wait up for you," said Ana, diverting her eyes to the floor.

The same tenderness lifted to Kian's face and this time he let it remain as he walked over to us. MJ dropped his arm from her shoulder, moving slightly away. While I knew that MJ wasn't Kian's biggest fan, he also seemed to respect the fact that he and Ana were trying to figure out their relationship. And one couldn't ignore the fact that he saved Ana's life.

"Don't wait up. You need your rest. Your body is still recovering," Kian said softly, mere inches from her.

She finally looked to him. "Wake me then, so I know you are back in one piece."

He smiled. "I will. I promise."

I glanced to Raef. The warmth generated by the two of them was infectious and I felt the heat climb up my back. I swallowed, but the motion made my throat ache. The discomfort triggered the memory of what happened in my bedroom and the urge to take a shower was overwhelming. Raef saw and stepped close to me.

"You okay?" he asked quietly.

I realized my hand was at my throat, rubbing the spot where my attacker had choked me. "I really just want to take a shower . . . and get some sleep," I replied, but I could tell he knew exactly why I needed to get clean. Darkness caressed his eyes for just a moment.

"You can take my bed. I'm going to stay up and keep watch."

I shook my head, refusing. "You need sleep as well. I'll just sleep on the couch."

He shook his head. "Technically I can go days without sleep and be unaffected. You, however, need a solid night's sleep. Take my bed – it's much more comfortable," he said, ending the conversation.

"Thanks." I fidgeted, desperately wanting to climb out of my skin. I headed to the stairs and Ana saw me leaving.

"I left you some clothes in the bathroom!" she called. I waved a thank you to her as I headed down to the lower deck and the lure of a hot shower.

Once in the bathroom, I stripped out of my clothes, happy to be rid of the day that was imprinted on them. I removed my bracelet and put in carefully by the sink. The large rainhead poured a hot stream of water downward in a thousand little drops inside the shower. I stepped through the glass door and let the liquid massage run all over my body, washing the day away.

My neck stung where Bridge Boy had grabbed me, and the sensation brought back the attack clearly in my mind. I closed my eyes tightly, trying to force the violent encounter from my head, but I only saw his face in more detail.

I washed my body and hair and was back out of the shower within minutes. I stepped over to the mirror, which was now completely fogged over, and wiped away the steam with my hand. I looked at myself in the blurred reflection, touching my neck where the killer teen's hand had nearly crushed my throat. There was no outward mark, but I could feel his fingers digging into my neck.

I dried my body and wrapped the towel around me as I looked to the shelf where Ana had left me something to sleep in. I was alarmed to see a black, silky concoction nestled inside. I slowly pulled the pile of smooth material free and it unfurled into a dark, daring nightgown with a long slit up one side and thin shoulder straps.

"Yeah . . . I think not." There was no way I was wearing the slinky outfit.

I found the black pair of underwear she had promised, price tags still attached. I snapped off the tags and stepped into them. Damn well determined NOT to wear the other thing she left me, I decided to borrow a shirt from Raef. I cracked open the door to the bathroom and looked down the hall to make sure I was alone.

With the coast clear, I darted across the hall and into Raef's bedroom. I moved past the round bed to his bureau. I pulled one of the dark mahogany drawers open and was rewarded with a neatly folded selection of high-end, button-down shirts. I selected a simple cream colored one from the top of the stack and shook it open. It reminded me of him and I brought the shirt to my face and breathed deeply.

I could smell his earthy scent on the fabric, a mixture of sand and sea and pine. I slipped into the shirt and it hung down to my mid-thigh, cool and smooth against my skin. I finished buttoning the shirt, leaving the top two undone so they wouldn't rub on my neck and remind me of the teen with a lust for murder in his eyes.

"I take it you didn't like Ana's choice of clothing?" I heard Raef ask from behind me. I spun around, surprised.

"Um . . . no. Not really. Is this okay?" I asked, pulling on the bottom of the shirt, willing it to hang lower.

"Of course," said Raef, walking into the room. "Are you cold? Silk is not exactly warm to sleep in."

"Just a little," I said, wrapping my arms around me. "How long were you standing there?" My face started to flush.

"Not long. I didn't see anything, I promise."

I couldn't tell if he was being 100% honest. He opened the door to his closet and pulled out a robe that looked just like Ana's. He brought it over to me and held it open.

"Thanks," I said as I slid it on, tying it in the front. We stood there, looking at each other for a moment.

Raef cleared his throat. "Try to get some sleep. If you need anything, I'll be on deck." He turned to leave, but I reached out and caught his arm.

"Thank you," I said.

"It's just a shirt, Eila," said Raef, but in his eyes I could tell he knew that's not what I meant. He reached out and tucked a lock of my hair behind my ear and let his fingers trail down the dark strand. Every time he touched me, heat followed his fingers. Since the night of the bonfire, his touch had intensified, creating an electric flame that scalded . . . but in a good way.

In an addictive, tempting way.

"Will you be okay in here?" he asked, concerned. I said yes, but he hesitated, trying to read the truth in my words. Finally he wished me goodnight and left me alone in his room.

I stood there, the glow of a single lamp throwing soft shadows around the room. I started pulling back the covers, layer after layer of luxuriant blankets and sheets in various tones of red, black and silver. I pulled a few of the pillows from the head of the bed and stacked them on the floor, dropping my robe onto a chair nearby. I flicked off the lamp and crawled into bed. The room was dark, except for the light from a neighboring yacht casting a yellow hue through the porthole window near the bureau.

As exhausted as I was, however, sleep brought with it nightmares. I'd drift off, but be jarred awake by various scenes of Bridge Boy chasing me, throwing me into a wall and at one point, crushing my neck.

By midnight, I finally gave up on sleep, pulled on the robe Raef had given me, and headed out into the hallway. The only lights in the lower deck were the small blue ones illuminating the hallway and a few under-cabinet lights in the galley.

The door to Kian's room was cracked open and I peeked in. Ana was asleep in his bed, tucked in with numerous pillows and blankets. Kian, however, was nowhere to be seen. I wondered if he had left to meet Collette and I prayed he'd be okay.

I continued down the hallway and climbed the stairs to the parlor. MJ was stretched out on one of the couches, snoring. He was in just his boxers and a thick burgundy blanket was twisted haphazardly over his body. I smiled. It was exactly how I would expect him to look, even in his sleep.

The parlor, like the lower deck, was dark, with just a few small running lights. Through the windows, the Boston skyline glowed beautifully, but the boats beside us had now gone dark. The warm deck lights of the *Cerberus* were still on and threw a gentle, golden aura onto the outer deck and the large, circular lounge. It looked inviting and I hoped the fresh air would clear my head.

I carefully pulled the glass door open so I wouldn't wake MJ and stepped out onto the aft deck. I walked around the side of the boat to the bow, my feet icy on the teak decking.

I sat down on the lounge and pulled my toes under me, wrapping the robe around me tightly. The cold October air created a crystal night sky, filled with stars and a spectacular white moon. I let the chilly air wrap around my face and breathed in the salty breeze.

I was wondering where Raef was, when from around the opposite side of the boat he appeared, the old photo book tucked under one arm. He placed the book on a table opposite from me and sat down on my lounge, turning so he could face me.

"Not tired?" he asked.

"Tired yes. Ability to sleep? No." I pulled the robe tighter against the cold.

Raef reached over the ottoman to a creamy throw and then cast the blanket around my back and pulled the edges closely together in front of me. I took hold of the velvet softness, holding it tightly to me.

"Thank you. I didn't realize it was so cold out tonight," I said, my words drifting into the darkness like little slivers of smoke.

"It's the air coming down from Canada. They already have snow up north," said Raef, looking out over the harbor.

The vista was so beautiful. It reminded me of the night on the beach, before it went so terribly wrong. I embraced the memory of sitting on that ratty old red blanket and looking out over Cape Cod Bay.

That night, like now, had a moon that could encompass the sky and threw a path on the water like a bridge of light to heaven. I remembered how he handed me my bracelet. I could still feel his touch on my skin as he slid it onto my wrist and tightened the ball to lock it in place. I knew that moment would stay with me all my life, even if my life turned out to be brief.

I ran my hand over my wrist and realized I had left the bracelet in the bathroom when I had showered. My wrist looked so plain without it, as if I were missing a piece of myself.

"What's wrong?" asked Raef, quietly.

"Nothing," I whispered as I looked up from my hand.

He reached out, carefully, and slowly swept his thumb over my cheek, taking with it a tear I didn't even realize was there. I reached up to his hand on my cheek and covered it with my own. "I'm just remembering a better night," I said, trying to smile.

"Tell me. Let me in on what you're thinking."

"I was remembering the night on the beach when you gave me my bracelet." He nodded, taking his hand away from my face and reaching for my wrist, touching the spot where it normally resided.

"I forgot it in the bathroom," I confessed, guilt and sadness starting to overtake me, not just about the bracelet, but about my whole existence here. How thoroughly I had ruined all of their lives, dragged into my nightmare and unable to escape. "I'm sorry," I said, my mouth trembling.

"It's okay," he whispered.

"I'm so sorry, for everything," I cried, the words choking me. He took my face in his hands and I tried to look away, tears trailing down my cheeks. I tried in vain to pull myself together, but I couldn't.

"Look at me," instructed Raef gently and I looked up to his beautiful eyes, now darker in the nightfall.

"This is not your fault. None of this is your fault. You're a pawn in a war that is centuries old. It's a pointless hatred that has been passed down for generations. Don't apologize. This is not your fault," he said, quietly stroking the side of my face.

I looked at him, wiping the tears from my face. My wet cheeks stung in the cold, night air. "But it *is* ultimately my fault. Had I never returned, you and Kian would've been able to carry on as you always had. And Ana and MJ would've never been diverted into a future that is no longer theirs. It *IS* my fault," I said drawing a deep breath of icy oxygen. The cold in my lungs helped me regain control of my emotions.

Raef studied me for a moment and sighed, "While your appearance did in fact change our lives, I wouldn't necessarily say it was for the worse." I looked at him, irritated disbelief on my face.

He grabbed my hand. "No. Listen to me. Kian and I didn't have any purpose to our lives. We just existed, bouncing from one city to another, rarely knowing anyone. Our families are long since dead and friendships can become liabilities, even among our own kind," said Raef, his hand tightening around mine.

"And Ana had no one either. She was living over a garage, barely getting by and completely lost as to her own abilities. Last summer she met Kian and, for once, found happiness only to have it torn from her again. You brought them back together."

I watched his face and it seemed so trustworthy and safe.

He grasped my other hand. "And MJ. He has the raw talent of his kind that he never fully focused on until you came. You brought out the best in him. You brought out the best in all of us," said Raef. "Yes, you changed our lives, but in ways that we could have never done without you."

I looked down at his hands holding mine and I flexed my fingers in his strong palms, trying to ground myself in the prickly sensation.

"If I do not learn to use my talent, I will have signed everyone's death sentence," I said, quietly. "I want you to know that I release you, all of you, from any debt you feel you owe my grandmother. There's no need for everyone to lose their lives. They're only after me."

Raef opened his mouth to speak, but I held up my hand to silence him. "I need you to make sure Mae is okay if something happens to me. I need you to keep the others safe. Can you promise me that?" I asked.

Raef sat back and looked out over the slowly rolling water. He wrapped himself in a pensive silence as he watched the ocean flex. Finally he turned to me, "I promise to protect those who you love, but I need to also protect the one I cannot live without."

I thought I had heard wrong.

Misunderstood what he had just said.

He leaned closer to me. "Even without Elizabeth, I would've protected you," said Raef, touching my fingers as they lay in my lap. "I knew I would from the moment I saw you. Before I even understood fully who you were, I knew I would follow you, guard you, even if only from a distance."

I drew a deep, unstable breath as he continued, "We are here on our own accord. And for me, I am here because of you and only you, Lunaterra or not. Elizabeth's granddaughter or not. I will always be here for you, Eila. You have entangled yourself in my heart."

I tried to absorb what he had just said and simply began to smile. I smiled so wide, that I brought my hand to my mouth, trying to cover it. He watched me and moved closer until he was right next to me.

His blue eyes looked at mine and he slowly pulled my hand from my mouth, revealing my smile. He gently tucked a dark strand of hair behind my ear, as he always did, and let it tumble down my shoulder. He brought his hands to my face and softly drew one thumb across my mouth, numbing my lips.

A burning heat began weaving up my back and through my arms

and legs. Still cradling my face, he brought his own close to mine and stopped, his nose almost touching my own. My heart was hammering as he carefully, cautiously, brought his lips to mine and softly brushed them along my own, scorching every inch they touched.

It wasn't simply a kiss, but a chance to feel something entirely forbidden. I could feel the muscles in the palms of his hands tense and react as he held my face, the flames within me dancing along every area he touched.

My soul was branded by his kiss, and the electricity that bounced between us was like lightning skating over the water ahead of the darkest storm. I closed my eyes and lost myself in the moment, feeling everything as my body glowed relentlessly in response to him.

It was the most intimate and alive I had ever felt.

He drew his mouth away from mine and I opened my eyes, entirely light headed. He watched me, looking for a sign of rejection, his own breath ragged. Desire took over and I knocked the blanket off my shoulders, reaching up to tangle my fingers in his hair, as I pulled his lips to mine.

He deepened the kiss in response and wrapped his body-breaking arms around my back, pressing my body against his. I didn't feel the cold air sliding past us as heat radiated inside me, gliding across my skin and down my spine. It was entirely possible my heart would give out, for his kiss alone could steal my soul and I would've willingly given it to him.

He pulled back slightly, shaking and breathless. I opened my eyes and his face was covered in beautiful swirls and designs, all framing his now entirely black eyes. He was a flawless combination of beautiful hero and soulless assassin.

For a moment I was frozen, yet fearless, as I allowed myself to study the artwork covering his golden skin. The wind tossed a lock of his hair over one eye and he carefully brushed it away, unsure if he should show me his midnight eyes, which were slowly returning to their twilight blue.

The intensity of the moment finally rose to my face and I smiled as I never had before. Slowly he smiled back at me, realizing, no doubt, that we had crossed a line that could never be redrawn.

Still tightly embraced in his powerful arms, he leaned back into the leather lounge, dragging me with him. The heat slowly fading from my body, I shivered and he reached over and pulled the blanket onto me. Onto us. I snuggled my face into his chest with a glorious understanding that he was mine as I was his.

I rested my head on his shoulder and we watched the moon hover over the water, silently. He stroked the curve of my side with his fingertips, pulling wisps of heat down my hip. I sat there, tucked into him, watching the night, my heart in flames. I no longer feared the darkness or what might lie in wait for me within the shadows.

We stayed that way, in our own peaceful nirvana, until Raef whispered to me that he heard Kian return. I had forgotten entirely about Collette . . . and even tomorrow's ball. I felt Raef's broad shoulders shift slightly under me, the muscles flexing beneath his shirt.

Kian walked around to the bow to where we were, his arms loaded with black garment bags. He just looked at Raef and me and gave a knowing smile. "I'll watch over the boat, if you want," he said to Raef.

"I think I will take you up on the offer," said Raef, pulling me to my feet. "I take it Collette played nice?"

"I'm alive aren't I?" replied Kian, sarcasm coating his words.

I pulled the blanket tighter around me as Raef's hand rested on my hip. As we walked by Kian, I flashed an embarrassed smile, but then remembered Ana. I touched him on the arm and he looked down at me,

"Wake Ana. You promised."

Kian's face looked surprised for a moment, "I will."

Raef reached out and gave Kian's shoulder a brotherly squeeze and then led me around the side of the yacht to the aft deck. I felt completely at peace.

Back at his bedroom door he wished me goodnight but I didn't want him to leave. "Will you sleep with me?" I asked, his hand still in mine.

He looked surprised. "Eila . . . It's not a good idea . . ."

My face flushed. "Just SLEEP. I'm afraid to sleep alone," I said, butterflies going berserk. "I keep thinking about . . ."

Raef quickly understood and his face looked pained, thinking of what I had gone through and how it haunted me. He nodded and we walked into his room.

He watched me as I slipped out of my robe and climbed into his bed, pulling the covers over me. He climbed into bed next to me, his clothes still on, and hauled me to him. I rested my head on his heart as he kept one strong arm around my back. He was studying me intently, his fingers tracing swirls on my electrified back.

"Does that normally happen when you, uh, kiss someone," I asked, reaching up and drawing shapes on his markless face.

"No," he said roughly. His eyes closed in response to my exploring fingers. "When you touch me, it feels so . . . intense. Like ice, but . . . wow." I smiled, proud I had such an effect on him.

"What exactly are they? The marks?" I asked, my fingers trailing down his jaw. He drew a halted breath, which almost sounded like a low growl. As my hands reached his neck, he gently caught my fingers.

"If you keep touching me like that, my will to be noble is going to crumble, especially with you snuggled next to me." His voice rumbled in his chest and I grinned, pulling my hand back to rest over his shirt. "The marks are the language of the Fallen One. It is an ancient language that I do not understand. I actually have no clue what it says."

I played with one of the buttons on his shirt as he watched me. "They normally only appear when one gives or takes life," said Raef, his fingers stilling on my back.

"Then why did they appear when we kissed?" I whispered.

"I'm not sure. You are the first Lunaterra I have kissed." Raef's voice purred deep within his chest. "Maybe it has something to do with Elizabeth when she altered Kian and I."

Something occurred to me and I stopped playing with his shirt. "Do you . . . do you think our feelings, for one another . . . are from Elizabeth?" I swallowed and Raef didn't answer right away. The silence bored into me.

"I don't know," he said quietly as his arm curled around me tighter, like a band of steel.

What if that was all this was? A side effect of Elizabeth's energy release when she died. Were we just a chemical reaction to one another? I didn't want to think about it. I just wanted to live in this moment. Believe that we were soulmates and not because of my grandmother.
I felt Raef breathe slowly in and out and I closed my eyes. Before I knew it, I had fallen into a deep sleep, free, if only briefly, from the monsters that lived in my world and filled my dreams.

The next morning I woke in a soft, silken nest of blankets and pillows. I lay there, feeling the subtle rhythm of the boat as it floated on the water and turned to look at Raef, but he wasn't in bed. I sat up, slowly, remembering the evening before and wondering where he had gone.

Wondering if it had happened at all.

From the galley down the hall I could hear voices and laughter. The smell of coffee and cinnamon floated lightly in the air. I stretched and slipped my feet out from under the covers and pulled on the robe. I could hear Ana laughing loudly.

Ana. Laughing. It seemed too improbable.

I pulled open the door to Raef's room and stepped into the hallway, watching Kian, Ana and MJ, talking and laughing. MJ was telling a story, his hands waving animatedly. There was a delicious spread of food on the table and the flat screen on the wall played the news quietly.

I leaned against the door, the sight of them actually enjoying themselves warming my heart. They were either in complete denial or absolute acceptance of our current situation and were determined to make the best of it.

The door to the bathroom across from me opened and Raef stepped out. He had on a pair of black sweat pants and his hair was wild and damp, a towel still in his hands. His toned chest and arms looked as if they were sculpted by Michelangelo himself.

My pulse accelerated to 9000 when he looked at me and smiled. "Did you sleep well?" he asked, stepping over to me and tossing the towel over his shoulder.

"I did," I said, a silly smile blossoming on my face. I turned slightly so the trio in the galley couldn't see my expression of delight. "Thank you," I said quietly, looking up at him, my heart fluttering.

He stepped even closer and smiled down at me, "My pleasure. Seek my services anytime."

Oh hell. I was in so much trouble.

He pulled my bracelet from his pocket and placed it back on my wrist. "I thought you might want this back," he said securing the beautiful gift once again.

I had forgotten it was still in the bathroom. Typical me.

"I wanted to ask you something," he said, a slight crease to his brow as he finished with the bracelet, adjusting the way it sat against my skin.

"Of course. Shoot," I said, trying to calm the butterflies attempting to flee my body.

"Did you know the mark on your back looks like it matches the symbol on the back of that book you brought with you?"

"Seriously?" I asked, quickly reaching around my back to feel the raised brand, but my robe was too thick to feel anything. "Are you sure?" I never got a very close look at it since it was on my back and I couldn't twist my head like an owl.

"While you were sleeping I got a, uh, long, look at it. You rolled over and I saw it," he said, a light flush adding to his cheeks.

Good grief, was he BLUSHING?

He leaned in closer and my heart spazzed. "I guess I could check again, though," he said quietly, a delicious curve pulling up the corner of his mouth. I had to pry my eyes off his lips before my brain melted and I jumped the boy. I punched him in his rock hard arm, feigning insult, but my acting was pitiful.

Raef laughed lightly. It was the first time I had ever heard him laugh and I loved the sound of it. He reached out to my hip and pulled me closer, his breath grazing my cheek. "At some point we need to find out if those are the same. You just tell me when."

Yup, I was going to DIE.

My words stumbled slightly as his fingers danced over my hip, "You are, um . . . thinking the book might be important?" I asked, proud that I could actually compose a coherent sentence with him so flipping close.

"You're so smart," Raef teased, and urged me down the hall with that wayward hand of his. "Come on. Let's feed you," he said, sliding it around to the small of my back. A fading burn-line followed in the wake of his hand as we walked down the hallway to our friends.

"All right, what was so funny?" I asked as I arrived in the galley.

MJ leaned back in his chair, "I was just telling Kian about how Ana had a princess party when she was eight, but ended up wrestling with one of the girls over a tiara. It was awesome!"

"And the last time I ever dressed up in anything that fancy," said Ana with a wry smile.

"Except for tonight," declared MJ, begging for Ana to slap him. Ana just shook her head, resigned.

Raef and I sat down at the table and I pulled a bagel toward me. Kian was still leaning against the counter. I glanced over to him, "So did Collette ask about our clothing? Why we needed stuff?" I asked pouring some coffee.

"She did, but I was my awesome self and danced around the answer. Thoroughly pissed her off too, though I kept my arms. Apparently she liked my cars better than me. Your gowns are in my room, as well as the tuxes. You should try them on before we ship out."

Even though I was a hardcore, anti-frill girl, I felt like a kid on Christmas and was itching to see my dress. Bummer that the Grim Reaper may be lurking in with the presents.

Last night our plan sounded pretty slick. This morning however, I was certain we were about to reenact the first chapter of THE LUNATIC'S GUIDE TO IDIOT IDEAS. I stopped eating and dropped my hands into my lap, rubbing my lifeline like a nervous tick.

Raef saw my subtle move and wove his fingers into mine under the table, stopping my manic twitch. He slowly traced circles at the base of my thumb with his and my palm warmed like the sun. My fears started to fade ever so slightly as the warmth slid up my arm, teasing my heart.

Kian watched us and shifted slightly on his feet. He knew Raef and I disappeared last night together. The question was: would he keep his mouth shut?

"I also swung by the city morgue," he said to Raef.

"Good idea," Raef replied and looked at my shocked face. "The guy there is helpful to our kind."

"He knows about you?" I asked, surprised.

"He is one," replied Raef.

Kian smiled, "He sells the corpse blood as a side gig. One is always in need of emergency human essence." He looked at my food. "Still hungry?"

"Ugh . . . not so much. No." I said, sipping the coffee slowly. Raef's hand grazed my thigh and I thought I'd keel over. His lips quirked into a small, knowing grin for an instant.

"So what's the plan?" asked MJ. "Just walk into the Breakers and up to this Raines guy and say, 'Hey there, we know you are a Mortis 'cause Eila has a picture of you and her Grams from a century or two ago, so start talking'?"

I had to agree with MJ - I was seriously skeptical of how we were going to get this guy to open up. Kian and Raef looked at each other, no doubt trying to figure out the same question.

"Actually, that may be perfect," said Ana. "Raines will never be expecting to meet Eila at his fundraiser. Praise his party then just casually slide into the house information. Once you've got his attention, you tell him who you are and that you need information. We'll know quickly if he is going to be on your side or not, based on his reaction."

Raef frowned and his hand stilled. "No. I don't want her going near him," he said, a protective darkness filling his gaze.

Kian looked at Raef, "He's not going to try anything in front of a crowd. He won't risk it. Plus, there is a chance, a small one, that he will recognize you or me. MJ, Ana and Eila are no one to him."

"Thanks," muttered MJ.

"You know what I mean," said Kian. He looked at me, "If you're up to it, I think it will have more power - more influence - if you approach him. If he does something stupid, he's dead in an instant, crowd of deep pockets or not."

"I'm up for it. In fact, I want to meet this man. He knew Elizabeth after all," I said, still hoping Christian Raines was a friend. We had our fill of foes.

Raef's hold on my hand tightened, "I've had too many close calls with your safety. Taken too many chances. Even at the beach with that damn human." A muscle in his jaw jumped as rage seeped into him and his gaze drilled into the table.

"Human. What human?" asked Ana. "What are you talking about?" I tried to shake my head, encouraging her not to press for details for the sake of Raef, and maybe myself as well. I placed my hand on Raef's rigid arm and squeezed.

He had turned into a stone of anger and when he spoke his voice was deadly low, "I left Eila alone on the beach so I could help Jesse, but some drunken senior named Ted . . ." Raef swore, his hand clenching into an iron ball, " . . . assaulted her."

Everyone was frozen, their faces stricken. I quickly clarified the event, which seemed to have bothered Raef far more than I realized.

I rubbed his arm. "Nothing happened. Raef got there before, well, you know. And Ted probably has no recollection of what he did. Almost did. Whatever. I'm just thankful you didn't stay in his truck with him, Ana."

Ana was about to reply and almost managed to open her mouth to speak, but Kian was already at her side. His face was hard. "Did he touch you?" he asked, his voice low and dangerous, just like Raef's. I feared Ted was going to need his own bodyguard . . . or move to a different planet.

Raef's gaze slid to me, an obvious plot to permanently damage

Ted forming if Ana's answer was similar to mine.

So not good.

Thankfully Ana explained that she had only helped him get his truck restarted and set up the amplifiers. She gently extracted her wrist from Kian's grasp and he finally stepped back slightly, but Raef and he seemed to exchange some criminal, unspoken thought.

When we got back to the Cape, *if* we ever got back, Ana and I were going to need to diffuse our two bodyguards before they ran into Ted. Otherwise the football team would find itself down a player. While I definitely deserved an apology from the linebacker, he didn't deserve to be maimed. Or murdered.

I looked over to Ana, "Let's go try on the dresses and make sure they fit."

She readily agreed, as the fierce testosterone in the room was damn near suffocating. Raef and Kian hadn't moved, and MJ watched as Ana and I headed to Kian's room. I knew, just KNEW, they were going to plot what they wanted to do to Ted.

Ana and I had our work cut out for us when it came to calming our faithful guards. I leaned over to Ana as we walked.

"We can't let them kill Ted," I whispered.

"Ya think?" she replied.

Ana was a living flame as she inspected herself in the mirror. The shimmering, slinky, floor length concoction had a back cut nearly down to her tailbone, which was crisscrossed with a cobweb-like pattern of crystal strands. The blood-red material clung to every one of her athletic curves and showed off the soft, trailing divot of her spine. The entire outfit stopped just shy of indecent.

Kian was going to have a coronary.

"You look . . . incredible," I breathed, awestruck.

Ana smiled and I could tell that she actually felt like a Hollywood starlet. It was a rare moment for her and I hoped she would remember it forever.

Looking at myself however, I wasn't nearly so confident. Granted, the snowflake white gown did manage to hug my more ample curves perfectly, the tiers of silk fabric creating a flowing, full skirt. The beaded corset top managed to make my chest look full and Austen-worthy, even without straps. Small crystals were sewn delicately into various areas of the skirt and bodice causing it to twinkle like stars on a summer night. It was gorgeous . . . and 100% intimidating.

Ana adored it. "Raef is going to love it. It is so you – quiet elegance. A rare flower," she said, smiling at me.

I turned slowly in the gown and the layered skirt trailed slightly on the floor and twisted around my ankles as I moved. The back of the gown also dipped low, but nowhere near as far south as Ana's. I actually did feel a bit like a Victorian princess.

Collette had also supplied us with mile-high heels, make-up and jewelry, complete with a matching ruby headband for Ana and a diamond barrette for me. The sheer worth of what we were wearing made me insanely nervous, but the boys assured us that the baubles were not on loan from Tiffany's.

Instead, the thousands in jewels and gowns were ours and Raef and Kian had footed the bill. Ana had to remind me, repeatedly, that Raef and Kian had plenty of money, but still – I felt uneasy being unable to repay such an extravagant gift.

By late afternoon, we had docked in Newport and I had barely seen the boys all day. They had been pouring over information on the Breakers, plotting ways to leave in a hurry if needed.

Ana had helped me with my hair and make-up, both of which I had been terrible at during my solo attempt to beautify myself. She took pity on me and then she took over. Her killer ability to glamorize was shocking since she so often dressed like a tomboy without a speck of make-up.

She finished my hair by setting in the barrette, then left me to attend to her own needs. I sat in Raef's room, in front of the mirror with my robe on, watching myself. The elegant evening wear Collette had chosen for me hung from the hook by the door, and I wondered if it could ever hide my own self-doubt.

I sat there, alone in the room, and could hear MJ talking to Ana in the galley. They were only down the hall, but I suddenly felt truly alone. I couldn't help but wonder if the past three days had actually marked the beginning of the end of my life.

We were operating on assumptions. Utilizing a rough draft of a violent history between my kind and the Mortis, since neither Kian nor Raef ever actually saw those centuries of bloodshed. They were "born" into their dark lives at the close of the fighting and at the end of Rysse's reign. Their information was sketchy at best and only derived from battle-stories of older soul-thieves and the other clansmen.

And stories handed down through the ages often become warped and twisted. At best, facts were exaggerated, at worst, completely inaccurate. I feared we were utilizing the later as our baseline of knowledge.

And if the Mortis were such loathed enemies, freaking *why* would they leave me alive when they had several chances to kill me? Something was going on and I had a terrible feeling we were going to end up dead. I knew one thing for certain though: no one was going to die for me. If I could protect them, I would. If I could trade my life for theirs, I wouldn't hesitate.

I sat there, staring into the mirror for quite a while, when I heard Ana call to me through my door to hurry up. The limo was waiting. I glanced at the clock and was shocked to see it was 7pm.

I needed to pull myself together. "I'll be right there!" I called back as I got to my feet. I took the heavy gown from its hanger as I heard Ana walking down the hall toward the galley stairs.

I carefully stepped into the smooth fabric and shifted my body so I could reach around to my back to close the dress. I started to slowly pull up the zipper, but my hands were shaking, the fear wearing through my confidence jeans. My trembling caused me to fumble with the zipper and then it jammed. Frustrated, I tried to pull it back down and restart it, but it was stuck fast. I kept fiddling with it as the minutes slipped by.

Mercifully, Ana came back because the door started to open. "Oh Ana. Thank goodness. The damn zipper is . . ." I turned and saw Raef standing in the doorway. He stood there, looking at me, every inch the stunning, male model he was in a perfectly cut black tuxedo.

"Uh. My zipper is, um, stuck. Can you help me?" I asked, my body trembling slightly. I couldn't get over how his clothing took his already beautiful self and launched it to the stratosphere. Damn.

He took a deep breath, heat simmering in his gaze and my body began to ignite in response. Brain. Must keep brain functioning.

"Of course," he replied, stepping towards me. I turned so he could access the zipper, my arms still wrapped behind me, trying to hold the open fabric together. Suddenly I felt his strong hands holding my own, trying to soothe the trembling. My fingers instantly stilled under his and the electric flame licked up my arms.

Holy fish fry, my body wouldn't follow directions.

He leaned toward my ear, "You are going to be alright. You won't be alone and I promise to stay by your side, okay?"

I managed to nod as he released my hands, which I dropped to my sides, letting the fabric fall open on my back. He leaned back slightly to examine the zipper.

He had sacrificed so much to protect me. They all had. And here I was questioning our ability to survive this nightmare. Furious I could have such little faith in our crew, I shoved aside my doubts.

"You're caught on a crystal," said Raef softly as his hands brushed along my back, working the zipper free. I suspected he did so deliberately, conspiring with my mutinous body to overthrow my sanity. Yeah, Raef was absolutely a product of the darkside.

It was as if he was my power source, fueling my stupid hormones. Delicious ideas about his lips and my body raced through my head. I had to think of something else and get my mind off his hands. And lips. Visions of un-french fries and spiteful cheerleaders ran through my mind.

I felt a slight pull on the fabric and then he drew the zipper all the way down to my tailbone so he could restart it, but then he paused. "What? Did it rip?" I asked, breathless.

"Your mark does match the book," said Raef and I realized he was examining the brand on my back. My heart was slapping around in my chest like a ping-pong ball. I felt his finger softly trace the mark and electricity raced over my back.

His hand suddenly jerked away from my body and something painful sliced through my bliss where he had touched me.

I was instantly hit with the vision of Elizabeth, struggling to stand inside a blinding column of light, and Rysse enraged as he appeared locked to her. The brutal change of emotion caused me to stagger on my feet.

"Eila!" Raef exclaimed as I swayed, anchoring one strong arm around me from behind. He held my back tightly to his chest. "Are you alright?" he asked roughly, shaken himself.

"What . . what just happened? Something felt like it was cutting into my back." The vision of Elizabeth had faded, but the bliss was gone, replaced by the thoughts that haunted me when I had been alone.

"Your mark! It . . . glowed. When I touched it, it gave off a blue glow," breathed Raef.

I must have jumped slightly at the shock of hearing that my own mark came to life because his hands fell to my hips, as if he was convinced I was going to faint. I reached around between us to the brand.

"WHAT?" I yelped, my heart in my throat for more than one reason.

"It glowed! I've never seen . . . wait. You said it hurt? Does it still hurt?" he asked, now concerned, looking into my face as I glanced over my shoulder to him. I shook my head softly, the pain having evaporated.

I swallowed back the lump in my throat. My heart was torn between loving him freely, but understanding if I did so, he would only be more crushed if I died.

I should shut down the relationship that was growing between us. I should try to at least protect his heart, for mine was already beyond repair. My internal struggle must have shown on my face, for Raef looked pained as he watched me.

But then he turned my body into his and stroked my hair back from my face, cupping my cheeks. "Don't be afraid, E. I will always be with you," he said and he lowered his lips to mine and kissed me slowly, almost reverently.

I couldn't deny how deeply I loved him and I kissed him back fiercely, fueled by both my passion and pain. My need shocked him for only a moment, but with a throaty growl he amplified the fire and ice we seemed to create. He held me tightly to him, his hands pressing into my bare back. If my mark glowed when he lightly touched me, then it was an absolute beacon now.

We finally broke from each other and I remained in his tight embrace, breathless. Raef's body quivered like a live wire and his face was graced with elegant, cryptic symbols.

He drew a trembling breath as he swept a tendril of hair from my flushed face. "I will do whatever it takes to keep you safe."

"I know," I whispered, reeling in my pain. I rose on my tiptoes to press my mouth to his, kissing him deeply and knowing without doubt, I would die for him. I released my lips from his and dropped back down onto my flat feet.

"Damn E . . . you make it impossible for a soulless guy to concentrate, you know that?" he said with a smile, completely unaware of my doubts.

"E?" I asked, realizing he had apparently nicknamed me.

"Yeah. My E. My Everything," he said, smiling. His hands traveled gently up my spine and he pulled me tighter to him as he kissed me again, this time softer and full of gentle love. I let myself pretend, for just a moment, that I'd be with him forever. That not even fate could separate us.

I felt his hands shift on my back and the stubborn zipper was finally being pulled up.

Ana looked downright devastating. There were no other words for my friend in the fiery gown she wore, her short golden hair slightly wild with the ruby-headband tucked neatly behind her ears. It was a complete transformation from her typical look and I could tell Kian was having trouble keeping his eyes off her as we rode in the limo to The Breakers.

Kian, Raef and MJ were discussing what should happen if Raines turned out to have a serious distaste for the Lunaterra and, by extension, me. Ana and I just looked at each other silently across the car as the homes grew in size and elegance outside the window. I knew that she too was concerned for all of us. Tonight was a huge gamble.

I saw Kian glance at her again, but this time Ana saw it as well, and they held each other's gaze for a few seconds. She was afraid for him as she listened in on what was clearly a plan to use themselves as shields to get us out of The Breakers if needed. I took a deep breath and Raef, sitting next to me, squeezed my hand.

"We're just being careful, that's all," he said, looking at me. "It won't be necessary. It won't."

I was frightened, though not because of Raines. I feared the idea of ever having to leave Raef. He reached up and touched my face. "It's okay to be scared," he said. It was an intimate gesture, as if he forgot we were not alone.

I glanced over to our company. They seemed completely unfazed and I realized they knew about Raef and I. Even though we never showed the heat between us in front of them, they just knew. And they didn't seem to mind.

"Oh for crying out loud, just kiss her," said MJ, smiling. Raef glanced his way and, being the best gentleman he could, lifted my hand to his mouth and kissed my palm, causing my lifeline to tingle.

"Wimp," said MJ, slouching back in his seat.

"A gentleman is never an exhibitionist with his . . . lady. Such things should be reserved for private," said Raef.

I turned five shades of scarlet. Ana raised an eyebrow and I knew she was wondering exactly how far "intimate" went. I shook my head *no* very slightly but she gave me a disbelieving look. Oh hell.

Kian glanced at her again and tried to control a small smirk. She didn't miss it and he quickly turned and looked out the window at the iron scroll gates of The Breakers.

Was my love life destined to be a regular topic of curious conversation?

I wanted to crawl under the leather seat and hide.

Maybe with Raef.

Definitely with Raef.

* * * * *

To say that Mr. Vanderbilt likes his homes on the larger side was the biggest understatement of the century. It was a house . . . no, MANSION, overlooking the ocean.

Completely built of white stone with intricate carvings of cherubs, the home contained what seemed like 100 windows. The red roof three stories up was topped with more chimneys than I could count. It was opulence, glamour and an absolute fairytale in granite and gold leaf.

A red velvet runner led to the doors, which were open and flanked by men in topcoats and tails. A footman opened the door to our limo and stepped aside as MJ climbed out, tugging at his tux. He looked like a young GQ model, and several other women that were walking in glanced at him and nearly swooned. Hero Boy looked hot.

Kian got out next and helped Ana carefully. In the light of the mansion towering above, she glowed like the surface of Mars. Radiant, the other guests looked at her in awe. She hooked her arm in Kian's, equally stunning in a black, Armani-esque tux, and he leaned into her, whispering something in her ear. She actually giggled.

Raef looked at me as I gazed out the limo door at the entrance to The Breakers. "You ready?" he asked. Not really, but there was no turning back now.

Raef climbed out, turning to help me. "You are stunning," he said to me, quietly, "and I'm not the only one who thinks so."

He glanced at the people walking in past us and I was shocked to see they were actually looking at *me* and whispering to each other. One older woman, in a stunning red velvet gown, nodded to me and smiled. People actually thought I was . . . *beautiful.* I couldn't believe it.

As we entered the great hall that was the center of The Breakers, it was obvious why the Fire and Ice Ball was the party of the year. The room towered 30 feet above us with a massive balcony that ran the entire circumference of the area. Two imposing gold chandeliers hung from the center of the ornate ceiling, casting a warm light over the entire room.

A live band was slaying a jazz tune from the 1920s and a large group of people were dancing. There were easily 500 people inside the great hall and the sound of everyone talking and laughing and dancing created a physical hum that traveled through my body.

I noticed that the guests ran the gamut of age, race, and style but all were connected by one common thread: money, and lots of it.

Jewels glittered as dresses and suits moved like pieces of art. Even the slate of bands that were to perform read like a who's who of alternative rock and funky jazz. As requested by Mr. Raines, women could only wear red or white and the effect was amazing. It was surreal, a dream that you fall into when you pretend you are part of a music video shoot.

Before I knew it, Ana was rhythmically moving her slinky, glittering body toward the dance floor, Kian and MJ following. A beautiful girl with ebony skin and a cloud-colored gown spied MJ and slid her way over to him. Within a minute they were dancing together.

Kian and Ana moved in a liquid grace, seamlessly dancing as one. Occasionally he would spin her out and then gently back into his arms. The look between them could rival the center of a supernova. Anger and frustration melted away and their attraction to each other was undeniable. She was the sun and he could never break orbit from her overpowering gravitational pull.

I knew the feeling well as I glanced at Raef.

He reached for me and his hand slid to my lower back. I was sure my mark was shimmering beneath the three-grand worth of dress. "We're supposed to blend, remember?" he said gesturing toward the dance floor.

I gulped as he wove us through the crowd to where our friends were dancing and spun me out once, making me laugh as if the stress I carried was thrown away from me. He pulled me back to him and tucked me tightly to his chest, his hand between my shoulder blades guarding my back. I gave up control and just let him lead me on the dance floor. I'd allow myself to be seventeen for as long as I could. For as long as it would last.

We had been dancing and laughing for the entire first, hour-long set when the music stopped and applause rang out. Through the sound system a man's voice filled the room.

"Is everyone having a good time?" he roared. The crowd cheered in response. "Well, that's what I like to hear! I wanted to thank everyone for coming and helping to fund the restoration of some of our country's greatest gems, such as this magnificent home." Another wild round of cheers and applause filled the hall.

I was craning my neck to see if it was Raines. I looked to Kian and mouthed, "*Is it him?*" Kian shook his head, unable to see as well. I looked over my shoulder to Raef, who was standing right behind me.

He reached out and tapped Kian and MJ, gesturing to the edge of the hall and the stairs that led to the balcony. Kian nodded. From the balcony we could get a clear view.

We worked our way through the deafening room and climbed the stairs to the second floor. There were fewer people in the balcony so we walked to the edge and looked down. The man on stage did not appear to be Raines.

MJ shook his head, frustrated. "Where the heck is this guy?"

Raef leaned against one of the massive pillars that held up the third floor as a new, rock-laden music set started and the crowd howled. He crossed his arms and scanned the room below us. I sighed and began to think that maybe this brilliant plan would net us nothing. Well, except a fun, incredibly lavish evening.

I looked around the balcony and then I saw him.

Standing on the opposite side of the balcony from us, Christian Raines was 100% the Most Eligible Bachelor. A perfectly tailored tux hugged his broad shoulders and his picture perfect face was flawless.

A face, which had not aged since Elizabeth's party.

My heart took off at a sprint and I yanked Raef behind the pillar so he was out of sight. Kian saw my sudden dash to hide Raef and he quickly stepped back behind another pillar.

"What? Do you see him?" asked Raef, his arm protectively finding its way around my shoulders.

I nodded. "He's on the opposite side of the balcony," I gasped. My stomach was in knots. "He looks like he's just watching the crowd below."

"Damn," said Raef. "We can't follow her up here or he'll see us."

"Well, he doesn't know me, right?" asked MJ. "I'll head over there with Eila. You guys go back down to the hall and cross to the other staircase near Raines. That way, you'll be only a few feet below him if we need you. Which we won't, right?"

Raef looked at me, unsure. We came all this way to talk to Raines and now, here he was, in sight. I had to do it. "It's a good plan," I said trying to muster my courage, but Raef looked uneasy.

"I told you I would be by your side all night," he argued.

"And you will, but we knew you couldn't do this part with me.

Raines could recognize you." I glanced over to Raines who was talking with a few, star-struck women. Now was the perfect time.

I leaned up to Raef and kissed him, gently, on the lips. I could feel his hand tighten its grip on my own. I knew our friends looked away, out of respect, but MJ had a huge smile as he stared at the ceiling.

"Be careful. Take no chances. Please," whispered Raef. "Please."

I nodded and turned to MJ, "Let's go."

I hooked my arm in his and we started walking around the balcony toward Raines. I glanced back and Kian, Raef and Ana were quickly heading down the stairs. I could see them crossing the hall below us as we walked the massive balcony, coming closer and closer to Raines, who was still talking to the women.

I swallowed hard and MJ held my arm tighter. From below, I saw Raef glance up, watching my progress. He disappeared with Kian and Ana into the stairwell that came up behind Raines.

MJ and I slowed as we approached Raines, who was trying to gracefully persuade the adoring females to rejoin the dancing below and leave him alone. He saw us approach and smiled, apparently oblivious to whom we were and I took it as a good sign. A sign we might actually come away from this more informed and with our lives.

Finally the women started to disperse and Raines turned his attention to MJ and me. I felt my entire body tense. MJ could feel my stress ratchet up a few hundred notches and he decided to take the initiative as he spoke up.

"Mr. Raines?" he asked, acting ever the cool and confident wealthy young man he was supposed to be.

"Yes?" Raines' voice was akin to deep, burgundy velvet.

MJ cleared his throat, "We wanted to tell you that the party is fabulous. Well done." I started to relax a bit. Raines didn't scream soul-thirsty immortal and it helped. Although, at this point, I wasn't sure *any* Mortis actually looked like their real, inner demon.

"Why thank you, Mr . . .?"

"Oh, I'm sorry. I'm Marshall Williams and this is Eila," he said, deliberately leaving off my last name for the time being.

"It's a pleasure to meet you," said Raines, reaching out and shaking MJ's hand. I laced my fingers tightly together over my friend's arm so I wouldn't have to touch Raines, possibly revealing what I was a tad too soon. I nodded politely instead. "Are you from Newport?" He asked. I knew I had to answer. Lord, here goes nothing.

"We're from the Cape."

"Cape Cod? Beautiful place," said Raines, a bit nonplussed. The announcer below us introduced the next band and the crowd cheered. Raines watched the happy throng below and was about to excuse himself from us, but I spoke up.

"Mr. Raines, I was hoping you could help me with an antique I have acquired." *Be a friend, be a friend, be a friend.*

Raines seemed surprised that a 17-year-old would want to talk shop. "Oh? Well, I'm not sure how much help I can be, but I'll try," he said, glancing at the crowd. I only had his partial attention.

I swallowed back my nerves, which was like gulping a Slurpie in one shot, freezing my brain. "I, uh, currently own a sea captain home in Centerville. The Captain Josiah Walker House. I was digging through records and found out that your company used to care for the home, in a trust."

If Raines was only half listening before, I now had his full, unadulterated attention. A flash of something crossed his face, but he recovered himself quickly. "Why yes. It's a beautiful home that you purchased. At auction, correct?"

MJ must have felt my pulse racing and he gave my arm a bit of a squeeze. I knew Raef and Kian were just out of sight, waiting to save the day if anything went wrong, but I was still terrified.

"Actually, no. I was given the house, by an anonymous buyer," I said, trying not to choke on the words.

Raines visibly straightened. "Why?"

It was a single word and the answer was going to make or break us. Literally. "Because the buyer wanted the home to go back into the hands of the original family that built it, which is me. I'm Eila Walker. My 4th Great Grandmother was . . ."

"Elizabeth," said Raines, quietly, almost breathlessly. He looked shocked. I actually thought he might be having a heart attack, if such an ailment could even be possible in his kind.

He reached out his hand to me slowly. "I am very pleased to meet you Eila," he said carefully.

I knew what he was doing. He wanted to touch me. To confirm I was Elizabeth's descendant. I managed to force one of my hands to release MJ's now rock-hard arm, and I reached out to Raines. When our hands met, I was shocked to feel my palm turn cool then warm, almost in waves. He slowly released my hand and smiled lightly, almost as a father would look at his child. It was . . . strange.

I glanced at MJ and released his arm completely, stepping towards Raines. I saw Raef immediately appear out of the stairwell, no doubt a reaction to my movement toward our host. "I know *what* you are and I know you knew my grandmother. I need your help," I said, confidence growing inside me.

"Of course," said Raines, his velvet voice more serious.

I was surprised he answered so quickly. I glanced over to Raef, and Raines followed my eyes, nearly doing a double take. They walked over to MJ and me, Ana walking next to Kian. "Mr. Raines, this is . . ."

"Kian O'Reilly and Raef Paris," said Raines, still staring at them as if he was seeing ghosts.

Raef, always in bodyguard mode, was not sold on the safety factor with Raines. "How do you know us? We barely spoke back then," he asked, his voice dangerously low.

"Because Elizabeth was fond of both of you. When you disappeared, she feared you had been killed," Raines replied. "I see you are not dead, however."

Kian and Raef were still uneasy with Raines so close to me, but the odd sensation when he shook my hand filled me with a strange sort of familiarity. "We have questions we need answered Mr. Raines."

"I understand. But I need to clarify something, right now. That while you are most definitely the granddaughter of Elizabeth, you are not the granddaughter of Josiah Walker."

I was completely confused.

If I wasn't Josiah's granddaughter, who the . . .?

"You are *my* granddaughter. You are a *Raines*," he said, smiling again.

Oh, snap.

At first, Raef and Kian were dead set against going anywhere with Raines-the-Liar, but arguing in the balcony with the party raging beneath us seemed unwise. Raef, close beside me, finally agreed to follow Raines to one of the ornate bedrooms so we could all get up to speed with each other.

Once in the gilded boudoir, Raef immediately spoke up, "There is no way in hell you are related to Eila! Our kind cannot have children – especially with a Lunaterra!"

Kian nodded, "He's right Eila. My bullshit-meter just pinned on that one."

Raines put his hands up, casually defensive, "Look, I know it sounds impossible, but I'm telling you the absolute truth. Elizabeth and I were far more than friends and she did conceive a child with me. Trust me when I say that we were as completely shocked as you are now."

Raef was shaking his head, not changing his mind, "Not possible."

"It's true. And Eila is my descendant. I could tell the moment I touched her. You felt it as well, did you not?" Raines asked, looking to me for confirmation. I glanced to Raef and then back to Raines. "I felt an odd sensation, yes."

Raef stepped forward to me. "Eila," he pleaded, no doubt ready to argue about my sanity. I looked at him and he stopped where he was. He knew enough to stop talking. Instead he set himself like a fortress next to me. He crossed his arms, his stance screaming, *"Say the word and I snap his neck."*

"How did you know Elizabeth?" I asked. "How did you meet her?"

Raines looked at me and sat down in an ornate armchair near the bed. He rubbed his forehead, thinking.

"I met Elizabeth when she was only five years old in the northern part of France. I had been a Mortis for almost 90 years when I met her. She was one of the Lisles – a royal – and she had somehow gotten separated from her family. I found her wandering the woods, miles from her home."

"What do you mean 'a royal'?" I asked.

"Hers was the ruling family. She was heir to the empire," said Raines, plainly, as if any of us would've known this. "None of you knew this? That she was destined to be Empress?"

We all shook our heads. Yeah – that 411 we definitely missed.

"Then you don't know how the Lunaterra function?" Again, all heads shook *no*. I felt supremely ignorant, especially since I was supposed to be one of them.

"The Lunaterra royal family dictates the will of the rest of the

Lunaterra species. They are linked, in one mind-set, to their leader. Basically, no free will. It's genetic," said Raines. "But Elizabeth was born different, sort of handicapped. She didn't connect with the pack mentality of her kind. I have a feeling that is why she was able to wander off. But back then, her family didn't realize she was different."

I was completely intrigued.

"I had been hunting in the forest when I found her, crying and cold, in the hollow of the base of a tree. I knew what she was and, because of what she was, I should have killed her. Or left her to die. The Lunaterra were brutal to our kind. It didn't matter if you lived in peace with the humans. If you were a Mortis and a Lunaterra found you, you were dead. If you were lucky, they killed you instantly and if you were unlucky . . ." Raines shifted, as if he was remembering something, ". . .they killed you slowly."

Raef looked at me as I sat down slowly across from Raines. I couldn't help thinking he might never be able to see me as his "E" after this. The skeletons in my family closet were executioners. Somehow, I wasn't sure the Mortis were the soulless ones after all. I felt ill.

"I sensed there was something about her," continued Raines. "Her essence was so unique. She didn't look at me like I was to be loathed. She just gave a small smile and reached her little arms up to me. I knew, absolutely knew, she was not like the rest. Lunaterra are programmed to hate the soulless. As children they watched their parents kill and, like wolves, parents would sometimes bring a weakened Mortis back to their children so they could practice their ability."

I definitely was going to be sick. I put my hand over my mouth, horrified at what my kind had done. Raef sat down next to me and put his arm around my waist. It was an effort to show that this information didn't change how he saw me, although *I* wasn't sure my reflection would ever be the same. Kian and Ana sat down on a sofa across from us, but MJ stayed on his feet by the door, always the watchdog.

"I took her back to her family and left her close enough to the estate so she would be found. I didn't hear of her again until a decade later when rumors spread that an heiress was found to be 'abnormal.' Defective, because she didn't follow orders to kill. Word was that she had even helped a few of my kind escape by feeding them information on pending attacks. Her family decided to execute her, charging her with treason, but before they could, she ran." Raines shook his head, his eyes cast to the floor.

"I knew it had to be the little girl from the woods and I was determined to help her. It took me nearly a week to find her and when I did, she was in terrible shape. She had been living in the forest, exposed to the cold winter that had set in. She was thin, sick, and bruised from beatings at the hands of her own family. But she recognized me and knew she was safe. Even back then, at fifteen, she was beautiful, much like you," said Raines, looking at me.

I felt Raef move slightly, pulling me closer to him. He never took his eyes off of my possible grandfather.

"I guarded her and took care of her. She became critical in the fight against her own kind and started to hide those of us she knew were truly good people. By the time she was eighteen, her power was unlike any other Lunaterra I had ever seen, and that made her family furious. They hunted her relentlessly and I knew we had to put real distance between us and them. We came to Massachusetts and I posed as her brother due to our apparent age difference of nearly 10 years. For a brief time, her life was normal – she made friends at the school I sent her to and she was happy."

"But then word came that a Mortis named Jacob Rysse had

entered the fray in Europe and he was unlike any we had ever known. He was a killing machine and seemed to have a high tolerance when it came to the Lunaterra's power. He also had zero tolerance for the type of soulless people Elizabeth had tried to protect. He saw them as a weakness to his race. He started to build a small army, known as the Rysse Clan. They decimated the Lunaterra and started picking off our own race as well."

Raef glanced to me. I knew he had been one of them – a killing machine, though he went after humans. I wondered if he also eliminated the weaker Mortis.

Raines rubbed his face and leaned back farther in the chair. "There was always this spark between us, but I kept it buried. Forced it down. I felt that to become more than her guardian was unwise, but we had this link. I couldn't break it, couldn't talk her out of it. And one night, all that emotion and desire came out and she ended up carrying my child. Neither of us ever thought such a thing was possible, especially between the two of us. I panicked when I realized that she and the baby would be hunted by both of our families. So I did the only thing I could - I set her up to marry Walker immediately and hide who she was."

I realized I had stopped breathing and drew a deep lungful. My heart clenched for Elizabeth and what she had gone through at such a young age.

Raines locked his hands together and leaned forward in his seat, his head hanging. "She was furious and begged me to not make her do it. She was absolutely broken hearted and I just wanted to die. But she did it, for the child. I stood there and watched her marry him. Watched her leave with him, knowing it was their wedding night and that she was carrying our baby within her. It ripped me to pieces." Raines placed his face in his hands, his body stiff.

"Walker assumed the child, born eight months later, was his. Elizabeth kept her pregnancy and our son hidden from everyone. No one knew about our son. I got to hold him once, when Walker was away. He was a few weeks old," said Raines, choking up. "Elizabeth said when she was alone with our son, she called him Christian."

Raines shook his head, unable to continue speaking. His grief seemed to crush him and my heart went out to him. He sat back, blinking back tears and looking out past the massive glass windows. A silence fell on the room.

I glanced at Raef and Kian, then back to Raines. "Do you know how Elizabeth died?" I asked quietly.

Raines managed to pull himself together the best he could. "No. Not really, though I guessed Rysse attacked her and somehow they both ended up dead." Anger laced his words. "I found her body in the old harbor square. I even heard the blast. I buried her, but a local man did see her lying by the harbor fountain, before I got there. He believed she had been struck by lightning, but few believed him as he drank too much and the body wasn't there."

I glanced at my friends and cautiously spoke. "We believe that Rysse didn't kill Elizabeth. We think she allowed him to touch her and that something went wrong and her own power killed them both."

Raines looked shocked. Raef looked at me suspiciously, confused as to why I was bringing it up at all. We were supposed to be asking about the house, but I needed more answers than just the buyer's identity.

"She wouldn't do that. She hated him. You're wrong . . . you're . . . wait, why do you think this?" asked Raines, standing up slowly. Raef was immediately on his feet, a predatorial look in his dark eyes.

I slowly got to my feet, "Because I've seen her death in my

dreams and I think they're from Elizabeth. I think she is trying to tell me something. And I think Rysse believed he could do something to her. Maybe draw off her soul, or something." My friends looked downright floored at my hypothesis.

Raines looked at me, his brow dropping into a deep crease. "There was a rumor that Rysse *was* a Lunaterra who had been turned. But it was regarded as pure fiction because Lunaterra cannot be turned. Elizabeth, however, had her suspicions. And she herself was a flaw of nature, but an evolutionary jump as well. If the rumor was true, than it was possible that Rysse thought he could turn her." Raines slowly sank back to his chair. "In your vision, what exactly happened when Rysse touched her?"

I glanced at Raef, unsure if I should continue.

He didn't protest so I went on, "He grabbed her by the neck and they seemed to focus on one another. His face - it became marked. And then he suddenly panicked and appeared to be sort of chained to her, unable to let go. Elizabeth, however, didn't act afraid. A bright light wound around both of them, almost like a snake. When it became almost blinding, it turned into . . . "

" . . . A column of white fire," finished Raines, in a near whisper. "She . . . she triggered a Core collapse."

"A what?" asked Raef, shifting towards Raines.

Raines was lost to his own thoughts, staring down at his hands. It was then that I realized he was rubbing a fine gold ring on his pinkie finger. Delicate and wound with a braid-like pattern, it was definitely a woman's band.

Raines finally looked up and his eyes were glossy. "A . . . Core collapse. It's a DNA encoded trip wire in the Lunaterra. A self-destruct trigger that calls down the Web's core. That kind of energy no one can handle."

He swallowed hard and looked away from us, out toward the sea beyond the windows. "Rysse must have tried to push a stolen life-force into her as a way to corrupt her DNA and turn her. Why he thought he could do it, however, is beyond me. Knowing Elizabeth, I'm sure she orchestrated it to lure him in . . . and kill him."

Raines' gaze was distant, as if realizing for the first time that Elizabeth probably knew she was going to die. Knowingly lured in Rysse with a promise of being turned so she could kill him. I was not sure he'd ever find comfort in the knowledge that she left this world on her own terms.

I looked at Raef, whose own face was now tense. I spoke to him directly. "That explains why the Bridge Boy didn't kill me, the day he got into my house."

"Someone tried to KILL you?" asked Raines, alarmed, now looking pointedly at Raef. "Who?"

"A clansman who managed to get into the house without an invitation," said Raef, stepping in front of me. "He nearly killed Ana and tried to take Eila somewhere. He said that his orders were to secure her and the diary," said Raef. "Knowing what we do now, I think they are going to attempt to turn Eila."

I saw Ana wrap her arms around herself and Kian leaned closer to her so his body was just barely touching hers. Automatically, she angled closer to her lifeguard.

"Then the house has been breached," said Raines. "To do that takes someone powerful enough to disable the protective nature of the home. That's not good." Raines thought for a moment, "What about her diary? Did you find it?"

I shook my head, "No, just an unfinished photo book. That's

how we found your picture."

Raines suddenly looked brighter, stepping forward. "Did it have an engraved leather cover? With a round imprint in the center?"

"Yeah. That's it," I said, hope rising.

"That's the diary!" said Raines. "Elizabeth's necklace is the key that unlocks it. The necklace fits in the cover and reveals the written portion of the diary. Those blank pages are not really empty. We could have answers!"

"That's awesome!" I said, thrilled. Could fate actually be on our side? Was it possible? Dare I hope? Except . . . "Necklace? What necklace?"

"I gave Elizabeth a necklace for her 17th birthday. She had it altered by a friend at school so that it would act as a key to her diary. No necklace, no words. When she died, I sent the necklace back to her best friend, Katherine. She'd have kept it in the family, and handed it down through the female line. Last I heard, the Sheas had it."

My heart plummeted. "Any chance the Sheas were living on the Cape last you heard?"

"Yes, and they have a daughter around your age. Nikita, I think. Is she a friend?"

"Not exactly," I muttered. Finding the necklace would be difficult. Getting Nikki on our side, however, would be downright impossible. Game friggin over. I had better odds with the Clan.

"I'm sure the family would've kept it as an heirloom. What about the diary - is it safe?"

"Yes, it's in the . . ." I was about to say "yacht", but Raef squeezed my hand, a signal to not specify where it was. Raines still needed to earn his trust. "Yes. It's safe."

"Then that's all I care about," he replied.

As odd as it was, I did believe that Raines loved Elizabeth. And, while I wasn't entirely sure on the biological grandfather part, I believed that he was telling the truth as he knew it. He could be a valuable asset to us, once he proved to the boys that he was on our side.

"Eila, you said you needed my help when you first approached me. I can get you further protection. If you will allow me, in addition to myself, there are other Mortis who were very loyal friends to Elizabeth and me. They could help."

I felt Raef tense and glanced over to my other three friends. No one seemed ready to make that leap of faith yet. "Actually I wanted to ask you if you knew who would've bought the house and given it back to me. Our trail ends with you. We know that you kept the house in a trust for years until just after my parents died."

"I kept the home hidden from our descendants using the trust. I was worried that if one ever returned that *this* is what could happen. When your parents died, I let the trust run out since I thought Blaine was the last of our bloodline. I didn't know about you. If I had, I would've kept the house hidden," said Raines. "While a few humans would've known that Elizabeth had a child, no one knew the child was mine. Only those of us, here in this room, know that information and that you are a hybrid. It is critical that information never leaves this room."

"We understand," I said, a pale smile crossing my face.

"Eila, you should probably . . ." started Raines, but he was interrupted by a knock at the door. Everyone stiffened and became silent.

Raines, now hyper-alert, glanced to the massive bathroom attached to the bedroom. He looked at Raef and motioned to it. Raef nodded and we all moved silently and quickly through the bedroom and into the bathroom.

Kian carefully closed the door as Raef pulled me in tightly, his muscles twitching. We peeked through the crack in the door with Kian, while Ana and MJ stood back, tense and on alert. Through the crack I watched as Raines, glancing back once more to where we were hidden, walked to the door and opened it. I heard a man's voice from the hall.

"Mr. Raines?" asked a man, dressed in a black tuxedo. He was exceedingly handsome. Too handsome. I glanced up at Raef, a questioning look on my face. Was this man a Mortis as well?

Raef wasn't taking any chances and mouthed the word, *phase* to MJ, who immediately started to back further into the bathroom and strip out of his clothes. I could hear Raines and the visitor talking about the party as MJ moved behind a low bureau.

He stepped out of the last of his clothes, and I watched in awe as his skin shimmered into a million, mirror-like pieces. They cascaded down his body as his form disappeared behind the bureau. A moment passed and then the huge black head of Marsh appeared from around the mahogany chest, his teeth bared.

Raef pointed to the gilded glass doors that lead to a balcony on the outside of The Breakers. Marsh bolted silently from the room, pushing his way through the doors and disappearing onto the outer balcony.

There was a sudden shout from the bedroom and we looked back through the crack just in time to see Christian's body slump to the floor. I nearly screamed out, horrified that he might be dead. That I had just caused yet another person to be killed. Raef quickly covered my mouth however, and stifled my cry.

He yanked me away from the door and grabbed Ana as well,

while Kian stayed, acting as a guard to buy us time if needed. Ana, realizing we were going to leave him, suddenly pulled away from Raef, shaking her head *no*.

She ran back to Kian, trying to haul him away from the door, but she might as well have tried to move the entire mansion, because Kian wasn't leaving. She mouthed the word *come* over and over and her eyes welled with tears. She feared for his life and right then and there, showed her true heart.

He reached down and took her face gently in his hands, kissing her sweetly on the lips and she stilled. When he finally released her, she looked back to Raef and me, her eyes pleading with Raef to not leave the boy she loved behind.

Raef made a nod to Kian, who looked back through the crack in the door. "*Searching room,*" he mouthed to Raef.

Raef looked at Ana and then gestured for them both to come with us. Kian tucked Ana tightly against him and we all silently ran out to the balcony that overlooked the water. Marsh was nowhere to be seen.

We ran along the polished limestone that was framed by massive, sweeping arches that looked onto the pounding ocean below. Once we were safely away from the room, Raef spoke up, "We need to get out of here right now! MJ is making sure our route back to the car is clear."

We took the corner of the balcony that rounded the side of the building and nearly plowed into Dalca. I was shocked. Everyone was, except Ana.

"Dalca? You got my message!" said Ana, "Thank heavens! We've got to get out of here. We just saw a Mortis attack Christian Raines! It could be the Clan."

Dalca looked at Ana, irritated. "Why on earth are you even here? I got your voice message and couldn't figure out what you would be doing, heading to a party at a time like this!" Dalca was pissed.

"It's a long story," said Raef. "We need to keep moving."

Dalca nodded. She actually looked quite beautiful in the black velvet gown she wore, no doubt so that she could get into the party and look liked she belonged. Well, except that she was supposed to be in either red or white, but I wasn't about to tell her that. I was just happy to see her.

"There's a boiler room in the cellar. It used to hold the loads of coal that Vanderbilt would bring in through a private passageway so guests wouldn't see. We can get out that way without being seen," said Dalca.

Kian nodded, his arm protectively around Ana's waist, "Lead the way."

We followed her quickly across the balcony and back into an area of The Breakers that was cordoned off as a museum, empty of any guests. We hurried down a side staircase, finally arriving in the cellar and a towering set of wooden doors.

Raef reached the doors, pulling hard on the handles, allowing Dalca and me in first. The room was very dark and hard to see.

I turned to Dalca, but something struck me hard in the back of the head, and my world instantly went dark.

My head was pounding and my body felt stiff and cold. I managed to open my eyes, but the dark boiler room was still spinning.

"What the . . ."

I managed to moan, putting a hand to my throbbing head.

There was a soft light from a cluster of candles on the floor near me. The low light allowed my eyes to slowly focus and I saw Dalca standing above me, silver gun in her hand. It was pointed at the space between my eyes.

"Welcome back, sunshine," she said in a tight, superior voice.

She was standing next to a dark-haired, imposing figure of a man with eyes as black as an eclipse. It took me a moment to recognize him, but when I did, I knew Raef and Kian had been right. It appeared that Mr. Grant, my creepy history teacher, was definitely dangerous. He stood alongside Dalca, watching me.

"Dalca? What are you doing?" I managed to ask, my voice gravelly and panic clawing at my lungs.

I glanced around the room and saw, to my horror, Raef and Kian on their knees. Both were being restrained by three men each, all dressed in the same dark clothing. Raef's face was cut and scratched, as was Kian's, having obviously fought against their captors. Ana was standing, her back pinned to another man behind her, his hand around her throat preventing her from the slightest movement. Her lip was split and her eyes red with past tears.

Raef looked menacing, as did Kian. Their eyes were black and their bodies were covered in the Fallen symbols, elegantly displayed beneath the cuts. A murderous rage hummed through both their bodies, causing the black lines to pulse with each heartbeat.

I knew that the only people capable of restraining Kian and Raef were their own kind. Or mine. These, without doubt, were all Clansmen. While each looked physically different, they all shared the same black eyes, formal stance and cryptic markings.

They were fighters. Killers. A vigilante militia and I knew what they wanted. Any hopes I had for us disappeared.

I slowly rolled to my side, attempting to sit up so I could get to my feet. The movement caused a searing pain to run through my head, and I paused on my hands and knees, trying to let the throbbing subside. Dalca grabbed me by the arm, however, and yanked me to my feet, causing me to stagger.

"HEY!" growled Raef, furious that I was being manhandled. I managed to refocus, and I was now facing Dalca and Grant.

"Dalca, what are you doing?" I asked again, glancing to Grant. She just laughed, but Grant held up his hand and she immediately fell silent.

"Eila Walker. I must say that even I was surprised that you came to the house on Main. You should know that no one gets a home for free. Payment is always due," he chided as he reached over to Dalca's necklace and yanked the vial brutally from her neck. A flash of pain crossed her face for a mere fraction of a second, but she didn't move.

"You know, Elizabeth was quite the masterful Lunaterra. She took no prisoners, if you know what I mean." He stepped closer to me and I held my ground, refusing to give him the satisfaction of my fear.

"You are like her - an elegant statement of hidden violence. You and I, Ms. Walker, are not so different."

Like hell we weren't.

I looked over to Dalca and for the first time, really saw her. It was only then that I realized Mae and I had indeed been given a gift for the house.

"The witch ball," I said slowly. "*You* gave Mae a witch ball that you said would protect the house, but that was how the Bridge Boy got in, wasn't it?" I asked, angry that my home had been violated so easily.

She looked at me and smiled darkly, "Very good, Eila. It was a nice housewarming gift, I think. Quite generous of me, really, after buying you the house in the first place."

Oh god. Now I understood. Dalca was the buyer and was working for the clan. For Grant. She wanted me to return and, looking at our company, she was decidedly not playing for the good guys.

I glanced at Ana who had tears running down her face. Kian looked at her, enraged that she was in the hands of a man that was no doubt ruthless.

"Eila, I'm so sorry," cried Ana. "I had no idea, I couldn't read her. I thought it was just because . . ." The clansman holding her gave her a rough jerk and she fell silent. Kian threatened Ana's guard with decapitation when he had a chance. The guard just smiled.

I looked back to Grant, who was inserting Dalca's vial into a hypodermic needle that he had pulled from his coat pocket. The powdery material slowly swirled into the solution, creating a muddy liquid. "Dalca. How could you side with them?" I asked, anger rising inside me.

She snorted, "I'm a devoted admirer of Mr. Grant and his work. I intend to help what is left of the Clan return to their status as the superior ruling class with the help of your power, once turned. For my service, Mr. Grant has agreed to give me immortality."

I glanced back to Raef, and his eyes connected with mine. He looked enraged and tortured all in the same moment. I watched Grant ready the syringe and the steel needle reflected in the candlelight.

I thought back to the dream Elizabeth had kept sending me, and I knew I was right. Jacob Rysse wanted to turn Elizabeth. He wanted her as a Mortis with limitless power. Her uniqueness led Rysse to believe she was changeable and Elizabeth played into his selfish hands. She knew she could take him out by luring him in and I intended to do the same. I needed to repeat the past, but let them think I wasn't.

I knew what happened that night, but they did not. They were guessing at what Rysse had done. They wanted the diary so they could understand what Elizabeth had planned. They needed me to return so they could have a chance at getting into her home and securing the book.

Elizabeth may not have shown me how to live, but she had given me the details on how to die. I decided to gamble it all, hoping I was right and I swallowed back my fear.

"That's what is left of Jacob isn't it? After Elizabeth fried him," I asked, coldly. It was a guess, but one I had to gamble.

Grant paused slightly as he loaded the needle and glanced at me. "You're not as stupid as you appear," he said, stepping closer.

Dalca smiled with anticipation as he pulled one of my arms roughly from behind my back and extended it in front of me. He was going to inject me with the solution. That was their best guess on how to turn me, but I needed them to think it was the wrong way.

"Big, bad Jacob Rysse isn't half so scary when he's been reduced to dirt. Quite ironic too, since he was dumb as dirt when he was still kicking."

Raef looked at me like I had lost my mind. I was deliberately pissing off a Clansman, which, to me anyway, seemed like a sure-fire way to keep him from thinking clearly. Well, and probably get slapped.

Grant's hand ratcheted down tighter on my arm, but I kept my voice from cracking in pain. "Rysse got himself killed and blew his chance with Elizabeth because he did it wrong – just like you are about to do as well."

"Don't act like you know what you are talking about, girl," hissed Dalca, but I got Grant's attention.

I used his momentary pause to plow forward. "He tried to turn her, you know? He knew he could, but he did it wrong and you are about to make the same mistake." I was hanging onto my bravery by my fingernails, forcing away the idea of death.

I glanced at Raef and his eyes grew wide with alarm and understanding. "Eila! DON'T!" he begged, suddenly realizing what I was doing. Grant glanced at him and then back to me while Dalca looked furious at the delay.

"How would you know?" asked Grant, a lethal tone to his voice.

I pulled on every last thread of those damn confidence jeans and spoke directly to him, without flinching. "Because I have seen it.

Elizabeth showed me in visions. And, because . . . I have the diary."

Dalca looked stunned and Grant shot her a look of pure disgust.

"Jacob did the same thing that you're about to try," I said, nodding towards the needle. "Elizabeth convinced him to inject her, knowing that was the way to kill him by triggering her power. If you want to turn me, you need to force a stolen soul through me. Doing so will corrupt my DNA. It would've worked on Elizabeth, but Rysse did it wrong." I shut my brain down, not thinking about the next few minutes. I couldn't or I'd lose my nerve.

"Eila! STOP!" demanded Raef, desperate.

Grant looked at him, taking in his reaction. Taking it as a possible confirmation that I was speaking the truth, so I quickly continued, refusing to look at Raef.

"If you do as I say, it will work. If you inject me, however, you will lose your only chance to have me as your best weapon. Your last chance to turn an heir of Elizabeth's unique bloodline into a Mortis."

"Why would I believe you?" asked Grant suspiciously, still holding out my bare arm.

If he injected me, it would probably kill me, but I might not throw off my power as Elizabeth had. I'd be dead, and my friends would no doubt be killed. But if I copied Elizabeth, I should react as she had and hopefully incinerate Grant and his men. And if I was right, Kian and Raef should be immune thanks to Elizabeth. I was dead no matter what, but I might be able to save them and Mae would be safe.

I knew then that my destiny had never been to survive.

My destiny was to end the Clan.

I swallowed hard and willed myself to look at Raef, his agony clear. I drew a ragged breath so I could speak without crying.

"Because I have fallen in love with my protector and if you turn me, I'll help you do whatever you desire, because I will be with him. Forever," I said, a tear escaping my face. "He hates being a Mortis, so he doesn't want me to turn, but I will do anything to. . . ," I swallowed hard, " . . . stay with Raef. I don't want to die. You must spare them all and in return I will do whatever you ask of me."

Raef buckled over, the pain of knowing what I was attempting to do far too devastating.

"Don't listen to her!" said Dalca, angrily. "She lies. There is no proof that she is telling the truth! Don't be a fool! Don't be an idiot. You can' . . ."

I didn't even see Grant move, but one second Dalca had been yelling and the next second she was on the floor, her neck at an odd angle and her eyes staring lifelessly at the ceiling.

"She had outlived my good favor," said Grant, as if he had just tossed an old pair of socks.

I had to swallow back my fear and nausea and not look at her body lying on the stone floor. Grant bent down and pulled the gun from her still curled fingers as my heart hammered in my chest.

"I see this as a gamble either way. As such, we will do it the way I see best," he said placing the needle on the edge of the massive, unused boiler behind him. It was larger than the engine of a steam train and towered above us, a black, gothic beast.

"But, seeing as this is your idea, I'm not going to use one of my men to test your theory. Instead, we will use him." A chill went through me as Grant pointed to Raef.

"Never," growled my beloved guard, his marks becoming even more intricate.

Grant sighed dramatically and pressed the muzzle of the gun hard to my head, cocking the barrel. I closed my eyes, not wanting to think about the bullet passing through my skull.

"You have exactly five seconds to change your mind or I put a hole in her head, since injecting her will supposedly kill her anyway. Five, Four, Three . . ."

"WAIT!" yelled Raef and I opened my eyes, looking at him. He slowly got to his feet, the trio of Mortis still holding him tightly. He looked at me as though his heart was shattering. The muzzle of the gun was still pressed tightly to my temple, but my history teacher was no longer counting.

"Let him go," Grant commanded, looking at Raef. "Do something stupid and I will kill her."

Raef looked at me, agony covering his beautiful face. In that moment I knew my fate, as did he. All the rage and desperation that surrounded the two of us seemed so distant. But history was not to be denied. I was certain that in my death, they would survive, but one question remained: could Raef bring himself to kill me?

The clansmen let Raef go and he walked slowly over to me. Kian, sensing imminent failure, looked away to Ana whose tears raced down her face. I stepped forward slightly to Raef, unafraid of my beautiful angel.

He looked over to Grant, who still had the gun to my head. "I'll do it," he said quietly.

I knew it took everything he had, every ounce of strength, to form the words. Grant stepped back a few feet, but still had the gun aimed at me.

Raef reached out slowly, cupping my face in his hands. My throat tightened, sadness and fear starting to claw inside me. A tear ran down my face and onto his hand and his own eyes started to pool.

I reached up to his hands holding my face, "I love you, so much.

Forever. It's going to be okay. I'll just . . . see you on the other side. Okay?"

The pain on his face was hard to look at, but I held his gaze and he nodded slightly.

"On the other side," he said quietly and then pulled my face to his and kissed me as he never had before, love and pain ricocheting through his powerful grasp. It was everything he ever wanted to share with me. It was his entire heart in one, earth-shattering kiss that scorched my soul.

He wrapped his arms around me and fit my body against his, while his kisses traveled from my lips, to my face, to my cheek. He pulled me tighter to him still, wrapping his arms completely around my back, one hand bracing my shoulder blade.

His lips made my body glow and I let his love flow over me, wrapping me in warmth that held the fear at bay. I let myself feel his strong arms and his soft lips as they traveled to the edge of my face and slowly, gently down my neck.

He kept his face tucked into the side of my neck and I whispered one last time in his ear, "I love you."

I felt him take a ragged, painful breath and he brought his face back to mine. I touched his cheek with my hand as his eyes locked with mine. And then I felt it - an icy, brutal stab to my chest as he forced a virtual opening in my soul.

The pain was instantaneous and excruciating.

I gasped and staggered, but he held me fast, refusing to let me fall, his arms like stone. My body immediately reacted to his supernatural invasion, and my heart began to race, causing my head to spin. But then I felt something else as well - a pull, as if he was drawing on my own essence.

It was only then that I realized I had made a terrible error; that while he most likely had immunity from my lethal talent, my own essence may still be deadly – and he knew it.

"Raef," I gasped, hoping to stop him from drawing on me, but he continued mixing his stolen souls with my poisonous one. He knew I was going to die and he was going to go with me.

He rested his forehead to mine as he continued to bind our essence as his markings strobed, as if my life force was pumping through him.

Weakening, the icy burn began to bloom in my chest as my peripheral vision began to become blindingly bright. Even the pain was now becoming distant as I began to lose feeling in my body.

I tried to hold onto his shoulders, but I seemed to have lost all strength as my arms slowly slid down his back, now useless. My legs became leaden and buckled, but Raef, still strong, shifted his arms carefully to keep me from dropping to the floor. The arctic fire in my chest seemed to expand, spreading outward and my sight failed completely, turning to white.

And then I heard it.

The beginning of the Core's collapse, targeting me. It was a high-pitched whine, like a jet spooling its engine.

Grant began shouting, suddenly alarmed, but he was too late. The fire within raced through my body, as if a dam let go, and I heard the clansmen scream.

My heart shuddered to a stop as death draped over me, shrouding the world in a beautiful, endless silence.

It was my worst fear come true. I was stuck between the world of the living and the afterlife, I was sure.

I couldn't see a damn thing or even move, since gravity apparently had increased ten-fold. My skin felt cold, as if I had been chilled by the weather and Novocaine numb.

Death sucks.

I could even hear my ancestors, calling my name. Loudly. Repeatedly. Actually, it was getting a tad irritating. One was even saying that I was coming around and that something was wearing off.

Wait . . . *Wearing off?*

I refocused my mind and attempted to see through the blackness and suddenly there was a bright flash of light.

"She's trying to open her eyes! Eila! Can you hear me?" said the nagging male voice, almost breathless, as if he had run a marathon. I couldn't respond, but the voice sounded like . . . MJ? Oh god, did I somehow kill him too? I wanted to call to him, but all that came out was a low, ragged moan.

"She's coming around quickly," said a brisk, female voice followed by others jumbled together. I was starting to get feeling back in the tips of my fingers and toes. I tried to see again and I got another flash of light.

"Doctor, do you want me to give her some Versed?" asked the brisk voice.

Doctor? What doctor? What the...?

"No, let's just extubate her quickly before she starts fighting it," said an older male voice. "Eila, if you can hear me, this is Doctor Wainright. We are going to take the tube that has been helping you breathe out of your throat, since you are doing well on your own."

My first foggy thought was that I was thrilled to be alive, but that was quickly followed by panic about a tube down my throat, which I couldn't seem to feel.

I heard MJ's tense voice, "Her heart rate is up. She's not in pain is she?"

No one responded, but I did, in fact, start to feel a general ache through a large portion of my body. I suddenly had the urge to cough and in doing so my head started to pound.

Uh, yeah, *she* was definitely in pain. I felt like I had smacked into a brick wall doing 40.

"All done," said the male voice. "Let's get some oxygen on her."

I could hear sounds around me more clearly, including a rhythmic beeping and hissing. Someone had placed something over my nose and mouth and it caused cool air to flow over my face.

"Eila. Can you try and open your eyes?" asked the woman.

Though my body responded sluggishly to my requests, I managed to move my fingers and was rewarded with someone squeezing my hand. Another hand, which I realized, had been holding mine. "Eila? Eila - it's MJ. Can you open your eyes for me? Can you squeeze my hand again?"

Focusing every ounce of determination I had, I managed to flex my hand again and a strong squeeze clutched my fingers. I got another flash of light and realized I was blinking. After a few more attempts, I managed to keep my eyes open, though barely.

It was then that I could see the blurred but sterile environment of a hospital room. I looked around slowly and saw a doctor in a white, long coat standing next to my bed. Behind him were two nurses.

My hand was squeezed again and managed to turn my wobbly head to see MJ, sitting beside my bed, holding my hand. He was smiling at me, but his face looked like it had gone a few rounds with a WWF fighter in a cage of thorns. He had cuts over his cheekbone, eyebrow, and lip, and black and blue blotches on his face and arms. The cuts were held together with little white strips of tape.

"You're hurt," I managed to whisper in a raspy, dry voice through the oxygen mask. Speaking made my throat scream and I winced. He smiled broadly and let out a laugh that sounded almost like a sob, apparently relieved I was back with the living.

Well, sort of. I felt like I had just returned from Hell.

"Oh, thank God you're alright! You scared the life out of all of us," he said leaning down and kissing my hand, then glancing toward the far wall of the room. I followed his gaze and saw Ana smiling as she held herself up with crutches, her leg in a cast.

"Shit," I managed to croak as I realized how beaten and battered they looked. I heard MJ give a slight laugh, both at my foul language and the release of stress.

"Raef? Kian?" I whispered, worried.

"They're fine. We're all okay," said MJ, pressing my hand to his face. It was then that I noticed two men in dark suits stepping over to my bed, but the doctor stopped them.

"You've got five minutes. She needs to rest. And ask her yes or no questions only because of the intubation," said Dr. Whats-his-name. He turned to me, "Don't talk Eila. You've had that tube in for a while, so your throat will be raw. Just signal yes or no, alright?"

I nodded, surprised I was able to do so. My body was coming back to me and, damn, did everything hurt. Even my toenails.

"How's your pain?" he asked, seeing me wince. He looked over to MJ, who was once again watching me, worried. "Her I.V. is hooked to a pain pump. Press the button and it will self-administer the right dose of pain meds."

"Is that safe?" asked MJ.

Safe? Screw safe! My body was cranking up the torture dial!

Dr. So-and-So nodded. "It won't allow past a certain amount in a set time frame. You can't overdose her, but it can take a little while to take effect. I'd give her some now."

MJ nodded and glanced down at me. He reached over and thankfully pushed the button.

"Eila, it is an absolute miracle you survived so close to the explosion and for the length of time that you lacked a pulse. The pain you have is from a lot of internal bruising and roughly 30 micro-factures to your torso and arms," said the doctor. "If it wasn't for the quick actions of your friends and Mr. Raines, I doubt we would've been able to resuscitate you."

Resuscitate?? Oh man, I WAS dead.

MJ reached over and stroked my head as one of the suits, a 30-

something version of a Jonas Brother, cleared his throat. I looked over at him as the doctor left.

"Eila - I'll come back to check on you later," said Ana. I gave her a weak wave with my free hand and she hobbled out of the room. I felt terrible that she and MJ had been injured. What happened?

The suit with the tickle in his throat stepped up to my bed, followed by his "friend" who was shorter and stockier with reddish-blonde hair. He looked like he might be a few years younger than the dark haired one, perhaps mid 20s.

"Miss Walker, my name is Special Agent Anthony Sollen and this is my partner Special Agent Mark Howe. We are from the FBI. We need to get your statement about what happened four nights ago."

FB friggin I? This was not good. And . . . FOUR DAYS?

I glanced at MJ and pulled the mask away from my face. "Four days?" I asked, my question barely a whisper.

"It's Wednesday, Eila," said MJ, putting the mask back over my nose and mouth. "You've been out since the *boiler* exploded in The Breakers. Do you *remember?*"

I could see that MJ was trying to convey the idea to play along through his eyes, as surreptitiously as possible. I looked at him for a moment, then realized that my plan must have worked a tad too well. And I couldn't exactly tell the FBI that *I* was the malfunctioning boiler or I'd be stored with the aliens in Area 51.

I was going to have to lie and lie well - a talent I entirely lacked. I shook my head slowly *no* as if I was having trouble with my memory.

"You do not recall being in the coal room?" asked Agent Sollen.

I gave my best, perplexed look and shook my head *no*. I was doing pretty well at my first foray into acting and my pain was starting to subside, thanks to the drugs. I found it odd, however, that the FBI was investigating a boiler mishap, which obviously wasn't really a boiler mishap. Unless . . . they weren't buying the boiler story that MJ and whoever else had told.

Shit!

"We know you need your rest, but one more question: Did you know a Dalca Anescu?" asked Sollen.

Wow. Could this get any worse?

Now I didn't know whether to lie or not. I pretended to think hard and decided to go with the truth regarding Dalca, since Cape Cod was so freaking small it would've been nuts not to know her. I nodded *yes*. Then I realized they had just referred to her in the past tense . . .

"Did you recall seeing her at The Breakers the night of the Fire and Ice event?" he asked.

Heck yeah – right before I realized she had gone over to the dark side. But I shook my head *no* and winced accentuating my dramatics with a little moan, hoping they would get the hint and leave.

MJ got to his feet. "I think you need to leave. Eila needs her rest and obviously doesn't remember anything. We have all told you the same thing over and over. We had decided to explore the mansion and got lost, ending up in the boiler room where we encountered Dalca. She seemed agitated, possibly high on something. She saw us, and started screaming about how Raines had screwed her over and then, BOOM! I didn't even see the actual boiler explode, but it nearly killed us all. I'm just beyond grateful my girlfriend is alright," said MJ glancing down at me.

Girlfriend? Umm . . .

"If you need anything else, you know where to find all of us," said MJ, ending the interrogation.

The agents looked at each other, then gave a quick nod to me,

"Feel better, Miss Walker," said Sollen.

I gave them a weak wave and they turned to leave, closing the door behind them. As they passed by the massive window that looked over the nurses' station, Agent Howe glanced through the glass at me and disappeared down the hall.

I turned my head to MJ. "FBI and *girlfriend?*" I barely whispered through the mask, an eyebrow raised.

"The damage was . . . extensive. And they only let me stay because I was your *boyfriend*," said MJ, sitting back down next to me. "You need to stop talking. You'll have no voice left."

"Mae?" I asked, pulling the mask from my face. I worried that she had been told about me and was left to think the worst.

"Raines and Kian have flown over to Ireland to pick her up. They will have her back here by this evening at some point. It took a while to find her, since she was bouncing all over Europe on her tour."

"Raines is okay?" I coughed, relieved.

MJ nodded. "Yeah. The dude who came to the door knocked him out with some sort of sedative. It didn't last long though, because he found me outside and told me there were clansmen inside. That's when we both came looking for you guys. Raines thinks they wanted him alive because they must have known about the necklace, but not where it was hidden. And before you ask, Kian and I dumped the body from your bedroom, so Mae won't walk in on *that* fiasco."

MJ leaned forward, encasing my hands in his. "Raines was insanely worried about you. When they finally located Mae, and told her what had happened, he volunteered his private jet. Kian went just to make sure Raines . . . behaved."

I couldn't believe it. Raines really was on our side and we had doubted him but trusted Dalca. We had made some rotten choices that could've led to all our deaths. Although . . . "Were you even in the boiler room?" I asked in a ragged whisper, ignoring his demand.

"Raines and I got through the outer door of the boiler room, just as the . . . explosion happened. We got tossed back quite a ways. Everybody did, except for Raef, who managed to pull you away from the falling ceiling and shield you. You pack one hell of a punch," he smiled. "I've already healed a lot. Kian and Raef, too. Your energy seems to have interfered with their healing process. Slowed it down. But we're all ok. "

"Are Dalca and Grant dead?" I asked, my voice sounding like a dysfunctional squeak. MJ sighed, exasperated, and shook his head.

"Stop. Talking. And yes, the clan members were incinerated. All that we found after the blast was ash. Everywhere. Dalca was under a piece of the ceiling, crushed. Ana said that Grant had already killed her though. You don't remember that?"

I thought back and started to remember the boiler room more clearly. I remembered Grant breaking Dalca's neck and I nodded *yes* slowly. I was about to ask another question, but he put his finger to my lips to keep me from talking.

"How about I give you the long and the short of it, and you keep your mouth shut?" I frowned, but MJ just continued. "What you did, with Raef's help . . . well, it worked too well. The energy you emitted blew through three floors of The Breakers and instantly incinerated the Rysse guys. Kian managed to shield Ana the best he could, but her leg got hit by debris. Hopefully Dalca's post-mortem injuries will mask her broken neck, so the FBI doesn't get even more interested. We damaged a national treasure for crying out loud."

MJ played with my fingertips as he continued, "When Raines and I were finally able to reach you, I could tell immediately that your heart wasn't beating. Raef was unharmed, but beyond devastated. He wouldn't . . . let go of your body." MJ's voice caught in his throat.

"We finally convinced him to put you down so I could start CPR and Raines got you airlifted here, to Boston. It took nearly 20 minutes to restart your heart. No one knew if you would ever regain consciousness. Raef thought . . . we thought, we had lost you," said MJ, his voice shaking. I squeezed his hand, trying to reassure him.

He shook his head, "Eila, what were you thinking? You could've died!" MJ's face was lined with fear.

"We . . . needed a Hail Mary," I rasped.

He shook his head in frustration; "Promise me, right now, that you will never, *ever* do that again!"

The pain medications were starting to really kick in, and I was feeling warm and very sleepy, "I promise." MJ smiled at me. "Where's Raef?" I asked, longing to see him.

MJ's smile faded. "He is keeping a distance. He's watching over you, guarding the area, but Eila . . . he was destroyed over what happened. He killed you. *Killed you.*"

I was about to argue, but MJ held up his hand, already knowing what I was about to say. "I know. I know – you thought you had no choice. You never knew he'd be the one to do it. But he's having trouble coming to terms with what he did to you. He's going to need time. Can you give him time?"

I nodded, a tear falling down my face. "Tell him I need to see him. Please," I whispered.

MJ nodded, "Okay, but you need to stop talking. And rest," he said, placing the oxygen mask back on my face gently.

The pain meds were making my brain fuzzy. "Please," I whispered again groggily through the mask.

"I will," said MJ as I dozed off.

When I woke again, my hospital room was dark, except for the city skyline outside my window. A soft stream of light filtered in through the large glass wall that faced the corridor. Privacy, it seemed, was a distant second to being able to see the patients.

Out near the nurses' station, I could see a man and a woman talking, though their backs were to me. The shoulders of the woman started to shake, as though she was crying. She lowered her head and the broad-shouldered man reached out and pulled her close, hugging her.

As he turned his head, I could see that it was Raines. And he was hugging . . . Mae! She turned her head to look up at him and he was saying something to her, but not releasing her from his hold.

"You've GOT to be kidding me," I muttered to myself. So much for keeping Mae away from my world.

I heard something move in the far corner of my room and I turned my head toward the sound, suddenly alarmed.

"It's okay. It's just me." Raef's smooth voice floated from the shadows, preceding his beautiful face as he slipped into the slanted light.

I tried to sit up so I didn't look like such a weakling, but a bullet of pain sliced through my back. I froze automatically in reaction to the pain and couldn't help sucking in a sharp breath.

Raef was instantly beside me, cradling his arm behind my back. My fingers wrapped into the softness of his sweatshirt and I buried my face in the warmth of his chest.

"Eila. Please don't try to move," he said, his voice husky beside my face as he lowered me gently back to the bed. I felt entirely safe and at home in his powerful arms that so cautiously held onto me. His sea-storm blue eyes were tracing over my damaged body as he released me and lowered himself carefully to the edge of my bed.

He sat there, silently, studying me. His face spoke volumes of the tormented emotions he was battling inside. I reached out my hand and laced my fingers with his. He looked down at our hands and his tightened gently, possessively, over my own.

"I thought I was going to go with you," he said, in a quiet, near whisper. "But when I realized that I had survived and you weren't. . ." He closed his eyes tightly and his voice revealed the smallest crack.

I squeezed his hand tightly, "I'm here. Right here, and I'm okay."

His eyes flashed open. "YOU are not okay. You are in the ICU!" he said, in a near gasp. "I killed you! You died, in my arms. I felt your heart stop. I did that!"

"This isn't your fault. I chose what I chose because the alternative was a bullet in the head or death by injection, and either of those options left you all unprotected," I said, conviction ringing in my dry voice.

Raef started to shake his head, about to argue, but I kept going, "I was dead no matter what. Me, being here and talking to you, holding your hand and seeing your face again, is a gift. I survived because our friends cared enough to fight for me after I fought for them. You fought for me. For my life and my heart." I pulled his hand to my chest and tucked it under my chin. "You are my guardian and so much more."

He looked at me, his eyes trailing over my face and then down to my hand. He leaned forward and pressed his forehead to mine and sighed.

"I want to kiss you, I do," he whispered. "But I'm afraid that in doing so, in allowing myself those pleasures of kissing you and touching you and . . ." he drew a shaky breath and leaned back so he could look in my eyes. I knew what was coming.

"I will always be here for you. I'll always do whatever you ask of me, but until you know how to defend yourself without such extreme measures as dying. Without me having to . . ." he shook his head at what I was sure was the memory of my body crumpling in his arms.

I raised my other hand to his face and touched his lips to keep him from speaking. "I know. Until I can control my power, and you feel that I can defend myself, you are taking a step back from us, in that way." I watched his eyes and he looked away for a moment, giving a quick nod of agreement.

We sat for a moment, in silence. I glanced out the window to where Mae and Christian were still speaking, though he was now leaning against the desk. Mae was going to need protection as well. Thinking I could keep her out of this was irrational.

"Okay," I finally agreed. Raef turned to me, slightly surprised, no doubt, that I wasn't a bawling mess.

"You're right. There are other people relying on me to be the best I can be. I get that. And I can rise to the occasion despite my raging desire to kiss the life out of you in some darkened corner of the world." A small smile crept up my face.

Raef's own lips twisted into a sly grin, "So, *now* I'm supposed to be just a friend and a bodyguard, knowing your little fantasy about a liplock? Miss Walker, I do believe you intend to torture me."

"Think of it as endurance training," I said, still smiling. He raised my hand to his mouth and kissed my wrist softly, a wide smile gracing his perfect lips. Electricity tingled through my palm.

Who were we kidding? There was no way we were going to be able to keep our hands off each other. Talk about epic fail.

In the distance of the city, I could see the sky beginning to awaken as a warm glow chased away the darkness. Dawn was climbing the horizon and a new day, a new life, awaited me.

Awaited us all.

Catch up with the characters, author, and world of UNDERTOW at
CAPECODSCRIBE.COM and on Facebook at K.R. Conway.

Tweeting @Sharkprose

Instagram: k_r_conway

The story is just beginning.

R U Brave?

STORMFRONT (Book 2)

CRUEL SUMMER (Kian & Ana's Novella)

TRUE NORTH (Book 3)

K.R. CONWAY

ACKNOWLEDGMENTS

If it takes a village to raise a child, then it takes an army to build a story. I was lucky enough to have a fierce battalion behind UNDERTOW. I MUST thank all my warriors.

Many thanks to my late grandfather, Joseph Blackburn, without whom this story would have never even sparked in my head. At only 17, he landed as a Marine on Iwo Jima during WWII. He saw fighting and sacrifice but also humanity, compassion, forgiveness, and humor. He told us of the friendships and craziness of so many young men thrown together against the backdrop of desperation. I took his portrait of war and set it into a tale of a genetic hatred between two races, mixing brutality with friendship, fear with humor.

I also can never thank enough my team of Beta readers. They would re-read, over and over, scenes from UNDERTOW and even get into arguments about what a character should or shouldn't do. Layla, Bethany, Carrie, Kim, Katherine, Meghan, Mara and Clare - I could never have done it without you.

A huge round of applause for Charlotte, my mad-skills editor / Beta, who tirelessly read through UNDERTOW checking for issues. I would've lost my mind without her. And she did it all with a newborn. Talk about Wonderwoman!

Many thanks to my parents, brother, hubby and kids who I'd bounce ideas off of and who listened to me talk endlessly as I tried to work through a scene. They didn't strangle me, which is really impressive.

A shout out to Agent Query Connect, an online community of

writers who were always there to help hone a query letter or find leads. And another high-five to the Cape Cod Fiction Fanatics writing critique group that meets at Starbucks. Between the intense coffee and great conversation, I always had a reason to get back to my desk and write while staying up for hours thanks to the java jolt.

Thank you to my numerous editors at The Cape Cod Times who hired me as a freelancer right out of college. Their faith in me lead to other journalistic pursuits for the past 15 years. To this day I'm amazed they took a chance on me, especially since I was a Forensic Psych major in college. Writing? What the heck is that?

Thank you to my blog followers, Facebook fans and the nearly 500 people that swarmed the first few chapters of UNDERTOW in under five days on FICTIONPRESS. While I did pull it down on the advice of an agent, the cheers and praise of those readers helped me plow through the novel.

Many thanks to the real BHSers (past and present) that became cover models for UNDERTOW: Leslie (Eila), Colby (Raef), Christa (Ana), Justin (Kian), Sean (MJ), Megan (Nikki), Chris (Rilin), Sara (Eve), and Jeremy (Christian). They were insane enough to do it. Hooray for the wild bunch! Huge thanks to photographer Alex Daunais and graphic guru John Sullivan of Quahog Corner for their endless skills, and Carole Corcoran's stunning landscape shots of Cape Cod.

Endless thanks to the musical muses that overrun my iPod: Band of Skulls, The Black Ghosts, Creed, Evanescence, The Faders, Yeah Yeah Yeahs, Tristan Pettyman, Three Dog Night, Stateless, The Black Keys, Muse, Imagine Dragons, Little Big Town, Imogen Heap, Halestrom, Finger Eleven, and so many more. Long live the Rock N Roll Muse!

And lastly, a massive hug of gratitude to all of Cape Cod. The quirky people who live here, the shops and homes that inspire the imagination, and the stunning landscape that calls to the siren in us all.

STORMFRONT

TURN THE PAGE FOR A SNEEK PEEK
AT THE SECOND BOOK IN THE
UNDERTOW SERIES . . .

PROLOGUE

NEWPORT, RHODE ISLAND
FOUR WEEKS BEFORE THANKSGIVING

The largest mansion in Newport looked like a war zone.

At least, that was how Mark Howe remembered the Vanderbilt's historic estate. He would get another look today if the line ever moved, which at this point seemed doubtful. He couldn't believe how long it took to get a non-foamed, non-whipped, non-mucked-with cup of coffee in Newport. How was it even possible that so many Mercedes-driving blondes managed to squeeze into the corner cafe at the crack of dawn?

He would have left, ignoring his desperate need for caffeine, but his body was literally running on fumes. Since the Newport blast seven days ago, he had gotten the absolute minimum for functional sleep, as the case had become quite the media frenzy. Piecing together what the hell had happened in the boiler room had become priority numero uno for his office in Boston, yet he had not received a final report from forensics on the type of bomb used in the blast.

Yes, "bomb," because it damn well wasn't the boiler.

He was headed back to The Breakers mansion this morning if he ever got a damn coffee.

As he finally reached the counter his phone trilled in his pocket. He quickly gave an order for two, large hits of caffeine and snapped open his phone. "Howe," he answered, jostling the phone in the crook of his neck.

"Where are you?" demanded his imposing, seasoned partner of two years, Anthony Sollen.

"Getting us some coffee. You at The Breakers?"

A few faces in the shop glanced at him. The Breakers had Newport in a tizzy and getting the low down on what had happened during the Fire and Ice Ball was the talk of the town. Howe glanced around at his sudden audience and paid the cashier, quickly walking out to his sedan as Sollen talked into his ear.

"Yeah, I'm here, and Forensics wants to talk to us. Now," snapped Sollen.

"I'm on my way. Be there in three minutes." Howe snapped his phone shut, knocking the gearshift into drive.

He managed to swig half of the scalding drink before he pulled through the iron gates of the Vanderbilts's summer home, now being guarded round the clock as a crime scene. He parked in front of the massive entrance and headed inside with his partner's cup of joe.

Numerous members of the local and national Historical Society had been the biggest pains in the ass when it came to dealing with the blast scene. They were there, as always, watching every move the FBI made, making sure nothing was further damaged. They were chomping at the bit to start repairs before winter set in and possibly caused further damage to the historic home. Millionaire Christian Raines, whose fundraiser fete had been in full swing inside the mansion during the explosion, volunteered to foot the bill for all repairs. Supposedly he was devastated by the damage to the historic estate.

Devastated my ass, thought Howe. He was certain something was up with Newport's Most Eligible Man.

As he entered the boiler room for the umpteenth time since the night of the Fire and Ice party, Howe was still amazed that the only fatality in the blast was Dalca Anescu, who had been crushed by a piece of the ceiling.

The beastly, cast iron boiler that filled one side of the room looked like a concrete truck had hit it doing 90 mph. The floors and walls of the brick room all sustained structural damage and showed it via hundreds of cracks. A gaping hole in the ceiling gave a clear view up from the cellar through three floors and clean through the roof, where the energy of the explosion had been funneled. Damage estimates were easily in the millions, all of which Raines seemed willing to pay.

Howe thought of the kids from Cape Cod that had survived the carnage. There were the two O'Reilly brothers, deep pocketed themselves, who were the least injured. Ana Lane and the boy, Williams, had minor injuries, but the girl, Walker, was nearly killed and had obvious concussive injuries consistent with close proximity to a blast.

If they were all in the same room, why on earth would they not have all sustained the same injuries?

How in the hell were they not all dead?

Something was just wrong with the whole picture and Howe hoped the forensics team finally had a lead on the actual source of the blast. He walked to the center of the room where Sollen was standing with an older, balding man.

"So? I'm right, right? Plastique like C-4 right?" asked Howe handing the coffee to his partner, who nodded his thanks.

Sollen gestured to the man beside him, "Mark Howe, this is Dr. Carl Leeland. He does some work for the DC office from time to time when we are stuck." The forensic geek gave a stiff smile.

Howe reached out and shook the doctor's hand, "We're stuck, I take it?"

"Nice to meet you Agent Howe, though I wish the circumstances were better. I've worked some terrorism attacks for the government when unusual materials are used in bombs."

"So it was a bomb," said Sollen, rubbing the back of his neck, the tension literally forcing his muscles to seize. "Type?"

Dr. Leeland cleared his throat, "Well, that's just it. I cannot find any bomb residue of any kind, anywhere in the building, let alone this room. Any explosive that we know of that can create this kind of damage leaves a residue and there is none."

"Couldn't it have burned off?" asked Howe, hopeful as visions of a more simplified end to the Breakers case began to evaporate.

Leeland smoothed back his few remaining hairs as he spoke, "There is no indication of any sort of fire, anywhere. Which tells me that this was not chemical in any way. It had to be a physical bomb."

"Like what? Compressed gas or something?" asked Howe.

"Well, if the blast was far, far smaller, yes. But a blast this huge?" Leeland shook his head. "The only thing that comes to mind that can do this damage without leaving a chemical trail, is nature."

"What?" asked Howe and Sollen, nearly in unison.

"Nature, like a tornado. Although, my guess, in here, it would have been something like a bolt of lightning.

"Why lightning?" asked Sollen.

Leeland looked down at his clipboard as his glasses slipped

slightly on his narrow nose. "According to the statements your office took from the guests that night, nearly all said they heard a boom that reminded them of a lightning strike."

Howe shook his head, this idea of lightning being just too damn far fetched and the boiler looking better by the second. "Are we certain it wasn't the boiler? Maybe it actually did malfunctioned and blow?"

Leeland shook his head. "No. The boiler would be in pieces and right now it is flattened to the wall. Something threw it there with incredible force." Leeland suddenly snapped his fingers, as if remembering something, "Oh! And wait until you see this!" He picked up a flashlight out of a black duffle bag and walked over to the boiler. Sollen and Howe followed.

Leeland flicked on the flashlight and trained the beam of light into the depths of the crushed boiler. The light found its target and Leeland held it steady, "I believe the saying in Boston is 'How do you like them apples?'" he asked, triumphant.

Howe squinted as he looked into the darkness at the small, silver object at the end of the light. It was jammed among the pipes within the boiler. "Is that a handgun?" he asked, stunned.

Sollen looked as well, his brow furrowed with lines. "I think that is a Korth. See the check mark near the end of the barrel. Damn expensive handgun."

Howe knew without doubt that the kids from the Cape knew far more than they were saying. "None of those kids said a thing about a handgun." He shook his head, trying to sort the outrageous intel. "Okay, just so I have this all straight, you are basically saying this was a bomb that causes no fire, but major structural damage, and manages to kill only one person, but levels half of a mansion? Does this sound crazy only to me?"

Leeland tossed his hands, "I'm saying that if this is, in fact, a weapon, then I have never seen it before and it is one hell of a device."

Sollen looked at Howe, lines of stress clearly across his face. Someone had a new type of bomb in the United States and it wasn't the home team.

"What's the chance that Anescu was a brilliant physicist and that this all ends with her?" asked Howe, sarcastically.

"Slim to none," replied Sollen. "Ever been to Cape Cod?"

"Only once when I was stuck in traffic for three hours trying to cross the Sagamore Bridge," replied Howe. "Let me guess – you want some salt-water taffy?"

Sollen, never one to joke, pulled his Blackberry from his jacket pocket. He pressed a button and looked at the screen that showed information on the five survivors of the blast. "I say we pay the charming town of Centerville a visit and start with . . . 408 Main Street. I hear the Walker girl just got released from the hospital and I'm sure she'd just love to see us again."

Howe just shook his head, "I hate the beach."

CHAPTER 1
EILA

NAUSET BEACH, CAPE COD MASSACHUSETTS
ONE DAY BEFORE THANKSGIVING

I had a kill mark.

At least, that's what Christian had called it.

He said mine was darker, deeper . . . more distinct, even than my 4th great grandmother, Elizabeth's. From what I had managed to see, the small brand on my back that deemed me a murderer had also begun to change, growing upwards on my spine like a gnarled vine.

Christian said it was normal, considering what I had done a few weeks before. Considering how many I had slaughtered inside the coal room of the Newport mansion. A kill mark, he said, was the badge of the truly lethal and appeared only on those like me - those who could torch soul thieves and nearly flatten a national treasure . . . though I was sure my wrecking-ball capability was a shocker for Christian.

I've got to say, I could do without it.

In fact, I could do without the whole assassin genes in general. It would be awesome if we were given a chance to choose our gene pool. A chance to mull over the options and pick what we wanted and what we would pass on, like the ability to channel the energy of souls and thus, fry soul thieves.

That would have been a big, fat pass for me.

I remember watching Sleeping Beauty as a child with Mae, and the Three Good Fairies chose what the princess got for endowments. They opted for a sick singing ability and good looks. Apparently everyone in the kingdom was stupid, because no one gave the poor girl any BRAINS and she went and touched the damn spindle. I mean, for crying out loud, if you get to choose the genetics ya get, belting out show tunes and rosy lips should be low on the list of must-haves.

Sometimes I felt like I too was destined to screw up and touch the proverbial spindle . . . unless I could torch the spinning wheel first. The only problem was a certain soul thief, who didn't seem too keen on having me test my wheel-frying abilities at all, especially after the Newport fiasco five weeks ago.

I needed a do-over from that night. We all did.

I glanced at Ana standing next to me. The snowflakes had begun to coat the top of her jacket's hood. A few brave flakes descended onto her long eyelashes and she blinked them away as she rolled her lips, willing them to not freeze off.

She huffed out her disgust at our current state, the cold air turning her words into slanted puffs of smoky vapor. "This is the dumbest pastime on the planet. I mean, who thinks up activities like this? Does some moron decide that hypothermia prior to turkey is a great idea and everyone jumps on the bandwagon?" She brutally scrubbed the flakes off her parka, evicting them without remorse.

Truth was, as a Kansas native now calling Cape Cod home, I didn't see the logic of surfing on Thanksgiving Eve either. Especially prior to the Nor' Easter that was heading towards us and churning up some monster waves. That said, however, this brilliant plan to freeze our butts off at Nauset beach was her idea. I decided not to remind her of that bit of info, since she was looking like a fairly pissed Popsicle anyway. I didn't think that the stiff walking boot encasing her left leg helped either.

She wouldn't have the darn thing if it wasn't for me.

Of course, she might not have her life anymore either, if I hadn't done what I did. Luckily, she only had to wear it when we went out of the house for any length of time, as she was basically healed.

"Let's give them ten more minutes, and then we can head back home," I replied, giving her a small smile. She eyed me with a steely glare and then just shook her head, resigned, her eyes going back to the two soulless surfers in the waves.

I must admit that when I first moved to the Cape, nearly three months ago, I didn't think Ana Lane and I would ever be more than classmates. But now? Now I couldn't imagine life without her. Through all the chaos that rained down on our lives over the past couple of months, she became more than just a short-statured blonde with a sharp tongue.

She became my best girl-pal ever.

She became the one I could divulge secrets to, horde chocolate with, and spill my guts to in the dead of night. And we stayed up until late every Friday night, watching movies in her room.

Her room, which was now across from mine, since she had

moved into 408 Main Street with me and my legal guardian Mae. She was my mother's best friend until the night both my parents were killed in a car accident. I was only two when they died, and Mae had only just graduated high school, but she took me in. She loved me as her own and I have never seen her as anything other than a sister-like Mom who I have loved for the past sixteen years.

As for Ana, she wasn't just a live-in BFF either. She was also one heck of an asset, especially in our motley crew. She was like an emotional psychic with a super-charged mind. She could understand what a person FELT, deep inside. Pick apart their true desire, and either blab about it or modify it. She could take someone who was simply miffed and make her a raging maniac. She could take someone who was shy and make him crumble into oblivion. Or, she could make that one, quiet wallflower become a fearless captain.

She was also getting better and better at reading memories. A few weeks ago she was able to link to my mind and view my nightmares regarding Elizabeth's death. A death that happened nearly two centuries ago, and that I had begun reliving in my dreams.

Unfortunately Ana couldn't read the future, nor see the train wreck we hit head-on during the Fire and Ice Ball at The Newport Breakers.

Hey – nobody's perfect.

If there was a plus side to my body going nuclear in the coal room of the Vanderbilt's summer mansion, it was the simple fact that the bad guys were dead. Fried into dust by the soul-channeling energy I command.

Well, "command" may be a bit too strong of a word. I think I more or less barfed up a solar flare.

Luckily I didn't remember much of it.

On the downside, I did nearly croak. Plus, I put a hole in the mansion that looked like a comet had struck. And while the mansion and I were finally on the mend, the fallout of what I did with Raef's help was not soon forgotten.

Since the ball, Raef had been treating me with kid gloves and avoiding all physical contact – as if I resided inside a glass bubble. I was also sure he was haunted by the fact that he basically killed me that night in Newport. He never talked about it, which I didn't think helped when it came to his new title: Worry-Wart of the World.

I've gotta say, having the boy who previously could make a kiss scorch right to your toenails, now start acting like one giant mother hen, was SO not sexy.

I missed his touch, his kisses, and the way his face became marked with beautiful black symbols when we were in one another's arms. I missed him, all of him, but he seemed lost in his own, painful world and he wouldn't let me in.

In the first days after my weeklong hospital stay, it was a miracle if I was even able to escape to the bathroom alone. Mae was hovering, Raef was obsessing, Kian was patrolling, and poor MJ was semi-grounded. But Ana? Ana found it downright hilarious until she became more mobile and instantly joined my ranks in the dreaded "buddy-system."

See, this was the problem with having immortal, semi-boyfriends and an ice-cream wielding, shape-shifter as bodyguards – they are great at their jobs, but go a bit overboard. Determined to not have Ana and I in danger again, the boys had devised the "Buddy System," which basically meant we needed a male sidekick wherever we went. The feminist in both Ana and me bristled at the mandatory babysitting, and defiantly referred to the boys plan as "BS."

They weren't amused.

So it was with no small amount of arm-twisting that we had managed to get Kian and Raef to go surfing, a whole sand dune and 50 yards of rolling ocean away from us. I think the only reason they finally agreed was because no one else was out here, freezing to death prior to a storm, and therefore the threat was minimized. We were also instructed to STAY at the top of the dune's staircase, where they could easily see us. Of course, such a demand made the devilish urge to go and hide all the more tempting.

Like I said – it was all BS.

I watched as Kian and Raef sat on their new surfboards out in the water. They were talking to one another as they straddled the boards in their wetsuits, though Raef kept looking at me every two seconds. Technically, as immortal soul thieves, they didn't need the protection from the frosty Atlantic, but flinging them out there in just some swim trunks would have drawn attention if anyone else had been as insane as we were.

Luckily, we were the only psychos on the beach.

The thickening storm clouds had blocked out the sun, and the brilliantly blue sky from earlier was now a brutish gray, speckled with hyperactive snowflakes. Ana said that a Thanksgiving storm like this was a rarity on the Cape. Of course, she also had extolled the virtues of surfing prior to pumpkin pie and, well, that wasn't exactly accurate either.

"What do you think they're talking about?" I asked, watching the waves where our bodyguards bobbed up and down.

"Pfft – wadda ya think? What they always obsess about. You. Me. How to lock us up in a tower with ten-foot thick walls and a fully outfitted army." She stepped back slightly and brushed the snow off a small bench to sit down. I noticed Kian and Raef instantly stopped talking the second she moved, and were now watching her and scanning the surrounding area. They really needed to chill.

"How's physical therapy?" I asked.

Ana sighed as she sat, "It's fine. I swear though, they book me more often than everyone else just because of Kian. All the therapists just want to see him leaning against that damn back wall, looking all sorts of sexy. Drives me nuts. And he insists on taking me. Honestly, I don't even think my therapist knows my last name! She sure as hell knows Kian's though. My last session is Monday afternoon, thank goodness."

I gave a small chuckle and she glared at me. Kian O'Reilly and Ana had met the summer before I came to Cape Cod. While both were somewhat tight-lipped about what had happened that summer, I knew one things for certain: Ana and Kian had been desperately in love . . . until her abusive father had a heart attack and Kian refused to save him.

As soul thieves, Kian and Raef could steal the life force of their victims, but they also could share what they had stolen in a filtered form to heal a human. Kian had told Ana that her father was too weak to be saved and would have turned into a soul thief, like him. Ana didn't believe him, calling him a murderer and banishing him from her life.

A year later, I arrived on the Cape and they collided once again. Kian had returned to sell his yacht, Cerberus, and Raef had come along. Raef soon figured out that I was the 4th great daughter of his former friend, Elizabeth, and he decided to protect me – because he failed to protect her in 1851. Kian had zero interest in the protection detail thing until he realized Ana was hanging out with me and she became a target by association. Pretty soon, I had two immortal guards that were technically my genetic enemies.

Fate works in some crackpot ways.

As for Ana and Kian . . . their relationship was a work in progress. I suspected Raef and I had a long way to go as well.

CHAPTER 2
RAEF

Five weeks ago, I nearly killed the girl I loved.

It wasn't an accident. It wasn't a mistake.

I did it deliberately, and the feeling of her body weakening in my arms haunts me still, as if branded into my hands. The sound of her last, thin breath replays over and over in my mind, a taunting reminder of what I am capable of and what I had done.

She carries the mark of where I had forced a stolen soul into her - a thin, finger-long scar engraved between her breasts.

She tries to hide it, but I know it's there.

She will carry that scar to her grave, a permanent reminder of who I truly am - a killer, designed by the darker hand of fate.

The scar had bled down her beautiful, fair skin that night, turning the bodice of the white ball gown she had worn into a sickening, mottled pink. In my mind I see her, lifeless, tucked under me as I try to shield her from the pieces of falling stone and wood that rain down around us. Debris that was from the massive hole her energy had drilled through the Breakers. Energy that was unleashed when her body switched to overload, and her DNA hit the self-destruct button because of me.

Her power had wound around us like a snake of light and rocketed through the ceiling only to fall back, collapsing onto us. It had killed the clansman instantly . . . and halted Eila's heart.

I tried to go with her. Tried to poison myself with her life-force by drawing it into my body, but I failed. She wasn't toxic to me – she never was and never could be. I was left alive, desperately trying to restart her heart with MJ and Kian frantically attempting to help. Trying to save this one girl who had so profoundly changed all our lives, and who had sacrificed herself to protect us. To protect me, her historic enemy.

She had whispered into my cheek that she loved me, moments before I caused that scar. I hear her voice speak those words when I stand, alone at night, watching over her home. Praying I will catch anyone who means her harm before they come too close.

Before they have a chance to take her life . . . as I had.

I watch her now, standing with Ana as the snow swirls around them. She seems happy, healthy, and against all odds, alive.

She had told me, repeatedly, that it wasn't my fault. That we had no choice, that night in Newport, surrounded by Mortis who wanted her power. She said she was dead no matter what, but at least she could give the rest of us a fighting chance at survival.

But I was, and am, her guard. I should have been more careful, more vigilant. I should have known, somehow, but I didn't see a friend's betrayal coming. None of us did, and it was Eila who paid the price, and

I the one who demanded the ultimate payment.

She was, is, my everything. My need to love her is like a physical demand that must be met for my survival, and for that reason, the fear that I may hurt her again is crushing. The terror that I may fail her again, as I failed her grandmother a century and a half ago, weighs more than the world.

She trusts me, loves me, and I *will not* lose her again.

But to protect her, I know I need to be stronger. Faster. A perfect killer. I needed a Dealer, no matter the cost, no matter the risk. I would do it for her.

I wasn't sure if I could tell Kian, because he may try to stop me, though he had no problem picking off a few people if it were necessary. And Christian I still didn't quite trust, though I was certain he had the right connections to introduce me to the darkest corners of our kind.

So for now, I do what I can. I am hyper-vigilant, I try to stay nearby, and I try not to breech the wall I have built between us. A wall that is a necessity, because when I hold her, kiss her, and run my hands down her slender frame, I forget who I am. In her soft lips and breathy gasps I lose myself, and in doing so, she becomes vulnerable. Unprotected, because I am entirely distracted when she presses her beautiful body against mine. That wall, however, was beginning to feel more precariously erected with every passing day. As Eila grew stronger, my will to keep her at arm's length weakened.

In the hospital we had made a deal: keep our hands off one another until she could use her power like the dangerous weapon it was designed to be and protect herself. I assumed I wouldn't worry so much about her if I knew she could defend herself and I could draw her into my arms once again. Unfortunately, I overlooked one thing: I would NEVER stop worrying about Eila Walker. Even if she could crush the planet, I would still worry.

As I watched her in the center of the swirling snow, her chocolate hair twisting around her face, I knew I was in trouble.

She wanted to fight. I wanted her safe.

As she grew stronger, she began talking about training more and more. She wanted to attempt to call her power again and see if she could control it. But I had seen her power nearly kill her and take out half of a mansion. I saw it kill her grandmother, Elizabeth.

Kian, traitor that he was, told Eila it was her birthright to learn about her gift and protect herself. I wanted to stab him, even though I knew he was right.

But I couldn't let her use her gift again, for I feared what her power could do to her. What if it collapsed on her again, and this time I couldn't restart her heart? What if she practiced when I wasn't there, and it injured her? Or even worse, what if she failed to protect herself from one of my kind and she was killed? The vision of her dying at the hands of a Mortis ran a bitter knife through my heart.

"What's going through that thick head of yours?" asked Kian, rapping his knuckles on the edge of my board. A froth-tipped swell raised us a few feet and then dipped us into a watery valley, obscuring Eila from my view for a moment. I craned my neck to see her.

"She's fine Raef. If you stare at her any longer, your eyeballs are going to burn a hole through the atmosphere."

I glanced to Kian, his blonde hair swept back from his face, and wondered how he could be so calm. Ana had nearly died two days before the Fire and Ice Ball, attacked by a Mortis who had gotten into Eila's house and threw her down a flight of stairs. He too knew what it was like to watch the girl he loved nearly fade from this world.

He had saved her life by sharing his pilfered life-forces with her, nearly ending his own in the process. She didn't know how far he had pushed himself to save her that day and he didn't want her to know. I knew he had wanted to also heal her leg, but Eila's energy release inside the Breakers had temporarily disabled our ability to heal . . . both ourselves and others. Thus, Ana was on the mend the old fashioned way, which bothered Kian more than he let on.

While there was no arguing that Kian could be a complete egotistical ass, he was loyal to our dysfunctional crew and endlessly devoted to keeping Ana safe. And because Ana went where Eila did, he guarded them both, and for his help, I was truly grateful.

To say we were tight friends however, would be seriously overstating our relationship. We tolerated each other, disagreed on most things, but when it came to Eila and Ana, we were in perfect sync.

I also knew that his mind drifted to Ana like mine did to Eila. How far they got physically last summer was something he did not discuss. Yes, he was a jerk on occasion, but he also protected Ana's privacy. God help the man who ever dared to touch Ana wrong . . . or Eila.

My Eila.

Not long ago, a drunken footballer named Teddy Bencourt nearly took something from her that she wasn't willing to part with. I was almost too late, and seeing her fight him off caused the killer in me to burn like an Olympic torch. She had calmed me and I had yet to see the kid again, but if I did . . . not good.

"Do you hear me, man? You've got to ease up a bit. You look like roadkill."

I turned to him, giving him an unmistakable gesture with a certain finger.

He glanced over at Ana. She was talking to Eila and dusting off the pine bench near the top of the dunes. She moved to sit down and we automatically shifted our gazes to watch her and scan the area for any threat.

He looked back to me. "I'm serious though. When the hell was the last time you slept?"

"The night before the Breakers," I replied, fully aware that even for my kind, 35 days without sleep was pushing past our supernatural limits. It was also the one and only time I had slept beside Eila. The memory of that night rushed into me and I closed my eyes to clear my head.

Complicating my fatigue was the fact that I wasn't hunting animals very often. I never liked leaving Eila in anyone's care but mine, but not stealing animal life-forces on a regular basis was wearing me down. When I was truly desperate for a hit, injecting myself with corpse blood, which contained traces of a human life-force, would work. Briefly.

But what I really needed was a pure hit of power. I needed the soul of a living person.

"You are some kind of stupid, you know that?" grumbled Kian, shaking his head, which caused his board to subtly bounce in the water. "I know you are obsessed with her safety, but you are going to crash and burn at this rate, and you'll be of no use to anyone. Get it together before you become a liability."

I shook my head, "I'm okay. I'll be fine."

Kian looked at me and his face was serious, "No you're not, and soon you won't be."

I knew he was right, but more importantly I knew that only as my true self could I ever be Eila's savior. Only as a killer of mankind could I fully protect the girl I loved.

Which was why I needed to find a Dealer . . . and soon.

CHAPTER 3
EILA

By the time we got back to my house, the snow had really begun to fly. Thankfully my awesomely awesome Wrangler navigated the white roads easily. Our secret service duo followed us in Kian's new Range Rover, complete with surf-boards strapped to the top.

It looked entirely ridiculous.

They were about as stealthy as a hippo riding a tricycle.

Kian had bought the black, rock-stomper of a vehicle soon after his immortal ex-girlfriend, Collettte, had taken his Corvette. It was a trade he grudgingly agreed to in order to acquire designer clothes for all of us when we went to the Fire and Ice Ball. The clothing was fantastic, but Kian was pissed about the loss of his fast machine. Luckily, he still had Cerberus – his multi-million dollar yacht that had become, briefly, our home away from home. It was the ultimate clubhouse, rolling on the sea.

Cerberus, however, had been shipped down to West Palm Beach for the winter and I honestly missed the yacht and the memories it held. MJ was supposed to check on it while visiting his family in Florida for Thanksgiving – lucky.

The yacht also became our salvation when my house was breeched by an uninvited visitor with lethal intents. While Cerberus was technically just a boat, it was also a weird sort of pal and we all missed her fabulosity.

I pulled my Jeep up to the side door of the house and cut the engine. The boys pulled in behind us just as I was getting out of the car, and I watched as the two killer bodyguards stepped out of the Rover and walked towards us in the falling snow. Their presence seemed almost surreal – my whole life did.

I was the owner of a magnificent Sea Captain home on Cape Cod, built by my 4th great grandparents, including Elizabeth who was one of the fiercest rebel fighters the Lunaterra and Mortis had ever known. I had inherited her dangerous talent, plus that of her guard and lover, Christian Raines. Supposedly I was a hybrid – a mix of two warring enemies, thanks to their forbidden affair.

Unfortunately, all I really wanted to be was a Barnstable High School senior and not look like an idiot in my school picture. Instead I was a rare, zillion-watt light bulb.

I bet if I shook my family tree hard enough, Big Foot, Nessy, and even the Sea Witch would come tumbling out and squash me.

I got up close and personal with the Lunaterra side of me when I went all "mega-bomb" inside the Breakers. The Mortis part, however, didn't seem to show itself. I had no desire to suck the soul out of anyone, and I wasn't fast or strong . . . or immortal. At least I didn't think I was immortal. I was 17, soon to be 18, and "immortal" was decades away.

Raef and Kian were thankfully immune to my power, though they did have a few dings and dents after my epic light show. We had known they were unaffected by my power since they had witnessed Elizabeth's death when she called on the limitless energy of the Core within the Web of Souls. Her lightning-like energy incinerated nut-job, Jacob Rysse, but didn't kill Raef or Kian – a fact for which I was extremely grateful. Her death sparked the local town myth that claimed she was struck by lightning.

Yeah – not quite.

It was entirely possible that the healing ability of the Mortis part of me allowed me to survive the Core collapse of my power inside the Breakers. When Elizabeth had tried it in 1851, she had been killed. Christian said he had found her, lifeless, in the harbor square after she had eliminated Rysse. He said he took her body and buried her and sent her necklace back to the young woman named Katherine who had altered it for her.

A necklace that unlocked Elizabeth's diary, and was now in the hands of my most loathed classmate: Nikki Shea.

I could kiss that sucker goodbye.

I slammed the driver's door shut and walked around the back towards Ana who was sliding out her side. Her walking boot was awkward, but soon would thankfully be retired. She wobbled slightly on the slick ground, but Kian was quickly next to her, one broad hand on her back.

"I am not a total clutz you know?" she protested, growling at the slushy driveway.

Kian slid her a sly smile. "Yeah, well . . . knowing your luck, you will slip and break the other leg and then I will be giving you piggy back rides everywhere. Actually, I could get down with that arrangement."

Ana punched him in the arm, but then slipped. He grabbed her quickly and pinned her to his side. "Jeez woman! It wasn't a dare!"

"Will you just help me get inside already?" she sighed, gripping the front of his leather jacket tighter as she slowly made her way across the slick ground to the door. I followed, trying not to smile as she and Kian continued to argue about everything, including the size of the snowflakes.

Raef stepped in next to me, his hands in his black coat pockets. "So Kian and I are going to head back to Torrent Road briefly, get changed and then we'll be back."

I nodded, but a biting wind tore around the house and I tried to tuck my face down into my coat. Raef moved in front of me, shielding my face and body from the brutal gust. The treetops slashed back and forth violently in the gale, as if an invisible giant was pounding through the woods, but just as suddenly as it started, the wind died, and I was mere inches from Raef's chest.

He looked at me while he dusted the snow from my jacket hood. "I have a feeling we might lose power tonight. I'll make sure the fireplaces are ready to go, just in case."

"Mae will appreciate that. Thanks Raef," I replied as we finally made it through the side door to the house.

Mae appeared from the laundry room, a basket of folded linens in her arms, her crazy red hair pinned up in a bun. "Hi Guys! How was the surfing?" she asked, sliding the basket onto the counter.

"Excellent Ma'am," replied Kian, who helped Ana to sit at the table. He knelt before her and started unstrapping the walking boot from her leg. Ana, never one to be pampered, immediately leaned forward to help, but instead cracked heads with Kian. She bit back a swear as Kian sat back on his heels, "Can you just sit still for two seconds?"

"I can do it," she demanded, rubbing her head.

"I KNOW you can, but there is snow caked in the buckles. Just chill for one moment. Please."

Ana slouched, resigned, as Kian continued working on the boot. I hung my jacket by the door as Raef walked over to Mae. He smiled at her as he reached for the basket. "The waves were terrific. Perfect swells. Do you want this on the second floor landing as usual, Ms. Johnson?" he asked, shifting the basket in his hands.

"For the twentieth time, it's Mae. Please. And you don't need to do that. You and Kian have already done so much these past weeks. I would have been lost without you. All of you. Even Mr. Raines."

Ugh. The way the word *Raines* curled off her lip, I knew she had a serious crush on my soul-stealing, ultra-great grandfather.

I laid down the law with Christian Raines weeks ago; Mae was off limits. And while Christian had obeyed, having him a few miles away at his new Torrent Road home was causing quite the kerfuffle in both our house and throughout the town. He was, after all, Newport's Most Eligible bachelor three years running, and now he was living in a massive stone villa known to the locals as the Island House, though we called it simply Torrent Road. Mae had no clue about Christian's darker side – or mine for that matter.

MJ argued that Raines should be disqualified from Newport's hot-hunk competition, since he was a Mortis. Soul-sharks, he said, had an unfair advantage in the looks department and as I studied Kian and Raef, I knew he was absolutely right.

Raef, with his very dark-blonde hair, chiseled physique, flawless face, and stunning deep blue eyes, looked as though he fell off the front of a Hollister shopping bag. Kian, equally perfect, was taller, with blonde hair that fell straight near his broad shoulders, as if he was a posterboy for a surfing company. Like Raef, his deep blue eyes hid a blackness that could blot out the blue, and his hands, so gentle with Ana, were capable of incredible violence. I saw him kill someone in front of me with those hands and witnessed the rage that encompassed his body when he did so. No remorse, no regret, but he saved my life and Ana's.

I wasn't super keen on having Christian so close, especially with the adoring stars in Mae's eyes. But Christian had helped us, enormously. He paid all my medical bills and he opened his house to both Kian and Raef, who needed somewhere to stay now that Cerberus was in southern waters for the winter.

Christian had also managed to charm the crap out of MJ's folks, convincing them that he would be an excellent silent partner at the Milk Way – basically he was their personal bank at a zero-percent interest rate. I'm pretty sure he did it to smooth over MJ's mom, whose anger about her son being involved in my crazy life was still at Code Red level.

Raines's home was also where all the books and papers from Dalca Anescu's shop, the Crimson Moon, were stashed. A shop that no longer existed, because Kian and Raef had burned the building to the ground, after removing any shred of evidence that could reveal our world to the FBI.

Torching the building was a risk. FBI Agents Mark Howe and Anthony Sollen had visited me in the hospital and several times at my house. They asked many questions, over and over, about what happened in the Breakers and if I knew what happened to the Crimson Moon. I was worried that somehow, some way, they would realize I was the cause of the damage to the Breakers. But who in their right mind would ever believe that a teenager could channel a mythic power so brutal that it shattered a large portion of a famed, national treasure?

Yes, the FBI was sniffing around, but they were also chasing their tail.

I nodded to Ana, who was finally free of her black boot. "Want to go change? It's a fuzzy-pjs kind of day."

"Hell yes. I'm frozen," she replied as Kian pulled her to her feet. He pouted and Ana gave him a questioning look, "What?"

He shook his head, "I don't have any fuzzy PJs. I'm bummed." He gave her a smile and she shook her head, but a twisted grin escaped her lips. He turned to Mae and began chatting about the storm as Ana and I followed Raef out of the kitchen and up the main staircase to our rooms.

Raef set the basket of laundry near the door to the bathroom, which Ana and I shared. I pushed open my bedroom door as Ana did the same across the hall from me.

"You feeling okay?" asked Raef, as he leaned back against the wall next to the bathroom. To anyone else, Raef acted like a polite, helpful high schooler, which was what made his true identity all the more chilling. A Mortis was impossible for anyone to identify until it was too late. Mortis couldn't even pick out one another from a crowd, just as humans can't identify a convict in a room full of bikers.

"I feel good. I'm going to get into some cozy clothes and help Mae prep some food for tomorrow. You know she expects you and Kian to come to dinner, right?"

He nodded, "Yeah. Not sure how we are going to work around the food thing though." The reality was, Mortis didn't eat food. They noshed on life-forces, and the turkey downstairs in the fridge was definitely lacking in that department.

"Just come. You guys can make up an excuse – some strange

fasting for an unknown religion or something. She is so excited to have company for Thanksgiving. We never do. It's always just the two of us, and Ana hasn't celebrated Turkey Day or Christmas since her dad died last year."

"I haven't celebrated either holiday since 1850," replied Raef, a smile pulling at his mouth. He stepped over to me and leaned down so he was eyeball-to-eyeball with me. "I'm actually looking forward to it."

"Really?" I squeaked. I was super excited to be having the holidays in my new home with my friends, Mae, and Raef. Sometimes I even laid in bed, thinking about finding that ideal tree with my four friends. Of course, Ana and MJ would argue over which evergreen was perfect, and she would make him spin each frothy spruce about 100 times, but I was silly-giddy about the whole season. I shook my fists dweebily and started to squeal, thrilled that he was happy.

"Okay - well it's not THAT exciting," he laughed and I couldn't help it - I crossed our hidden line and hugged him.

He stilled for just a moment and my heart damn near stopped, but then he wrapped his arms around me and pressed me into his solid chest. My throat tightened and I managed to whisper into his chest, "Don't take too long at Christian's."

He pulled back from me, just enough to see my face and my glassy eyes. "Am I ever gone long?"

I laughed, "No, I guess not. Am I just that addictive?"

He swallowed and looked more serious, "I'd say that's an understatement."

I heard the door click shut across the hall, and Raef released me, turning to see Ana in a pair of mis-matched PJs. Raef nodded to her fuzzy pants, covered with a certain green, Dr. Suess character. "Is that Elmo?"

Ana looked horrified, "Elmo? Are you color blind? Elmo is red and this . . ." she pointed to one of the emerald faces, " . . . is THE GRINCH! You know, for someone who has been around for almost two centuries, you really are lacking in your furry-monster identification skills."

"I'll be sure to work on that," replied Raef, amused. He looked back at me as I bit back a smile. "I've got to go so I can get back before the storm really hits. Do you two want anything while I'm out?"

"Christmas Tree Peeps!" said Ana, raising her hand.

I shrugged, "Works for me."

"What in the world is a Peep?" asked Raef.

Ana slapped her hand to her forehead, "Oh my god, you guys are like aliens. How do you not know what Peeps are? Are you from another planet?"

Raef just shrugged, "I don't exactly go the grocery store."

"It's okay Raef. Ana and I are going to help Mae, and maybe overdose on some cookie dough, so forget the Peeps," I smiled.

"Okay then. I'll be back, sans Peeps . . . whatever they are." He turned to Ana, "And I'll see you soon as well, Elmo."

As he headed down the stairs, Ana yelled after him, "IT'S NOT ELMO!"

Lord, I love the holidays.

ABOUT THE AUTHOR

K.R. Conway has been a journalist for fifteen years and is a member of the SCBWI. She teaches Fiction Craft classes for teens and adults and drives a 16-ton school bus during the school year.

In addition to working jobs that should come with a warning label, Conway holds a BA in Scary Crazy People (Forensic Psych), torments the tourists about Jaws, and occasionally jumps from Eila's bridge with the local teens. She lives on Cape Cod with two house-crashing humans that look a bit like her, a fishing-obsessed husband, and a weird collection of critters.

Stalker Info:
Instagram: k_r_conway
Twitter: @sharkprose
Blog: CapeCodScribe.Com
Facebook: K.R. Conway

46675878R00223

Made in the USA
Middletown, DE
06 August 2017